THE MINI BREAKERS

THE MINI BREAKERS

LUCY KENNEDY

First published in the UK in 2026 by Eriu
An imprint of Bonnier Books UK
5th Floor, HYLO, 105 Bunhill Row,
London, EC1Y 8LZ

A CIP catalogue record for this book is available from the British Library.

Trade Paperback ISBN: 978-1-80444-213-5

Also available as an ebook and an audiobook

1 3 5 7 9 10 8 6 4 2

Typeset by IDSUK (Data Connection) Ltd
Printed and bound in Great Britain by CPI (UK) Ltd, Croydon CR0 4YY

The authorised representative in the EEA is
Bonnier Books UK (Ireland) Limited.
Registered office address:
Block B, The Crescent Building
Northwood, Santry
Dublin 9, D09 C6X8
Ireland
compliance@bonnierbooks.ie
www.bonnierbooks.co.uk

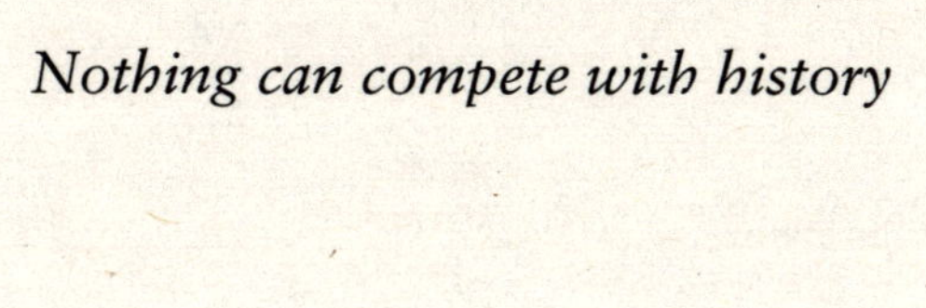

Nothing can compete with history

Chapter One

Dublin Airport
Saturday 8 a.m.

'How are ya, bee-atches?!'

Beth's scream echoed across the airport. Running through the departure lounge, bag slapping against her thigh, she looked eighteen all over again, post-Leaving Cert and heading off on a package holiday with the girls.

The "girls" in question, Kate and her partner Ariana (now both forty-one) watched Beth's approach, grinning apprehensively. Their friend was wearing a silver shimmery jumpsuit, purple shoes and various necklaces and bracelets. She was also dragging a huge purple suitcase.

'Beth!' Kate said, laughing, as her friend flung herself at her. She must have arrived in a taxi, Kate thought, as there were no kids in tow, just a faint smell of Jo Malone and white wine.

'It's only eight a.m. Give me a break. The shite coffee hasn't kicked in yet.'

'God, it is so good that we are doing this.' Beth beamed. 'I really need a break from my kids. I've taken a Xanax, and I am definitely drinking on the plane.'

She grinned at Ariana.

'I'll look after Kate for you, I promise. I know what a wild risk-taker she is.'

Ariana gave a forced laugh.

'I'm not worried about Kate taking risks,' she said lightly. 'It's not her style.' Kate could see a flicker of something – sadness? – in her eyes. She and Ariana were in the middle of a decade-long argument about whether or not to get married and her friends knew it. Ariana was desperate for commitment. She wanted to buy a place of their own. Kate was the one stalling.

Maybe, Kate thought, this holiday would give her the push she needed to commit. Because what was Kate waiting for? Even Kate herself couldn't answer that one. All she knew was that she couldn't even think about the next step without panicking. Ariana was watching her so she plastered a smile on her face that she knew wasn't quite reaching her eyes. She suddenly felt claustrophobic and needed some air.

Ariana reached out to her.

'Are you okay?' she said, frowning. It was typical of Ariana that, even when she was furious and hadn't slept, she would still think about other people, even those who were hurting her, like Kate.

'It's all good,' Kate said, as she wiped her sweaty brow. 'I hope that you don't miss me too much!' She forced out a strained laugh.

Ariana smiled back weakly.

'You'll have great fun, Kate, just please take the time to think.'

About us, she thought to herself.

Meanwhile, Beth was chattering on.

'I mean, I adore the kids. And Jack, of course. But it's no harm if he sees how much I do at home twenty-four seven, when he's off keeping the streets safe and all that.'

Beth's husband Jack was a burly, handsome detective, measured and careful, the opposite of chaotic, impulsive Beth. Beth was the last person Kate had imagined would wind up staying at home, married to a police officer with four kids, but it seemed to work. At least, Beth never seriously complained. She was always her usual giddy, good-humoured self.

'Yeah, he'll realise how hard you work keeping the home going,' Kate said firmly.

'It'll be good for him.' She smiled at Beth.

'I should go,' said Ariana, glancing at her watch.

'Don't let freedom go to your head now, girls.'

'Don't worry. We've got a motto,' Beth told her. 'No one pregnant, arrested or dead!'

'Reassuring,' murmured Ariana. She gave Kate a peck on the cheek, her breath cool on Kate's skin. Kate briefly closed her eyes. Why did she worry so much? She and Ariana might actually be okay.

'Namaste, friends,' they heard from a distance and turned to watch Georgie walking towards them, her toned arms spread wide. Even in her faded Joni Mitchell t-shirt and worn, ripped jeans, she looked stunning. Kate glanced down at her own expensive-but-crumpled linen t-shirt and jeans. How did Georgie do it?! She was beautiful, with big, blue eyes, perfect skin, and long, wavy blonde hair. She didn't care much about clothes or makeup or getting her hair done but she had an innate sense of style that meant she always looked right. Even at school she had been the golden girl, effortlessly nailing her grades, her social life and her extra-curricular activities without breaking a sweat. She could have been a nightmare, but she wasn't, Kate thought. She was ultra-kind and thoughtful, remembering the birthdays of all her friends and her friends' children, sending Mass cards, anniversary cards, you name it. She never forgot anything if she knew that it was important to someone else. She would drop everything for a friend. Gorgeous, inside and out. Kate had never heard her say a cross word about anyone. If anything, Georgie was too nice, which explained Paddy.

If anyone is punching above their weight, Kate thought grimly, it's Paddy, Georgie's horrible husband. He was as self-centred as Georgie was kind, as rude as she was polite, and he had a way of putting her down that the rest of the girls hated. An outing in which Paddy was involved would always end in embarrassed silence as he complimented his wife while managing to make her feel bad at the same time.

'I like smart casual,' he'd say, if someone admired his jacket or shirt, 'but my wife is more of a patchouli-and-unwashed-armpits type.' Unfortunately, Georgie seemed determined to see the good in him and they had just celebrated their twentieth wedding anniversary. How they'd got so far, nobody knew.

'Gorgeous outfit,' Kate said to her, as always feeling slightly jealous and slightly in awe of her friend, dressed now in white-linen wide-legged trousers and a gorgeous sleeveless top with a bold print. 'You look like an off-duty supermodel.'

'Don't be ridiculous,' said Georgie, glancing carelessly down at her outfit, her silver bangles tinkling as she did so. 'I just threw a few things together, you know me. Girls, I am so excited.'

'Same. Shall we check in now?' Kate said, eyeing the departures board nervously. She always had an irrational fear that the flight would leave without them. The thought of running to the plane after having her name called out in the airport was one of her middle-of-the-night, wake-up-for-a-wee fears. Her others included: the state of the world, her elderly parents, her business – she ran a successful life-coaching business – oh, and that little matter of her entire future with Ariana.

She turned now to talk to her girlfriend.

'Keep me posted on your dad, promise?'

'Of course I will,' said Ariana. She wasn't quite meeting Kate's eye. That blazing argument they'd had last night was clearly still in the air.

'But honestly, don't think twice about it, it's just a routine kidney checkup, he'll be fine. You just go and have a ball. Say "hi" to Dee and Sam when you get there.'

Dee and Sam lived in New York and London respectively, so they'd flown directly to sunny Portugal. They'd be waiting for the three of them in Albufeira, rocking the holiday-beach-wear look, Kate thought, thinking of her practical outfit sadly. She had no sense of style. With her, it was all comfort – it could hide everything she didn't want others to see.

'Will do.'

As Kate looked at her gorgeous, clever, kind, perfect girl-friend, she was suddenly hit with a wave of anxiety. She hated being apart at a time like this, when it felt like their entire relationship was hanging by a thread. But at the same time, she knew they needed the break.

They had been together for more than twenty years, ever since school, and Ariana was getting impatient. She had always been clear that she wanted a future with Kate. Kate had stalled for long enough. She knew deep down what her problem was: she'd spent her childhood watching her parents argue or when they weren't arguing, sitting in tense silence. She knew that her relationship with Ariana wasn't like that, but a little part of her always worried. Ariana, after years of patient conversations, after couples therapy, after endless long, circular discussions, had finally given her an ultimatum over dinner the night before.

'You need to figure this out, Kate. I'm sick of waiting. Use this trip to decide what you want – or I'm out of here,' Ariana had warned her.

Now, Kate swallowed. Maybe a few days away with her friends would help her get her head around it all. Maybe.

As though reading her mind, Ariana wrapped her arms around Kate and whispered in her ear.

'Hey,' she said. 'It's okay. Have a good time.'

She pulled back.

'You know what your problem is? You worry too much. You overthink things, Kate.'

Kate forced a laugh.

'I know.'

It was true. Kate worried and over-analysed everything. Oh, the irony of being a life coach. She could sort out strangers' lives within seconds but struggled with her own in every way.

'Come on, Kate!' yelled Beth, who was hovering with Georgie.

'I thought you were stressing about the time. Let's get this party started!'

Off the three best friends went, making their way through the busy and tempting Duty Free.

'It's all so cheap,' murmured Kate, eyeing up the gorgeous body lotions and makeup as they sped past.

'Blinkers on,' Beth told her, 'Don't even look at the giant Toblerones.'

'Everything will be cheaper in Albufeira. And none of us need cigs and all that these days. We're all clean-living girls now, aren't we? Apart from me, that is!'

'Sure,' Kate said. It was true. Well, true-ish and clean-ish. Occasionally, Ariana would sneak the odd vape. Kate knew that was what she was doing when she went for one of her long walks.

'I've never smoked,' said Georgie. 'Not since you gave me a cigarette that time, Beth, and I was sick behind the bus stop outside school.'

'You should keep that one quiet. Not a good look for a yoga influencer,' Beth said, 'What would all your followers say if your terrible past came to light?'

Georgie giggled. 'I'd probably have to do a public apology.'

Kate grinned over at her two friends as they pounded through Duty Free. Soon they would be reunited: Dee, Sam, Kate, Beth and Georgie. Other friends had come and gone over the years, and they all had other groups of course, work colleagues and family, but nothing as tight as the central five. They had something magic that only existed when it was them. As soon as they'd met, in Irish college in their second year at St

Mary's secondary school, they'd clicked. It was hard to explain but it just worked. Maybe because they were all so different. Dreamy Georgie, funny Beth, sensible Kate, Princess Dee and down-to-earth Sam. Or maybe it was because, even though they'd gone their separate ways since leaving school, they had always made their friendship a priority. Even Dee, with her high-flying broadcasting career in the US, would always come back to reality when they met up (or as back to reality as Dee ever came these days). When they were back together, they were just themselves: five girls with the world at their feet. Kate felt anticipation bubbling up: this break was going to be amazing. Just what she needed.

'I need coffee, a strong one,' Beth announced, once they were through security. She began to march towards one of the coffee counters.

Kate consulted her watch. 'We have a few minutes,' she said cautiously. Why can't I just relax, she thought to herself. She was on holiday after all.

'Double espresso please,' said Beth to the twenty-something behind the counter.

'I'm wrecked,' she went on loudly, 'I had to put out last night cause I'm gone for the few days. A goodbye shag, you know?'

The barista widened her eyes. 'Okay, wow. Cash or card?'

'Card,' said Beth. She picked up the coffee and downed it. 'Another one, please. Thanks for that.'

'Jesus, Beth!' whispered Kate. Beth had never cared much what people thought, but it seemed she cared less and less as she got older. 'You sound deranged.' She had to admit though, that it was funny. Even Georgie was laughing, and she was normally too worried about hurting other people's feelings.

'Ah, why not be honest with the young people about married life?' said Beth, completely oblivious to the barista, who was now whispering and giggling with her friend. Probably talking about the randy old weirdos, Kate thought. Cringe. 'Since the twins, I'm always wrecked.' Beth downed the second coffee. 'Anyway, shall we?'

They boarded on time, to Kate's immense relief. She felt her shoulders drop as they shuffled along the cabin looking for their seats. Beth hugged the Aer Lingus flight attendants as if she had known them all her life.

'Is she drunk or over-caffeinated?' whispered Georgie to Kate as they walked down the aisle of the plane. 'She's always been a lot, but this is something else.'

'Just exuberant, I think,' said Kate, eyeing Beth nervously as she settled into her seat. 'Maybe we've forgotten what she's like. It's been a while.' The girls hadn't seen each other for a couple of years. They'd wanted to, but life kept getting in the way. Kids, jobs, personal lives, there was always something, Kate reflected. It used to be so simple, the five of them huddled over their lunches at school, giggling, telling silly jokes, talking Beth down from one of her outlandish ideas, covering for each other when one of them was late or homework wasn't done. Now, life is so complicated, she thought. An image of Ariana's sad face and her last words to Kate at the airport floated in her mind.

Decide what you want . . . or I'm out of here.

Kate shivered as she settled into her seat beside them.

'I guess,' whispered Georgie, tucking her backpack into the overhead locker. 'I hope she chills out a bit, poor pet. I want her to enjoy her time away from the kids,' she murmured as she sat down across from them.

'Good morning, this is your captain speaking,' came a deep voice over the tannoy.

'He sounds sexy, doesn't he?' said Beth loudly as she settled into her seat. 'Like he's wearing an Aran polo-neck jumper and hasn't shaved in a few days, smells of Davidoff. You know the vibes?'

'So long as he does his job and gets us there safely, I don't care what he sounds like,' said Kate, squirting Rescue Remedy onto her tongue. Now that her fear of being late for the flight had passed, she could focus on her next fear: the fear of flying itself. She'd taken a course that was meant to help with her anxiety by showing her statistics about plane crashes. Unfortunately, it seemed to have made her worse. And then she had watched that documentary the other week about a plane that had crashed in the desert. She was pretty sure their seats were in the danger zone should the plane land nose-down.

'Hey, hey,' said Beth, nudging her, placing a warm hand on Kate's.

'Smile, you're on holiday. Seriously, you look terrified. When do you think the drinks trolley comes round?'

*

Ten minutes into the flight, the crew indeed came round with a full trolley of clinking bottles.

'We'll have something, please and thank you,' said Beth, ready with her card. She beamed at the crew member and pointed at Georgie sitting across the aisle. 'After all, it's this girl's birthday!'

'Shut up,' hissed Georgie, feeling mortified. How long had it been since they'd pulled that prank? It must be twenty years. It was how they used to score free drinks at restaurants and bars when they were younger, but weren't they a bit old for that now? She also hated being the centre of attention.

'Not funny, Beth.'

She lifted up the inflight magazine to shield her face from the curious gazes of the other passengers.

'In that case, fizz it is,' said the flight attendant, smiling at Beth, who beamed back.

'Oh, no thank you,' said Georgie, flushing, as the crew member proffered an open bottle of prosecco.

'Just some sparkling water is fine. Or green tea if you have it, please.'

'Everyone, in case you didn't catch that, this is my friend's birthday trip!' yelled Beth, standing and gesturing at Georgie.

'Want to wish her a happy birthday?' She took a glass of fizz from the crew member and winked at Georgie.

'Go on, stand up Georgie, do a twirl.'

Bright red, Georgie had no choice but to stand up. She didn't know if she should wave or just smile.

'Round of applause for my friend!' shouted Beth. There was some scattered clapping from the confused passengers.

'We can do better than that,' said Beth.

'Come on, people. One, two, three . . . Happy Birthday to You . . . '

Georgie stood there as a plane load of strangers sang to her and clapped, some in a different language, others silent, clearly trying to sleep. Why did Beth always have to start off their middle-aged, relaxing holidays like a hen party?

'I'm going to kill you for this,' Georgie whispered, sitting back down at last, still scarlet.

'Kill me? Not very zen of you,' said Beth, downing her bubbles. 'I thought you were all about the peaceful life?'

Just breathe, Georgie reminded herself. Breathe in, breathe out. You teach mindfulness every day; you can do this. It's your job after all.

Kate shot her a sympathetic look over the aisle, clearly feeling Georgie's pain and embarrassment; she had suffered from Beth's low-shame threshold plenty over the years. Beth was fun and funny, but sometimes she could overdo it.

Georgie decided the best course of action was to ignore Beth now, in case she set her off again. She took a sip of her sparkling water, put on a lavender-scented eye mask, and relaxed into the flight. She could hear Beth asking for shots but being politely refused by the crew. They seemed to have cottoned on to her ruses. Then she remembered that she was trying to push Beth and her antics out of her mind and smiled. She was looking forward to this holiday more than anything. Because while Georgie knew her life looked idyllic on the outside, with her gorgeous husband, beautiful cottage and thriving mindfulness business, the truth was, it was anything but. It was the story of her life. Disney princess meets bad boy and reforms him. Except she hadn't. Everything about her life had been a fairytale – until it wasn't. *I won't think about Paddy now*, she thought. She would deal with that later. She hadn't told the girls about the state of her marriage yet. *Breathe in, breathe out, breathe–*

Georgie frowned under her eye mask. She had the strangest feeling that someone was watching her. Yes, she definitely had the feeling that someone was staring right at . . . She sat up abruptly and tugged off her eye mask, to find that someone was indeed watching her intently. The elderly woman sitting next to her had her eyes fixed on Georgie's face.

'Is everything okay?' Georgie asked her.

'I'm so sorry, love,' whispered the grey-haired woman. She had gone pink with embarrassment.

'I know it's rude to stare. It's just, I'm terrified of flying and . . . well, you just looked so peaceful.'

Georgie smiled.

'I'm a yoga and meditation teacher, so I should be,' she joked. The plane dipped slightly, and the woman yelped and clutched the arm of her seat. 'Why don't I talk you through some exercises? We've still got an hour to go.'

'Thanks,' the old woman whispered. 'You're a very kind young girl.'

'I'm forty-two, so I'm not sure anyone could describe me as young, but thanks,' Georgie whispered back.

'Age is relative,' the woman said, her knuckles still white on the armrest. 'You'll realise that when you're my age.'

'Let's do this together,' Georgie said soothingly. 'It's all about how you breathe. You're gulping air, which is bound to raise your stress threshold. So, breathe in and out, in and out. . . .' she encouraged, as her new friend closed her eyes. Her hand slipped into Georgie's and gripped it tightly.

The ladies breathed together for the best part of an hour until the plane started its descent.

'This bit's always a bit scary,' Georgie said softly. 'But I've got you.'

'Thanks. I'm Katherine by the way,' the woman whimpered, eyes closed in terror.

'And I'm Georgie. Now, keep breathing.'

They landed with a bump of wheels on tarmac, and the woman let out a gasp of relief.

'Thank you so much, dear!' she exclaimed as they taxied to a halt. 'That was really very kind of you.'

She opened her eyes, which Georgie saw were a bright blue.

'Why are you going to Albufeira?' asked Georgie curiously, 'If you hate flying so much?'

This shy, painfully nervous woman seemed different to the crowds of holidaymakers on the plane.

'Well,' Katherine confided. 'I'm actually here to scatter my husband's ashes. Martin.'

She patted the brightly coloured woven bag on her lap.

'We were childhood sweethearts, and we came here on holiday once, a long, long time ago. It was wonderful. He always said, "If I ever kick the bucket, scatter my ashes in Albufeira, where we had such a good time."'

She sighed, looking out the window.

'That was a long time ago. The seventies. I wonder if it's changed much?'

'I'm so sorry for your loss,' said Georgie.

'I miss his face every day,' Katherine sighed as her eyes filled up. 'He always made me laugh and now, I don't find any reason to,' she said sadly.

The plane taxied down the runway and drew to a halt. Georgie swallowed. She had imagined growing old like that, once upon a time.

'It sounds like you were soulmates,' she said in a small voice.

'I don't believe in any of that soulmate rot,' Katherine said vigorously. 'There's plenty of soulmates in the sea. But I did love him. To be honest, he worshipped me, right to the end.' She smiled, clearly thinking of how spoilt she had been. 'He watched me follow all my dreams and was always the first person to congratulate me when I did well. All my friends would tell me how lucky I was. And I was, I suppose.'

Her voice caught slightly and she coughed.

'Have you got a person, my dear?'

'I've been married for twenty years,' said Georgie, hearing the hollow note in her own voice. 'He's called Paddy.'

'I hope he knows how lucky he is,' Katherine said firmly, 'I can tell you're something special. You deserve to be appreciated by someone who knows that.'

Georgie tried to muster a smile.

'Oh yeah. I'm sure he does.'

She was lying, and she sensed that Katherine knew it by the way she was looking at her. The older woman patted Georgie's hand.

Paddy had never been all that keen on her travelling, maybe because she was doing more of it since her yoga Instagram page had taken off – she had started being invited to wellness retreats in Morocco, Sardinia, Rome. She'd been on a panel or two and a famous wellness celebrity had even invited her on her podcast.

Paddy hadn't been keen on this holiday either.

'Really?' he had said, wrinkling his nose when she told him. He was just back from the gym and was wearing a tank top with a slogan on it that read No Pain No Gain.

'You're going away with those girls? The ones from school?'

'Why not?' Georgie had answered defensively.

Paddy had put down his creatine drink. He'd started weight-lifting, which he said was real exercise, unlike yoga. He had given one of his patronising little smiles.

'They're just a lot, aren't they? Kate is so weird and inse-cure, and she dresses like my mother. Dee is a legend in her own mind, even if no one on this side of the Atlantic has a clue who she is. Sam is probably the dullest person I've ever met. And Beth . . . '

Paddy had smirked again.

'Well, she's just plain nuts.'

'Those are my friends you're talking about,' Georgie had said. 'We haven't had a holiday together in ages. You're busy all hours with this latest start-up anyway. So, I'm going.'

He had shrugged.

'Fine. But I'm surprised, Georgie. You should be thinking about making more useful friends these days.'

He had walked away, leaving Georgie staring after him. Use-ful friends. He meant the primped, glossy wives of his business associates, who drove massive Land Rovers with personalised number plates and lived in huge McMansions and did their nails and Botox religiously. That was the sort of wife Paddy wanted now. In fact, she had an uncomfortable suspicion he wanted to upgrade the whole package. He had always hated their crumbling old cottage and her hippy-dippy lifestyle.

As his wife, Georgie could tell she was disappointing him massively, with her baggy yoga trousers and unkempt hair. The truth was, Georgie thought, he had never liked her girlfriends, even back at school. He always said they were stuck up, but Georgie wasn't sure it was that. She wondered whether, all this time, they had just been able to see through him.

*

The seatbelt sign was turned off and everyone stood up.

'Oooooohhhhhh, Georgie – did you make a new friend?' Beth slurred, waving at Katherine. Her gaze was unfocused. How had she got so pissed so fast? thought Georgie. But then they'd been on the plane for just shy of three hours, so Beth had probably knocked them back.

Beth beamed at Katherine.

'Are you in Albufeira for the clubbing then?'

The woman looked flustered.

'Well, no,' she said. 'I'm–'

'Because you look very spry,' Beth continued. 'Like you could really hammer it at three a.m.'

Beth giggled at her own joke.

Georgie sighed.

'Ignore her. Good luck with everything,' she told Katherine. 'I hope you manage to enjoy yourself here, too. It sounds like that's what Martin would have wanted.'

Katherine smiled and began fussing with her passport and boarding pass.

'I'll do my best, dear.'

Georgie glared at Beth as her friend stumbled around, retrieving her luggage from the overhead locker. Honestly, asking an elderly lady clutching her dead husband's ashes if she was here for the clubbing. How old was she? Twelve?

'What?' Beth said, as she caught Georgie's eye, 'Why are you looking at me like that?'

She's definitely slurring, Georgie thought.

'Aaaaaaand breathe,' Georgie said aloud, as the aeroplane door was opened. Finally. A wash of hot petrol-fuelled air passed right through the cabin. A holiday smell.

Heaven.

Beth was just Beth, Georgie thought. Well-meaning, kind, full of silly fun. And with a heart of gold. Ready to party before the party had started! Like the time she'd snogged a Greek waiter on Kos or did the Kate Winslet thing from *Titanic* on the cruise they'd taken three years before. She'd clambered onto the bow of the ship and had had to be talked down by the captain. The girls had seen her run wild enough times over the years, overdoing the booze and racing ahead of everyone else. This holiday would clearly be no different. Besides, she'd be asleep in the taxi soon, snoring loudly. Beth always burned out pretty quickly.

*

Across the aisle from her friend, smiling to hide her real thoughts, Beth's heart quickened again. This had happened to her a lot recently. She'd be chatting away, perfectly fine, and then her heartbeat would speed up and she would feel really weird: like she couldn't really breathe. Claustrophobic and confined in her own clothes. She pulled at the collar of her jumpsuit. Her neck was getting warm and itchy. She tried to take deep breaths like Georgie, but her heart thumped even louder than before. Not this again. Get a grip, she told herself. There was nothing wrong, so why did she feel this sense of dread? Jack had the list of instructions for the kids. The fridge was groaning with well-balanced meals, the WhatsApp parent-and-hobbies groups were up to date. They would be fine, surely.

It was only for a few days, and she really needed this break with the girls. Jack had wanted her to go. To cut loose, to get in touch with her old self. So why was she so stressed? She never got stressed. Kate got stressed. Beth was carefree, happy-go-lucky . . . .

'Earth to Beth,' Kate said, waving her hand in front of Beth's face. 'Ready to go?'

'Yeah!' Beth jumped up, plastering an even bigger smile on her face. She could see the old lady who Georgie had been talking to walking down the aisle, carrying a brightly coloured bag carefully, as if it were made of precious glass. Beth headed after her, hugging each of the cabin crew goodbye – they'd been lovely even if they had been a bit stingy with the booze – then followed the others off the plane. Whatever was wrong with her could wait.

Ten minutes later, Kate and Georgie were standing in baggage reclaim, keeping their eyes on the conveyor belt. Beth sat cross-legged on the floor, her head pounding, her chest still tight, trying to take in little gulps of air without the others noticing. 'Come onnn,' she muttered, pushing her sweaty hair back from her face. 'Where are these bags? I'm dying for a shower and a cool drink. It's boiling. And I'm bored.'

'You sound like one of your kids,' said Kate, her eyes fixed on the carousel. 'God, I hope our suitcases haven't got lost. I never take a suitcase. I hope it wasn't a mistake,' she said anxiously.

'If it is, we'll know who to blame,' wailed Beth. She hated waiting for things. It made her feel impatient and itchy. She could do with a few of Georgie's mindfulness mantras right now.

'There's mine,' said Kate in relief, spotting her sensible navy case. 'And yours, Georgie.'

'Where's mine?' said Beth, from the floor.

'It was marked "heavy" when you checked in,' Kate reminded her. 'Did you not check it fell within the right weight range before you left?'

'Oh shit!' Beth said, scrambling to her feet as a huge purple suitcase, which had somehow burst open, emerged onto the conveyor belt. At the top of the bag was what looked like a black inflatable sheep and . . .

'Are those sex toys?' hissed Kate. 'What the hell?'

Georgie groaned and shifted her battered canvas bag onto her shoulder, as Beth scurried over and began jamming an impressive selection of whips and dildos back into her bag.

'I think she does this to torture us,' Georgie said to Kate, who grimaced.

Beth could hear them and blushed bright red. How was she going to explain this?

'Guys, those baggage controllers are absolute pervs,' she yelled, lugging her suitcase over. 'They went through my luggage. Whatta cheek!'

She'd decided there was nothing for it but to brazen it out.

'What,' said Georgie slowly, pointing, 'is that? Is that an inflatable sheep?'

'Oh.'

Beth looked down at her open suitcase.

'It's just a silly thing. One of the school mums had a sex-toy party. She's joined some MLM pyramid type of thing, where she has to flog a certain number a month. Anyway, I bought some joke rude bits for us to have a laugh.'

She looked expectantly at her friends, who were staring back at her blankly. Surely, they'd think this was funny.

Surely.

'Ah, Beth, are you not a bit old for these gags now?' said Kate at last.

'Gags, eh?' Beth winked. 'Didn't bring any gags for you, Kate, but I've plenty of other things.'

Georgie peered at the heap of items. 'Is that a litre bottle of lubricant? Jeez, Beth.'

She rifled in her canvas bag and pulled out a tote that read I Am Peace.

'Do you want to borrow this to carry it all?'

'Why? Are you embarrassed?' teased Beth.

'Well yeah, kind of. We're three middle-aged women who are here on a relaxing holiday, not a sex odyssey,' said Kate bluntly. 'I don't really want to walk through the airport carrying armfuls of glow-in-the-dark lube.'

'Fine,' said Beth after a pause. 'I'll put them in the tote bag.' She felt put out. She'd thought the girls would find her selection hilarious. What was wrong with a bit of fun, even if they were in their forties? Kate could be a bit of a granny sometimes.

As quickly as they could, the girls gathered up the sheep, vibrators, Kegel balls and neon lubricants and put them all into the tote bag.

'You carry them,' Beth said, thrusting the now-heavy bag at Georgie, 'because you have the best upper-body strength. All that downward-dog action is paying off by the way, you look fab.'

How was it that Georgie managed to look completely unflustered, while she was a hot, sweaty mess, Beth wondered, as Georgie sighed and took the bag. Try as she might, she couldn't stuff the sheep in, so its head poked out.

*

Outside, Faro airport was terribly busy, swarming with family holidaymakers, drivers holding collection cards, loud hen parties and the now-somewhat-subdued mini breakers.

'Taxi!' Kate called, marching over to the rank.

Beth shot off after her.

'C'mon, Georgie,' she said, keen to put the sex-toy incident behind her, waving to her now from the waiting taxi. 'Let's get this holiday started!'

The taxi was hot and stuffy. Beth sat in the front with the driver the way she always did because she liked the chat. Kate and Georgie were in the back. As they set off, Beth turned around to talk to them but noticed that Kate had gone pale. It only took five minutes for her to get sick in a car.

'Are you okay back there?' called the taxi driver, as he drove, watching Kate closely in the mirror.

Georgie stroked Kate's sweaty head.

'He's worried you're going to puke, Kate, love,' she whispered gently.

'I am, I think,' Kate whispered back, trying to roll down the window.

'Breathe slowly and steadily,' Georgie told her. 'Breathe in, one-two-three-four – and out, one-two-three-four–'

Kate didn't need breathing exercises, Beth thought impatiently. She needed medication.

'Does she have the squits?' she asked turning around. 'I've got some Imodium in my suitcase?' The driver winced and put on the radio.

'I'm fine, Beth,' said Kate, through gritted teeth.

Really? Beth thought. What's wrong with them? You'd swear they weren't on holiday at all.

'Easy, tiger, I was just trying to help,' she said, with a shrug.

'Well, don't,' said Kate quickly.

Georgie caught Beth's eye in the mirror and Beth pulled a face.

'Touchy,' she mouthed. Kate noticed and Georgie saw laughter creep into her eyes, in spite of her nausea. They all knew that if she let it out, it would start them all off. They were back in school again, messing, with Mrs Casey staring at them from the front of the class. The feeling never changed, no matter what age they were.

'The Hotel Edene, please,' Georgie said with a smile, as they pulled onto the motorway. The girls could always make each other laugh. That part hadn't changed.

Chapter Two

They got their suitcases and the tote bag of sex toys out of the boot and turned around to look at the hotel – a big, beautiful, whitewashed paradise. And there was that gorgeous, heavy heat – perfect when you were sitting by an inviting pool, not waiting at the airport or sitting in a hot taxi.

'Isn't it great we're all here together at last? I love you guys,' Georgie said, suddenly overcome with a rush of love and gratitude for her friends. She'd been right to come, she thought. Screw Paddy. Then she felt guilty. He was her husband and she should at least be trying to make it work, even if he seemed to despise her.

'Love you, too,' said Kate weakly, taking in great gulps of air.

'Same,' said Beth. She squinted down at her jumpsuit. 'Can you see this damp patch on my crotch? Honestly, every time we went over a bump, I wee'd myself.'

'Well, olá, girls!'

They turned to see their friend Sam walking out of the hotel with a sangria in one hand, ice cubes clinking in the glass. Kate took her in admiringly – the long, flowing burnt-orange dress and matching espadrilles, a chunky gold bangle on her brown right arm, flawless olive skin, and her long silky, shiny dark hair. She looks great, was Kate's first thought, trying to ignore her own wrinkled clothing and churning stomach. She hoped that Sam was happy – she usually was. She had sailed quietly and cheerfully through school with the modicum of drama, met her perfect husband, Jeff, at her perfect first job, had a perfect wedding, had been headhunted for an even more perfect PR role, and had a perfect house. And right now, standing here in front of them, she didn't look as if she had a care in the world. If anything, it looked like the hotel was her own property.

The only fly in the ointment that Kate could see was that Sam and Jeff had been trying for a baby without success. But even that didn't seem to bother Sam too much. She always shrugged and said that maybe it wasn't meant to be. Kate had no idea if she was really as relaxed about it as she seemed.

'Sammy Bear!' Beth ran over to her and grabbed her for a big, squeezy hug. 'Look at your lovely face! What is it with you? Have you a portrait in the attic? Do you get hotter every year?'

'No, but I have a really great aesthetician,' said Sam, grinning. 'Lovely to see you, too. All of you.'

'Where's Dee?' Georgie asked, looking behind Sam. 'Our glamorous New Yorker? Is she in the bar signing autographs?'

'There's a spa in the basement and she's gone for a colonic. Don't ask.'

Sam rolled her eyes.

'She booked it in as soon as she got here. Apparently, the flight has had a negative effect on her, you know, arse, and she need cleansing or detoxing or something. She'll be back in thirty mins she said, unless she explodes and then has to get a flight back to JFK. Shall we get a jug of sangria and decompress?'

They didn't need any persuasion and were soon sitting on the hotel patio around a jug of delicious sangria stuffed with ice cubes and fruit.

'This definitely takes the edge off travel fatigue,' said Beth, pouring another glass of the ice-cold drink. 'And it's almost healthy, right? All that fruit.'

'Right,' said Kate wryly. 'I'm sure the fruit will make up for all the airplane wine, too. Shall we take a tour?'

They strolled around the hotel, taking it all in. The reception area was all white walls and bamboo, very clean and modern, with a slight smell of chlorine in the air from the pool. A holiday smell.

'Amazing, adults only,' said Beth dreamily, eyeing the peaceful pool area. 'Not a rubber ring or plate of chicken nuggets in sight. Bliss. And it's so calm.'

'We can have some proper chats,' said Kate. Whenever she had a dilemma, the girls would always be there for her. And now, she had a dilemma. She tried not to think about what Ariana had said to her in the airport. That she was sick of waiting. That Kate had to figure out what she wanted out of life.

The resort was a horseshoe of elegant, whitewashed villas, surrounded by bright purple flowers, two gorgeous swimming pools in the middle. Behind the inviting pool area, down a pebbled pathway, lay a spa. Light music pumped through the speakers in a relaxing rhythm.

'It's so pretty,' murmured Georgie, the breeze ruffling her honey-blonde waves. 'I'd love to host a yoga retreat here one day. And it's going to be perfect for my writing.'

'Oh, are you writing, Georgie?' asked Sam.

'Yes, actually,' said Georgie, smiling modestly as they strolled back out onto the terrace. 'A big lifestyle publisher has commissioned me to write about well-being in middle age. They've got loads of wellness people on their list. Pretty wild, isn't it? Me? A book deal?'

'Seriously?' Beth screamed and flung her arms around Georgie. 'I am so proud,' she mumbled into Georgie's back.

'Go on, tell us more about it,' said Kate, who was also beaming with pride.

'It's sort of a lifestyle-journal type of thing aimed at women our age. Lots of gorgeous pics, focusing on mindfulness, self-help, slowing down. Good, nutritious, low-carb, high-protein recipes, simple yoga, some breathing exercises. A literary agent saw my Instagram page and we put together a proposal and . . . well, the publisher loved it. There was an auction and everything.' Georgie laughed at the delighted looks on her friends' faces. 'It's not actually that big a deal,' she added. 'I'm not exactly the new Gwyneth Paltrow.'

'Georgie, you have nearly four hundred thousand followers and are the face of several major ad campaigns,' said Kate briskly. 'Stop being humble and say it out loud: "I, Georgie Geraghty, am a serious businesswoman, entrepreneur and podcast guest." And now you can add author to the list.'

Georgie went even more pink. It was true, thought Kate. Georgie was a brilliant businesswoman, but she had almost zero confidence. She didn't realise how charismatic she was. The way that everyone was drawn to her like a magnet. Being around Georgie was like being near the sun: you felt warm and great and uplifted. Her husband was the only negative thing about her. Kate bet that he was jealous of her book deal.

'I can't believe all my friends are so high-powered,' said Beth. She pointed a finger round the group. 'Georgie – wellness influencer and author. Kate – massively successful life-coach business. Dee – currently having a colonic, but a famous NYC-based newsreader and TV interviewer. Sam, head of PR for a massive airline . . . ' She pointed at herself. 'And then we have moi. Chiselling fish fingers off the floor and running late for the school run. A big, unwashed failure.'

There was a silence. Beth laughed loudly to fill it.

'Beth, that's not what you really think of yourself is it?' said Kate. Poor Beth. Things must be worse than she'd thought.

'Some might say that motherhood is the most important job of all,' said Georgie gently.

'Oh, sure,' said Beth cheerfully.

'God, don't look so serious, I wasn't complaining or any-thing. I'm very happy with my lot. The kids would really love it here,' she added, looking around, clearly trying to change the subject.

'Especially the twins. Their swimming is really coming on from their Saturday classes, it's so cute–'

She stopped herself then.

'Listen to me. So boring. I guess I've become indoctrinated into finding my own children fascinating. Jesus, things must be bad.' She laughed, but her face turned bright red and Kate could see that her t-shirt was sticking to her. She looked panicky.

'Well, everyone loves their own children. It's natural,' Kate said, giving her friend a supportive look, while thinking, but no one else gives a shit.

'Now, shall we find our rooms?'

They'd booked three twin rooms: Georgie and Sam together as always, Dee with Beth – the short straw – and Kate on her own, which suited her fine. It meant space to think and, thank-fully, not sharing with Beth, who could be a handful. The group even had a side WhatsApp to decide who would room with her this time. They all adored Beth, but she was the wild card – smuggling in booze, or guys before Jack came along, even hosting a full-blown party in her room once, with Sam waking up to chaos around her.

'She won't do that now,' Kate had said reasonably, when Sam had pointed this out on WhatsApp. 'Will she?'

'I don't know,' Sam had replied. 'It's Beth. You literally never know.'

In the end, Dee had taken one for the team. 'I see her the least,' she had said. 'So, I find her the most amusing. Anyone is hilarious when you only see them once in a while.' The others knew that Dee was secretly fond of Beth and the two of them actually got on, which was surprising given that Beth was as mad as a hare and Dee was full of icy self-control. Fair deal, the others had thought.

They headed to reception to get their room cards. One by one, they offered their wrists to the friendly receptionist, who wrapped the green band around their wrists that said, 'all inclusive'.

'Free booze!' whooped Beth. 'God, I love Portugal already.'

The receptionist flinched. 'A lot of our guests come here for the peace and quiet,' she said firmly. 'We have an older clientele. Some come back year after year.' Don't ruin this for them was the subtext.

'We're here to relax, too,' Sam told her, smiling and kicking Beth slyly. 'A nice, relaxing few days, that's what we want.' She gave Beth a stern look.

They were all on the first floor, their rooms in a row next to each other. It reminded Kate of their first time in Irish college in Spiddal. She'd been so homesick, she remembered, that she thought she wouldn't last the course. Then, on the second day, this girl had come up to her at breakfast time, pushed her Ray-Bans down her nose, looked Kate up and down and said, 'Are you going to the céilí tonight?'

'Yeah?' Kate had replied. She hadn't been planning to, but the girl looked as if she wouldn't take no for an answer. Kate knew that she was from St Mary's, but she'd never dared approach her. She had a certain aura about her.

'Good,' the girl had said smartly. 'See you at eight at the shop. We can go together.' She'd wafted off on a cloud of Opium perfume, before turning and saying, 'My name's Dee, by the way.'

'Kate,' she'd replied softly. Later, when she'd nervously walked towards the shop in her cleanest t-shirt and skinny jeans, she'd been surprised to see Dee there, waiting. With her was a small gang of others, whom Kate recognised from school, but hadn't really spoken to before now: Beth, Georgie and Sam. They'd clicked straight away and for the rest of their time in school, they'd stuck together.

Besides, they had so much history at this point that none of them could imagine life without the others in it, no matter how far away. Sometimes, all a friendship needed was deep roots. And regular get-togethers to remind themselves that they loved being together.

'Do you think that Dee will cope with being the most A-list celeb in the resort?' said Kate, as she and the others clattered up the stairs, making a ton of noise in the quiet corridor.

'I'm sure she'll talk about how tough it is being recognised, while walking around indoors with her massive Gucci shades on, dropping the names of all her famous friends,' giggled Beth. 'Remember that time in Berlin after she first signed her contract with TV Gold? No one had a clue who she was, but she kept asking if the paps were after her.'

'She loves it though, doesn't she?' said Kate. 'All of the fame and everything that comes with it: freebies, nights out, an adoring public . . .'

'I'm sure there are snags,' said Georgie, as usual trying to see both sides of the story. 'Imagine people taking pictures of you all the time. It must get annoying for her, no?'

'Yeah, but you can't have it both ways,' Sam said practically. 'We have our fair share of A-listers to deal with at work. Sometimes it's all awards ceremonies and glamour. Other times, it's a fan wanting a photo when you have a sweaty moustache and bad period bloat. Tough. That's the life that you chose. You can't decide when to be recognised, can you?' She stopped outside her room. 'But yeah, Dee does love it. Too much, I think. I'm surprised she deigned to come on holiday with us.'

'We're her oldest friends,' said Georgie, looking hurt, 'Of course she wanted to come on holiday with us.'

'Hmm,' said Sam, shrugging. She opened the door to hers and Georgie's room. 'Well, this is gorgeous.'

Georgie followed her inside and drew in a happy sigh.

'I've seen my share of five-star villas on my trips, but this is perfect, so calm and elegant. And look at the view of the pool!'

She drew back the curtains to show a bright turquoise pool glinting in the sunlight. The walls of the room were painted a willow-green colour, and the bed linen was crisp and fresh. Lovely, thick, white sheets and beautiful cream-coloured scatter cushions on top of a willow-green bedspread.

'Plenty of wardrobe space,' said Sam, when she'd marched over and flung open the wardrobe doors. 'Which is good because, you know, I like my outfits.'

'You are our style queen,' said Georgie warmly.

Sam beamed.

'Why, thank you, Georgie!' She was the style queen of their little team, always looking just right, whether she'd thrown on a tracksuit to walk the dog or was in her finest for an exclusive product launch. She never looked as if she was anything less than put together. Now, she explored the rest of their room, casting her critical PR eye over it.

'Decent-sized bath, shower and plenty of space,' she said. 'Fluffy towels. Good toiletries, nothing's been refilled with something cheap. Yeah, Kate's done good.'

'Thank you!' Kate shouted back from her room. They always left the choice of hotel to Kate, because she was the organiser in the group. She might get anxious about it but knew she had the knack of bringing it all together. Ariana would often say, 'Would you not leave the others to do a bit of work for a change?' She wouldn't have it any other way, Kate thought now, opening her suitcase, trying to push the image of her girlfriend out of her mind.

As usual, everyone had contributed their non negotiables and Kate had pulled together a list of requirements, most of which came from Dee.

The hotel must:

- Have access to a spa
- Have organic, sulphite-free wine
- Be adults only
- Be all inclusive
- Be a short flight
- Have guaranteed sunshine
- Be near designer outlets
- Come with a driver.

Apart from the last one, Kate had managed to find a selection of hotels that met Dee's requirements and the Hotel Edene was booked. And now Kate was finally here. Here with her friends, to relax and switch off.

'I never thought I'd be so excited by towels,' Beth called from the other room. 'The little luxuries you appreciate at our age.'

She gave a shriek.

'Oh my God, Dee's luggage is Louis Vuitton! Hilarious! And she's taken up the whole wardrobe.'

Each room had a pretty balcony looking out over the main pool and beautiful gardens, with its own table and two chairs. There was a bottle of chilled prosecco waiting on each table, stuffed into an ice bucket full to the brim with ice. Two crystal glasses glistened in the sun. Temptation overload.

As soon as this vision was spotted, they all opened their sliding doors at the same time and laughed as they stepped out onto their balconies together.

'Let's crack this one open, shall we?' said Beth, holding her bottle in the air. 'I'll do some for Dee, too. If she's allowed it after a full colonic.'

She took in a deep breath of sweet, warm Portuguese air and then a gulp of prosecco.

I hope Dee's not on another weird diet, Kate thought. Dee was always trying something – macrobiotic, keto, high-protein – and it made Kate self-conscious. She'd always been the biggest of the group. Curvy, was how she was described when she was younger, which had felt super annoying. Though she'd left behind the anxious dieting of her teens and twenties, the mentality lingered. She hated the thought of having to wear her swimming togs in public, so she had picked a black, oversized all-in-one swimsuit with extra give at the stomach and plenty of sarongs.

'It's so beautiful here, Kate,' Georgie sighed. 'Thanks for organising it all. I know we're not easy to pin down. Multiple countries, jobs, families . . .'

Kate smiled over at her friends. God, she was glad to see them all.

'Not at all,' she said. 'It's worth it to get us together again. Some nice meals, good chats and tasty wine. That's us happy, isn't it?' she smiled. 'We deserve this.'

She drew a breath. 'I really need this,' she added honestly.

'All okay at home?' said Sam, who'd appeared on the balcony beside her, eyeing her shrewdly.

Kate shook her head. 'Let's talk about it later, ok?' she said. She didn't want to spoil the magic by introducing the painful subject of her love life.

Sam gave her a sympathetic look but said nothing further. Taking their fizz inside, they each unpacked clothes, bikinis and washbags, shouting at each other across the balconies, just like they had at Irish college all those years ago, or when they went island-hopping around Greece together after their Leaving Certs. They'd lain on the beach getting sunburned, ate in the same taverna every night and Beth had met a local bus driver whom she'd declared the love of her life, before dumping him for a waiter. Kate wondered if they'd be friends forever. She hoped so.

As they were hanging up their clothes, the door to Georgie and Sam's room was flung open so dramatically that it banged against the wall behind it. Dee, looking very Coco Chanel in a black-and-white checked blazer with matching shorts, came striding in.

'Hi there,' she said, pausing elegantly, like a model, and not someone who had just had a tube up her backside.

She was also, Sam noticed, wearing a massive hat and even bigger sunglasses. Indoors. Her legs looked smooth and tanned, like in an ad for a stockings brand. Only Dee would look this good after a colonic. When she smiled, her teeth were white against her bright-red lipstick. She was Manhattan glam all the way.

'Dee, you look phenomenal,' Sam said. 'And you know how seriously I take personal maintenance.'

'Thanks,' Dee purred, air-kissing Sam and then Georgie. 'I work hard at it. My personal trainer arrives at four a.m. most mornings.'

'Wow,' said Georgie, eyes wide. 'Sometimes I get up for sunrise yoga, but–'

'Everyone does it in New York,' Dee said. 'Everyone in the media business, that is.'

'Look at you, Dee!' Kate said, hurrying in from her room to hug her friend. 'Incredible.'

Dee smiled modestly. 'Oh, I know. And you look . . . well, Kate.'

Kate bit back a smile; Dee didn't do compliments, so 'well' was about as much as could be expected.

Beth came running in too. Within seconds, there was tears, laughter and snot everywhere. Anyone watching would have thought a national event had taken place rather than a face-to-face reunion of five best friends after a longer-than-usual break from each other. They all held tight. The kind of hug that you get from family, a real one. A babble of indistinct words rose up from the huddle.

'Ah, it's so nice to be together!'

'I love you so, so much.'

'You look amazing.'

'Can I feel your arms, Dee?'

'Beth, are you pissed already?'

We might as well be back in our school uniforms, thought Kate happily. All laughing, all talking at the same time and hugging. She knew she had been right to pin them all down for this holiday. It had been worth it.

Chapter Three

After Kate had dragged the others off for another drop of prosecco before they went down to the pool, Sam turned to Georgie, her eyes dancing with devilment.

'Jesus, the size of Dee's boobs!'

She burst out laughing. 'Bloody hell, they are like two feckin'
watermelons! What are we thinking? A boob job? Anything
else since we saw her last?'

'She looks gorgeous to me,' said Georgie absently, as she
arranged a lavender-scented candle on her bedside table next
to a book of Buddhist teachings. She was planning to get in
touch with her spiritual self while she was here, doing some
writing as well as taking lots of pictures for the Gram. She
knew her followers would expect it, and she liked doing
it, too. Her agent said she was that rare thing – an organic
content creator.

'Sure, but I think she's had something else done,' said Sam,
heading into the shower and pulling off her top. 'Come on,
Georgie. Don't pretend you haven't noticed anything. Her face
looks different, maybe a bit puffy, around the cheeks and eye
area, no?'

'Shhh,' whispered Georgie, closing her eyes and settling on
the bed. 'I'm just doing a short gratitude practice.'

Sam sighed and headed into the bathroom to shower. Georgie
wasn't the kind of girl to speculate about facelifts and boob
jobs. She was too pure. And she hadn't spent two decades in

the dirty trenches of PR either. Sam would have to wait to analyse with Kate and Beth. She put on the shower, adjusted the temperature so that it was perfect, and stood under the cool water, massaging the expensive specialist shampoo she had packed into her long dark hair. This is bliss, she thought. Peace and quiet in Portugal with my best friends. She had so much to tell them, so much to get off her chest.

Sam knew full well that she inspired envy in people. She was, she acknowledged, pretty lucky. She had a ridiculously well-paid job, a gorgeous husband, and a beautiful house. She had great friends, great hair and a walk-in wardrobe stuffed with designer clothes. Occasionally, underneath it all, Sam still felt like that scrappy little girl who had navigated her parents' divorce and the subsequent financial fall-out. The brave one, who protected her siblings, who had got a job at fifteen so she could give her sisters cash when they needed to get books and bus fare. Sam had learned a good lesson early on: make it happen for yourself, because no one else is going to help you.

All of her sisters were still in Ireland. She was the one who had broken away, travelled, grabbed hold of the glamorous lifestyle with both hands. Her company leased private jets to celebrities and the super-rich, to oligarchs and musicians, tech bros and Hollywood actors. As PR director, Sam had to deal with riders, PAs, agents, managers, entourages. The job was twenty-four seven, and she loved it. It kept her busy. Distracted. It had given her a gorgeous life in London, a beautiful period home and a sexy husband, Jeff, a pilot who she had fallen in love with at first sight at a work event. She had been told a thousand times she looked like Salma Hayek. Yes. Things were perfect.

If only . . .

If only they could have a baby.

Jeff had said he wanted kids from the start but for the first few years of their relationship, it was a conversation Sam had successfully kicked down the road. 'Let's pick it up when we've lived a bit,' she would say. Back then, Sam was not a baby person. She liked the idea of kids, of course, the cute baby in beautiful clothes and a tiny hat, just not the reality. And truthfully, friends like Beth had put her off over the years, with stories of the chaos, the mess, the bodily fluids and the extreme noise. Beth made parenthood look stressful. And Sam liked her life as it was, thank you very much. Great restaurants, travel, the best hotels. Mingling with the rich and famous.

After a decade of putting it off, they had finally started trying in Sam's mid-thirties. She had come home from work one day and Jeff had poured two glasses of wine – a Côtes du Rhône they had brought back from a wine tour of Provence the previous summer – and taken her hand and said, 'Sam. I think I'd like to pick that baby conversation up again.'

Sam's heart had plummeted. 'I'm just not sure I'm cut out for parenthood,' Sam had said. 'All I saw growing up was arguments about money. Besides. You want me to give up my fags? My cocktails? My cream carpet?'

'You'd be the best mum,' Jeff had told her, his dark eyes locking on hers, cutting through her attempt at humour. There was a pleading expression in them that Sam could never resist. 'I think it would bring us so much joy. It would make us a family.'

'We're a family already,' Sam had said. 'A family of two.'

'This would complete it,' Jeff insisted. 'I know it would.'

Sometimes, over the next painful few years, Sam would wonder why Jeff wanted to bring a baby into their perfect life and change everything. But he did. And, eventually, so did she. At first, Sam had gone along with it because she loved Jeff and wanted him to be happy. Then something had shifted. Suddenly, she had wanted this too. She had wanted it more than anything.

And it just. Wasn't. Happening.

Sam had quit smoking completely. She'd reduced her alcohol and coffee intake. She'd eaten more vegetables and exercised and cut back on her hours and did acupuncture and made sure she got eight hours' sleep a night. They'd followed the schedules and apps to the letter: between the ovulation kit, the oil of evening primrose, the zinc for Jeff, the monthly pregnancy tests, it all added up! Not that they were short of money, but even so . . . it wasn't cheap trying to make a baby, especially when you were older.

The clock was about to run down on their plans when they started to discuss IVF, which really wasn't cheap. The doctors were optimistic, however, because of Sam's good health. They had tried: one, two rounds without success and now, they had agreed to just one more cycle. But would that really be it, Sam thought, or would they keep on and on? Sam couldn't really believe it. She had spent most of her life trying not to get pregnant and now, nothing. The irony of it, really. Typical!

Even sex – which had always been great with them, exciting and creative – had lost all romance and it was now methodical and clinical. Gone were the sexy nighties and candles. Now the twelve-hour fertile window felt like more pressure than landing a plane in a storm. There was nothing romantic about timetables and thermometers and lying with your legs up against the wall after sex. It all felt pretty undignified. In the end, they had pressed pause. Sam couldn't take it anymore. She needed a break, a few months without thinking about it. She needed to remember who she was without the dizzying anticipation and crushing disappointment every month.

Her friends kept telling her to relax. In fact, they told her lots of things:

It'll happen when you're chilled out.

When you least expect it.

Why don't you try a holiday?

I wish they'd all shut up, Sam thought viciously now. She turned off the shower and stepped out, feeling fresh again. She needed to block out those voices this week, to give herself a break. This was switch-off time with her besties. Even Jeff had been happy to see her heading off. 'Relax and enjoy yourself, Sammy,' he'd said, wrapping his arms around her. 'You work hard, so now go and play hard, okay? When you come home, we'll try another go of IVF, okay? And everything will be fine,' he'd smiled.

She hoped that it would be. She was not a patient woman.

'It's a load of middled-aged women,' she had said laughing. 'I don't think we'll do much playing hard.'

'Come on,' he had said. 'You're with Beth. So, it's bound to be dangerous.'

He had a point there, Sam thought. She looked at her calm face in the mirror and wished that she felt as together as she looked. Maybe this break in the sun with her favourite people would help her to switch off and relax. Jeff always said that when she was with her friends, she laughed the most and he was right.

*

Sam looked different, Georgie thought, as she breathed in the delicate lavender scent of her candle. She couldn't quite put her finger on what it was. Her skin looked dewier or something. Sam liked to take care of herself. Maybe she'd invested in some fancy new face cream or laser. All Georgie used was a dab of Rosehip oil.

As she heard the shower going on, she closed her eyes and breathed in for four and out for four. It was her favourite way to relax. She didn't want to bring the mood down on this holiday, but she'd had enough of keeping her home life to herself.

She needed to tell them. All this time she'd been keeping it in, like a dark secret, and now it wanted to come bursting out.

Where had it gone wrong with her and Paddy? They had been childhood sweethearts, together since the age of fifteen, and now they were like strangers. They had met at a teenage disco in Donnybrook called Wesley and had kissed that first night. Back then, Paddy was cheeky and funny and a bit daring and as a self-confessed swot, Georgie had fallen for him straight away. They had been together ever since. All through school, through exam stress, uni, work, they'd stuck together.

They were different, of course. Paddy had been into rugby, beer and sports, like so many of the lads they knew. Nothing wrong with that, Georgie had thought, but he also got into fights. Gave cheek to the teacher. Georgie was smart, polite, shy. The teachers adored her, while they gave Paddy the side-eye. Still, the two of them clicked. People made jokes about them being an odd couple, but they stuck together, year after year. When Paddy proposed one day, Georgie said yes without hesitation. With Paddy, she had that feeling of security, of familiarity, no matter how much of an idiot he could be after a few drinks.

Paddy had always wanted to live in Dalkey village because of the contacts and the upmarket neighbours that he could meet. It was a classy area, he said, perfect for an entrepreneur like him. Georgie didn't care about that, but she loved the little cottage that she'd found on a walk one day, with its wild garden and wonky floorboards. Paddy wasn't sure that it gave the 'entrepreneur' vibes he was looking for, but agreed that as a starter home, it might work. They settled in. Paddy's business went from strength to strength. Georgie taught yoga. She found Paddy's friends a bit much, she had to admit. He liked Georgie to turn on the charm, to throw elegant dinner parties, no expense spared. Paddy liked to show his beautiful wife off. He talked about getting a bigger place one day. A better car.

Georgie tried not to think about that too much. If it made him happy, then fine.

But the thing was, she wasn't sure it was making Paddy happy. The more successful he became, the less close they seemed. Over the years, he had become less affectionate with her, working away a lot, going out with the lads a lot more. Expecting her to drop everything when he got home.

'I do have a job, you know,' Georgie had told him mildly when he'd given out to her for not being there to meet him after one trip.

'You teach menopausal women how to stretch and you run an Instagram account, it's not exactly running a business!' he would say.

And then, when he'd had a few drinks and his friends were around, he would say other things, too. When Georgie was in bed, door closed on their adolescent banter, Paddy would read out Georgie's Insta captions, using a fake-soulful voice, to their howls of laughter.

'"Sunrise is the most spiritual time. Tune into the real you."'

Georgie would lie there, wondering how the funny, cheeky boy she'd first loved had turned into this man.

'He's just jealous, babe,' Sam had told her on the phone one night. 'Because your star is shining so much more brightly and you make him look like the boring old fart he is in comparison.'

They'd both laughed, but Georgie knew that the others had never understood his appeal. But once, she'd loved the way he had of not taking life too seriously; of always finding the fun in things. When had it changed?

Paddy had always liked having Georgie to show off at corporate events – his hot wife did the deal for him, he always said. But now, even her looks seemed to annoy him. Recently, he'd suggested she dye her hair a lighter shade of blonde, look at some tweakments, like the other wives they hung out with.

The sex had started to become less frequent. And then they were hardly having sex at all. She had suggested romantic get-aways and dinner dates together, but he made excuses. He'd prefer to watch football in the den with a beer, alone.

When she'd tried to seduce him one night in a lacy nightie – not very her at all, but she was happy to give it a go – he'd turned her down. 'This is a bit embarrassing, George. You're a middle-aged woman.' And he had turned over and started reading the *Which? Guide to TVs*.

Georgie had felt stunned. Paddy clearly no longer found her attractive. But he was adamant he didn't want to break up. He didn't want their lives to change. He just didn't want to have sex with her, to touch her, or to talk to her much. How had this happened? She and Paddy had always been so close.

Or had they? Georgie had blocked out a lot over their last twenty years together – his occasional flings, the way they'd never discussed having a family of their own, the way he put her down in public – but when she dug deep, she wondered if they had ever had much in common. When she'd first seen him as a shy, serious teenager, she'd thought he was gorgeous but once attraction faded, what was there? She would examine her face in the mirror, stand naked and look at her body from all angles. She didn't look bad for a forty-two-year-old. Her lifestyle meant that she was toned and trim, her skin glowing. What had changed for him? And was this enough for her? If she left Paddy, could she be with someone else? She had been with Paddy, and only Paddy since she was a teenager. He had been her first kiss. She wasn't sure she had the courage to leave him.

One, two, three, four. Georgie brought herself back to her breathing, just as she told her clients. She would use this time to think and reflect.

She worried about her closest friends; they all had so much on their plates, too. Sam always teased her for having her head in the clouds, but Georgie knew she was intuitive. She picked up on a lot. Sam was deeply sad about the IVF not working; Kate was stressing about Ariana; Dee looked more tense than usual; and Beth was undervalued and overstretched. Mind you, life was intense in your forties and that was all there was to it. Peri-menopause, menopause, anger, emotions, hormonal imbalances. Symptoms that hit you out of nowhere. It was almost as if you didn't recognise yourself anymore, that the body and mind that you'd known for forty years, had suddenly been invaded by someone else. A more anxious, sad someone else.

You were not you. Georgie knew that from most of the women in her class.

Some women put on weight or complained of hot flushes. Some went off the charts and had a total mid-life crisis, exploring their sexuality, or having an affair. Some just changed their hair. And then some sailed right though it with ease. There was no way of telling which way it would go. All Georgie knew was that she was sick of middle-aged women being invisible. Sick of 'menopause' still being something of a taboo word. It was what had inspired her to write her book proposal. 'Write from the heart, Georgie,' her agent had said. 'The publisher wants this because they want you. You're genuine and authentic, a rarity in the world of influencers who promote mascara they've never tried or steam mops they've never used. You're the real deal. Write this for women like yourself and they'll love it.'

And Georgie had taken that advice on board. The words had tumbled out of her onto the screen, writing for other women who felt confused, blindsided, in spite of how great everything seemed on paper. Whose husbands also didn't seem to like them anymore. Women like her.

'I'm only forty-two, for God's sake,' Georgie muttered now as she heard Sam turn the shower off. 'If I have to start over again, without Paddy, surely, I can.'

When Sam came out of the bathroom, Georgie smiled at her. 'It's so good to be together again Sam,' she said, feeling grateful. That meditation must have worked. 'I know this is going to be the best holiday ever.'

'You're such an optimist, Georgie,' Sam said, brushing out her long, dark waves. 'But yeah. It'll be great . . . so long as Beth doesn't piss us all off with her antics, Kate parks her neuroses, Dee doesn't throw her weight around and give us the whole A-list routine, and you and I manage to survive with our egos and sanity intact.'

Georgie laughed, blew out the candle, and headed into the bathroom. 'It is going to be great, you'll see,' she called.

And it would be. Five best friends, sun, the pool, all-inclusive drinks . . .

What could go wrong?

Chapter Four

In the room just next door, to Dee's horror, Beth was crying.

'What is wrong with you?' Dee called from her perch on the toilet, trying to sound patient and caring but really wanting Beth to shut up. She was still feeling the effects of the colonic, and this was the last thing she needed. But the sobs, which had started quietly, were now impossible to ignore.

'I just miss you all,' wailed Beth on the other side of the bathroom door. 'And I feel sad that this is only an occasional thing. You guys mean so much to me.'

Jesus, thought Dee. Beth's getting seriously emotional in her old age. And Dee didn't do emotions, at least, she hadn't until a week ago. She'd been sitting on the toilet so long she felt like her bum was engrained on it. Not a very pleasant experience but then sometimes beauty was painful. Dee had had first-hand experience from being in the public eye for the last few years.

'I know Beth, it is sad,' she said, wondering if she'd ever manage to get off the toilet. The colonic had seemed like a great idea at the time, promising detoxification, and better digestion but she hadn't realised it would make her feel so sick. Maybe it was her overdue period on the way at last. 'Um, how about you go and unpack?' she suggested. 'I'll be out in a minute.'

After a few more wails and sobs, she heard Beth stumble to her feet and start pulling drawers open. Thank God she had moved on. 'Bloody inflatable sheep,' she could hear her muttering. 'I thought it would be funny, Dee, you know?'

'I'm sure it was,' called Dee soothingly, not having a clue what Beth was on about. Cautiously, she stood up from the toilet. She thought it might be safe to attempt a shower.

She could hear some more muttering, a few drawers opening and shutting. It was all a bit strange. Beth really wasn't a crier. She might laugh till she was sick, but Dee had never seen her cry. Still, Beth had form for being unpredictable. Because of Beth, they had been barred from several restaurants in Dublin over the years. There had even been that mooning incident fairly recently. Not funny at the time and very embarrassing for Dee, who was papped as she pulled up Beth's black-and-white polka-dot knickers. Beth had reminded the group several times that they weren't her 'usual' choice of underwear, although the girls suspected otherwise.

Beth was super fun and great craic. She had always been popular in school. She attracted friends like magnets and was also great at staying connected. She was loyal, too. Kate might be the organiser, but Beth was the glue that held their group together. She made these holidays happen. Once, Dee would have said how grateful she was to her for that. Only now Dee wasn't sure . . . did she want to be a part of this group of old school friends anymore? Had they always been this annoying or had she just moved on? Seeing them today had been a bit of a wake-up call. Kate was so needy and weird and always dressed in those awful, frumpy clothes. Sam thought she was God's gift and was wrapped up in her boring PR job. Beth had all those children and seemed to be in the middle of a nervous breakdown, with all this weeping. And Georgie . . . Well, Georgie was just so bloody self-righteous. With her, 'Oh, I just use a bit of rosehip oil,' and, 'I cut my hair myself' bollocks. Dee flipped on the shower angrily. She had always had a slight issue with Georgie, ever since school. She wasn't jealous – who could be jealous of Little Miss Holistic? – but still. Something about Georgie had always wound her up. She stepped under the spray, let the hot water flow over her, and drew deep, soothing breaths.

After Dee had showered, she came out to get dressed and found Beth asleep on the bed, hugging Dee's pyjamas like a child. She is regressing, thought Dee with curiosity. What the hell was wrong with this woman! She was nearly forty-two and acting like they were island hopping in Greece again. God, she'd never forget that holiday. Sunburn, food poisoning, ill-advised flings. It had been fun, so much fun, she thought wistfully. And whatever her life was now, she had to admit that it wasn't much fun at all. She'd got what she wanted, but somewhere deep down she wondered if it was enough, when you could be discarded like yesterday's old newspapers. What would Mum and Dad say about it? Probably something like 'Pride comes before a fall'. Dee's parents were chilly and reserved and had always been horrified at her choice of career.

'Couldn't you do something respectable, like teaching?' her mum had said to her once, her only comment on Dee's success.

Strange behaviour, Dee thought now, looking at Beth as she took out her magnifying makeup mirror and vanity case. She flicked on her ring light and laid out her makeup. It was all Chanel, Charlotte Tilbury and Dior. Only the best for herself. When she had received her first TV paycheck, Dee had ordered a complete set of Louis Vuitton luggage. She had decided then and there to keep her standards high and to pick only the best. She worked hard, so she deserved nice things – this was how she saw it. Including her flawless face. Not a line in sight or an unwanted hair to be seen.

She examined the results of her recent lip filler, which had actually been quite sore this time. It was a non-negotiable though – she had to look her best. The pressure of being single in the city that never sleeps was intense. In New York, people were ruthless when it came to dating. You had to look the part at work, too. Dee was the lead news anchor on TV Gold, a big deal in US telly. She was, quite frankly, incredible at her job. Some people thought that anchors just read off the autocue, but that was crap. Dee knew every single story intimately. She had to be fully prepared at all times, should the autocue ever fail, writing up the stories herself in hard copy and reading them carefully before she went on air. She couldn't afford to mess up. This job had been hard-won, and she wasn't about to throw this chance away.

Dee had moved to Manhattan twenty years ago, but she had been dreaming about it her whole life. Her original plan had been to be a dancer on Broadway – that had always been her teenage dream. She'd watched *Riverdance* on the Eurovision in 1994 and she'd fallen in love with Irish dancing, then she'd changed to ballet and then settled on jazz improv. Dancing was her world. Unfortunately, she was no Michael Flatley or Jean Butler. It turned out she was an average dancer at best. Dee could accept feedback and the feedback from her auditions wasn't good. After a year of painful auditions, rejections and with all her hard-earned savings spent, she had succumbed to an office job, first in sales and then she had moved to a film and TV agency, thinking that at least this way she was close to showbiz. After the pain of rejection as a dancer, she set her heart on being a TV sensation. But she had hated the agency from the first day. She knew she was destined for more than this. She was so close to the heart of it all – the famous people walking in and out every day – and yet here she was, stuck behind a desk on reception.

Still. You never knew. She had kept her megawatt smile in place as she filed, took calls, organised meetings. She had laughed and flirted and chatted with the casting directors who walked past her desk. It was exhausting, talking to strangers and trying to make an impression, having to be 'on' every second of the day.

She'd stayed there for four years dealing with idiots, while also auditioning and sending her showreel to all the radio stations, production companies and TV channels; keeping her hair glossy and blow-dried, her clothes glam, her smile in place, haemorrhaging money on rent, telling everyone back home she was 'just getting her foot in the door', all the while praying for a miracle.

And then, on a random rainy Wednesday morning, when she was slightly hungover at work, the miracle happened. She got a call from a TV Gold producer who worked in the building. 'You're an actor, right?' The woman came right out with it.

'That's right,' said Dee, determined not to sound taken aback. She knew the woman produced a news and current affairs programme so she'd added swiftly, 'With a background in journalism'. That wasn't exactly true, but Dee did watch the news. She didn't mention the fact that she'd scraped through her school exams and had failed history.

'I see you every morning. You look like a modern Lois Lane,' the woman told her. 'Feisty. Exactly how people want their news reporters to look. And you seem sharp, too. I'll be honest – we've been looking for a new face for months and we've had no luck, so I'm getting desperate. Come up for a chat.' And she hung up.

This was it, Dee had thought, her hands shaking. Or, at least, it could be. She had bolted into the toilets and done herself up to the nines in record time. She had taken a deep breath and taken the elevator all the way up to the producer's office, opened the door, walked in and turned on that megawatt smile.

Within the week, Dee had been interviewed, camera-tested and sent to the newsroom to learn how to read autocue properly, how to write stories and speed read. Her big break, just like that. It was a story she liked to tell in interviews. 'Always be on, because you never know who is watching,' she'd told *The New York Times* only the previous year.

It turned out the American public loved the straight-talking Irishwoman with the dark good looks and sharp suits. Soon, Dee was allowed to add her own little asides and ad libs to the script. Ten years later, she was still there, doing the same job day in and out, researching newsworthy stories, sharing them with the American public and just waiting for her own chat show. *Deirdre Byrne Talks*. It would happen one day; she was sure of it. Meanwhile, her ratings were steady. She might not be the hot new thing any more, but she was a safe pair of hands. Women still stopped her in the street, told her how cool she was, putting this or that politician in their place; asked her who did her hair, her nails, her Botox.

But then, two days ago, in the ladies toilet at the network building, everything had changed.

Dee had been in the bathroom, when she'd overheard two of the network assistants chatting as they washed their hands. She knew they worked for one of the key producers, so she'd tucked her feet up in the cubicle and pricked up her ears. It never hurt to hear what the higher-ups were doing.

'I'm so sick of working overtime and being expected to like it,' said one girl and Dee had rolled her eyes. The younger generation had zero work ethic. They expected everything to be handed to them on a plate.

'He's such an asshole,' the younger girl had agreed. 'They're all assholes. Sexist, ageist pigs. Speaking of which, did you hear that Dee's up for reconsideration?'

In the stall, Dee had frozen. Up for reconsideration? Her?

'Surely not. The ratings are great,' the other girl had replied.

'Hmm, but Tom's talking about getting in someone younger. Someone with more of a social-media following. You know how things are right now. Besides, Dee is getting pretty expensive.'

Someone younger, Dee had heard the words in horror. They were looking for a new her, only half her age. Someone who was probably cheaper, too. While Dee was doing the job and doing it well. What did it matter nowadays, when everyone had to be young?

The girls had strolled out, still gossiping. Dee had slowly lowered her feet to the ground. She had felt ill. This was terrifying, overwhelming and most of all, humiliating. She'd emerged cautiously and washed her hands at the sink. She'd stared at her gorgeous face in the mirror – flawless as always. Then her phone had beeped, and she'd taken it out of her bag. A message on the girls' group WhatsApp from Beth: Hey bee-atches! Hope you've sorted your packing! Tick-tock! I'm gonna bring us all some saucy treats.

Dee had swallowed. Of course – her girls' holiday to Portugal. She had felt even more sick. What would she tell them? She had always been the famous one in the group. They'd admired her career. Thought she was living the high life. What would they think of her when she was a nobody? Cringe.

Still, Dee had left the toilet smiling. There was no way she would let anyone know how she felt inside. She tried to push the thought out of her mind for the rest of that week, but it was impossible. She had spent so many hours mastering her craft and making herself a flawless anchor. Questions had whirled in her mind. Would she have to leave New York? Would she ever get another job?

Between that day in the toilet and her flight to Portugal, she'd barely slept. On the flight, she stared at the movie playing out on her personal screen, her mind whirling too fast to take in the dialogue. Who was she really, if she didn't have her job? She had nothing else. No partner. Not even a cat. A few one-night stands now and then – particularly over the past few weeks – but that was it. She had friends, of course, but industry friends who were always looking for the next deal, the next big break. No one really ever relaxed in Manhattan; people were too aware and too focused. It was almost as if people were scared to sleep! Dee had always thrived off that atmosphere. Now, she wasn't so sure.

Had she made a terrible mistake, throwing everything into this show?

This holiday would be good for her, she had told herself, as the plane circled the airport to land. She would come back rejuvenated. She would find another job. Her agent, Freddy, kept telling her that she was best friends with Oprah. Well, she could pull a few strings and land Dee a new gig. A better one. It would all be ok. It had to be.

Now, while Beth snored beside her in this poky little room, Dee stared at her perfect face in the mirror. Her porcelain skin and green eyes. She still had her good looks, thank God. She drew a shaky breath. Her stomach was heaving and she was sure she looked a bit paler than normal. Slightly sweaty. That was the last time she did a colonic treatment far from home. Unless . . . She thought about her overdue period and shivered. The recent one-night stands. Surely . . .

No. She was not going to go there. Because that was a ridiculous idea. And Dee could not take literally one more thing in her life going wrong.

She leaned over and shook Beth's shoulder. Beth made a little grumbling noise and snuggled deeper into Dee's pyjamas. Dee shook her again, a bit less gently. 'Hey, sleepyhead,' she said. 'Thought you might want to get ready.' Dee tapped the face of her Cartier watch with a long, pointy red nail.

Beth rolled over and beamed at her. 'I feel like a new woman,' she said, sitting up and rubbing her eyes. 'Refreshed.'

'That's a relief,' said Dee. 'You seemed a little . . . emotional, before?' She was trying to be tactful, which wasn't really her thing. Dee liked to be direct.

'Oh, I'm fine,' said Beth, waving her hand. She had the wrinkles from Dee's pyjamas imprinted on her cheek and her hair was dishevelled.

Dee felt her hard heart soften a bit. 'It's not like you to cry,' she said, hoping Beth wasn't about to make a habit of it this week.

The last thing she needed when she was feeling like this was a weepy roommate.

'Yeah, it just hits me from time to time these days,' said Beth. 'I feel sad for no reason. I know how lucky I am, it's just. . .' She glanced at Dee and said tentatively, 'You don't ever feel that way, do you, Dee?'

Dee hesitated. Once, the honest answer would have been 'no'. She hadn't cried since she was six. She had even laughed through *A Star Is Born*. Ex-boyfriends said she was made of steel, like it was a bad thing. Dee prided herself on it. But now . . . well, now she had had her heart ripped out by the network she had given the best years of her life to. She still didn't feel like crying, but she did feel sad inside. She just didn't want to admit it. She was Dee Byrne – tough, smart, famous. I must talk this through with my therapist when I get back to New York, she thought. It wouldn't do to start developing feelings at this age. And she wasn't about to start showing weakness now either. Not in her world, or the sharks would definitely start circling.

'Not so much Beth,' she said. 'Maybe it's hormones, you know? Your time of life?' Technically, Dee supposed they were both at the same time of life, given they were the same age. But still, she thought of Beth and the others in a different category to her.

Beth sighed. 'That's what everyone's been saying,' she said. 'So, I guess they're right.'

'C'mon,' Dee said, pulling Beth gently up off the bed. 'An hour by the pool and you won't know yourself.'

Beth brightened. 'God, yes! That sun, that cool water. Not to mention the free booze,' she added happily.

'Go easy, Beth,' Dee said. 'Hormones and alcohol don't mix well.' She picked up her Hermès beach bag and put it over her shoulder. Who was she talking to about hormones, she thought – Beth or herself?

Chapter Five

Hormones. Blame everything on bloody hormones, Beth thought miserably. Could it be as simple as that? Or was there another reason she kept bursting into tears at random times? Another reason why she felt so confused and insecure and . . . lost? Shouldn't she be happy to be here on her own, with no kids, she thought, as she followed Dee into the bar. Still, as much as she adored them all, four children was a lot. In so many ways. The supermarket was the worst. You got looks. Judgmental ones, and usually from other mothers, of all people.

Go for a third child, she and Jack had thought. And then, bam. Twins. And twins were great! They were so lucky. Beth loved them to pieces. It was just the stage they were at. Asking for everything or worse, throwing massive toys into the trolley. Beth couldn't even go into Woodies without them asking for something at the tills, as she would stand there sweating and hissing at the kids to 'put that back'. Only the other week she had left with too many paint samples and plants that she didn't need, just to avoid the embarrassment.

Of course, it wasn't that she didn't absolutely adore her four children, but still, they were exhausting. She never had time for herself any more, she couldn't even sit on the toilet and breathe in peace without the door flying open – or, at least one child watching her, which was pretty off-putting, to be honest. That was why she had her dirty secret. The attic. She didn't do anything dirty up there, of course. Only snuck up the ladder and pulled it up behind her. Just for five minutes' peace.

There was no real reason for her to be hiding out from her family like this. Jack was so lovely and such a great dad but he was so busy.

Beth had always imagined she would go back to work after her third kid. She had loved her job as a dental secretary, getting to know the regulars and keeping the nervous patients calm. But then the nursery prices had gone up and Jack's hours were so long . . . well, it hadn't made financial sense for her to work. She had understood that. Again, she was lucky. How many women got to stay at home with their beautiful babies and to prepare meals for their handsome husbands without worrying about money? But then the years had gone by and now the twins were going to start school. And occasionally, in small, treacherous moments, Beth thought about all that she had said goodbye to.

Goodbye, daily adult interaction.

Goodbye, regular patients she had loved.

Goodbye, cheering up the little ones in for their first checkup.

Hello, dirty nappies and kids' TV.

It was Groundhog Day for her – the same time, at the same place, doing the same thing. Weeks passed and she felt as if she had achieved nothing except for what went on inside the four walls of their house. She dreamt of returning to work. She had actual dreams of popping on some lip gloss, walking in with a takeaway coffee, planning the schedule, joking with her colleagues.

How sad was that?

Truthfully, nowadays, the most exciting part of her day came at five p.m. when she opened her bottle of chilled, cheapish Chardonnay. Sometimes, her anticipation of that moment worried her. But lots of people loved wine, didn't they? Especially from April to September when the weather was sunny and inviting. It was so tempting and hard to resist. Hot skin, 'a sundowner' as she liked to call it, just a glass or two.

Or three. Then you might as well finish the bottle. And then in the autumn, a glass of red was so cosy. The truth was that the wine made everything better. Made Beth feel calm and relaxed. A better mum. A fun mum, reading the bedtime stories with funny voices, making the kids laugh. Nicer to Jack when he got in, late and tired.

That was normal, wasn't it? It wasn't a drink problem. Or was it? The questions had cycled round and round Beth's anxious mind. What was going on with her? The crying, the feeling of anxiety in the pit of her stomach. That wasn't her. She was the laid-back, relaxed one. The life and soul of every party – or, let's face it, every WhatsApp group these days. Not this overwhelmed, panicky woman hiding in the attic from her children.

Before the holiday, her fits of sudden tears, racing heart and three a.m. wakeups had taken her to the doctor.

'You're probably perimenopausal,' her doctor had said casually, taking a blood sample. 'You could have years of this yet before the actual menopause hits. Don't look so shocked,' she'd added. 'Let me suggest a few things that might help. We can adjust this, of course, at your next appointment . . .'

But I'm only forty-one, Beth had thought pathetically. She hadn't said it aloud though because the doctor was so busy scribbling things down. At the reception desk she had accepted the prescription for Vagifem, a HRT pump and progesterone tablets and left. She hadn't filled the prescription though. She didn't need any of that stuff. Perimenopause was years off. She was fine. Wasn't she?

Still, Beth thought, as she queued at the bar behind Dee, admiring her perfectly pert bottom, she could talk to the girls about it now. They were all the same age, so maybe they were in the thick of this stage as well. Kate usually kept an agenda for their holidays and surely the menopause could go on it. And in the meantime, Beth was determined to channel her zesty teenaged – or at least mid-twenties' – self for this holiday. She had already horrified Dee with her show of emotion – that was enough of that. She wasn't about to embarrass the others either. She didn't want them to think she'd turned into some lame housewife who couldn't cope with life.

'Hurry up,' Dee called back to her now as they headed to a pretty table outside. She looked a bit pale, Beth thought. Or even slightly green.

Dee frowned at her. 'What is it? You're not about to start crying again, are you?'

'Don't be daft. Cocktail before dinner will sort me right out,' Beth said, smiling.

Chapter Six

Kate had fully unpacked her suitcase and carefully hung each piece of clothing in the wardrobe. She made sure every toiletry was lined up neatly and had arranged her book, sleep mask and pillow spray on the bedside table. Then she sat down on the bed and sighed.

'Get your act together, Kate,' Ariana had told her the night before. 'Or else you'll lose me. I mean it this time.'

Things between them always dissolved into recrimination and threats these says. Kate, always careful, cautious and a planner, had one big black spot when it came to the future. She didn't trust it. Whenever she thought about the things Ariana wanted to do – buy a house together, plan a wedding, a life neatly stretching out ahead of them, she felt sick. It made her want to pull the duvet over her head. And she knew that it wasn't just her parents' disastrous marriage. She didn't feel that she deserved it all: the home, the happy family, Ariana . . . She was just Kate, plain, overweight, not good enough for a gorgeous girlfriend and a happy life. So instead, she buried herself in her work, in her clients, her business plan – anything to shut it out.

She understood why Ariana wanted to get a move on, of course. They were both forty-one now and their friends were settled. It was normal to want to buy someplace together and make it gorgeous. Get a dog. Call each other 'my wife'. And yet Kate just couldn't do it. At every wedding they went to, they were asked the dreaded question: 'Are you two next?'

At first, they had laughed it off. Now, after ten years of weddings and christenings, Ariana would flinch, and Kate would feel tight-chested and panicked. And then they would fight when they were alone. 'You're going to lose me because you're too scared to take what you actually want from life, Kate. It's like you don't think you deserve to be happy,' Ariana would sob. 'You think that you don't deserve a better marriage than your mum and dad.'

Scared, thought Kate. That was probably right. Perhaps it was all the Catholic guilt of her childhood that made her feel undeserving. Perhaps it was that Ariana was so great, it was intimidating. Perhaps it was something else, some deep-rooted insecurity that had been with Kate since childhood. The voice that told Kate not to order the pasta she wanted but the salad instead, to dress in shapeless clothes so that people looked past her, to shy away from commitment in case it turned out wrong. Either way, she was screwing everything up.

The seeds for this recent argument had been planted years before, but the row itself had started weeks before the holiday. 'I'm not going to be able to eat a thing now in Portugal,' Kate had said, patting her tummy, as they walked hand in hand through Kilkenny after a pub lunch.

'Nonsense. You should enjoy yourself,' Ariana had replied. Her usually patient voice had a note of irritation in it. 'For goodness' sake, Kate. I hate that you can't look forward to a holiday without worrying about food. Can't you just get over this?'

Kate had flushed. 'Sorry for being so annoying.'

Ariana had sighed. 'You're not being annoying, Kate. It's just . . . you've been like this since you were, what – fifteen? Fretting about eating too much, wearing the wrong thing. What you could have done differently or better. Are you going to beat yourself up your whole life? It sucks the joy out of everything. Besides,' she'd added. 'I think you're just perfect.'

'Thanks,' Kate had managed a smile. It was true. Over the years, Kate had battled with her weight, and no matter whether she was slim in her mind, or gorgeously curvy in Ariana's, she was never happy. She'd tried Atkins, fasting, cabbage soup – the more ridiculous the diet, the better. It wasn't all in her head – she knew there was prejudice against her every day. She had experienced cabin crew looking at her with distaste as she took up a little bit more than one seat, strangers on public transport, children (not their fault but it still hurt) and randomers walking down the street, nudging and sniggering as Kate walked slowly along. She used to pretend that she didn't notice but she did. Sometimes, she could actually feel her own heart in her ears, feel the embarrassment and shame rising up like a wave.

It had started with puberty, and a convent school on Dublin's south side was pretty much the worst place to be a bit larger. Not to mention the acne, braces and thick-lensed glasses. It was only when she met Dee, Sam, Georgie and Beth that she'd been accepted for who she was. And they'd all stuck up for her. But still, it hurt. She'd told herself she couldn't go to parties and discos. 'I've got my period,' she would say, unable to look them in the eye. She'd hated deceiving her friends but going just wasn't an option. She knew that everyone would look at her and whisper about the fat girl in the too-small jeans. Instead, she would stay in her room and write in her diary about how ugly and lame she was.

Tomorrow I'll change, she would write. Then she would fall asleep crying and wake up again and do it all the same. Sometimes, she'd looked back at helpless fifteen-year-old Kate and her heart broke for her. But was she really that different now, aged forty-one? Inside, she was the same Kate she'd always been, she thought sadly.

At least she had good friends, now and back then. The five of them – and, on the outskirts, Ariana, for whom Kate's feelings had never been simple.

It had started in school, around fifth year, so she would have been sixteen. She was never sure when she had first known that she fancied her classmate with the glamorous glasses and honey-brown bob, but one day, she realised that she did. For a long time, she had ignored the feelings. Didn't admit it to herself. Fancying another girl was a bit weird, wasn't it? She hoped that one day she would just wake up and feel 'normal'. She couldn't be attracted to another girl. Not in Ireland.

And even though Kate's parents had long since stopped getting on, outside the house, they liked to put on a united front. They were Mass-goers. Her mum was the social queen of Blackrock. It just wouldn't do! And, Kate thought, what would the nuns think! They would be shocked and disappointed. And her friends would surely laugh. No, she couldn't fancy Ariana.

Still, she and Ariana had started to hang out, just the two of them. A lot. Phoning each other and chatting for hours. They were different personalities: Kate was shy, quiet, anxious, always dressed in baggy tracksuits. Ariana was cool, with trendy clothes and shiny hair and parents who let her stay out late. She had been the first of all of them to get a boyfriend, although she'd ditched him after six weeks and snogged Carrie White instead. No one seemed to mind that, Kate had noticed, but then everyone liked Ariana. They listened to her, didn't look through her like they did Kate. But Ariana didn't look through her. She laughed at Kate's jokes and listened to her stories. To Ariana, Kate was interesting and Kate had never been interesting before.

You'd never have put Kate and Ariana together. They were the oddest of odd couples. But they got on so well. They loved the same music, the same books and the same films. Each dreamed of art school in the city, of freedom.

They were soulmates, Kate would think, alone in her bedroom. None of her friends had realised their feelings for each other, thank God, until Dee did. Which was weird, given that

Dee was the most self-absorbed out of all of them. All the same, she had a keen, observant eye and was always the first to pick up on gossip. She had certainly picked up on this. One morning in a fourth year maths class, she'd leaned across to Kate and whispered, 'I've seen how you look at Ariana.' And she'd smiled.

Kate had stared at her, aghast, then had immediately turned puce and burst out crying.

'What's wrong now, Kate?' their teacher had said wearily. Kate was always having panic attacks, another thing that no one seemed to understand. She didn't have them on purpose. It was just that life seemed overwhelming sometimes.

'I'll take her to the office, shall I?' Dee had said, getting up and bustling Kate out.

In the corridor, Kate had leaned against the wall, taking in gulps of air. Her palms were sweating.

'Jesus,' Dee had said, leaning back against the door. Her tone had been half-kindly, half irritable. 'Take deep breaths or whatever you're meant to do. Come on, that's it.'

'Please don't tell anyone, Dee,' Kate had pleaded, as soon as she could take a breath. 'My mum would kill me if she thought I liked girls. She'll think she's failed me as a mother.'

Dee had rolled her eyes. 'For feck's sake Kate, I wouldn't have said anything if I'd known you'd be so dramatic. Who cares if it's two boys, or two girls, or anything else?' She had put her arm around her, an unusual gesture from Dee. 'Kate, be who you are. Who are you trying to impress? Your parents? The nuns? It is your life, and you only have one, so feck everyone else and be who you truly are and with who you genuinely want to be with.'

'Fine for you to say,' Kate had whispered. Dee was gorgeous and cool, and everyone tried to copy her. She was one of the 'popular, pretty girls' in the school, not an ugly, confused idiot. Every girl wanted to be like Dee and every boy wanted to date her.

She was ultra confident in her own skin and didn't care what anyone thought of her, including the teachers. She took no crap from anyone!

'You worry too much Kate,' Dee had told her, taking a crumpled packet of Marlboro Lights out of her blazer. Kate had already heard that plenty of times over the years. 'Come on, let's take the long way to the nurse's office and have a fag. You always assume the worst. If you ask me, you should stop staring at Ariana all the time and tell her how you feel.' She had winked. 'It might pay off.'

'Again. fine for you to say,' Kate had said, wiping her face. 'Has anyone ever said no to you?'

'No,' Dee had giggled, leading the way out to the bike sheds.

All the same, Kate had taken Dee's words to heart. It is your life, and you only have one, so feck everyone else and be who you truly are and with who you genuinely want to be with. She had carried them with her throughout school, the mantra running through her head. Be who you truly are and with who you genuinely want to be with. She trusted Dee. Dee wasn't the sort to say something she didn't mean, just to be kind. And Kate wanted to be with Ariana. They were clearly soulmates. Kate, who doubted everything in life, had no doubt about that. She was sure that one day the rest of the world would know it too and that they would be with each other forever. She just hadn't got around to telling Ariana yet.

And then, in their first year of art college, where they were studying together, Kate had decided it was time. Sitting on the rug in their student accommodation, slightly stoned, listening to PJ Harvey, Kate had just come out with it. 'Ariana. I like you. Really like you.'

'Thank God,' Ariana had said, putting out the joint. 'I thought I was going to have to be even more obvious than following you to the same art school.'

'Wait. You like me too?' Kate had asked incredulously.

'You idiot,' Ariana had said fondly. 'Now come here.' Kate had gone to sit beside Ariana and wrapped her arms around her friend. Then, after a good hour of passionate, intermittent snogging, Ariana had said, 'What the hell are your parents going to say? Mine are cool but yours are not.'

To Kate's astonishment, though, her parents didn't seem to care much. Maybe the state of their own marriage didn't qualify them to comment. Neither did Ariana's. Neither did all their neighbours. In fact, no one batted an eyelid. They were all simply happy that the girls were happy. The only worry that anyone had was how young they both were.

'You don't want to tie yourself down too early,' her mum had told Kate one day, after she and Ariana had graduated art college and were looking for a flat together. 'See what else is out there, you know? God knows, I wish I had.'

'Good to know,' Kate's dad had muttered.

For once, Mum ignored him. 'But seriously, Kate,' her mum said. 'There are other fish in the sea, you know.'

But Ariana and Kate had proved them wrong. They had lasted and twenty-two years later they had settled into their careers and lives together, renting a small home in Co. Kilkenny, where Ariana ran her art gallery and Kate had established her life-coaching business.

Professionally, Kate was someone else. Someone super tough and capable. She was renowned for her client presentations, and she'd stood at many podiums oozing confidence. She felt in control and comfortable when she was giving a talk. Her small team of five life coaches had the Kilkenny, Carlow and Kildare area covered and were spreading their good reputation to Dublin. She had always wanted to be successful in work, so that people would think that she was super confident and happy in her own skin. They would see more than the fat girl in ill-fitting clothes.

Only now, Ariana wanted more. And the old, insecure Kate had resurfaced. Now, in her pretty room at Hotel Edene, Kate looked down at the flowing skirt she had put on. As usual, it was a sort of murky, greenish-greyish-brownish colour. If her wardrobe was nondescript, she hoped she wouldn't stand out. Getting engaged, planning a wedding, having kids . . . all of those decisions waited for Kate back home. But for now, she could put her head in the sand and pretend none of them existed. Or at least, run them past the girls so they seemed less huge and scary. Kate could hear Beth's loud voice on the corridor, chattering to Dee as they headed towards the bar. She smiled. It was time to head down and find her friends.

Chapter Seven

'To us!' The girls toasted each other with iced sangria in the bar a few minutes later. 'To the Mini Breakers!'

'I'm so glad we managed this,' said Kate, beaming. 'I know it's hard what with work and children, but we did it. I don't want us to ever grow apart, you know? You are my long-term friends, my history, and you mean the world to me.'

'What a speech, Kate,' said Sam, smiling. 'It must be all those motivational talks you keep giving.'

'I mean it,' insisted Kate. 'We're living in other countries now. It's important for us to find time for each other. We don't want to grow apart!'

'No way,' said Beth firmly. 'That would literally never happen.'

'Of course not,' said Georgie, pushing back her fair waves.

Oh God, Dee thought, smoothing down her designer beach dress and glancing around the room. Was it just her or did it suddenly feel three sizes too small for her? And her friends, whom she loved and had kept in touch with all of these years, seemed . . . well, old and tired. Was she old and tired? Dee felt herself grow hot. She thought of the incident in the bathroom at work, about how she was 'up for review', like an old, rusty banger.

Kate touched her elbow. 'You okay?' she mouthed.

'Fine,' Dee snapped irritably.

'Are we going to eat lunch, girls?' Beth broke into her thoughts. 'I'm starving.'

'Defo,' they all agreed in unison standing up and heading out to the pretty, shaded terrace. They sat under a pergola filled with bright pink flowers. A gentle breeze broke the heat. As they all took their seats, a tall Portuguese waiter came over to their table. His eyes were chocolate brown, and he smelled gorgeous. Dee saw all the girls sit up straighter and try to look pretty, the way they would at sports day when one of the football boys walked past. Some things never change, she thought, sitting up even straighter, fixing him with a beam.

'The menus, ladies,' he said as he passed them around. He made direct eye contact with each of them for two seconds each time.

'It feels like we are getting communion from the priest in Mass,' whispered Beth to Kate. 'Only better.' The others tried to stifle their laughter. It would only take one of them to set the others off.

'This looks delicious,' said Kate. She scanned the menu, looking at the gorgeous pastas and fritto misto. 'I might just get a starter though. Something small, like the bruschetta.'

For God's sake, Dee thought. Was Kate still obsessing about food at her age? She flicked her eye over the dishes and decided a small salade Niçoise would be perfect. She wasn't that hungry anyway.

'Is that a proper meal though?' said Georgie to Kate. 'You need nutrients. Something with protein, like the chicken salad. I've got a whole section on this in my book.'

Kate bit her lip. 'You're right,' she said.

'Bruschetta makes me very constipated,' Dee blurted in her clear newsreader's voice just as the poor waiter, whom they all thought had gone, said, 'Anything to drink?'

Mortified, Dee pretended to look for something important in her bag. 'I think it's all the tomatoes,' she whispered. 'Is he still standing there? Jesus, how embarrassing.'

Ever since she'd joined TV Gold, she hadn't allowed herself to be anything other than the polished newsreader with the megawatt smile, so to be discussing her . . . bowels, was mortifying. What had gotten into her? And the others were trying not to laugh.

'Sounds like the old Dee,' Sam said. 'It's great to see her.'

'Oh yes please. Just all the bottles of Pinot Grigio that you have. Everything. The full stock, thank you,' Beth said, completely seriously, closing the wine menu and smiling sweetly.

'Um, maybe we should just start with one bottle for now please,' Kate said to the confused waiter. 'And I'll have the chicken salad.'

She smiled weakly at Georgie. 'Plenty of protein, right?'

'I have a few questions about the menu,' Dee told the waiter, with a dazzling smile. That smile always won people over. Lord knows she'd used it enough.

'Here we go,' whispered Beth to Kate.

'What?' Dee said.

'Nothing!' Beth piped up. 'You go ahead.'

'Can I have the Niçoise salad?' said Dee. 'But light on the anchovies and remove the olives, and if there's garlic in the dressing, please put it on the side.' She frowned at the menu. 'Are the eggs organic, can I ask?' she said. She hated the idea of eating eggs from battery hens.

'I, um. Yes,' the waiter said. 'I'm sure they are. At least, I think so.'

Dee narrowed her eyes. 'You don't sound sure. Lose the eggs but in that case, I want extra croutons, ok?'

The waiter scribbled down their orders and left. Kate picked up the bread, then put it back down again.

Just eat the bread, Dee thought. You're an adult! No one cares. Nonetheless, she kept her hand firmly away from the bread basket. It wouldn't do to put on weight on this holiday – although, come to think of it, maybe it wouldn't matter anymore, she thought sadly.

The table looked so pretty, with the baskets of bread and their wine glasses. Georgie pulled out her phone and took some snaps.

'Is that for your Instagram page?' said Sam.

'Yeah,' said Georgie. 'Apparently, followers like to see a slice of ordinary life alongside the yoga stuff.'

'How sweet,' said Dee. 'All those housewives in the 'burbs. Got a few followers on your little page now, have you?'

'Actually Dee, you may not be aware, but she has four hundred thousand followers,' said Sam tartly. 'It's not really a "little" Instagram page – it's a business. And she's getting a book deal.'

Dee's startled gaze whipped round to Georgie, who went pink.

'What?'

There was Dee, facing the chop while unassuming Georgie was building an audience for wafting around on a yoga mat.

'A book deal? You didn't tell me that,' said Dee accusingly. Why did she feel so incredibly jealous of her friend? The girls had a rule that they always celebrated each other's successes, but Dee was so used to the successes all being hers. She looked down at her plate, willing herself not to say something sarcastic or mean.

'Um, well they're still ironing out the contract,' Georgie said apologetically.

'But the publisher loves it, right? said Beth.

'Yeah, pretty much,' said Georgie, smiling shyly. 'For three books. There's talk of some TV appearances. You'll have to give me some tips, Dee.'

'Of course,' Dee said brightly. She raised her glass, 'Here's to Georgie, our new media star!' The others raised theirs too, clinking and yelling 'congratulations'. Only Georgie looked at Dee nervously. She knows, Dee thought. She can see that I'm not happy for her. How the hell can I be when my life is falling apart? She was jealous. That was it. Jealous of poor little Georgie.

'Hands up who has their period?' Beth asked suddenly, raising hers, just as the waiter brought their salads. Dee was sure he gave a weary sigh. 'You know, because we are always in synch. We always have been!'

'Not yet,' said Sam, 'but I'm due today, I think.' She sighed heavily, and the others looked at her gently. She shrugged and tried to put a brave face. What a pity she wasn't a mum, Dee thought. Motherhood was absolutely not for her, but Sam would be a great one. Dee had bigger fish to fry. Although come to think of it, her period was late. Very late. And she usually ran like clockwork.

'I'm running late,' she said softly to no one in particular.

'Not to worry, I have shitloads of tampons,' said Beth, again oblivious to any undercurrents. 'My periods these days are off the scale. The flow, wow. I power through tampons, period pants, the lot. Sometimes I have to double up–'

'Beth, please stop talking about tampons,' said Dee, noticing a woman at the next table shoot them a dirty look. She just wasn't able for Beth today. Why did she always have to yell like that?

'Okay, relax, Dee.' Beth laughed, taking a sip of wine, clearly feeling merry and loving life already. 'We can talk about this stuff, right?' We're middle-aged.'

'Speak for yourself,' said Dee. She hadn't spent all that money on her face and body to be called 'middle-aged'. Although maybe that's the way others saw her now.

Beth took another sip of wine, looking embarrassed in spite of herself. Dee knew what she was thinking: they had always talked about everything together. Their first periods. First kisses. First sex. Nothing had been too weird or embarrassing to share with the group. When had that all suddenly changed?

'Speaking of middle-aged,' said Kate quickly, 'Has anyone read that we're meant to get a surge of sexual energy in your early forties?'

'Now, that's interesting,' said Dee, leaning forward, relieved that the others hadn't heard her talking about being late. 'I have never felt more desirable to be honest, guys.' She licked her glossy lips. It was true. As much as the network might think she was past it, she felt gloriously alive. For some reason, her skin glowed and her boobs were larger than usual. She almost wished she'd had them done a size smaller.

'You do look amazing,' Georgie said automatically.

Dee preened happily. 'That's probably my wellness regime.'

'Which is?' said Sam. 'Because I like to think I take care of myself too. Regular mani-pedis, that sort of thing. The odd bit of Botox.'

Dee laughed pityingly. 'Oh, are you still doing Botox? It's all about polynucleotides these days.' She began to tell them all about the latest discoveries, on which she'd spent an awful lot of money, but something was telling her that the source of her energy came from inside. God, listen to her, she'd be turning into Georgie any minute now, going on about her chakras.

'I waxed my own bikini line last night,' said Beth. 'Or at least half of it before one of the kids woke up.'

'Poor you,' Sam said sympathetically. Then her phone beeped and she glanced at it and went pale.

'What's up, pet?' Beth said.

'It's from Jeff. He's made the IVF appointment,' Sam was staring at the phone as if expecting it to jump off the table at her.

'Oh wow! Congratulations,' Kate said. 'I didn't know that you were still trying.' Her voice trailed off as she took in Sam's expression. 'Is everything okay?'

Sam sighed. 'I don't know. Jeff really wants a baby, but I'm not so sure. I like what we have. A baby will change all that.' She looked at Beth. 'Sorry, Beth, yours are gorgeous, it's just . . .'

'I get it,' Beth laughed. 'They're a handful. And your life changes completely once you have them. There's no going back really.'

'You make it sound like so much fun,' Dee said dryly and they all managed a laugh.

Beth squeezed Sam's hand. 'You're on holiday. Talk to Jeff when you get home.'

'There's our food,' Kate said, clearly relieved at the opportunity to change the subject.

*

After lunch and a couple of glasses of wine, the mood among the women quietened. They'd done their catching up, the sun was beating down and after the journey, it was clear that they were all feeling it.

'Why don't we go over there?' said Georgie, as they finished their meal. She pointed to a quiet pool area away from the other guests. They could have a chat in peace. And if Dee insisted on banging on about every celebrity she had ever met and Beth wanted to talk about her flow, they could do it without everyone else having to hear them. She smiled. Was it just her, or were the girls even more . . . themselves on this holiday? Kate was more uptight than usual, Sam more preoccupied, Beth louder and more eccentric. Dee was more of an egomaniac than ever. And her? Well, she was probably a people-pleaser, a peacekeeper, as usual. She'd even managed to ignore Dee's barbed comments about her publishing contract.

As if on cue, she jumped up and said, 'I'll go and get us a few supplies for the afternoon. Can't do without the factor thirty!' As she got up to head to her room, she could see Beth spin around.

'Are you ready? Okay, one, two, three!' Beth yelled, before dropping her towel dramatically.

'Always good to announce yourself,' said Sam lazily. 'Hey, love the bikini.'

Beth beamed at her. 'Great, isn't it? From Penney's, only two euro in the sale.'

'I'll have to check it out,' said Dee insincerely, removing her flimsy cover-up and glancing down at her toned stomach in her Hunza G bikini.

'Jesus Christ, hello, Katie Price!' Beth screamed.

'Bloody hell,' Dee hissed. 'I don't want the whole pool looking over. And Katie Price wasn't exactly what I was going for, thank you very much.' She glanced uncertainly down at her boobs.

'You didn't tell me you were inviting two more girls along on this trip,' smirked Beth, 'Did you pay for the excess luggage?' She burst out laughing.

'Funny,' snapped Dee.

'Shut up Beth,' said Sam, fighting a smile. 'Sorry Dee. They're just . . . hard to miss, you know?'

'Can you all just be grown up about this?' said Dee, looking hurt.

'Yeah, sorry,' said Sam, shooting Beth a look. 'You look fab, Dee.'

'Thanks,' said Dee, looking somewhat mollified, picking up a copy of the Hollywood edition of *Vanity Fair* and settling down. She dropped her towel again just as Georgie was walking over with chilled bottles of water and huge bags of crisps in her tote.

'Dee! Your boobs!' she gasped, dropping the bag and covering her mouth. She couldn't help herself. They were huge.

'Right, that's it!' Dee aggressively slammed down her magazine. 'I'm going to sunbathe somewhere else if you guys are going to treat me like some sort of tourist attraction.'

There was a moment of silence.

'Can we feel them before you go?' Beth asked. 'Just for a sec?'

'See you later, guys.' Dee stood up, grabbing her towel and bag. 'I'm going to find a quiet place to read my magazine in peace. Somewhere people aren't dissecting my boobs or my, my career, or . . . argh!' she stomped off, beach bag and magazine in hand.

'Shit,' said Kate as they all lay down on their sunbeds and got comfortable. 'That is one annoyed Deirdre Byrne.'

'Yeah, I feel a bit bad now,' Georgie said. 'I shouldn't have wound her up like that.'

They all knew that when Dee was cross, it took her a long time to cool down and she found it difficult to let things go and move on. Dee was more sensitive than she let on.

Beth started giggling and then broke into a dirty laugh and couldn't stop. 'But they're so big. Surely, they're a lot bigger than when we saw them last?'

'I imagine she's had something done,' said Sam.

'And – and Georgie's face . . .' Beth managed, laughing uncontrollably. 'Oh no, I've wee'd myself,' she added in between wheezing gasps.

'Beth!' Georgie started to giggle at Beth's infectious laugh. 'Guys, I feel so bad. Her tits look great and I shouldn't have reacted like that.' She sat up. 'I'm going to go and find her and say sorry.'

'I'd leave her to cool down,' said Kate, the voice of reason from the sun lounger.

'Well, do you think we should at least text her?' said Georgie nervously. 'I hate the idea that she's angry with me.' She fidgeted with her sunglasses.

The others exchanged glances. 'Dee is just in a mood,' said Beth at last.

'Yeah, and . . .' Kate hesitated.

'And she's always been jealous of you,' said Sam bluntly.

'Dee? Jealous? Of me?' said Georgie, frowning. 'But why?' Dee had everything, Georgie thought. A fabulous career, a great lifestyle. She didn't even have a Paddy around to bring her down.

'There's only room for one A-lister in the group,' Sam explained. 'Dee's used to it being her but lately, with your Instagram and stuff, you're giving her a run for her money, I think.'

'And you're beautiful and you don't even know it,' added Kate. 'It's always driven Dee wild.'

'That's silly,' said Georgie flushing uncomfortably. 'She can't be threatened by me. Dee is an actual famous person. I'm famous to a load of middle-aged yoga fans.'

'That's where it's at nowadays,' Sam said. 'Maybe Dee's feeling a bit past it. Anyway, something is winding her up,' she said thoughtfully, 'We'll just have to wait to find out what, I suppose.'

They all nodded. They'd seen Dee lose her rag plenty of times before and it wasn't pretty. She could bear a serious grudge. In sixth year in school, she once hadn't spoken to them for two solid weeks because they had forgotten to wait for her at the bus stop.

'Look at that sweet old couple,' said Sam, looking over her sunglasses a few minutes later. 'Look at them holding hands. I hope me and Jeff are like that when we're eighty.'

Kate pulled down her own sunglasses to look. The couple seemed to notice them and gave then a wave as they walked past to the pool. The lady was small and pretty, with wide-set, innocent eyes and fluffy white hair and the man looked digni-fied, like a retired army type, with a neat white moustache. The girls all waved back.

'Hello, girls. I'm Margie,' the woman said, pausing. 'And this is Roger. We come here with our friends every year! A whole gang of us. Some of us have been friends since school.'

'How lovely,' said Sam. 'To stay friends all this time and plan holidays together.'

Another handsome, older man joined them and gave them all a courtly little bow. 'And this is Davey,' said Margie. 'We have some little games nights up in the boardroom. You young things will have to join us! Seven o'clock tonight – don't be late!'

'Maybe,' said Sam, hiding a smile. 'Nice to meet you, Margie.'

The trio strolled off, chatting away.

'Nice to be one of the youngest for a change, isn't it?' said Kate, rolling over onto her stomach.

'It's amazing,' said Beth, stretching luxuriously. 'The sun . . . No children anywhere . . . ' She bit her lip. 'Speaking of which, I wonder how Jack is getting on with the kids. It's Scouts tonight. I hope he won't forget. I've left big reminders all over the place on Post-it notes and I've added it to his Google calendar . . .'

'I'm sure he can cope without you for a few days, Beth,' said Sam. 'He's a grown man with a serious job, so if he can't take care of his own children by now, maybe he should learn. Now remember. Give yourself a break – no kid talk.' Georgie looked at Sam. Maybe the IVF message had hit home. After all, they'd been waiting for years and Sam didn't like to wait for anything. She caught Beth's eye and Beth nodded in agreement. No more kid talk.

'Jack will be fine,' Georgie said softly. 'He's Big Jack, isn't he? He can handle anything. Criminals. Gangsters. Small children.' She winked. 'Even you.'

Beth smiled.

'See? I'm right,' Georgie said. 'You're a lucky woman, Beth.' You don't know how lucky, she thought.

'I know,' Beth said happily.

The afternoon passed in a pleasant haze of lazy reading, dips in the pool and giggling over stories so old they could recite them from memory. Now and then, Georgie thought of Dee, wondered if she should go and find her, but Kate was right. She'd be better after a nap and a vodka martini before dinner. Eventually, feeling relaxed after a lovely afternoon in the sun, she eased herself off her sun lounger. 'Ladies, I think I'll go upstairs to change,' she said, stretching and yawning. 'See you in an hour!' They'd booked a taxi into town for dinner earlier and Georgie was starving. She thought about the seafood she'd have and her stomach began to rumble.

*

Dee wasn't in the room when Beth came up to get ready. Weird, she thought. Maybe she had stormed off somewhere to drown her sorrows. Still, Beth could use the peace and quiet. She had a long, cool, peaceful shower, dried her hair, got dressed and drafted a text to Jack. They had agreed not to text except in case of emergency, so that Beth could properly switch off, but one little text couldn't hurt, could it?

Beth began to type.

All ok with the kids?

No, too controlling. Of course everything was okay! That made it look as if she didn't have faith in him.

Hope all good!!!!

Too perky. Too many exclamation marks.

She thought about just calling Jack and then she could speak to the kids too. But no – that was lame and boring of her. She wasn't that much of a desperate housewife that she couldn't enjoy a few nights away. And no one else was worrying about what was happening at home.

She was just drafting a third, even-more-casual text when there was a knock on the door. Sam and Georgie appeared in the doorway, both looking gorgeous. 'Where's Dee?' asked Sam.

'No idea, not here,' said Beth, 'She can text us if she needs us. Shall we check out this OAP gathering before dinner then?'

'Why not?' said Sam. 'I'd like to hear that sweet old couple's stories. Find out how to make my marriage last. And I got the impression they'd like a few young things like us livening the place up. They must get a bit bored, coming to the same place every year with the same crew.'

'You don't think we should look for Dee, do you?' said Georgie.

Sam shook her head. 'You know what her tantrums are like. Vicious, but they'll blow over eventually.'

The three girls walked downstairs, laughing and chatting and met Kate in reception. It was buzzing, with disco music playing and people milling around. The receptionist was on a call, looking exasperated. 'I'm so sorry, miss, I'm not sure how the mosquito got in but there's not much we can do now . . .'

'Where is the boardroom?' Georgie mouthed at her. 'We're looking for the–'

The receptionist covered the phone with her hand. 'For the party? Room fourteen and don't forget to knock three times or you will not get in. Do you understand, Madame?'

She gave her a serious look from behind her glasses.

'Riiiiiight, okay, thank you,' Georgie said.

'Three times?' said Beth, bewildered. 'What the hell?'

'I don't know,' said Sam. 'Maybe it's a . . . secret party?' she giggled.

'A secret Scrabble party?'

'Well, let's check it out and if it's weird or boring, we can go and get a drink,' said Kate.

They headed along the corridor, listening for laughter, until they reached a room with a small sign on the door marked BOARDROOM. But just as they were about to knock three times, they heard Dee's voice right behind them.

'Well, thanks a lot!'

They all jumped and turned to see her limping up the corridor towards them.

'Dee?' said Georgie nervously. 'W-we were wondering where you were.'

'Oh really?' she said coldly. 'Looking all over for me, were you?'

'Well, where have you been?' said Sam matter-of-factly.

'My stomach was upset, as you all knew,' said Dee with dignity. 'So, I went to the pool toilet, only I got locked in for three hours and none of you came to my rescue! I had to kick the door down and I hurt my ankle. I might have fractured it. Some best friends you are!'

She spat out the last bit venomously. Her eyes were black with rage. This was bad. When Dee was really angry, she could terrify everyone in her path. And, for some reason, she was even angrier now than they remembered.

Kate gave the others a look that said, 'remind me, why are we still friends with this woman?'

Beth returned it, frowning and the others understood. Way back when they were fourteen, they had sworn to remain friends forever, no matter what changed. That promise was more important than any one of them, Beth thought.

'Jesus, Dee, I'm sorry,' she said guiltily. 'We thought you were just off somewhere on your own.' She put a hand on Dee's arm. It was shaking.

'And then you decided to go off without me,' snapped Dee. 'Brilliant. Amazing.' She looked hot, sweaty, dishevelled and a bit anxious. Very un-Dee.

'Let's go back and get you cleaned up before dinner?' Sam suggested.

'Fine,' snarled Dee.

The others glanced at each other as she hobbled back up the corridor. This was extreme even for Dee.

When they got back to the room, the girls all sat on her bed, like grounded teenagers, watching Dee storm into the shower and slam the door. They looked at each other again.

'What is going on?' Kate whispered. 'This is a bit much, even for her.'

'It's that colonic,' said Georgie worriedly. 'It's not good to mess with your mind-body balance like that.'

'You can handle her, can't you Beth?' whispered Sam. 'Let the rest of us have a breather?'

'Fine,' sighed Beth. 'I am used to dealing with tantrum-throwing children. You guys go. Save yourselves. We'll catch up with you in a bit.'

The girls slipped out of the room as soon as they heard the running water stop. Beth waited on the bed. Dee swept out at last, clean, wearing a silk dressing gown, and smothered in expensive-smelling moisturiser.

Beth said nothing for a long time, letting Dee sit down at the dressing table and begin to apply make-up. Eventually, she said meekly, 'Do you want some Imodium? If your tummy is bad?'

Dee sighed.

'No thanks.' She sounded tired, but not angry any more. 'And sorry about losing my rag earlier. I overreacted.'

'Talk to me,' Beth said in her kind voice. She recognised a tired and anxious child when she saw one. 'Are you a bit stressed, lovey?'

Dee sighed again, heavier this time.

'No. I mean, I am stressed, but . . . well. I'm pregnant, Beth.'

Chapter Eight

There was a stunned silence.

'Pregnant?! How?!' Beth shouted, her calm manner deserting her. 'And – and by who?!'

Dee groaned.

'Can you not shout, Beth? It's a frickin' secret, first of all, and secondly . . . well, you of all people must know how you get pregnant, for God's sake.'

'Okay,' said Beth in a loud whisper. 'I understand how you got pregnant, obviously. But with whom? You never talk about guys on our calls.' Beth made a point of FaceTiming Dee every Saturday morning, when the kids were in front of the telly, so she could hear all about Dee's glamorous lifestyle and live it vicariously through her. In spite of Dee's tantrums, Beth understood her and the drive that had got her to Manhattan. Plus, she was a very generous godmother to the twins. The others called Beth the 'Dee Whisperer'.

Dee thought before answering her. 'I don't know, to be honest,' she said at last. 'I've been trying to work out the dates while I was stuck in that bastard toilet. I've narrowed it down though.'

'To whom?' said Beth.

'Well, to one of three guys,' said Dee.

'One of three guys?' said Beth, looking stunned.

'Don't look so judgmental. Work has been pretty stressful lately, and I wanted to have a bit of fun,' said Dee defensively. 'I'm single, what's the problem?'

'Bloody hell,' said Beth. 'I'm impressed. So, that's how dating works in the Big Apple. Did you think you might be pregnant when you came on holiday then?'

'No!' wailed Dee. 'Of course I didn't. But my period was super late, so I bought a test in JFK just to be safe. I thought I'd do it by the pool but then I wee'd on my hand because it was my first time ever using a pregnancy test and then the main door of the women's toilets slammed shut and then I was stuck. It was dark, too. I had to use my phone light to see the test and that's when I saw the two red lines.' She shuddered. 'It was a serious shock.'

'Right,' said Beth slowly. 'Two red lines. That sounds pretty pregnant all right.' She kept her voice steady as she could see Dee's hands shaking.

Dee sighed. 'This was not part of the plan, not at all, Beth. Babies. I'm just not wired like that, you know?' she said. 'There's nothing wrong with kids – they're just not for me.' She tried to control her breathing; it was getting faster and soon she was gasping for air.

'Well, then you won't have the baby,' Beth said practically. 'Right?'

'Right,' said Dee slowly. 'Right. Yeah. Only the thing is . . .'

'What?' said Beth.

'I'm not sure,' said Dee, her voice catching. 'Whenever I think about getting rid of it, I want to cry. Maybe that's the pregnancy hormones talking, but . . . part of me thinks . . . maybe I do want this baby. Maybe I'm maternal after all.'

Beth stared at her. Deirdre Byrne? Maternal? This was a twist she hadn't seen coming. She gathered herself. 'Look, I'll call the girls. We can cancel dinner and have an emergency meeting here.'

Beth went to reach for her mobile phone, but Dee grabbed her arm. 'No, not yet – please, Beth. I need more time to think,' she said. 'If I want to go ahead, and it's a seriously big if, I need to make that call by myself. Georgie will be talking about my pelvic floor and the importance of my core and whether or not this baby is in tune with the moon, Kate will be going through my healthcare plan and worrying about scans and folic acid. And Sam . . .' Dee trailed off. 'Well, Sam's been trying for years to get pregnant herself, hasn't she? I don't want this to upset her, especially when I haven't decided what to do yet.'

Beth nodded. 'That's true,' she said. It was uncharacteristically thoughtful of Dee, but she had that in her when she wasn't storming around being the big star. 'And you really have no idea which one of this, er, three blokes it was?' she asked curiously. She was in full investigation mode now. If only she could get hold of Dee's calendar and cross-reference it with her cycle . . .

'No,' said Dee. 'I can't even remember their names.' She thought for a bit. 'One guy was called . . . was it, Paul? Something beginning with a 'P' anyway. He stayed over and left his number. He was nice. The other guy was an accountant, I think. Or an actuary. Boring. And the other guy was a dancer. Super flexible, kept his socks on. I can't remember their names at all.'

She sighed and then in a small voice added, 'I never thought I'd need to, you see.'

Beth pulled her friend towards her in a hug. She pushed Dee's head onto her shoulder and patted it. 'We'll figure this out,' she told her. 'If you go ahead with this, and, yes, I get it's a big "if", you'll be a great mum.' She smiled reassuringly, trying to imagine Dee as a mother, covered in baby sick. She couldn't imagine it exactly, but she knew that that didn't mean anything. Motherhood was anyone's guess. Dee stood as good a chance of being a great mum as anyone.

'Really?' sniffed Dee against Beth's shoulder. 'Because you know how selfish my parents were. I've always tried so hard to be independent, to avoid attachment. And now, look what's happened. If I do this, it's the ultimate attachment.'

Beth nodded. 'You're not your mum and dad. And we'll figure it out together. Somehow.' She wiped Dee's eyes with the corner of her dress. 'Now. Shall we go get a drink?'

Dee managed a small smile. 'An orange juice.'

'With a large vodka in mine,' Beth laughed.

*

In the bar, the girls were on the high stools, posing and looking lovely. They were laughing but sobered up sharpish when they saw Dee.

'Dee, how are you?' Kate jumped up. 'I'm sorry we didn't come looking for you.' She peered at her friend. 'You look a bit pale. Are you not feeling well?'

'I'm okay now,' Dee said, flashing Beth a firm look. Beth was known for not being able to hold her water when it came to secrets. Dee hoped she could at least keep this one to herself.

'Oh good. Listen, I booked us a table at an Italian place, Romanzo,' said Kate, holding out her phone. 'The reviews are amazing. I had to put our names down months ago. And I've got a taxi waiting.'

'Great, amazing, let's go,' Beth said, avoiding their gaze.

They drove through the old town, with its quiet cobbled streets, to the restaurant. From the car, they could see couples and families queuing outside, trying to be patient. It was very satisfying being able to stroll past them all and ask for their table. Not for the first time, Beth thanked Kate silently for being the organiser in the group. The restaurant was small and stunning, all outdoors, but set against a stone wall down which trailed bright red flowers. The tables and chairs were made of mahogany, covered in crisp white tablecloths with pretty silver cutlery. The coloured glasses shone in the candlelight and the pianist played quietly under a canopy of fairy lights. It was like a beautiful dream, Beth thought, one far away from fish fingers and *KPop Demon Hunters*.

'This is nice, isn't it?' said Georgie, taking a seat and looking around. 'Thanks so much for sorting it, Kate.'

'No worries. Now, guys,' Kate said, pulling a notebook out from her bag. 'Agenda time.' There was a chorus of loud groans and Kate hurried on. 'I know, I know, but we only get together once a year – and it's been more than that recently – and there's so much to get through . . . '

'Fine,' Dee said irritably. 'But do we have to do everything the same every single time? Let's just get this over with.'

'Okay then,' said Kate, shooting her a look. She continued determinedly. 'Number one on the agenda is . . . a quick life update from everyone. Starting with . . . Beth.'

Beth jumped. 'With me?' she said. 'But literally nothing happens in my life. It's all about the kids.'

'Yeah, to be fair that's true,' said Dee, clearly not realising how bitchy she sounded. 'We should start with someone who has a bit more–'

'Hush, Dee,' interrupted Sam. 'I'm sure Beth has plenty going on. Go on, Beth,' she said encouragingly. 'What do you do when you're not with the kids?'

'Oh, I never get space for myself,' Beth said. 'I used to hide in the toilet, but the kids would always find me. So now, when I don't want anyone to know where I am, I go to the attic.'

'The attic?' Sam laughed. 'You hide in the attic? Wow, you're really making motherhood sound appealing.' Her smile faded. 'Wait, you're serious?'

'And Beth,' Georgie said frowning. 'Are there even stairs to the attic?'

'There's a ladder,' said Beth calmly. 'A ladder I can pull up after me.'

'You're not . . . ' Kate began to giggle. 'You're not pulling up the ladder every time, are you?'

They all laughed. Except for Beth. She was clenching her jaw. 'Yes, guys, I pull down the little ladder and then I climb up and pull it up behind me and then no one can get to me. Look, you try and get peace in a house where your husband is gone twenty-four-seven and you have four children, including feral twins, who follow you everywhere including the toilet!' She paused, breathing hard.

The others went quiet.

'Is everything okay at home, Beth?' Georgie said at last, as the chilled Romeo & Juliet Pinot Grigio was poured.

Beth sighed, her anger fading as quickly as it had arrived. 'Before you all judge me, I'm up there a few minutes, tops. But I need it. Sometimes, I feel like it's just me and the kids, all day, all of the time. I'm like a taxi-cum-kids'-entertainer. No thanks either. Most nights I fall into bed so tired that I'm narky and the day starts over again, like *Groundhog Day*. Only a bit less funny than the movie.' To everyone's surprise, including her own, her eyes filled up. 'I've lost my purpose, guys; I've lost my identity. I used to be Beth, who was hilarious and had a good job and a social life and a terrific sense of style . . .'

'I mean, the sense of style was debatable,' Dee murmured. 'But you had a great life, in fairness,' she added when Sam shot her a look.

'And now I'm just . . . Mum. I'm nothing,' Beth trailed off, looking down at her hands.

There was another long silence. Then: 'You need to get back to work,' Sam said simply.

'Sam,' said Georgie gently. 'Being a mother is wo–'

Beth interrupted. 'No, she's right. I desperately want to go back to work. Doing what though?' Beth asked. 'Dental surgery was nine to five. What if one of the kids is sick? It's really tricky for Jack to get out of work. Besides, I quit that job. They replaced me. I need something else.'

'Listen,' said Kate, pulling her notebook towards her. 'We can sort this.' She flipped to a fresh page. 'Operation Get Original Beth Back. To your old self, or your new self. We just need to find out what that is.' Kate was in her lane now, life coaching and advising. 'Maybe being a dental receptionist was perfect for old Beth,' she went on. 'But maybe the new Beth wants something else. A new challenge. You're forty-one. You have the rest of your life ahead of you. Maybe that door shutting opens a window somewhere else. What sort of window would that be?'

Dee snorted. 'Doors? Windows? Whatevs. Just think, Beth. What do you love to do? What are you missing?'

Beth looked around at them. 'Purpose. You all have a purpose,' she said slowly. 'Kate and Sam, you both run successful businesses. Georgie, you love growing your account and helping people feel better through yoga. You're soon to be a published author. Dee, you're famous on the telly, you love what you do. And you're amazing at it.'

'Er, yeah,' said Dee, looking at her lap. Now was not the time to tell her that she, like most people, was dispensable.

'So, what's your purpose?' said Kate, looking at her intently, clearly determined to get to the bottom of this. 'What have you always dreamed of doing but have never had the courage to try?'

'Well, I've always loved the idea of . . .' Beth started, looking sheepish. 'Um. Well, I love the idea of midwifery.'

'Really?' said Dee, wrinkling her nose. 'Being around more babies all the time?'

'Shut up, Dee. Beth, midwifery is totally you!' Sam said. 'You're caring, you're funny, you're smart.'

Beth flushed. 'Seriously?'

'Absolutely,' said Georgie. 'I can imagine you bringing great energy to the delivery room.' Chaos too, maybe, but great energy.

'Having a baby is such a vulnerable time for women and they need to feel safe and empowered,' Beth went on. 'They need the best support during the birth, whatever that birth looks like. And before and afterwards too. I didn't realise till I went through it four bloody times how important that is.'

'You were always really good at science at school,' said Sam. 'When you weren't pissing about,' she grinned. 'Seriously, this makes total sense.'

'And the twins are starting school at the end of the summer, right?' said Kate. 'So, this is the perfect time.'

'It's a whole other degree though,' said Beth. 'Four years of study.'

'So, you have looked into it?' said Sam.

'Yeah, a bit. But . . . it sounds a lot when I say it out loud.'

'If anyone can do it, it's you,' said Georgie firmly. 'You have so much to give, Beth. I've never known someone put people at ease so fast. You can make anyone laugh.'

'They're mostly laughing at me,' said Beth, going pink again. 'I'll think about it, though. Talk to Jack about how we could make it work. He'd be supportive. Maybe his mum could help me when I have a lecture on and sure, I know all about the practical side of things. Jack is always saying I should start thinking about what I might want to do now the kids are older. Thanks guys.' She smiled and wiped her nose. 'And sorry that I got a bit emotional earlier, Dee.'

'It was weird,' said Dee flatly. 'I've never seen you cry, not even when you broke your ankle outside that club in Crete.'

'Sorry for what?' Kate replied 'Never, ever say sorry. That's why we're here. Now, before we move onto the next item on the agenda, shall we order? I think the waiter is hovering.'

They all chose the same: calamari salad and seafood spaghetti from the specials board. 'Sounds delicious,' Sam said. At the last minute, Dee grabbed the waiter's sleeve. 'Wait,' she said. 'Scrap the calamari, just bread.'

'Bread?' he said, looking bewildered. 'With anything else?'

'Plain bread,' said Dee firmly, belching slightly. She felt rotten. And she also had some dim memory that seafood wasn't okay for a baby. Or was that just oysters? Or cheese? Why had she never paid attention to any of her pregnant friends? Oh, wait, because pregnancy was incredibly boring, she thought. So, why on earth was she even considering going ahead with it? Could it be because she wanted it? The thought made her feel queasy all over again.

'What about you Kate?' Georgie asked. 'What's your life update?'

'Oh.' Kate fiddled with the stem of her wine glass. 'Well, I'm doing okay. I've been trying to do some exercise and lift weights: we need to do that in our forties, you know? And it's made me feel . . . kind of all right about my body for the first time in forever. Strong, you know? I'm still dithering about the Ozempic, mind. Still, I feel good, but my anxiety has flared up again. You see, Ariana . . .' She looked around at them all, 'She wants commitment.'

There was a silence in which the other girls exchanged glances.

'Commitment? After over twenty years? Wow, what a bunny boiler,' Sam said dryly at last.

'Yeah, I can't really blame the girl for that,' said Beth. 'Ariana is awesome but she's not a pushover. It's fair enough she wants to firm things up a bit.'

'I guess,' said Kate. 'Of course we're committed. But she wants more. She wants to move out of our rental, buy somewhere.' She drew in a shaky breath.

'Ariana really wants to put a ring on it, doesn't she?' said Beth sympathetically. 'I mean, she's a total catch, Kate. How you got that lucky aged nineteen, I'll never know. The perfect woman, straight out of the gate.'

'She is perfect,' said Kate gloomily.

'So, what's stopping you?' Beth said.

Kate gave a shaky laugh. 'You know what I'm like. When the anxiety kicks in, I can't think straight.'

'I mean, you've been thinking about this for decades,' said Georgie gently. 'And keeping Ariana hanging. It's probably time to make up your mind.'

'I might have no choice about that,' said Kate. 'Ariana's given me an ultimatum.'

'Woah,' said Sam, drawing in a breath. 'Seriously?'

'Yeah. She said she's sick of arguing and she wants to start living. She says I have to get over myself and start making some positive decisions in life or she's walking. I'm going to take his trip to think and hopefully, the answer will come to me. I can't go home undecided, or I really will lose her.' Kate dropped her head in her hands and her voice came out muffled. 'Which would obviously be a disaster. So why can't I just say yes? To life with Ariana? Maybe it's my own parents, or that I'm just scared I'm not good enough for her.'

'Maybe you're afraid of getting what you want,' Dee said, putting her finger on it with her usual bluntness.

There was a short pause.

'We're here when you want to talk.' Sam touched Kate's arm. 'I know you'll make the right decision when you're ready. You just need to get your head straight.'

Kate took her head out of her hands and stabbed at calamari moodily. 'Let's hope I can do that in the next few days.' She chewed and brightened up. 'This is amazing.'

It was amazing. The calamari were tossed in a garlic and lemon dressing on a bed of fresh rocket. Everything was fresh, colourful and crunchy. The others tucked in, but Dee shuddered and picked at the bread. She just couldn't think about seafood right now, but she didn't want to say anything or the others would cotton on to her. Besides, Kate, who'd been so on edge around food for her whole life, finally seemed to be loosening up a bit and Dee didn't want to spoil it.

'Listen, Kate,' said Georgie, swallowing a mouthful. 'Try and see the bigger picture instead of the small steps that are freaking you out. Big picture? You adore Ariana and she adores you. If marriage is important to her, it should be important to you. Is it something you definitely don't want or are you just scared?'

'It's such a big commitment, promising to be with one person forever,' said Kate. 'Not that I want to be with anyone else.' She sighed. 'Plus, I fancy her more than anyone else I've ever met. Not that many people can say that after nearly two-and-a-half decades, can they?'

'No, they can't,' Georgie said with what sounded like deep unhappiness. Then she took out her phone and snapped a picture of their table – the delicious plates of food, the glasses of wine, the whole gorgeous disarray.

'What are you doing now?' Dee snapped. 'You're like one of those Gen Zs, always taking photos of their food.'

Georgie went red. 'Sorry. I thought I could put a post up later. You know, about friendship.'

'Right,' said Dee through gritted teeth. 'God forbid your followers aren't updated on your every move.'

Georgie put her phone away.

'You're right, I should be more present,' she said guiltily. 'I'm always trying to strike a balance. The irony of being a mindfulness Instagrammer, I guess.'

'You're ok, Georgie,' said Sam, shooting daggers at Dee.

Their main courses arrived and the spaghetti was perfect, full of local prawns, mussels and clams that dripped with butter and garlic oil. Fresh parsley was sprinkled on the top. Kate couldn't stop putting huge forkfuls in her mouth, to Dee's surprise. She seemed to relish every bit.

'It's so good to be here with my friends, eating this delicious food and drinking this gorgeous wine,' she said.

'Cheers!' Beth said loudly, clinking her glass against the others. Then she gulped down her wine and went to fill her glass again. She was drinking a lot, Dee thought.

'So, what's the vibe for the book, Georgie?' asked Kate, mouth full of pasta.

'Well,' Georgie said, 'the designer I met when I went into the publishers was talking about keeping it simple and pretty. I'm going to start each chapter as a month, using the chakras and colours of that month. Simple exercises – physical and mental ones – and journalling prompts and meditations. Like a sort of . . . well-being bible for the busy woman. Totally judgement-free. That's what Davina said. Davina McCall,' she said. 'She's going to do a cover quote.'

Dee said nothing but the nausea came sweeping back. She gripped her water glass harder. She was the big name here, not Georgie, who – let's face it – teaches yoga. Not exactly the same as bringing the public up to speed on world news! She looked around at her friends' admiring faces and Georgie's embarrassed, but happy one. She knew that it was better to be pleased for her friend and she was – sort of – but it just wasn't fair. There she was, being kicked to the kerb, while a woman who stretched for a living had zillions of followers.

'To Georgie's new book,' Beth cried loudly and raised her wine glass again. Everyone toasted Georgie, so, of course, Dee had to as well. She put her glass down as soon as she could and shoved a piece of bread angrily into her mouth. She couldn't wait for this meal to be over. She felt unbelievably sleepy – in fact, she could have put her head on the table and nodded off. Must be the hormones.

There was yet more chatter about Georgie's book, the TV appearances she had lined up to promote it, the potential tour. Then the bill came. The girls always divided it equally, no matter who had eaten what, but now, Beth yelled, 'Wait, Dee didn't have any wine, so we'll pay for that.'

The others looked up, before Beth hastily improvised.

'It's the colonic.'

'Yes,' Dee said, glaring at Beth. 'Couldn't touch a drop after.'

Beth flushed.

'I think I drank your share.'

She had drunk a lot more than the rest of them. Maybe she had a drink problem, Dee thought, as Beth offered the waiter their combined cash.

Three minutes later and they were back in a taxi to the hotel. Everyone was still chatting but Dee said nothing. She looked around the taxi at her friends, laughing and chatting about their, let's face it, pretty boring lives. Lives that were better than hers, it would seem. Georgie, that quiet little mouse, had a book deal. Sam was loved up – ok, she had her upcoming IVF stress, but she had a gorgeous husband and amazing life, and it would work out for her. Beth was happy: sure she kept bursting into tears, but she was probably just overtired. And Kate had an adoring girlfriend at home who really wanted to marry her. Why did these girls complain?! They envied her but they were lucky, all of them. Meanwhile, she'd given everything to her career and now, here she was, forty-one, unemployed and unable to name the father of her baby.

Chapter Nine

At dawn, Beth gave up on sleep altogether. She had tossed and turned all night, unable to get comfy and switch her mind off. She would fall into a fitful sleep, only to dream about Dee going into labour and trying to push out triplets while presenting the news. It was too much.

At six a.m., she decided it was a waste of time. She got up and, still in her nightie, headed down to the lobby in search of coffee. *Should I offer to go and stay with Dee in New York for the birth?* she wondered, as she walked through the quiet corridors. *Maybe Jack could get time off to mind the kids. Yes, Dee would have access to expensive doctors, doulas, and childcare, but it wasn't the same as having friends with you, to really help you. And Dee's parents had always been checked out, so she doubted they'd take much interest. She would really be on her own.*

There was a bit of life stirring downstairs. The morning sun was rising as the staff got the breakfast tables ready. It was the nicest time of the day and all the guests were missing it. Somewhere, Beth could hear the faint sound of a vacuum cleaner. She persuaded a member of staff to make her a coffee and sat drinking it quietly. She could see herself in the full-length mirror on the pool wall. God, she looked haggard. Older than any of the others, she thought. Sam was obviously looking after herself – good diet, exercise, hair immaculately dyed. Georgie had always possessed an infuriating inner glow. Dee was beautiful, plus she threw money at the situation. And even Kate, the most insecure of them all, had transformed herself in the last year. She looked fit, secure, strong, confident. Whereas Beth? In the harsh morning light, she took in her hair, with its ragged split ends, her nails, which she'd frantically painted badly in the taxi on the way to the airport, hot red from Rimmel. Her short, bright-pink Dunnes' nightie. Everyone else had somehow grown up while she wasn't looking. She had stayed where she was – if you didn't count the four kids and a load of grey hair. Older but definitely no wiser. She'd spent too much time at home and now had the mental age of a nine-year-old, blurting out any old thing. Her behaviour on the plane made her blush now that she thought about it. It was fine to have fun, but maybe she needed to tone it down a bit.

As usual, she had managed to put away more wine than anyone else last night. Her head throbbed from dehydration and lack of sleep as she walked outside to the pool area, holding her coffee. Maybe I should give Georgie's meditation a shot, she thought. Maybe she would become as serene and beautiful as her friend if she just sat down and breathed for five minutes instead of hiding in the attic or downing shit white wine. She would start with this meditation stuff right now. Beth lay down on the plastic sunbed and closed her eyes. She farted, opened her eyes quickly, and looked around. Clearly no one had heard. She tried again. Breathe in . . . breathe out.

She had forgotten what life was like on her own really. What it was like to leave the house every day and go to work. She thought back to life before her babies, when she would get a nice coffee before work and stroll in. Chatting to colleagues, gossiping about silly things. There'd be drinks after work, dinners with friends. Now, it was all sports days and bake sales . . . *maybe* a coffee at another parent's house after the school run. Then it was home to piles of washing and tidying toys away, only for them to be tossed all over the living room hours later.

The old Beth. It seemed like a distant memory, a different life.

The idea of the midwifery course popped into her head again. It made her smile to herself. The girls were right. She had always loved science at school, especially the science of the human body. She was fascinated by the process of pregnancy, of birth in all its forms, and the early days of a baby's life. God knows, she had gone through the process herself often enough and had been around enough different people to know there was a wide range of experiences. She loved the idea of nursing the new mums and giving them a good start with their newborns. She was at her happiest looking after people. It was her natural skill, and she enjoyed it. Yes, midwifery ticked all the boxes.

She could hear the girls' supportive voices in her head. So, what was stopping her? Well, for a start, a massive dose of self-doubt. What if she didn't get in to college or couldn't complete the course? What if she was too out of it to study, after all these years pushing trucks around the carpet? What if . . . Stop it, Beth. She started breathing again, deep breaths in for four and out for four.

*

A splash startled Beth awake. The pool waterfall was turned on and the low pool music started. She sat up and looked around, surprised that she had passed out. She hadn't heard a thing. Did falling asleep count as meditation? A couple walked out of the hotel and waved to her. It was that lovely old English couple who'd been chatting to Sam yesterday. Margie and Roger. Wait – was that a love bite on the lady's neck? Beth squinted. Without her contacts or glasses, most of life was a blur.

'Hello, love,' the old lady called. 'Early bird gets the sun loungers!'

Beth laughed back. She was being silly. A love bite indeed! It was probably a birthmark. The lady was in her seventies at least, and delicate looking. She'd probably never even heard of the word 'love bite'. Beth was aware again of her quite short, bright-pink Dunnes' nightie. Then she saw Kate heading towards the pool area, carting five towels and her beach bag, organising them as usual. Kate didn't see Beth, as she was hidden behind the towel, snack, and water stack, and Beth didn't catch her attention. She needed to talk to Dee, she thought. Pregnant, at her age, without a partner or family, not even in her own country . . . she must be in real shock and turmoil about her next move. Beth would help her. She stood up and headed back inside.

And, while she was feeling saintly, she decided to ignore the phone ban and check in on Jack too. The poor love was probably struggling. He must have a list of questions as long as his arm to ask her.

She rang him as she entered the cool of the lobby.

'Hello,' she said when she heard his deep voice down the phone. 'How are you–'

'Hey. Thought we agreed no calls?' he said. His voice was raspy, the way it always was in the morning, before he'd had his coffee. She could hear the kids chattering happily in the background and the faint sound of the radio. The sounds of home.

'Right, we did,' she said, nodding. 'But I just wanted to check how you–'

'We're fine, love. All happy, all fed, the kids are great. Now you enjoy yourself,' he said, and she could hear the laughter in his voice as he went on to say, 'Just not too much, I know what you're like. We love you, miss you, now, bye. Don't call us again except in an emergency and we'll see you at the airport.'

He hung up. Beth stared at the phone. He had sounded so calm. She supposed it was easy to be relaxed when you'd done solo parenting for a few days, rather than day-in-day-out for years and years and years.

All the same. Wasn't he even the slightest bit stressed? Were the kids not arguing or throwing food? Was she completely redundant?

She felt a bit put out. Still . . .

She parked these thoughts for now and headed back up to Dee. Her friend was her priority. Dee had seemed so snappy last night, especially with poor George, and it was all because of worry, Beth was sure of it. She was probably hiding under the sheets right now, too scared to face her dilemma. She was probably sobbing her poor heart out.

She paused on the threshold of their room. Was that singing that Beth heard from the bathroom? Surely not. Maybe it was the sound of Dee crying.

When she walked in, Dee's bed was empty, and she was indeed singing in the shower. Probably trying to distract herself from her worries, Beth thought. Still, she sounded surprisingly upbeat. Beth sat down on the floor, facing the bathroom door and waited, like a good supportive friend. As she did, she practised her speech.

'I'll support you whatever you decide to do about this pregnancy. And if you decide you do want to go ahead, I was thinking I could fly out to New York and come to your appointments with you. After the baby is born, I could stay at yours for a week or two and be a sort of night nurse. The first few months are quite tough, but I know you have this in you.'

She would be useful again, Beth thought. Needed. Maybe this was her purpose in–

'Jesus Christ!'

Dee was standing above her, clutching the towel to her chest. She was enveloped in a cloud of steam – very 'Tonight, Matthew, I'm going to be a pregnant woman having a meltdown', Beth thought, remembering the catchphrase from *Stars in their Eyes*.

'What the hell are you doing sitting on the floor staring at the door, you weirdo?'

'I . . .'

All the grand words about supporting her friend flew out of Beth's head. Dee seemed so casual and normal, and not the expected emotional mess – it suddenly felt ridiculous to offer to fly out to New York to help with the baby. It felt ridiculous to even mention the baby. 'Er, I was just relaxing,' Beth replied, and she got up in silence and went into the shower herself. As the water poured down on her face and body, her dull headache subsided. What had she been thinking? Dee was the same age as her, an adult, for God's sake, so she could do what she wanted. Dee was tougher than the rest of them put together. She didn't need mothering.

What a waste of my worry, Beth thought as she scrubbed her scalp. Mind you, it didn't take much to start her worrying these days. Random periods every few weeks would do that to you, she supposed. She was permanently exhausted, had no interest in intimacy, emotional or otherwise, she was always on the brink of rage or tears, her boobs were always tender, her hair was like straw, her bones ached, especially her knees: the endless list just went on and on and on. No wonder she wasn't glowing along with the rest of them. It felt a bit unfair – four pregnancies, four kids, then straight into this. She was grateful for it all, but she wouldn't have minded a bit of a breather. A few years where her body behaved normally.

Beth got dressed, putting a long sarong over her black bikini and put on a bit of mascara and lip gloss. She found her flip-flops by the apartment door. 'All set,' she yelled in Dee's general direction. Dee was putting a towel into her beach bag, wearing a pretty pink-and-white short linen sun dress that looked expensive. Beth looked at her bargain sarong, thinking that it didn't look all that fabulous now.

'All set,' Dee said. 'Oh, and don't tell the others yet, will you? About you-know-what.'

'Of course not,' said Beth, pouncing. 'But have you had any, er, more thoughts about it?'

'I'm still no clearer than I was yesterday.' Dee chewed her lip. 'I'm hoping I'll make up my mind soon. It'd help if I knew who the father was.'

'Of course,' said Beth. 'In your own time, Dee.'

She could keep a secret – for once. This was a big one.

*

Kate and Georgie were already in the breakfast area as they walked in. The smell of bacon and fresh coffee wafted out of the dining room. Bliss.

'Morning girls.' Dee flashed her signature smile and waved as she walked – well, shimmied – into the breakfast area. 'Good sleep, everyone?'

'Fab. God, I'm hungry. Breakfast buffets are dangerous, aren't they?' said Sam, shovelling beans onto her plate. She looked at Dee warmly, clearly deciding to put last night's behaviour behind her.

'Hard to resist,' said Beth, piling her own plate high with egg, bacon, and sausage. She did enjoy a good breakfast, especially a free one.

'Yeah, it looks good,' said Kate, cautiously putting some scrambled egg on her own plate. Beth felt sorry for her. She'd enjoyed her dinner so much last night, now there she was, wondering if she should help herself to a bit of bacon. As if sensing Beth's eyes on her, Kate put down the plate. 'On second thoughts, I'll just take a banana. I might go and stake out our sun loungers, okay? I put towels down, but you never know with some of these old folk. See you there.' Kate said, her head down, moving towards the doors.

Beth looked at her walking away. It's rotten, she thought, that Kate s is so hung up on what everyone thinks. All these years later, a loving relationship and a massively successful business, and she was still the worried teenager they'd known at school. She'd love to see Kate happy and content in her body. Even though Kate looked great, she couldn't see it.

'Gosh,' said Dee, looking a little green. 'You know what? I think I'll just start with some toast. Dry toast.'

Right, Beth thought, better get on with lunch. She piled her plate with rolls, ham and butter.

'What,' hissed Dee, looking appalled, 'are you doing, Beth?'

'Making us a packed lunch, of course,' whispered Beth. 'We always do it at these sorts of places. Remember? When we were working in that hotel in Italy that summer? 2002?' She laughed thinking back, of the charming hotel perched high on a clifftop. They were paid next to nothing, so her job had been to make up the rolls for the beach at breakfast while the others had distracted the managers. She was in full secret-chef mode again now, as she buttered and filled the rolls to put into her napkins, strategically placed on her knee near her beach bag. She felt pleased with herself that she was able to be useful.

'We used to do that in our twenties, Beth, when we were broke,' Dee said.

'Yeah, I don't think I'm going to fancy some squashed ham roll in a few hours, thanks,' said Sam, grinning.

'Cured meat isn't good for inflammation,' murmured Georgie.

Beth flushed. She'd been half-joking, making the rolls. But it was their holiday tradition.

Just then she felt an arm brush against her, smelling of Heno de Pravia soap, that lovely smell that always reminded her of holidays, and a quiet, slightly judgmental voice said. 'Can I get you another plate for your . . . second breakfast?'

Beth froze, the knife in mid-air, and looked up slowly. The manager, a stern-looking woman with a tight bun and navy blazer, glared back at her. Caught red-handed, she thought. What would she say?

'Perhaps you didn't have enough to eat this morning?' the manager asked Beth. Very passive aggressive, she thought.

'Yes, thank you, I did, it was delicious,' Beth managed. 'These rolls are for my friend, Sam. She asked me to bring them to her room because she is very . . . drunk.'

Sam had been looking out the window, pretending to ignore all of this, but now, she whipped her head round to face Beth. Beth felt as if she were back in the classroom telling random, bald-faced lies to get out of something she had been caught doing.

'The poor thing,' said the manager, giving a close-lipped smile. 'In that case, I will take the rolls to her for you. What is her room number?' She raised her hand at a young waiter who was already busy cleaning up breakfast tables. 'Juan, can you please bring these rolls up to room . . .?' She looked at Beth.

'Twenty-five please,' Beth squeaked, not able to make eye contact with Sam. 'Um. And there's these too.' All eyes fell on her as she quietly removed the five ham and cheese rolls from her beach bag, some falling out of the napkin in the process. Beth picked pieces of ham and cheese off her sarong and stuffed them back into the rolls. Silence.

'Thank you,' was all that she could muster.

The waiter and manager left, carrying the tower of rolls. Nobody said a word. Beth felt suddenly so silly and childish. They weren't teenagers anymore and they didn't need the free lunch. She looked up to see a woman giving her a disapproving look from the table beside theirs. But she was only trying to help!

'Shall we head out?' said Sam, pushing back her chair. 'If I can walk, given that I'm apparently drunk and in need of five ham and cheese rolls at nine a.m.'

'What's going to happen when they get to room twenty-five and there's no one there?' said Dee as they walked out into the corridor.

'Good point. You have to go to the room now, Sam!' Beth hissed as they closed the restaurant door behind them. 'Please, otherwise they'll know I was lying. Run!'

'Run?! Beth, have you lost your marbles? You told them that I'm drunk, for God's sake. I'm laying low now and pretending that that girl Sam in room twenty-five is dead,' Sam said cheerfully, walking past Beth and over to the sunbed area.

'Come on, Beth,' Georgie said kindly. 'I'll buy you lunch later in case you're in need,' she smiled as she tucked her arm into Beth's.

'I can afford lunch, you know,' Beth said sulkily. 'I just wanted it to be like old times.'

'I know,' Georgie said, 'but everything changes, Beth, even us.'

I don't want anything to change, Beth thought, following her friend over to where Kate was waving eagerly. Particularly us.

*

'Are you guys okay?' Kate said as they approached the sun loungers, which she'd carefully laid out for the five of them. 'You're all very quiet.'

Sam laid out her lotions and book and her water. She looked sick and pale and Beth was mortified. She hadn't meant to upset her. 'Beth was trying to steal our lunch from the breakfast buffet,' Sam said.

'Woah, you let us down there, Beth,' Kate laughed. 'Where are all these rolls now?'

'Outside room twenty-five', Sam said, applying lotion, not looking up. 'Beth wanted me to sprint up and pretend to be drunk enough to want them.'

'It was just a silly joke,' Beth said and started to read her book. It was a thriller about a housewife who was so bored that she started to suspect her husband of poisoning her. A bit close to the bone, thought Beth. She was feeling frazzled.

The way the other girls had looked at her, like she was an embarrassment – it was only a few rolls, for goodness' sake. But maybe they were right. Maybe she'd spent so long around her children she hadn't grown up properly, like the rest of them. And the burden of Dee's secret was stressing her out. She'd never liked secrets. Was it too early to have a glass of something strong? She might need to sneak off soon and have a cheeky little mid-morning swiftie. She glanced around. The girls were all immersed in their books. It was nearly eleven – practically midday and totally acceptable to have a drink. She'd go to the pool bar when the girls were distracted.

*

Georgie, meanwhile, was eyeing the lifeguard over her copy of *Eat, Pray, Love*. God, he was gorgeous: tall, broad shouldered and bronzed. She wondered if he was looking at her – she kept thinking that he was. But she was being ridiculous, surely. She had forgotten what it was like to fancy or to be fancied. She wouldn't do anything, of course. That would be disloyal to Paddy.

But then Paddy didn't want to touch her.

She stared over at him sitting in his chair above the pool, willing him to look back at her. Although what would she do if he did? Georgie had never been any good at flirting and she'd been with Paddy for so long. It would be nice to feel desirable again. Her friends always told her that she looked well, but not her own husband. If anything, he told her to make more of an effort with her appearance. 'Get some of that Botox, dye your hair', he would say. 'Buy some decent clothes instead of those ratty old things. The other wives look really well turned out and you're just . . .'

He would trail off there.

She was just what?

Old? Boring?

The lifeguard turned suddenly, as if reading Georgie's mind. He really was handsome, with wavy dark hair and bright blue eyes. Then he smiled at them and waved, his eyes crinkling. Georgie was no good at flirting, but she did observe how Dee moved through the world and suddenly she thought she could take a leaf out of her book. She pouted in what she hoped was a sexy way and kind of arched her back, trying to look pretty and flexible – all that yoga – but also as though she was unaware she was being watched. She darted a look at the lifeguard and saw that he was looking at her, but then quickly turned to face away from him.

Rolling over, Georgie dug through her bag. She rarely wore makeup, but she had an old lip balm and some mascara in there somewhere. She ducked her head as if to peer at her book and quickly applied the makeup. She looked down at her ancient one-piece. The other girls were in bikinis, even Kate, who was pretty resistant to wearing anything revealing. Instantly, Georgie felt ridiculous. What was she thinking, trying to flirt with a gorgeous young bloke! She needed to cop on; the sun had clearly had an effect on her loins. She turned back around, composed herself and pretended to read her book.

'Good morning, ladies,' the lifeguard called over. Was he staring at her? Surely not.

'Good morning to you, too,' Beth said back to him. 'Are you new here? I didn't see you yesterday.'

'Yeah, I was at another hotel for years,' the lifeguard said cheerfully. 'I fancied a change.'

Beth leaned forward, nodding intently as they talked and Georgie cringed. Beth had a habit of interviewing everyone and getting their life story. It was one of her endearing qualities, but she couldn't face it just now. She tuned out Beth's and the lifeguard's chat, pulled out her phone and took a photo of the pool, bright blue and calm. Then she began typing her caption.

Sometimes you need to clear your mind and just breathe. Somewhere beautiful helps. Blue is a colour that induces calm. It represents serenity and peace. It evokes emotions of trust and honesty and–

'Guys,' Kate's voice interrupted her. Georgie looked over as she pulled out a notebook and put her glasses on. 'Agenda time!'

'Oh, not again,' Dee grunted from her sunbed, closing her eyes. 'Why do we have to do this stupid tradition rather than have a normal adult conversation?'

'Just to make sure we don't miss anything,' said Kate defensively, not looking at Dee. 'Okay,' said Kate. 'Beth suggested this topic. Number two on the agenda, ladies . . . '

'The menopause!' Beth shouted, loud and clear from her position on the sunbed.

Georgie groaned internally and looked to see if the lifeguard had heard her. He was grinning, so it would seem that he had. Imagine him hearing all about hot flashes and vaginal dryness. Honestly, Beth could be so loud sometimes. There was no way that they hadn't heard her in the old town of Albufeira and maybe even in Lisbon.

'Beth, can you lower your voice a bit? she whispered, her eyes darting towards the lifeguard's chair.

'Okay, sure, fine,' Beth replied. 'Let's start with why I have suddenly lost control of my body. One period a month? Two? Who knows? And my facial hair has gone wild.'

'Ugh, yeah,' said Sam. 'It's like, the minute I turned forty, I needed to watch my chin like a hawk.'

Dee giggled. 'Too right. My laser-hair-removal appointments have really stepped up,' she said. 'And that's just above the neck–'

'I know!' Beth continued, ignoring Georgie's nervous glances across the pool. 'What about your libido? Mine is literally zero, I'm dead from the waist down. I've told Jack that I love him, but he thinks that the mystique is gone.'

She hooted.

'What mystique? That's normal though, right? I'd rather read a book or watch something decent on Netflix.'

'The weight is harder to shift now, too, isn't it?' Sam chimed in.

'Yes, I agree. I am permanently bloated and nothing fits me anymore. I should have shares in Spanx,' Beth laughed.

'And what about really heavy periods, like every two weeks? Blood literally everywhere, leaking in public, at parent-teacher meetings?'

Beth was on a roll.

'Even now, look,' she looked down at her bikini bottoms.

Georgie jumped up.

'Who wants to swim?' she asked in a loud voice, thinking on her feet. She was desperate to cut this conversation short. But then, it wasn't like her to worry about impressing some random guy on holiday. She wasn't sure what had got into her.

Years' worth of neglect, maybe.

She pushed the thought out of her mind.

'I'll come,' said Beth, jumping up too. Together they headed to the pool. It was only as she stepped into the water that Georgie noticed that her left hand was bare. She had left her wedding ring on her bedside table. She never took it off.

Again, what had gotten into her?

She knew she looked toned – all that yoga – but all the same, she felt suddenly self-conscious. She ruffled her beachy waves and hoped her light dusting of makeup would stay intact. Perhaps if she tried not to get her face wet–

'Party time!' Beth screamed, cannonballing into the pool beside her.

Before she could turn, Georgie was engulfed in a tidal wave. She found herself swept beneath the surface, water filling her eyes, her mouth, her nose. Was she drowning?! In the pool at the all-inclusive? Sputtering and coughing, Georgie broke the surface and started sneezing, snot all over her face.

'Are you okay, ladies?' came a voice from the lifeguard's chair.

'We're grand! Just fooling about!' Beth called back.

Through her streaming, stinging eyes, Georgie could see Mr Hot just staring at them, not impressed. Not impressed at all.

Beside her, Beth beamed, seemingly oblivious to the fact Georgie had just had a near-death experience. 'Haven't dive-bombed in years. God, I love it here. Isn't it awesome to relax and be ourselves for a change?'

'Awesome,' wheezed Georgie.

'Georgie, are you wearing mascara in the water?' Beth looked closer at the black rivers streaming down Georgie's face. 'You never wear makeup.'

'I know,' said Georgie grimly. 'I'm just going to sort myself out.' She was still blinded by tears and mascara. She managed to grab the pool step bar, and she crab-walked out of the pool and over to her sunbed. She must look an absolute sight. Presumably this was why people didn't wear mascara in the water.

And then a voice said, 'Excuse me – would you like a, um, tissue?'

She turned around and there was Mr Hot, the lifeguard, holding out a packet of Kleenex.

'Thanks,' Georgie muttered, mortified. She took the tissues, unable to look in the direction of Beth, who was now dive-bombing into the pool again. She sat down on her bed and got another towel to dry herself, patting down her hair, which was standing around her head like a mad wig.

'I'm Marco, by the way,' the lifeguard said. 'Would you like me to call First Aid?'

'Thanks Marco, I'm Georgie,' Georgie said, wiping under her eyes. 'No, don't worry. I think I had some sort of allergic reaction to the chlorine.' She handed him back the packet.

'Keep it,' he said hastily. 'Are you sure you don't want to get checked out? Because . . . your nose is bleeding.'

Her nose was bleeding? She touched her nose, and her fingers came away covered in a mixture of blood and snot. Georgie hadn't had a nosebleed since she was a kid. For God's sake. 'Really, I'm fine,' she said firmly. 'My friend just smacked into me by accident. Thanks for checking though.'

To her relief, he turned and walked back to his chair. 'Let me know if you need anything,' he said as he climbed back up to his perch above the pool.

'Sure!' Georgie said weakly.

'Georgie, he's right. Your nose is bleeding,' Kate said, concerned. She sat up and dug through her bag for a mirror, handing it to Georgie. Georgie held it up and actually squealed when she saw her face. She looked like a wet clown from a horror film, with black streaks from her eyes and blood trickling down her nose. 'Beth is the pits,' she hissed. 'She dive-bombed me, gave me a nosebleed and made me look like an idiot. Why can't she just behave like the adult she is, for once?'

'That's the eternal question,' drawled Dee, smiling from under her giant hat.

'Ah, try not to let her get to you,' Sam said. 'She spends her life being an adult now. She's just trying to let loose! She didn't mean to hurt or embarrass you; you know that she's just a messer, especially with us. We bring her back to her happy, irresponsible years!'

'You weren't so chill when she told everyone you were drunk at nine a.m.,' said Georgie. She took a deep breath. No harm done. It was on her anyway, for putting on makeup and trying to flirt with the lifeguard like some desperado. Honestly. She was married. Unhappily married, true, but still married. Georgie finished wiping her face and lay back down on the bed. She took another deep breath and visualised a deep, shaded woodland pool. Soon, she began to relax.

*

The girls lay on the sun loungers and read books, trying to ignore the vigorous splashing from the pool from Beth. She had made friends with a group of older ladies also splashing about and was really enjoying herself.

'You girls should come to one of our little games-night parties while you're here,' a woman called Dawn said breathlessly. 'It would be lovely to have some young people in the mix.'

'I keep hearing about those! We definitely will,' Beth assured her.

'Come on, girls, it's nearly midday – let's have a little drink!' said a woman with a serious perm called Tracey.

'You too, Beth,' said Dawn.

Beth hesitated. Why not? A small glass of wine, to erase the memory of the ham rolls that morning or Georgie's startled face as she had dive-bombed her in the pool. Was she a bit of a sad embarrassment to her friends? Well, at least this lot seemed to think she was fun.

She glanced at the other girls who were all engrossed in their books, magazines and Insta. 'Sure thing,' she said, following her new friends out of the pool.

'Shots of sambuca all round, please,' Tracey declared at the poolside bar. Beth downed the shot and felt her chest get all warm. This is even better than my evening glass of wine, she thought. Not that she'd be doing shots while she was looking after the kids, of course. Things weren't that bad. This was different. She was on holiday; she was allowed to have fun. 'One more please and that's me.'

When she got back to the others, after one more 'last shot', which had been closer to three, she felt pleasantly giddy and cheerful. She didn't notice her scrappy nails or the way her hair stuck out or how flimsy and cheap her clothes were alongside the others'. She felt good.

They skipped lunch after their full brekkie but had smoothies at the pool bar. Banana, strawberry, raspberry and oat milk, sprinkled with chia seeds and frozen sweetened orange peel. This totally balances out the sambuca, Beth thought happily.

'What are we thinking of doing dins-wise tonight, guys? The old town? Now that we all have a tan, let's go and show it off!' Georgie suggested.

'Absolutely,' said Beth, kicking a leg up, Victoria Beckham style. Ever since the sambuca, she was feeling full of energy, ready for anything.

'Time to show the public our beauty,' Sam agreed. 'But let's have a siesta first, shall we?' She yawned. 'I'm so tired, I don't know what's got into me.'

'Yeah, and I'll do some yoga,' said Georgie, standing and stretching. 'See you guys later.'

After they'd walked off, Dee whispered to the others, 'Georgie looks sad, don't you think?'

'Maybe,' said Kate, looking after her. Beth just murmured, settling down onto her sun lounger for another hour in the sun.

'I think something must be up,' Dee said insistently. 'She looks haggard too. So old.'

'Georgie looks about nineteen,' said Kate tartly.

'I assume things are all right with her and Paddy?' Dee asked.

Kate shrugged. 'You know Georgie. She keeps her cards close to her chest. But actually, I don't get the impression that she and Paddy are great. She's barely mentioned him.'

'He's a cocky bastard,' muttered Beth. They'd all disliked Paddy at school because he'd been a bit of a player, so they'd been pretty shocked when he and Georgie had got together – and stayed that way. He was everything Georgie wasn't: selfish, rude, loud, brash. They had assumed the relationship would run its course, especially when they finished school, but Georgie and Paddy had stuck with each other. And then they had got married and he was still hanging around, decades later, much to their surprise.

'Georgie can never see it,' Beth said. 'She thinks the sun shines out of him. That she's lucky to have him. When actually, it's the other way round.'

'I hope they're okay,' said Dee, rather unconvincingly, Beth thought. Clearly, Dee wouldn't mind if Georgie's perfect life hit a few bumps in the road. Dee could be fun and as a journalist she knew just about everything, but jealousy was her weak spot. 'We should talk to her later, over a drink,' Dee suggested.

'Oh, I don't know,' said Kate uneasily. 'Georgie is private, you know. I think she'd talk about it if she wanted us to–'

'I agree,' said Beth. If Georgie didn't want to say anything, it was none of their business.

'No, we should ask,' Dee said keenly. 'In fact, you should do it, Kate. You're the one who always takes the initiative. The organised one. You're our leader.'

'Really?' said Kate shyly, looking flattered. It probably distracted her from her indecision about her own life, Beth thought, which was understandable.

'Of course!' Dee went on, buttering her up. 'Who was the one who told boys we liked them at school? Who helped clear up our sick? Who was the best person to negotiate a late curfew with our parents?'

She pointed at Kate, who smiled. 'Me, I guess.'

'And besides,' Dee said, 'I'm too blunt, Sam's too tough-love and Beth – well, you wouldn't expect tact from Beth, would you?'

'Hey,' Beth murmured from her sun lounger. That remark hurt, but after the shots, she only had the energy to protest faintly and sleepily from her sun lounger. Dee was hardly one to talk about tact, when she was homing in on Georgie's love life like a missile, manipulating Kate into doing the questioning.

'No,' admitted Kate. 'I wouldn't.'

Cheek, thought Beth. Did they all think that she was completely tactless? They must do.

'All right, I'll bring it up when we're having a drink, suss out the lay of the land. Hopefully, Georgie is okay and Paddy is behaving himself.'

'He can be a bit free with other women,' Beth acknowledged. 'Which is wrong, obviously.' Dee settled back in her sun lounger and Beth could see that behind her faux concern lay a smidge of real worry. Maybe she felt a bit guilty for being so jealous. What if something really was wrong with Georgie, Beth thought sleepily, her eyes closing.

After an hour, Georgie returned, looking sweaty but happy. 'That's better,' she said cheerfully. 'Anyone want a drink?' She headed off to the bar and soon the girls were sitting over their drinks – a jug of piña colada and four chilled glasses and an orange juice for Dee, who was still claiming to have a dodgy tummy – in the golden light of the late afternoon. What bliss, thought Beth sleepily. Hot skin and sipping a cool drink with the smell of coconut suntan lotion filling the air.

'The golden hour. Paddy always used to say this was the best time of any holiday,' Georgie said dreamily. And then she looked sad, as if it wasn't like that anymore.

'Um, how is Paddy?' Kate asked, seizing the opening, her diplomatic face on.

'He's good.' Georgie sighed.

'Then why the big sigh? What's going on?' asked Kate kindly. 'You never come out and say it, but we know something is up. You used to chat about Paddy all the time but it's as if he has gone into Witness Protection.' She narrowed her eyes. 'Has he had an affair, Georgie? Do we need to take him out?'

'N-no . . . ' Georgie stammered. 'Nothing like that. Paddy is really loyal,' she said. 'But I barely see him, what with his work trips and golf outings.'

The others exchanged glances.

'Then what?' asked Beth, taking a gulp of her drink. 'He's stolen the company funds? Taken up gambling? Been caught with a–'

'No!' Georgie looked around, clearly not wanting anyone else overhearing their private chat. 'Jeez, nothing like that. But the thing is . . . '

She hesitated and Kate quickly poured her another piña colada. 'I know, it's full of sugar and ultra-processed whatever,' she said. 'But once in a while won't hurt you.'

Georgie gave a shaky laugh and took a sip of the creamy drink. 'Ok, well, the thing is, Paddy doesn't want to have sex with me ever again.'

Chapter Ten

There was a silence.

Then: 'Oh, is that all?' said Beth, sloshing some more booze into her glass. 'That's just marriage, long-term commitment. Me and Jack sometimes don't get round to it for months.'

Georgie shook her head. 'I don't think it's just marriage,' she said quietly.

'Okay,' said Kate, glaring at Beth to hint she should shut up. 'Go on.'

'Well, I tried a few times, you know. To get things going. He kept putting me off.' Georgie set down her glass and twisted her hands in her lap. 'And it's not a few months,' she whispered. 'It's been . . . longer.'

'Years?' asked Kate.

'Years. At first, I didn't care and then I thought we'd get round to it eventually. Then I talked to him about it. He says he still wants our life together. He doesn't want us to break up or anything like that. He just . . . doesn't want to have sex with me. Or hug me, or touch me, or even. . . .' Her voice faltered. 'He doesn't seem to want to talk to me.'

There was a long silence.

Then Dee said, 'Have you tried counselling?'

'I persuaded Paddy to see one,' Georgie said. 'But he said the therapist was wrong. We only went to three sessions, and he stormed out and we never went back. He says my expectations are too high and to get over myself and that plenty of couples our age don't have sex or spend much time together.'

'And what do you think?' asked Kate gently. 'Is that enough for you?'

What an arse Paddy was, she thought angrily.

'Sometimes I think so, yeah,' said Georgie. 'It's not necessarily the sex. I could understand that if we had a better connection. It's just . . . sometimes I wonder if he even likes me.'

Beth drained her glass.

'I've got it,' she said, her voice slightly loose. 'You're hot, Georgie, but you've always been a bit Earth Mother. Men are simple creatures. You hit the boutiques here, get a spot of slinky lingerie, a bit of kinky stuff, get it home and there.' She snapped her fingers.

'You'll have Paddy's attention in no time.'

Georgie bit her lip. 'It's not that simple–' she began.

'Men are simple,' slurred Beth.

Kate frowned. Beth sounded absolutely wasted. How had that happened on a piña colada?

'You should just get something seriously kinky. Enough of all this linen and Birkenstocks–'

Georgie flinched.

'Shut up, Beth,' snapped Sam, her eyes on Georgie. 'You don't know what you're talking about.'

'I'm talking latex, I'm talking wipe-clean . . . '

Georgie stood abruptly. 'I'll get us some more drinks,' she said, her voice shaking, and walked off.

Dee whipped round and shot Beth daggers.

'What the hell is wrong with you?' she said. She was clearly fuming, Kate thought, probably because she thought that only she was allowed to bring Georgie down a peg or two.

'Yeah, Beth, that was totally uncalled for and insensitive,' Sam added.

Kate loved Beth but she was exasperated with the behaviour. 'Georgie's clearly having a really hard time, she's the most private person I know and she finally tells us what's going on and you tell her to get some kink gear?' Kate shook her head. 'You must understand it's more complicated than a sexy nightie. Come on. Grow up, Beth.'

'I . . . yeah,' said Beth, chastened. 'I'm sorry,' she said, lying back down, a look of guilt rushing over her. 'I – maybe I had a bit too much to drink,' she admitted. 'The cocktails went to my head.'

'No shit,' muttered Dee. 'Not to mention the sambuca with the oldies.'

So that was it, Kate thought. She might have known.

Beth smoothed down her hair. 'I'll stop talking. I'll just listen,' she said.

'Good idea,' Sam said sharply.

When Georgie came back, Beth sat up again. 'Sorry, Georgie,' Beth whispered.

'Don't worry,' Georgie said. 'I get it. It's just hard for me to talk about. Look, I know that you guys have never exactly clicked with Paddy–'

'No!' interrupted Beth. 'That's not right. It's not that we never exactly clicked with him. We just don't like him.'

There was a pause, and the girls all stared at her. Then Georgie started laughing.

'Sorry,' muttered Beth. 'I was being tactless again.'

'In this instance, I think it's okay to be honest,' said Sam with a grin. 'Look, whether we've hit it off with Paddy or not is beside the point. I don't have to love all my friends' partners. But we haven't always felt he's been very nice to you.'

Georgie smiled sadly. 'He wasn't always like this, you know,' she said softly. 'He could be funny and sweet, when he wasn't showing off. But these last few years . . . I'm starting to wonder. Maybe I do deserve more. Maybe he's not my forever person. My soulmate.'

'You'll get there,' Kate said. 'I always tell my clients that the big shifts start in the smallest of ways. Maybe yours will happen on this holiday, you know? And whatever happens, we're here for you.' She glanced at her watch. 'Come on. I think it's time for us to hit the showers and then the town. Let's put this to one side and have a great evening. But if you need us, we're there for you, Georgie.'

'Of course we are!' echoed Beth and Sam.

Only Dee was silent.

*

They all took their time getting ready that evening except Beth, who spent her time reading and then darted into the shower at the last minute. But she was used to moving at speed. 'Ready,' she said, scooping her damp hair into a bun and grabbing her bag. 'Shall we?'

'Not so fast,' said Dee, pointing at Beth's feet. 'What are those?'

'They're Crocs, Dee.' She stuck out a foot proudly. 'Do they have them in America? Fantastically comfortable.'

'Off,' snapped Dee. 'Now, this instant.'

'Comfort is key Deirdre,' Beth sulked, but Dee was having none of it.

'Beth, you are not a six-year-old, wearing unicorn Crocs is inappropriate for a woman of your age and it's embarrassing for us to be seen with you.'

Beth said nothing. How could she argue with a pregnant woman? She'd have to wait nine months to tackle Dee again. But also, she could hear the judgmental tone in Dee's voice. She was an embarrassment. How had this happened? She had always been fun, the life and soul. The girl everyone wanted at their parties. And now she had to be told how to behave and what shoes to wear. She sighed and went to change into a pair of clean white trainers. Dee looked slightly more impressed. But it was as if there was something inside her, driving her onwards, because when she went downstairs to the lobby, she spotted the grand piano in the corner and made a beeline for it. She'd always loved the piano. 'Wait,' she cried, running over. 'Let's see if I can remember anything from Mr Gillespie's class.'

'Oh please God, no,' murmured Dee, as the others gathered around.

Beth rattled through the Spice Girls' 'Two Become One', 'Kumbaya', 'Imagine', Stevie Wonder's 'Happy Birthday' and then urged them all into a raucous rendition of Elton John's 'Your Song'. The older couples gathered round, and someone – Roger, it looked like – launched into a sing-song of 'Come on Eileen'. Dee stood several feet away, pretending she didn't know any of them.

'The car's here!' called Kate, gesturing from the doorway, just as Beth crashed to a close and everyone cheered her. 'Thank God,' she added under her breath.

'Right, I've got to go, you've been a great audience!' Beth yelled as they headed out into the night. She followed the others into the air-conditioned seven-seater, still giggling at the memory of Dawn hitting the falsetto notes on Queen's 'Somebody to Love'. She still knew how to get a room going: if she couldn't be the coolest any more, maybe she could still be the loudest.

Dee could barely squeeze her enormous sunhat, tied with a scarf, into the car. 'Thanks for sorting this, Kate,' Georgie said, craning her neck to see past Dee's sunhat. 'I've decided that I'm going to switch off and enjoy tonight and keep Paddy out of my mind. I've even left my phone in the hotel bedroom, so I won't keep checking it. He used to send me such sweet texts,' her voice trailed off, 'Not that he can be bothered these days.'

Kate squeezed her hand. 'No problem. Besides, the hotel kindly ordered it, quite quickly too.' Kate grinned. 'Maybe it was because Beth found the lobby piano.'

It was beautiful in the old town and busy – very busy, full of Irish and English accents as well as Portuguese. There was a lovely warm, garlicky smell in the hot air. The smell of holidays. Children ran past, aiming for the toy shops as couples strolled along at leisure, hand in hand, clearly on a love buzz. The little shops on the cobbled streets were lit up invitingly and staff from the various restaurants stood outside, encouraging the hungry tourists to look at their menus.

'Hey, beautiful, come in for a Portuguese meal?' one man said as they strolled through the main street.

'They probably think that we are a famous girl band,' Beth said, fluffing her hair and giggling.

Dee rolled her eyes irritably. 'It's obvious they've recognised me. I wish that they would leave me alone, I'm just a person, like everyone else here,' she sulked. 'I'm entitled to my privacy.'

Beth opened her mouth to tell Dee that no one here had a clue who she was, when she caught Kate's eye and shut it again.

'Yes,' Beth said, 'it must be so hard for you being recognised everywhere. At least you have your disguise.'

'My disguise?' said Dee, frowning.

'Yeah,' said Beth, gesturing. 'That massive hat.'

Kate burst out laughing.

'This is just my sunhat,' said Dee coldly. 'It's Chloé.'

'Oh,' said Beth. 'Well, if it's Chloé . . .'

They reached the huge square at the centre of the town and took it all in. The middle of the square was filled with henna and braid stalls, little girls sitting down to have their hair braided in brightly coloured thread. Around the edge were the restaurants and bars, people gathered at tables having an aperitif and nibbling on snacks. The noise of chat and music filled the air.

'I think we should have some local cuisine,' said Kate, consulting her itinerary. 'There's a place round here . . .'

'Something simple,' said Dee, putting a hand uneasily to her stomach.

'And vegan options?' said Georgie.

'And wine please,' said Beth smiling and rubbing her hands together.

In the end, they found a cheap Portuguese petiscos, or tapas restaurant, just off the square. It was full of locals and it was always a good sign when the restaurant was busy and there weren't photos of the food on a massive menu board outside.

'Can we have a table outside please?' Kate asked. The waiter showed them to a cosy table and she smoothed down her linen trousers as she sat down. She felt hot and uncomfortable – the other girls were in skimpy tops, but as usual, she was wearing a cardigan. How many holidays had she spent swathing herself in heavy layers? Or, worse, hidden inside her hotel room, worried to come out because her swimsuit didn't fit? Why, she wondered suddenly. It's not like anyone here gave a toss. And she'd sat at the hotel pool earlier in her bikini, which was a first. She tugged off her cardigan and slung it over the back of her chair, revealing her toned arms in her white vest. No one noticed. No one so much as glanced at her. Kate shook her head. Like so many of her insecurities, this one might just be in her head.

The other girls sat down as the waiters fussed around them, pushing the tables and chairs together.

'Right. Let's get locked,' Beth announced, the Irish accent drawing attention from other tables immediately.

'Shhhhhhh, Beth,' hissed Dee. 'It's only seven and there are families here. And we're adults, for God's sake.'

'Okay, okay,' Beth said, putting her fingers to her lips, like a child in school. 'When did you all get so old and boring? I mean, we're on holidays, guys, come on!'

'Will we just get a bit of everything?' Sam asked, obviously tuning her out. 'I'm absolutely starving over here, must be the heat.' She grinned. 'Or the fact that for the first time in ages, I'm not fretting about doctors' appointments and scrolling the fertility app. God, that's a relief.'

'Glad to hear it, Sam,' Kate said. 'Maybe taking some time off from trying is a good thing, hey? Try and relax a bit.'

'Don't tell me I just need to relax and I'll get knocked up,' Sam warned her. 'It makes me want to scream. But yeah, it's a good feeling.'

'What can I get you guys?' said the waiter smiling around the table. 'Some bread and olives to star–'

'One of each,' Dee said under her hat, without looking up from the menu. 'Actually make that four portions of bread.'

The waiter looked startled.

'She's from New York,' Kate said, smiling up at the waiter. 'And also, she forgot to say please. And we're thinking we'd take one of every starter and share them.'

'Make it two,' said Sam.

'Really?' said Kate.

'Oh, come on, we're on holidays, I'll treat you,' Sam said. 'And five chips please,' she added.

'Wait, five?' said Georgie. 'Isn't that a bit . . . '

'Make it six,' said Dee, perking up at the sound of the word 'chips'.

As the bottles of chilled Portuguese Pinot arrived. Kate pulled out her notebook. 'Romance!' she said. 'That's what's next on the agenda.'

'I think we've established there's nothing happening for me in that area,' said Georgie miserably.

'Same, to be honest,' said Beth. 'Jack's idea of romance is a takeaway curry on a Friday night. Mind you, I'm happy with that! Maybe it is romance, in its way.'

'And my romance went out the window with the first ovulation cycle,' said Sam, with a laugh that didn't reach her eyes.

'Fine. Come on, Dee,' Kate said. 'What about you?'

All eyes darted over to her.

'What about me?' said Dee, startled. Oh God, she thought. Why were they trying to get deep with her? It just made her sweaty and uncomfortable. She wasn't really an open-up person, or at least, not in public. If they only knew, her life was in bits, she was not in a position to even talk about anything right now, let alone her non-existent love life, not to mention pregnancy with a stranger! If only they knew how scared she was.

All eyes were on her as she casually swallowed and took a sip of water.

'Well, go on. There are no journalists here, so you can speak off the record. How are things with you on the romance front? Any blokes on the scene since . . . who was the last one? Mark? Matthew?'

'Oh, that guy. Mark, the CNN journalist. Jeez, him. I'd forgotten all about him,' said Dee. She studied her nails. 'Well, I've had some shags, that's all.'

'I don't think I'd be up for that,' said Kate. 'One-night stands.'

'It's pretty normal, Kate,' said Dee icily. 'You wouldn't know because you've been with one person your whole life and they adore you. But the rest of us have to deal with this shit.' Her voice caught and she adjusted herself before continuing. 'Actually, dating lots of people and broadening your sexual horizons can be a very rich and rewarding experience. I've tried shibari, for instance.'

'What's that?' asked Beth, fascinated.

'It's a very classy style of Japanese rope play,' Dee explained.

'Bondage,' breathed Beth. 'Wow, am I boring.'

'I know, me too,' said Kate. 'New York must be a small pool. And you're dating on these exclusive showbiz apps, right?'

'Of course,' said Dee. 'Raya, all the executive ones.' She smirked. 'Sometimes I slum it with Tinder.'

'Anyone nice on the apps then, Dee?' Georgie asked, just as the starters arrived. There were so many, the waiter had to bring an extra table to add to theirs, full of food. Their food!

'Act casual,' said Sam, as cutlery and glasses were rearranged to accommodate the huge number of plates. 'It's a bit of extra food, that's all.'

'It's a whole extra table,' giggled Kate. 'What must they think? That we don't get decent food in Ireland?' She turned back to Dee. 'Go on. You're avoiding the question. Any blokes in the mix aside from the bondage stuff?'

'Well, um. I had three dates recently. The first one was hot. Buff. He's a dancer, an exotic dancer.'

'A stripper?' asked Sam.

'No,' said Dee, glaring at her. 'Well, actually he's dabbled in the past, but recently he's supported some really big acts.'

'Stripper,' Beth murmured.

'Sounds promising,' Georgie said.

'And then there was some other guy, a celebrity accountant. Loaded. Kept showing me photos of his jet. But he was a bit boring and very boring in bed. I couldn't wait for him to leave. And then the last one was this guy . . .' Dee frowned, thinking back. 'I want to say he was called Paul, maybe? I met him on a work outing. We'd just won a very prestigious award. He was nice though,' she continued. 'He was fun and genuine, not your usual guy in a bar. He was cute too, tall with dimples.'

Kate noticed that Beth downed her wine quickly at this. What was wrong with her?

'He sounds lovely, what does he do?' asked Georgie encouragingly.

'It's all a bit hazy,' admitted Dee. 'I think he's a paramedic or a forest ranger. Or with the CIA.'

'Hot,' said Sam approvingly. 'Wildly hot jobs. Although I'm not sure he'd be allowed to tell you if he really was with the CIA.'

'It was definitely something physical and brave,' Dee said, trying to recall.

'But you haven't seen him since?' asked Georgie.

'Well, he asked for my number, and I said no, I'd take his,' explained Dee. 'I didn't want to wait around for him to call me, you know?'

They all nodded. Dee didn't wait for men to call.

'But my phone was dead, so I wrote it down somewhere and . . . I lost it.' She sighed. 'How did we manage in the old days with all those bits of paper?'

'So, it was a guy whose name began with "P" with a physical, brave type of job,' said Kate. 'Not much to go on. Oh, well. At least you had some fun.'

'Some fun,' Dee said quietly. 'Maybe . . .'

'Well, I'd love to see you happy, Dee,' Georgie said, and her wide, innocent blue eyes looked straight into Dee's heart.

'Thank you.' Unexpectedly, Dee choked up and the table went quiet. The others looked at each other in shock. They hadn't realised that Deirdre even had tear ducts. Only Beth avoided their gaze and drank another glass of wine, very fast.

'Me too,' Dee added quietly as she gnawed on a tiny piece of cucumber, like a rat. 'I'd love to see me happy too.'

'And you will be,' Georgie said softly, putting her hand on Dee's.

'Come on guys,' said Beth, changing the tone. 'We need to get cracking on this food. Some lunatic has ordered half the restaurant.' They all laughed.

'God. At least things have improved since we were fifteen,' Sam said. 'Remember that guy at the Year Five dance with the train tracks, Dee? You got stuck to each other when you were snogging.'

'The organisers had to put the lights on so they could detach you,' giggled Beth. They all tucked into the food, passing plates and urging each other to take seconds, declaring the food delicious.

*

Kate joked and laughed along with the others about the Year Five disco, even though she had missed that disco, as she had missed all of them. She hadn't wanted to be the friend that never got asked to slow dance, so she hid away at home, lying to her friends about being sick, lying to her parents. Lying to everyone because she was just so scared. Scared of living. Really living.

And here she was, forty-one and still scared.

Kate popped a garlic prawn into her mouth. It tasted oily, salty and garlicky and so delicious. Sometimes the biggest transformations happen with the smallest of steps. How many times had she told a client that? But had she ever believed it about herself? She ate another prawn. She picked up a piece of bread and swiped it in the oil.

Something inside Kate's head just clicked, as she finished her food. She would be absolutely lost without Ariana so what the hell was she doing, even needing to think about this! She was going to propose. Yes, that's what she was going to do. She was going to say yes, for the first time in her life, rather than just going along with what happened to her. 'What are you smiling at?' Georgie broke into her daydream. 'You look very happy all of a sudden.'

'Oh, it's just ... the food was good, wasn't it?' Kate responded, not giving anything way, *yet*.

'Yeah, seriously good. God, I wolfed that down,' Sam said as they came up for air. 'I was starving. Weird, because I don't usually fancy eating when it's hot.'

'After-dinner drinks anyone, anyone?' Beth suggested half an hour later as they tumbled out of the restaurant and onto the pavement outside. 'Or shall we head now and find a club?'

'A club?' said Kate, grinning. 'I think you've overestimated us, Beth.'

'Yeah, I'm too stuffed,' Sam said. She suppressed a yawn. 'But you guys go for it, I'm easy, I can get a tea back at the hotel.'

'A tea!' shrieked Beth. 'A tea, Mrs Doyle! We're in Portugal, for God's sake.'

'Well, I'll be going back to the hotel,' said Dee, eyeing Beth sharply as people turned to look at her.

'Me too,' said Kate apologetically. She was dying to phone Ariana just to tell her how much she loved her, but they'd agreed on no-contact this week while they 'took some time to think.' Panic seized her. What if Ariana decided to ditch her just as Kate finally decided to step up?

'Oh, come on,' said Beth, pleadingly. 'Just one little sambuca? How often do we get time off the leash?' She had her begging face on, with her hands in the praying position.

'Speak for yourself,' said Dee. 'And you're the one who chose to have a load of kids.' She stuck her hand out for a taxi.

'You'll come for a drink with me, won't you Georgie?' Beth said, fixing Georgie with big eyes. 'Please. Come on, I bet you're in bed by nine every night normally after doing your sun salutations or whatever.'

Georgie hesitated. 'Fine,' she said, as the taxi pulled up. 'One drink, okay, Beth?'

'Just try not to let her embarrass herself too much,' said Dee, as she, Sam and Kate piled in to the cab to head back to the hotel. 'I'm the one who has to share a room with her and I'm too old for wiping up sick.'

The taxi pulled away and Georgie and Beth began to stroll along the narrow, winding street, looking out for a decent bar. 'Look at us, out on the town,' Georgie said. She hesitated. 'Do you think that Dee's been in a bit of a bad mood on this trip?'

'Em,' Beth said, 'Maybe, but I think she'll be better after a night's sleep. Hey, look. Home from home!' She was pointing at an Irish bar, which was heaving with crowds of people, blasting out traditional Irish music onto the street.

'Perfect,' Beth said, with a devilish smile.

'Isn't it a bit noisy?' Georgie said. 'We could keep going and find . . .'

'No, come on! We need to embrace being Irish abroad,' Beth said firmly, pulling Georgie into the noise.

As they walked in, they were hit with a wall of sound and heat. There was a trad band playing in the corner, two fiddles and an accordion and some guy on the spoons. Pints were being spilled and everyone was talking loudly. Just like home.

'Hello hot stuff!' a very drunk man burped in Beth's face.

'Woah, someone needs to brush their teeth!' Beth laughed and wafted her hand in front of her face.

'I know you,' he said, pointing at her. 'Don't I?'

'Doubt it,' Beth said breezily, craning her neck to see past him to the bar. 'Unless you're at pick-up and drop-off every morning at St Ursula's. That's pretty much the only place I go.'

'No, I do,' he said insistently. 'I know you. I–'

'Ah, there you are ladies!' said a guy with an American accent. 'I was looking for you!' said the handsome stranger to Beth. He was tall with broad shoulders, warm brown eyes and a dimple in his chin. Cute.

'Thank you,' the knight in shining armour said to the drunk man. 'I can take over from here.' He blocked out the muttering mess.

'Wait, do you also think we know you?' said Beth confused.

'No,' he said. 'I was just trying to get that guy to leave you alone.' He grinned. 'I'll leave you alone now too.' Then his eyes shifted past Beth and widened as he saw Georgie. He did an almost visible double take. 'Unless – unless I could get you both a drink?' he said. 'I take it you're on holiday here too?'

'That's right.' Beth looked down at her bright red shoulders and said, 'Now this is going to shock you, but we are not Portuguese.'

'I can tell that you're not from around here,' Georgie said playfully.

Beth blinked at her in surprise. Was Georgie flirting with the guy? She was lots of things, but a flirt was not one of them. And she had sounded definitely flirtatious just then.

'I'm Pete.' He offered his hand and said, 'Yeah, I'm not a local either. I'm from New York actually.'

Chapter Eleven

'New York! Oh, our friend lives in New York!' Beth got excited, possibly overexcited. 'Have you met her? Deirdre Byrne?'

'Deirdre? Nope, afraid not.' Pete smiled at her. 'New York is a big place, you know.'

'Damn,' said Beth. 'Well, anyway, I'm Beth and this is Georgie.'

'Beth and Georgie. So, what about it? Can I get you two a drink? I'm getting a round in for my friends anyway and, since we're all Irish, it would be rude not to.'

'You're Irish?' said Georgie sceptically.

He smiled again, a very sexy smile, thought Georgie, with his dimples.

'Well, my great-great-great-great grandfather was. A bit.'

'Two double vodkas please.' Beth went for it.

'Coming up,' he said. His eyes met Georgie's then, and she felt a rush of warmth that left her breathless and tingling all over. What, she thought, was this?

Pete left them to head in the direction of the bar.

'Are you all right?' said Beth. 'You look like you've been hit by a truck.'

'I think I have been,' murmured Georgie. 'Do you have any lip gloss, Beth?'

'Nope,' said Beth. 'And calm down. You already look hotter than any other girl in here without making any effort. It's annoying.' She looked after Pete's broad, departing back. 'He looks hot – kind of firefighter-hot.'

'I feel giddy, Beth, what's going on with me?' Georgie groaned. 'He looked at me just then and it was like this wave of attraction washed over me. Is this some sort of perimenopausal hormone rush? Or have we connected on a spiritual level?'

'He is good looking,' Beth said slowly. 'Really good looking. Kind eyes. But . . . what about Paddy? Your, er, husband?'

'What about him?' said Georgie, her eyes filling with sadness. 'All this time I've tried to deal with his issues. For years I've put up with him talking over me, making snide comments about my work. And then ignoring me when we're on our own. It's always been about him. Well, what about me? I'm on holiday, aren't I allowed to have some fun?'

'Of course,' said Beth, startled. 'But – far be it for me to be the sensible one – you are, er, married and–'

'My marriage is over, Beth,' Georgie said, lifting her chin. She was admitting it out loud for the first time and it felt . . . okay. 'I can't go on like this with Paddy. It's not good for either of us. There is no love anymore, it's all gone.' She waved her hands dramatically. Yes. It definitely felt quite good having got it off her chest.

'Oh, love,' said Beth. 'You know I've got nothing against fun. And I would never judge you. I just don't want you to do anything you'll–'

'Here we go, ladies.' Pete came back over balancing everything in his huge hands. He handed two glasses to the girls.

'Well, thank you, Pete,' Georgie said and nudged Beth meaningfully.

'Oh yeah, thank you,' said Beth stagily. 'Pete, would you mind keeping my friend Georgie here company while I go to the loo? For a weeeeeeee.' She did jazz hands to accompany *weeeeeeee*, like she did for her toddlers.

'Sure thing,' said Pete, blinking a bit at the jazz hands.

Beth fought her way through the crowd to the toilets, leaving Pete and Georgie standing in silence. Georgie was thinking that she loved his smile – a slow, shy smile for such a gorgeous man. She wondered what sort of job he did, with those broad shoulders . . .

'I feel like you're looking right through me. Are you reading my mind?' he said.

'Maybe,' Georgie responded. God, was she flirting?

'But actually, yes. In fact, I am very intuitive and you're particularly open and easy to read right now. It's partly because of my star sign and partly because of the lunar phase we're in.' He stared at her, and she shrugged. Paddy would tell her that was all a load of bull, that she was being embarrassing, but she might as well be her real self now, star signs, lunar cycles and all. After all, she'd never see this guy again.

'Okay,' he said at last, his eyes teasing, as her heart thumped quickly. 'In that case, why don't you tell me all about myself, Georgie?'

'Well, I think that . . . you do a physical job,' she said. She laid a hand lightly on his arm. 'Very physical.' She was definitely flirting. And she liked it.

'Wow, that lunar energy is spot on,' he said admiringly. 'I'm a firefighter in Manhattan.'

'You're a firefighter?' said Georgie frowning. 'That's a hot, heroic job . . . Wait.' She laughed. 'I know this is silly, but . . . are sure you don't know a Deirdre Byrne?'

'Told you, nope,' he said. 'Why do you guys keep asking?'

'Oh, nothing,' said Georgie. She giggled. It was silly – she had spent too long in a small village in Ireland and she assumed everyone knew each other. New York was massive. It was presumably full of hot, square-jawed men with heroic jobs. 'What's brought you to Portugal?'

'Stag do,' he said. 'Old friend from school is getting married. We live all over the world so we were looking for somewhere in the middle to meet up.'

'So, you chose Portugal,' Georgie said.

'I did and I'm glad now.' He gave that shy smile again. Georgie flushed. She knew some guys did the whole bashful act to pull women, but she was sure it wasn't the case here. He seemed genuinely, adorably shy, but with a quiet confidence. Like he could get you a drink at any bar, see you home safe in a crowd, rescue a cat from a tree.

'What about you?' he asked, his eyes fixed on hers, as if she was the only person in the room.

'Same,' she said. 'A group of us from school, scattered all over. So, we arranged a holiday here. We've kept in touch ever since we were kids,' she added.

'Wow, that's pretty special,' he grinned. 'And what about your work?' he said.

'I'm a yoga instructor and I've got a sort of Instagram account thing going on.' She flushed. 'I know, I know. It's a bit silly.'

'It doesn't sound silly,' Pete said. He looked genuinely interested. 'I'm a bit old for social media though. Have you managed to make that a business then?'

Hesitantly at first, and then with growing confidence, Georgie began to tell him about how her page had started as a way for her to upload her yoga reels and the snapshots of her daily life that she thought might help other people. And then how she had connected with her followers, the brand deals, the representation, the team her agent had provided to advise her on how to keep her business organic and warm and authentic while also reaching a wider audience. The book deal, the podcast appearances, the wellness retreats.

'This all sounds incredible,' Pete said, his gaze fixed on hers. 'You really seem to know your stuff.'

'Yeah,' said Georgie, thinking about it. Over the last five years, her account had blossomed and grown into something real and substantial. Something that brought in income equal to, if not greater, than Paddy's. She did know her stuff. 'Yeah, I'm starting to think I do.'

Someone jostled Georgie from behind and she found herself stepping forward, closer to Pete's broad chest. He didn't move away and neither did she. What was she doing? They only had another couple of days here. But really, what would be wrong with a holiday fling? She tilted her head, looking up at his face – those big brown eyes, the dimple in one cheek . . .

If I can look at a stranger this way and not Paddy, there's something very wrong, she was thinking. But I don't want to think about Paddy right now . . .

'Jesus!'

Georgie jumped as Beth broke the magic.

'The queue for the ladies was rude! I honestly thought that I would just wee standing there. Heavy babies,' she added confidingly to Pete. 'My pelvic floor's been screwed ever since.'

To Georgie's relief, he laughed. Thank God he had a sense of humour, she thought. Beth certainly wasn't for the faint hearted! Then his gaze returned to her and Georgie felt like a teenager all over again. He was lovely. She actually didn't want the night to end – she could stay standing here in this stuffy Portuguese Irish bar forever.

But Beth was chattering on. 'God, it's hot in here,' she said. 'And actually, I don't feel so good. I might go outside for a sec, Georgie,' she said swaying and off she went, charging right through the rowdy crowd without looking back.

'I . . . ' Georgie hesitated. She wanted to stay with Pete and gaze into his eyes some more. But her friend was wasted, and she didn't like the look of her. A bit pale and green. 'Excuse me,' she said hastily, and followed Beth, who was scattering people before her as she hurried out.

'Oh, I feel awful,' Beth was slurring as they got outside into the fresh, hot air. She slumped onto the pavement and put her head in her hands.

'That's weird,' said Georgie, sitting beside her and putting a hand on her back. 'You had the wine with dinner but otherwise, it's just been that vodka, right?'

'Yesh, I promish.'

'Maybe you've got a bug.' Georgie bit her lip as she rubbed Beth's back. She wasn't sure how to get Beth back to the hotel like this. She was lolling all over the place. Would a taxi even take her, in this state?

'Excuse me,' said a familiar, gentle voice. 'Can I help?'

Georgie looked up and there was Pete, a light jacket slung over those broad shoulders, bathed in a glow from the pub door. A heroic glow. He was a hero, she thought. So handsome and brave and those shoulders . . . She wished suddenly that the night could have gone differently. That they could have both ditched their friends and had gone back to his room. They would start by kissing passionately and then he would push her gently onto the bed and kiss her neck and. . . .

'Woah is she okay?' he asked, interrupting Georgie's dirty thoughts. She looked down to see that Beth had passed out against her shoulder. 'You girls had a lot to drink beforehand?' he asked, crouching down and looking concerned.

'I don't think so,' said Georgie, bewildered. 'Just a few glasses of wine over dinner. Maybe Beth took some medication or something.' She pushed her friend's hair back from her sweaty forehead. Beth had mentioned seeing a doctor about perimenopause – was she on some meds that would mix badly with booze?

'I think she needs to lie down somewhere other than the street,' Pete said decisively. 'Okay, let's go' he said and bent down. Before Georgie could say anything, he had scooped Beth into his arms. Georgie's heart skipped a beat. She practically swooned. 'Where's your hotel, Georgie?' he asked casually, as if this was a perfectly normal situation. He was holding Beth as if he was Superman.

'The Hotel Edene – it's just up the hill, five minutes away in a taxi.'

'The taxis are this way,' Pete said, nodding in the direction of the street. They set off together. Beth burped loudly on Pete's chest. I'll never see this hero again, Georgie thought, mortified. Beth was an animal. Wait till she spoke to her in the morning . . .

'Taxi!' Pete called and a reluctant driver pulled up, eyeing Beth suspiciously. Pete rattled off some flawless Portuguese and the driver gave the thumbs-up.

'We're good,' said Pete. 'He'll take us to the hotel. I'll come along and give you a hand the other end.'

'Thanks,' said Georgie casually; while thinking, and he speaks Portuguese! He's actually perfect!

Pete deposited Beth gently in the back with Georgie then climbed in the front.

'What about your friends?' asked Georgie, supporting Beth's head. 'Don't you need to stay with them?'

'I told them on the way out I'd met a gorgeous damsel in distress,' he said softly. 'And I needed five minutes.'

The driver snorted, his eyes on the road. Georgie grinned at Pete, who had flipped down the sun visor and was looking at her in the makeup mirror. This was so romantic, even with Beth snoring loudly on her shoulder.

'Over there on the right.' Georgie pointed as they approached the Hotel Edene a few minutes later. 'I can take it from here.'

'Are you sure?' Pete asked.

'Positive,' said Georgie, hauling Beth out onto the drive.

'Is this the sun lounger?' said Beth, giggling. 'I want a piña colada.'

The giggling was reassuring, Georgie thought. 'Well,' she said, turning to face Pete, trying to hold Beth upright. 'Thanks for everything.'

'No problem,' he said. Then he added quickly, 'Listen, I was wondering . . . tell me if you're not keen, if I'm way out of line, but, well . . . maybe we could go out again, while we're both here?' He glanced at Beth then back to Georgie. 'Just you and me, I mean. Not that your friend isn't fun, but . . . '

Georgie laughed. He was blushing. It was so endearing, given his massive bulk and manly shoulders. 'I'd love that actually,' Georgie said, firmly pushing all thoughts of Paddy well down. Why shouldn't she have a holiday fling? She'd spent her whole life doing the right thing – well, now she felt like being selfish for a change.

'Great,' he said, beaming. He patted his pockets and his face fell. 'Only I think I left my phone at the bar. Hopefully one of the lads saw it and picked it up.'

'Mine's up in my room. But I guess you know where I live,' Georgie said, gesturing up at the hotel. 'So . . . come and get me here?' she said.

'Sounds great,' he whispered and leaned over Beth to kiss Georgie lightly on the lips. It was the briefest touch, but her whole body tingled, her legs felt shaky, and her heart started racing. This was the first man she'd kissed in years. Decades. Since she'd met Paddy. They had a spiritual connection. She knew it. Soulmates did exist.

He pulled away and smiled down at her. 'I'll see you, Georgie,' he said softly.

'Yeah. Great,' she said as she dragged herself reluctantly away from him, hauling Beth along beside her. In the hotel doorway she stopped and watched as the taxi disappeared down the hill. Would she really see Pete again? God, she hoped so. She hadn't felt anything like this before, not even with Paddy.

She staggered through the lobby with Beth. Using her yoga strength, she managed to dump her friend into a chair and she went off to find a water cooler. The lobby was empty, but she could hear some chattering along the corridor, and then several of the older couples bustled past her and up the stairs. She recognised the handful they had met – Margie, Roger, Davey and Dawn – among others. That was a late night for them, she thought, as she filled a glass for Beth. Maybe they were having another one of their little card parties. It was sweet. She hoped she was still hanging out with her friends when she was in her eighties.

She made a sleepy Beth drink the glass of water, then walked her to the lift and along the corridor to her bedroom door. She was quite limp, but it was doable. As Beth leaned up against the wall, Georgie managed to root through her friend's bag and find her room key. She dropped most of her items on the ground: lip-gloss, hairbrush, makeup bag, perfume, aftersun, paracetamol, everything, but at last managed to grab the card and tap it to the door. As she opened it, she could see that the room was completely dark and silent. Georgie swallowed nervously. They would be dead meat if they woke Lady Dee.

In the dim light of the hallway, Georgie could see that Dee was asleep under a hydrating eye mask and whale ocean sounds were coming from her phone. The room smelled of lavender and orange, like in a spa.

'Let's get you into bed,' Georgie whispered to Beth, leading her inside. Beth mumbled loudly and Georgie shushed her. 'Don't say a word, everything is fine, good girl,' she kept whispering reassuringly. She was suddenly so tired that she might just fall asleep here herself.

She tucked a sweaty, dribbling Beth into bed quietly and kissed her forehead. Her hair was stuck to it, like an overheated child. Georgie stood for a moment, looking down at her friend. It was a mystery how Beth had got so locked so quickly. Maybe with the heat and the exhaustion, the booze had just gone straight to her head. These things happened. But all the same, it was weird. And actually, Beth had seemed off all day – slurring, playing the piano. All that yelling. Georgie shook her head. She would think about this properly tomorrow, maybe after a coffee and a quick stretch.

She tiptoed quieter than a mouse towards the door, tummy muscles working overtime and holding her breath with each step. She was nearly at the door when–

'Who's that?' she heard Dee say.

Georgie jumped. 'It's just me, Georgie. I was bringing Beth to bed,' she whispered. 'See you in the morning,' she said, trying to creep out.

'Good night?' Dee asked. 'I haven't been able to get a wink of sleep.' She sat up in bed and lifted the eye mask onto her forehead.

'Yeah, great actually,' Georgie said. 'I met a lovely guy named Pete in the Irish bar, as it happens.'

Dee looked surprised, then yelled 'Pete!'

'Yes, that's right, Pete,' Georgie said, surprised. What was so exciting about his name?

'I knew it,' Dee said cryptically. 'I knew I'd remember eventually.'

Georgie had no idea what she was talking about.

'Well, that's good,' she said. 'Night, Dee.' She wandered back to her room, high on the memory of him leaning in to kiss her, of the cute way his eyes crinkled when he smiled. She hoped he'd remember to call.

Chapter Twelve

'I'm not one for the drama, as you know, but I think I might have been poisoned last night,' Beth whispered loudly from her sick bed. She felt terrible. Her head was throbbing and every time she moved, the room seemed to move with her, leaving her nauseous. She felt like death.

'I don't think you were poisoned,' said Georgie, who'd dropped in to check on the patient. 'I was with you the whole night except for when you went to the loo. After you announced that you were going to wee.'

She did jazz hands at Beth.

'Oh God,' Beth said, mortified. She sat up in bed, realising that she was still wearing last night's clothes, like a teenager who'd snuck back into her bedroom through the window. 'I don't understand how I got so wrecked.'

'Me neither,' said Georgie. 'We didn't have that much wine at dinner, and we had enough food to sink that. Six bowls of chips, in fact.' She gave Beth a thoughtful look. 'I wonder why it went to your head like that?'

'Maybe it's the sun,' said Beth. 'Or maybe I ate something–' God, this was mortifying. Passing out at the age of forty-one. 'Listen,' Beth said, suddenly desperate to be alone, 'it's your holidays, George, so head to the pool. You shouldn't be stuck inside with me.'

'Not at all,' Georgie said firmly, spraying her lavender spray around the room to try and take the edge off the hangover fug.

'Beth, don't be silly. Come on, we had fun yesterday, didn't we? Remember jumping on my head in the pool?'

At this, Beth burst out crying. A proper, deep-from-her-soul kind of crying.

'I'm so sorry, you must hate me, Georgie. Does everyone hate me? Dee does, I know that she wants me dead,' Beth sobbed.

The day before was flooding back to her in waves of mortification. She had been loud and obnoxious. She had annoyed Dee in the restaurant. She had told Georgie to buy some latex. She had annoyed everyone.

'Beth, what's wrong?' said Georgie, bewildered. 'Do you miss the kids?'

'Sure,' Beth sobbed, thinking of their little happy faces. 'But I'm also happy to be away. I don't know, Georgie, I'm all confused.' She pulled up the sheet over her and wailed.

'Hey, hey, easy tiger!' Georgie came over and sat beside her. 'You've got the hangover fear. You know, where you second-guess all your life choices and fall into a pit of self-loathing? But it's okay, we can get you out of it. I'll tell you what you need.'

'If it's yoga, I'll actually start crying again,' sniffed Beth.

'You need to sleep, swim, drink four litres of water and then have some chips,' Georgie said firmly.

Beth gave a watery laugh. 'Okay. I can do that.'

Georgie went to the bathroom and ran a flannel under the cold tap. Then she came back and handed it to Beth. 'Put that on your eyes,' she said. 'Be a bit kind to yourself Beth. Everyone gets pissed sometimes. You'll be right as rain after my prescription.'

Beth smiled and took the cloth. 'Remind me, last night, in the bar . . . were we talking to some hottie?' she asked wiping her eyes on the wet facecloth. 'Some hottie who seemed very, very into you?'

'Actually, yes.' Georgie smiled. 'Now you mention it, we were.'

'Go on then,' said Beth, snuggling down. 'Tell me everything. I remember tall . . . dark . . . handsome . . .'

'All of that,' said Georgie. 'He's a firefighter in Manhattan. Really broad shoulders. He picked you up – I mean, literally picked you up. In his arms.'

'Oh God,' said Beth. 'My fantasy finally came true, and I barely remember it.' She rubbed her temples.

'He carried you to a taxi. He spoke Portuguese, such a nice guy. Stopped some drunk guy from hassling us. We chatted right up until you came back from the loo. He's so easy to talk to.' Georgie sighed dreamily. Then she laughed. 'You know I had a bit of a panic though.'

'How come?' said Beth sleepily.

'Well, he lives in Manhattan and his name starts with a P. Did Dee say that about her one-night stand, having a powerful job, name starting with "P", remember?'

Beth sat bolt upright in bed. 'What did you say?' Her heart was thumping and she felt that she might throw up.

'His name begins with a "P".'

There was no way, Beth thought. No way whatsoever. 'What would the chances be though, Georgie?' she improvised.

'I know! What am I like? Anyway, it turns out it's not him because, oddly enough, New York is a big place. So, I'm safe.' Georgie giggled. 'Can you imagine if I got my hands on Dee's fling? She'd hunt me down and . . .'

'Kill you,' Beth said quietly.

*

Sam thought that Georgie looked flustered when she emerged onto the patio.

'Well, how's the patient?' asked Dee. 'After keeping me up half the night,' she added tiredly.

Georgie settled herself on her sunbed, rubbing in suncream. 'She's asleep,' she replied. 'She was totally out of it though, muttering and babbling about God knows what.'

'Thank God she's silent,' Dee snapped.

'What's that supposed to mean?' Sam said. Dee could be so bitchy sometimes.

'Well, the snoring last night,' Dee said.

Ah. Beth was an epic snorer, Sam remembered. The others nodded in agreement. Then Dee's features softened. 'Look, I think there's something wrong with Beth. Really wrong. It seems to me that Beth is having a mid-life crisis and she's decided to go large this holiday, forgetting she's forty-one, not twenty-one. The drinking, the stupid behaviour, the crying – she's a woman on the edge.'

'I think Dee's right,' said Georgie unexpectedly. 'To be honest, I'm worried about Beth, too. She seems really unhappy.'

'Now that you mention it, when I call her to catch up in the evenings at home,' said Sam, 'she's always having a small glass. But, like, every time.' She felt suddenly guilty that she hadn't kept up with Beth, hadn't asked her properly about what her life was like, but then it was tough with the kids screaming and yelling in the background all the time.

'And hiding in the attic isn't great, is it?' said Georgie. 'She sounds low to me.'

'I told you,' said Dee. 'She's in a bad place and she's drinking more than she should. Not that I'm anyone to lecture,' she added quietly. She looked guilty and Sam wondered if she'd been a bit much with poor Beth.

'We all drink more than we should probably,' said Sam. 'Except Georgie. But it seems Beth is leaning on it a bit too much.'

'Beth is always the life and soul of every party, so she hides it all so well,' Kate said frowning. 'But I think that there's an underlying sadness to her these days. I don't think that it's Jack or the kids, she adores them.'

'Maybe getting back to work would be good for her, like you said,' suggested Georgie. 'That midwifery course she was talking about.'

'Yeah, maybe. She's been a full-time mum for seven years. Seven years of putting herself last,' Sam said thoughtfully. 'Jack's great but I think that in terms of the house, shopping, cooking etc, he's pretty old-school.' She shifted uncomfortably on the sun lounger. Her boobs felt heavy and sore. She knew her period was due even though she'd ditched the apps for the holiday. Any minute now, she would see blood on the loo paper and feel that familiar pang of sadness. But she had to keep smiling. And focus on her friend.

'Shall we talk to her about it?' Kate asked. 'I don't want to say the wrong thing and put her back up. But I don't want to ignore it either.'

'What exactly happened last night?' asked Sam, her antennae alert.

'Well, we went to some Irish bar in the new town–'

'Natch,' said Dee with a smirk. 'Classy as always.'

'Don't be such a snob,' said Kate. 'Go on, George.'

'And we had a double vodka and Diet Coke each,' Georgie said. 'I was absolutely fine but then when I was talking to this guy–'

'Wait, what guy?' demanded Sam.

'Just this nice American guy that we met,' Georgie continued, blushing bright red. Interesting, Sam thought.

'One minute, Beth was fine, and then she went to the toilet and suddenly she wasn't. She was slurring, falling over, trying not to be sick. I don't know how it happened.'

'Because you were too busy talking to this American guy,' teased Kate.

'Continue, Georgie,' Dee said impatiently.

'Then she passed out and we had to get her back here in a taxi.'

'We?' said Sam, watching Georgie closely.

Georgie blushed again. 'The guy helped me. But she was pretty out of it. Like, way more than she should have been, unless . . . ' She paused. 'Unless she drank more at the bar than I thought,' she finished.

'There you go,' said Dee. 'Case closed. We just need to decide on a strategy to tackle her. An intervention.'

'Hmm. Maybe you're right. If there's one thing I'm good at, it's strategy. But while we work out what to do . . . let's have a drink?' Kate asked and they all giggled, relieved at the release of tension.

Sam offered to go up to the bar to get some sangrias. She could do with stretching her legs. Beth sounded as if she was in a poor state, but hopefully a sleep would make her feel better. 'Four sangrias please,' she asked the pool barman. 'Unless you think it's too early?' she joked.

'Not at all.' As he mixed the jug, he nodded over to the older ladies in the pool. 'You're nothing compared to those guys. They were on the sambuca at midday. With your friend.'

Aha, Sam thought. So that's why Beth had been so drunk. She'd been day drinking with the oldies. As if on cue, one of them waved over at her. Dawn, Sam thought her name was. 'Fancy a drink with us?'

Sam forced a smile. 'I'm just taking these to my friends – another time!' she called back.

'Just don't get too carried away! I know what you young people are like. Don't make us come over there!'

'Oh, don't be daft,' said the woman called Tracey. 'You have fun, love. Your young friend Beth was partying with us the other day!'

Sam laughed weakly. Piss off, she thought, feeling uncharacteristically annoyed. Old biddies without a care in the world. And suddenly Sam felt like crying. Her friend Beth, her sunny, cheerful, optimistic friend had been doing shots with these strangers.

Crying in her room. She'd felt that low and desperate. She must have been feeling this way for a while for things to get this bad. And none of them had noticed and helped.

By the time she reached the beds, she couldn't control herself, Sam felt sick and suddenly burst out crying. The tears flowed down onto her chest.

'Sam!' the girls said as one. 'What happened?'

'It's just . . . ' Sam said between sobs. 'I hate the idea of our Beth this unhappy. I think we let her slip through the cracks a bit, you know?'

The girls drank their drinks in silence. Sam tossed hers into the grass verge. 'Don't fancy it suddenly,' she said as the others looked at her, startled.

'I wonder if we should talk to Jack first, or would she kill us–' Georgie started.

'No,' Kate said decisively. 'I've been thinking and our strategy should be to be direct. Beth's our friend. If we think she has a problem, we shouldn't go to Jack behind her back, not yet. She's straightforward and loyal. Let's just talk to her. Find out what's going on.'

'Well, why don't I go up now and see how she is?' Sam suggested. 'I'll suss things out and we can make a call on what to do.' Sam headed up to the room, her mind whirling. How had they let it get this bad? But now that she thought about it, really thought about it – how often did they properly catch up these days? They checked in and asked each other how they were on WhatsApp and FaceTime, but everyone always said, 'good thanks'. What if they were honest? What would they each really say?

Beth's behaviour has been a cry for help all this time and I didn't even notice, Sam reproached herself. She knocked at the bedroom door of room number twenty-six.

'Come in,' she heard Beth's croaky voice from inside, so she used the key card to let herself into the room. It was a sweaty fog of wine fumes and anxiety, with top notes of lavender.

'How are you doing, Beth?' Sam asked as she went to the window and casually cracked it open a good few inches, letting in the refreshing breeze.

'Sam, thank you so much for visiting me.' Beth sat up, like a hospital patient, with her eyes full. She looked pale and exhausted. 'I'm so embarrassed. A middle-aged woman on holiday, getting this wrecked. Honestly, right now, I just want to be back at home.' She fixed her big dark eyes on Sam. 'Do you hate me?' Her eyes filled up.

'Of course not!' Sam almost laughed. 'I love you, you idiot! I've known you nearly thirty years, for God's sake. What's with the paranoia?'

Beth gave a sob. 'I don't know. I feel like shit.'

'I need to come to Ireland more often, hey,' said Sam, that guilt creeping up. Beth looked so young and vulnerable lying in the bed, like they were teenagers again. Sam took a breath, deciding to bite the bullet. 'Beth, we think something's wrong. With you, I mean.' She held up a hand as Beth rushed to speak. 'We know you're happy with Jack, we know you love the kids, we know you have a great life. But all the same, we think something is wrong.'

There was a long silence in which Beth fiddled with the sheet. Then she said in a small voice, 'Yeah, there is.'

'Well, talk to me. How do you feel?' Another silence. 'Or will I get Georgie?' said Sam. 'She's better at this than me. I do decisions and practicalities, not emotions and deep stuff.'

'It's okay. I like that you're practical,' Beth said. She drew a shuddering sigh. 'Well, like I said the other night, I think that I am maybe perimenopausal? The doctor seems to think so anyway.'

'Right,' said Sam. 'That might be a possibility . . .'

'I feel I don't know myself anymore,' Beth said quietly. 'I feel panicked the whole time, like overwhelmed with every day. I wake up in the middle of the night, my heart pounding.

I keep bursting into tears. And you're right, I am happy, but . . . but also, I'm not. I have no libido – poor Jack – and I feel like I just shout at the kids all day, it's horrible–' Beth broke off and rested her hand into her hands. 'I'm a mess.'

There was silence. Sam put out a hand and squeezed Beth's. 'You'll be okay,' she said softly. 'You're our Beth, the life and soul. You'll find your way back.' There, Sam thought. She'd said just the right thing. . . .

'Or,' said Beth, seeming to brighten up. 'Maybe I just need a Bloody Mary. Do you want one if I order room service?'

'A Bloody Mary, are you serious?' said Sam.

But Beth had cheered up now. Everything seemed a bit brighter at the thought of a Bloody Mary. 'Sammy Bear, we are all-inclusive, hello? Don't worry, it's free.'

'Beth,' Sam said, looking Beth right in the eye. 'I don't think you should have another drink. I think you should listen to what I'm saying. I think you're really down. Am I right?'

Beths face fell. 'Sam.' She laughed nervously. 'Are you joking? I'm absolutely fine, honestly. When I moaned about the kids the other day, I was just–'

'Beth, it's not just that. This whole trip has made me wonder. You're the life and soul like always, but something is missing.'

'What are you saying to me Sam?' Beth asked her friend, looking at her right in the eye. Sam could see the panic setting in. She looked like a naughty kid, who'd been caught stealing sweets. Only she wasn't a kid.

Sam met her gaze clearly. Sometimes the firm approach is the best one, she thought. 'I think that you might need some help, Beth. I think you should go back to the doctor and take this perimenopause stuff seriously. It might be that they're right. Booze for instance – it can affect us differently as we get older. Emotions can change, too. You might not think mental-health stuff is for you, but it's a spectrum, isn't it? Like physical health. It can dip when you least expect it.'

Beth said weakly, 'I'm the happiest person I know.'

The silence this time stretched on and on.

Beth just stared at her. Then, when Sam thought she might scream from the tension, Beth said easily, 'I'll have a think about what you've said. But I need a kip now if that's okay, Sam?' She turned to the side and pulled up the sheet over her body.

'Oh, of course,' Sam said surprised; Beth seemed so calm. Oddly calm, actually, given what Beth was like normally. Had she even heard what Sam had been saying? Was she ignoring it? Was this what happened if you confronted someone who had a drink problem – they went into denial? Still, at least she had started the conversation. That was a start. Sam picked up Beth's arm and kissed her hand. She said, 'I love you, Beth, we all do. But we are worried about you, and we wonder if you're turning to drink and socialising and all this banter to cope with some other problems. And we want to help you feel better.'

Beth's head emerged from under the sheet. 'So, the others think the same?' whispered Beth.

'Yeah,' said Sam. 'Yeah, they do. And we all love you and–'

'Thank you,' said Beth, yawning. She was clearly pretending to be sleepy, Sam thought. She turned away and hid her face. 'Thanks for being honest with me and I'll think about what you said, I promise,' she said. 'I just need to rest now.'

'Okay,' Sam replied, leaving the room quietly. She hated leaving her friend alone like this. But she had a feeling this was something Beth had to go through all by herself.

*

In the bedroom, behind the recently closed door, Beth's mind was racing. Tears ran down her face as she stared at the wall. She lay there for a while, incidents rushing through her head. She couldn't put her behaviour down to just cutting loose on holiday. The crying happened all the time. She knew she was drinking just that bit too much. Hiding in the attic wasn't good either, was it? She was forgetting things. Going into rooms with no idea why she was there. Saying the wrong thing at exactly the wrong time. It was happening too often, and it was becoming too much. She thought of that doctor's prescription. Should she consider it?

Eventually, the slide-show of humiliation started whirring too fast and she groaned and kicked off the sheets. She'd had enough of lying here panicking. She could take this one step at a time. Right now, all she had to do was get up. She could do this. She was a forty-one-year-old mother of four and she could do this.

She got out of bed, her head swimming unpleasantly. Then she stood and walked very slowly over to the bathroom, pulled off the clothes she'd been wearing the night before, and got into the shower. She let the water pour over her to wake her up and she scrubbed her body clean, rubbing Dee's expensive shampoo into her hair until her scalp tingled. Once she was out, dressed and looking half normal again, she cleaned the room and flung the balcony door wide open, letting in the fresh air.

She had planned to come to this holiday as her old, fun self, not this weeping, miserable wreck. All the same, this was the Beth who had showed up. This wasn't exactly the holiday she had planned. But it might be the one she needed. Her best friends in all the world were here, right downstairs and all together. Now was the time to open up and express herself. She just had to be brave.

*

Beth found them all at the side of the pool. They didn't see her for a moment and she stood and watched them: Dee, looking like a fifties' movie star; Sam and Kate, laughing at something

155

in a magazine, their voices ringing out; Georgie, serene and sweet as always, busily scribbling in her notebook. She was so lucky to be a part of this group.

Then Georgie saw her and waved, and she went over.

'We kept you a bed,' Kate said and, at the simple gesture, Beth burst out crying.

'You – you saved me a bed?' she sobbed. 'That's so nice of you.'

'What on earth?' said Kate, putting an arm around her. 'It's the five of us, always – we wouldn't leave you out.'

'Come on.' Sam hugged her. 'Sit down and relax, you messer.'

Beth sat down and dried her eyes with her towel. 'Guys, I don't know what's wrong with me,' she started. 'I feel like I've gone mad, or lost myself, or both.'

'Sam said you'd been wondering about perimenopause?' said Georgia gently. 'Don't underestimate hormones, Beth. Mother Nature is a powerful beast.'

Sam rolled her eyes at Georgie who shrugged. 'What? She is.'

'Well, sure,' said Sam briskly. 'But I imagine it's eminently treatable. And that you should consider what the doctor told you and weigh up your options. There might be something to be said for a good dose of HRT.'

'I feel . . . ' Beth struggled to put into words the strange feeling. 'With kids hanging off me and not a minute to call my own, I feel . . . '

'Lonely,' said Dee softly. 'Is that it?'

Beth met her friend's eyes. Dee's usually hard, beautiful face was soft.

She was listening.

'Yes, I am lonely.' Beth gave a shaky laugh. 'Which I know sounds ridiculous because I'm never on my own! But I feel lonely sometimes, even in a crowded room.' Beth felt relieved revealing all of her feelings out loud. Getting it off her chest.

'And the drinking?' Sam said quietly. 'Do you think that you are drinking a lot at the moment?

'Yes,' Beth said. 'I was thinking in bed that I haven't had a day off in about two years. I think that it's habit, I don't think that I'm an alcoholic but I'm definitely . . . dangerously close to . . . going off the rails,' she said, and her eyes filled up again. 'I need to get this sorted when I get home. Have I ruined the trip?'

'Nooooooo,' the girls all said.

'We'll help you with this,' Kate said. 'I'm actually relieved.'

'How come?' said Beth.

'Well, I'm worried about you. And I thought you'd tell us you were fine, that we should calm down, that you'd crack some jokes, all the usual Beth stuff. I'm relieved you're listening to us. I guess we chose a moment when you were in a weakened state and couldn't protest too much.'

Beth giggled. 'Yeah, too right. I could barely move. A good moment to stage an intervention. I'm serious, when I get home, I'm easing off on the booze, going back to the doctor about my medical stuff and maybe hiring a therapist. Something has to change. This isn't me. I'm fun.'

'Maybe it's not that simple,' said Georgie softly. 'We could all be fun in our twenties because our lives were simpler then. And now . . .' She gestured around. 'Well, life got real. So maybe aiming for your old self isn't the thing to do. Maybe we aim for something else.'

Beth nodded slowly. 'You're getting wise in your old age, George.' She was feeling a bit better. These girls were her best friends. This was all going to be okay. She lay on the sunbed and took a few deep breaths. 'Hopefully, no more dramas for this holiday then girls,' she said. 'We can just relax and–'

'I'm pregnant,' Dee announced.

There was a brief silence, then they all burst out laughing.

Chapter Thirteen

'Guys, I'm pregnant,' Dee repeated. 'This isn't a joke.'

'Wait, you're serious?' said Kate, sitting up. 'Are you sure?'

'Yes, I'm sure,' Dee said. 'I did a test on the first day here just to be safe and it came up right away. One to two weeks.' Even saying it aloud didn't really help; if anything, the shocked looks on her friends' faces were making her feel more panicked. But if Beth could confront her issues, Dee could at least address her own secret. 'Beth knows, but I made her swear not to tell any of you, which I know has been absolutely killing her. So, I thought I'd do her a favour and come out with it.'

There was another silence that Dee could only describe as stunned.

'You're really pregnant?' Sam asked, her face white with shock. 'Do you think you'll go through with it?'

'Um, I don't know to be honest. A baby really wasn't part of the plan,' Dee confessed. 'I only found out two days ago, so it's still sinking in.'

'Of course,' Sam said quietly.

'But yeah,' said Dee, her voice shaking slightly. 'I think I do want the baby.' She swallowed. 'I know how wild that sounds. Me, a mother. But all the same . . . yeah, I th–think I want it. Maybe. Possibly.' She stuttered into silence. It was strange saying it out loud.

There was a third stunned silence. They were coming thick and fast.

Georgie gathered herself.

'In that case, congratulations, Dee,' she said, coming over to hug her. The others all came to hug her, following Georgie's example.

'Dare I ask who the father is?' said Kate. 'I know you've been quite . . . active. Three, er, recent dates, wasn't it?'

'I can't be too sure. But yes, I think there are three candidates. Accountant, dancer, guy with the fit job whose number I lost.' Dee sighed. 'Too bad. He was the only one I wouldn't mind seeing again.'

'I think this calls for a drink,' said Georgie. 'Er, soft drinks, it sounds like. Sam, give me a hand?'

They headed to the bar and hopped up on the stools.

'Let's have a cheeky one on our own,' said Georgie.

'Georgie!' Sam giggled. 'This is not like you.'

'I don't want to drink in front of Beth, but I need it. There's only so much that deep breathing can help with.'

'I never thought you'd say something like that.' Sam gestured to the barman. 'But yes, like what the actual? Dee, a mum? Really? She used to leave the room when Beth breastfed and mime puking.'

'Yep. She said babies are revolting,' Georgie said.

The barman walked over to them. 'Five Cokes, one iced water and two extra-large white wines please,' Georgie asked. Then the two of them snuck around the side of the bar – possibly to Beths sneaky sambuca spot – and sat down.

Georgie picked up her wine and Sam picked up hers.

'Cheers!' they said at the same time. Georgie's toast was loud and confident, but Sam's was doubtful and sad. They clinked their glasses softly together.

'How are you, Sam?' Georgie asked, now that they could talk in confidence. 'I was thinking that must have been tough, hearing about Dee's news.'

'I'm not great to be honest,' Sam replied. She took a sip of wine, but her stomach was churning, and she had a metallic taste in her mouth. 'This wasn't the plan, you know? Once Jeff convinced me we should go for it and try for a baby, I thought it would just . . . happen. Everything else in my life has, you know? Instead, it was a load of money and faff and no baby. And Dee gets pregnant, just like that, with some bloke she barely remembers.' She sighed. 'Anyway, yeah. Not great.'

'I know that is very hard to hear, Sam,' Georgie said, 'and I don't have experience with IVF, but from the sounds of things, you might have to accept you can't plan every aspect of this. There will be an element of fate.'

Sam winced. 'Ugh, I hate to say it, but I think you're right. Between Beth's mid-life crisis and Dee announcing her pregnancy, I think that I'll need a holiday after this one!'

Georgie laughed. 'There's something I haven't told you yet,' she said.

Sam groaned. 'Oh God. More drama?'

'No, don't worry. But that American guy I met last night, before I had to take Beth home?' Georgie smiled shyly. 'Well, we had a little kiss.'

'What?' said Sam, leaning forward. 'And, er, what about your husband?'

'Yeah, what about him?' said Georgie defiantly, then shook her head. 'I know what you're going to say – this isn't like me. But all the same, I kissed him. He's gorgeous. His name is Pete and he's a firefighter in New York. We only spoke for a few minutes, but I think we had a connection. And as for my husband who doesn't want to have sex with me? I'll think about him later.'

'Georgie, who are you?' shrieked Sam.

Georgie giggled. 'I know! This is not like me and I'm loving it, Sam. I feel alive again.'

'So exciting! So, when are you meeting again?' Sam asked. 'Because if he's in New York and you're back in Ireland, it had better be soon.'

'Well, that's the thing,' Georgie said. 'We got out of the taxi and neither of us had our phones and Beth was semi-conscious so we couldn't swap numbers. But he said he'd find me here.'

'So romantic, but I have to admit . . . a bit frustrating,' said Sam, who was too practical for all that. 'Given the time frame, you know. Ah, well. Try and take your own advice here, keep following your path. Let fate do its thing.'

'I will,' Georgie said. 'Here's to fate,' and they clinked their empty glasses.

'Come on. Back to the drama we go,' Sam said as she carried the tray of warm Cokes back to the girls. Georgie followed behind her. Keep following the path and fate will take over. That was one of her favourite mantras.

*

'Jesus, you wouldn't want to be thirsty,' Kate laughed as they joined the group again. They were all sitting up, mopping sweaty heads and upper lips. Dee was topless and the lifeguard's chair had moved closer.

All in ten minutes!

'I was working out Dee's cycle,' Beth said with her iPhone calendar open on her screen. 'I've figured out exactly when she ovulated.'

'Beth,' said Dee. 'I'm pregnant, what more do we need to know?'

'No, it's a good idea,' said Georgie. 'We can tune in to the pregnancy more holistically.'

'Urgh, please,' said Dee. Ovulation, cycles – she hadn't a clue about all of this, really, because it was never on her radar. She had tuned out Beth's endless-seeming pregnancies because it was so boring and gross. Now, she was all ears because it affected her! Her and her perfectly toned, tanned body!

'I can't believe you got pregnant by accident,' said Kate. 'After everything the nuns told us.'

'Mmm. They talked a lot, but they didn't get too specific, did they?' said Sam.

'I wish I'd paid more attention to this stuff,' admitted Dee. 'Although yeah, sex-ed in a convent school probably isn't the best.'

'Well, at least your boobs will get even bigger now,' Sam said with a straight face. 'Save you money on another boob job?'

This time Dee burst out laughing. She couldn't help it.

Then Dee sighed. 'Do I really want to be forty-one and a single mum though?'

Beth reached over and squeezed her hand. 'We'd be here for you, Dee.'

'You've all got your own lives,' Dee said. 'Let's be realistic – I'd be doing this completely on my own. Which you'd think I'd be used to by now.' There was a note of defiance mixed with sadness in her voice. Her parents had always done her own thing and as the only child, she'd learned independence quickly.

'Your work will give you a good package, right?' said Sam.

'Not sure,' said Dee evasively. 'Healthcare is insanely expensive in the States, you know, guys. I can't even imagine what having a baby would cost.'

'Yeah, and don't you get, like, four days off or something ridiculous?' asked Kate.

'It's four weeks, I checked,' said Dee. 'But yeah. Insane. That's if they keep me on.'

'What do you mean? Of course they'll keep you on. You're Deirdre Byrne, queen of TV Gold,' Beth said.

Dee looked unhappy for a second before saying, 'Look, guys, can we not talk about it for a bit? I really am going to engage with it, but I want a few days of denial first.'

'Okay,' agreed Beth. 'It's our third night, does anyone want to go out or will we keep it casual and stay here?'

'Here,' said Kate firmly. 'Let's just not bother tonight – no makeup, just t-shirts, nice chill night. I think we've all had enough drama for one holiday.'

*

How can I tell them, Dee thought, about the job? It's bad enough being pregnant but if they knew that I am a washed-up has-been, too . . . She applied the finishing touches to her face. She could look the part, even if she didn't feel it.

'Wow! You look great Dee,' Beth said when she came out of the shower, pulling on a pair of shorts and a wrinkled t-shirt. 'Um, I thought we were doing casual?'

Dee looked down at her very tight, skin-hugging, red-sequinned cocktail dress and kitten heels. Her brown hair was blow-dried to perfection and her lips were painted a glossy red. 'I don't really do casual. It's difficult when you're a public figure – you have to be always on.' She rotated and admired herself from all angles. 'My tits do look great, don't they?' At least there's one advantage to pregnancy, she thought.

'Just stunning,' said Beth. 'In fact, all of you looks stunning.'

'I know,' Dee responded, as she winked to herself in the mirror. She noticed that Beth hid a grin.

The girls got in the lift, Dee staring seductively at herself in the lift mirror, the whole way down. She looked fabulous. Just stunning, even if she said so herself. Pregnancy was clearly great for your skin, she thought. She looked glowing, like she'd had fantastic sex, followed by a martini and–

As the lift door opened, she stepped out in front of Beth and there he was.

The guy that she'd slept with the other month, the guy who had given her his phone number, which she had lost and whose name she had then forgotten and who might be the father of her baby!

In her hotel, in Albufeira, Portugal. Of all places.

Looking as shocked as she felt right now.

Dee gathered herself. At least she looked, although she said so herself, like a goddess. She couldn't have designed this reunion better. Although, come to think of it, what on earth was this guy doing here? Had he somehow tracked her down? She was used to men being intense, but this was something else. Was this restraining-order territory?

'What,' she began, 'are you–'

'Pete! No way!' Beth beamed up at him. 'It's me. The girl who passed out last night? Thank you so much for looking after me. Georgie told me all about it.'

Pete dragged his gaze from Dee to Beth. 'Oh, hi,' he said, still clearly stunned. 'Of course I remember you. Only I'm sorry, I can't quite remember your–'

'I'm Beth,' she said, holding out her hand, friendly as ever. He took it, his eyes locked on Dee, his mouth still open.

'Oh, sorry,' Beth said turning to Dee. 'I'm being rude. This is my friend, Deirdre – she lives in Manhattan like you.' She laughed. 'Remember I was asking you last night if you knew a Deirdre?'

Pete nodded, still looking stunned. 'Y-yeah, I remember. But–'

'Anyway,' said Beth, looking from one to the other, a curious expression on her face. 'Are you looking for Georgie? She's on her way down. We thought we'd have a chilled night tonight. Although,' she winked, 'things can always change.'

'Georgie?' he murmured faintly. 'Y–yes.' He shook his head, focusing his gaze again on Dee. 'Your name is Deirdre? Because that night in New York you told me–'

Ping.

The lift opened again, and Kate walked out.

'Hi guys! Who's this?' she said, oblivious to the tension in the lobby. When no one answered, she held out a hand to Pete.

'I'm Kate, how's it going?'

Pete shook her hand politely, in slow motion.

'I just don't understand,' he said, eyes still on Dee, 'why you told me your name was–'

Ping.

The lift doors opened again, this time revealing Georgie and Sam.

Beth glanced from Pete, who looked even more stunned, to Georgie, who looked perfect, like an angel, in a simple white crochet dress, which accentuated her tanned shimmering skin.

A shy smile spread across Pete's face and Georgie went a delicate pink. 'Georgie,' he said, his brow clearing.

'Pete!' she said.

'I just wanted to call by and, um, check on . . . you.'

Dee began to frown. The guy Georgie had met the other night. Surely not . . .

'Wait. Wait,' she said, the pieces falling into place. 'HE'S the guy you met at the Irish bar?' she said, pointing at Pete.

'Well, um, yes.' Georgie reddened, glaring at Dee. 'Pete kindly helped me get Beth home the other night,' she went on primly.

Dee stared at her for a moment, then gathered herself. 'What a funny coincidence,' she said, in her silkiest newsreader voice. 'You see, I also know Pete. Pete, can I talk to you a moment? Alone?'

'Sure, right,' he said, nodding quickly. The others watched as Dee led Pete around the corner.

There was a long silence, before Georgie said, 'Does Dee know Pete-from-the-Irish-bar?' bewildered. 'But how?'

Beth shook her head, frowning in confusion. 'It sounds as if she knows him from New York. But we asked him if he knew a Deirdre in New York and he said no.'

'Maybe he was lying,' said Georgie, the colour leaving her cheeks. 'Maybe Pete is the mystery man Dee slept with and . . . Oh God.' She couldn't finish her sentence.

'One of the possible fathers of her child?' whispered Beth. 'But why would he lie when we asked him? He had no reason to hide it. Even Dee only knew about the baby two days ago.'

Kate shook her head. 'I have literally no idea. But you're right about one thing, Georgie, Pete's very hot. I'm just sorry he's potentially Dee's baby daddy.'

They sat down at the bar in silence and ordered drinks – sparkling water for Beth, juice for Sam who was still feeling rough, large glasses of wine for the others – and waited, trying to make conversation but all the while frantically wondering what Dee and Pete were talking about.

Georgie felt an odd knot in her stomach. Clearly Dee and Pete had history. Georgie had seen the way Dee had looked at him. And if Dee wanted a guy, nothing would stand in her way.

What the hell was going on?

Chapter Fourteen

Around the corner from the reception area, Dee was asking Pete the same thing.

'What the hell is going on?' she said, her hand on her slim hip. 'Why are you here, in Portugal? In my hotel? Did you hunt me down?' She was used to guys becoming infatuated but not fly-out-to-Portugal infatuated. Usually, some flowers and marriage proposals were as intense as it got. This was a first. She wasn't sure whether to call the police or to be impressed.

'Hunted you . . . What?' Pete began to laugh. 'No, Jesus. I mean, we had one night together, what – six weeks ago?'

'Six weeks sounds about right,' said Dee grimly, thinking of Beth's ovulation chart.

'Right, well, I can assure you that when you didn't call, I presumed that you weren't interested. I didn't come here to Portugal to track you down!' Pete said.

'Then what are you doing here?'

'My friend Dan's stag party. I never expected to see you coming out of the lift!' He shook his head, smiling. 'That was a shock. But wait a second. Back in New York, you told me your name was Carla!'

'Ohhhh,' said Dee. 'Yes, you're right. I probably did.'

'But . . . why?' he said, looking bewildered. 'If your name is, what – Deirdre? – why would you give me a fake name?'

'It's difficult dating as a celebrity,' said Dee, smiling modestly. 'It's such a drag being swarmed by fans and it can make it difficult to form relationships. Especially when it comes to men.

I never know if someone likes me or they like the girl off the lunchtime news on TV, you know? Or if they're going to sell a story. It's exhausting, being this famous.'

'Oh, right,' said Pete politely. 'Are you on the TV then?'

'Yes, I am!' said Dee indignantly. 'Did you not recognise me?'

'No!' Pete said. 'I mean, I'm sure I would if I watched day-time TV,' he went on apologetically, 'but I don't. I'm usually at work.'

'Oh,' said Dee, deflated. Still, maybe it would be good to be with someone oblivious to her fame. More wholesome and real that way. 'Anyway, I often use a fake name on dates. I'd have told you the truth eventually, of course.'

'But you ghosted me first,' said Pete.

'I misplaced your number,' said Dee, giving him her most charming smile. He really was gorgeous, she thought. Even more than she remembered, with his liquid brown eyes and well-muscled arms, his shirt-sleeves rolled up. She couldn't have picked a more perfect father for her unborn child. She edged a little closer. 'Which I regret now, of course. So, I get why you're in Portugal. But what are you doing in this hotel?'

Pete ran his hand through his hair, sexily, Dee thought. 'I came to see the girls I met the other night. Who seem to be your friends, so that's also . . . strange.'

'Beth and Georgie,' Dee said. 'They mentioned they met a charming, American guy.'

Pete went red, which Dee also thought was adorable. 'Oh. Did they? Well. That was me,' he said. 'I helped them get into a taxi and back here. One of them – Beth, is it? – was a bit worse for wear. She seems great though. And Georgie, she's . . .' His blush deepened. 'She's lovely.'

Dee gathered herself. She wasn't sure if something was going on between Pete and Georgie, but she wanted to nip whatever it was in the bud. 'Beth is going through something, as you might have gathered. And Georgie is very sweet,' she said, with just the right patronising note in her voice. 'Maybe a little . . . well, you wouldn't call her exciting, you know?'

'I had a nice time with them,' said Pete, frowning.

'That's great.' Dee watched him from under her lashes. Should she tell him about the pregnancy? Was he the father? It seemed likely. And she would much rather it was him than the exotic dancer or the accountant guy – the guy who was so boring she could barely remember anything about him. Yes, she had to shut down anything between him and Georgie sharpish.

'How funny you ran into them,' she said. She gave a little giggle. 'Naughty Georgie – she looks so innocent but she's a real dark horse. She must have told you?'

'Told me what?' said Pete.

'When Georgie has a few drinks, she can be an awful flirt,' said Dee, lowering her voice. 'She can't resist. But the truth is, she's married.'

This time, the silence stretched out. Then Pete swallowed. 'I see,' he said quietly. 'Well, thank you for telling me.' He forced a laugh. 'Listen, it's been nice catching up,' he said. 'But I think I should–'

'Would you like to join us for a drink? With the others, I mean?'

She didn't want to let him go without pinning him down to another date. She would break the baby news to him once they'd had a chance to rekindle their flame from that night together all those weeks ago. A drink now and then a quiet date in town in a day or two, just the two of them . . . and then she would tell him the truth.

Pete shook his head. 'Um, I don't think I–'

But Dee practically hauled him towards the bar, where the girls had found a table and were crowded around it, a collection of glasses in front of them.

'Pete's going to join us,' Dee said.

*

'So, you two . . . know each other?' said Georgie, her eyes wide. Dee had her hand on Pete's arm and was smiling up at him through her lashes. In the soft candlelight of the bar, she looked even more stunningly beautiful than normal. This was a nightmare situation. An unexpected battle, and Georgie was already losing it.

'That's right,' purred Dee. 'Rather intimately, in fact.'

'From – from New York?' asked Georgie, her stomach sinking. Pete was so the baby daddy.

'Yes,' said Dee. She glanced seductively at Pete. 'We had one memorable night, didn't we, Pete?' She flashed her white teeth at him and licked her lips.

'Um, yes, we met briefly in a bar,' he started, 'and–'

'Right!' Beth said, widening her eyes at Georgie. 'I think Dee might have mentioned you although she couldn't precisely recall your name. She thought you were called Paul. Still, how nice. An unexpected reunion. Pete, I'll get you a beer,' Beth said standing and going to the bar.

'So, you're a forest ranger, is that right?' asked Sam.

'I knew it was a sexy job,' Dee said with a secretive smile.

Pete went almost purple with embarrassment. 'No. I'm a firefighter,' he managed to squeeze out.

'But we asked you if you knew a Deirdre,' said Beth, coming back with a bottle of chilled beer, which she handed to him. Then she pointed an accusing finger at Pete. 'And you said no.'

'She told me her name was Carla,' said Pete through gritted teeth.

He's lying, Georgie thought. He tried to catch Georgie's eye, but she stared down at the table, reeling. 'I didn't know a Deirdre. Or at least I thought I didn't,' he added, unconvincingly.

Beth whipped her gaze round to Dee. 'Why on earth would you tell him your name was Carla?' she demanded.

Dee gave a tinkling laugh. 'It's a showbiz thing,' she said. 'Celebrities do it all the time. In hotels and restaurants and . . .'

'In bed?' said Beth, aghast.

Georgie wanted the ground to open up and swallow her.

'You can't be too careful in my position,' Dee told her firmly. There was a pause.

'You could have used my name,' said Beth at last.

'Same,' said Sam. 'Why not Sam?'

'Yeah, or mine,' said Kate. 'Bit offended you didn't, to be honest. You don't even know a Carla.' She looked around and the girls nodded.

'Well, I chose Carla,' said Dee briskly. 'The point is it was a simple misunderstanding. But Pete knows my real name now and he found me in the end, didn't you?'

'Yes, well that was a surprise,' he said. 'Nice that we can be friends now.' He tried again to catch Georgie's eye, but she made sure to keep her head down. She wanted to run away, but she didn't want Dee to see how upset she was.

'We don't have to be just friends . . . ' Dee whispered audibly into Pete's ear.

At this, Georgie stood up abruptly. 'I'm going to the restaurant to eat,' she said, 'I'm starving.' She couldn't stand watching Dee in action any more. And as for Pete, Georgie felt like such a fool to have been taken in by those brown eyes. She'd clearly been out of the relationship game for far too long. It was better to remove herself from the scene altogether.

'I'll come with you.' Sam stood too. 'Nice to meet you, Pete,' she added.

'Me too, starving,' said Beth, jumping to her feet. 'C'mon, Kate,' she said, fixing Kate with a look. 'Thanks for the fireman's lift the other night, Pete.' She ran after the others.

'Nice to meet you all,' Pete said, shifting uncomfortably as Dee ran her hand unsubtly down his arm.

She was about to pick things up where they had left off.

*

Taking a seat at their table in the restaurant next door, Sam pressed her fingers to her forehead. 'Talk me through this slowly, Georgie,' she said. 'This is your Pete from the other night, yeah?'

Georgie also had her fingers pressed to her forehead. 'Yes, that's him, Sam, Pete. We connected and I really like him,' she said. 'But then . . .'

'But then ol' Big Jugs comes along and steals him,' Beth finished, dropping into a chair next to them. 'I mean, I wouldn't normally encourage cheating, Georgie, but, well, Paddy is an arse,' she added.

Georgie nodded sadly.

'To be fair, it sounds like they have prior history,' said Kate. 'A one-night stand that may or may not have resulted in a pregnancy. That's a big deal. Only why Dee's walking around Manhattan giving out fake names like J-Lo, I have no idea. Talk about delusions of grandeur.'

Georgie groaned.

'I'm over it,' she mumbled into her hands. 'I have to be. Dee's pregnant, Pete might be the actual father of her baby, and she clearly likes him. So, I'll just . . . pretend I don't.'

She looked up, plastering a smile on her beautiful, sad face. 'There, I'm over it already.'

'Sure, you are,' murmured Kate. 'I mean, Beth is right about cheating, I suppose, but all the same, who wouldn't want a holiday romance with a hot firefighter?'

*

The girls looked at the menus in silence. There was still no sign of Dee. She's probably licking his ear, thought Kate, doing her 'Deirdre Seduction'. She had been known for it in sixth year. It had a hundred per cent success rate. When Dee spotted what she wanted, nothing – not even her own granny – would get in her way. Kate felt bad for Georgie, but if Pete was prepared to go along with Dee's little story, maybe he wasn't right for Georgie after all.

'Sod it, I'm having a double-cheese pizza,' said Georgie putting the menu down. 'I can be plant-based and gut-friendly another time.'

'Good idea,' said Kate. 'And garlic bread, loads of it. And some antipasti starters.' She grinned at Georgie. 'I know it won't fix everything but it's a start.' Feck this body-worry business, it does no one any good in the long run, just gives me anxiety, she thought. Not worth it. Besides, Ariana loved her as she was and wasn't that good enough? She thought that it probably was. What had got into her this holiday? Had she finally had enough of overthinking? Was the warm air in Portugal chilling her out? Whatever it was, she liked it.

They ordered and sat chatting for a while, planning the next day and trying not to wonder what Dee was getting up to. But as their starters arrived, so did Dee, looking pretty pleased with herself. Her smile was almost shark-like, the way she showed off her teeth. 'Well. How weird is that?' she said to the table, sitting down and picking up the menu, as if everything was normal. 'Pete, my Pete, turning up here!'

Your Pete, eh? thought Kate. Subtle as a hammer. You didn't know his name yesterday.

'What did you do with him, send him up to our room?' said Beth tartly.

Dee smiled at her sweetly, not rising to the bait. 'He's gone – for now. I've given him my number and he took it, so we'll see.' She shrugged. 'We've said we'll probably meet in town in the next few days. Get a drink or something. And then, if the moment is right, I'll tell him about the baby.' She tossed down her menu. 'I think I'll have the grilled chicken. I've got an appetite for something other than bread for a change.'

'There are two other candidates, right?' Kate pointed out. 'I mean, there's a 66.6 per cent chance this isn't Pete's baby,

Dee.' As she said this, she looked carefully over at Georgie, who was staring blankly at her menu.

Dee shrugged. 'I have a feeling it's him,' she said. 'I've always been very intuitive. It's why I'm such a good interviewer.' She looked at them all, as if she couldn't understand why they were so upset.

The girls had ordered four large double cheese pizzas drizzled in hot honey. Food for the soul. Dee flashed a smile at the waiter. 'Grilled chicken, chips, spinach salad, dressing on the side. Extra spinach. Large sparkling water, heavy on the lemon. Thanks.' She smiled around at the girls. 'I need all the vitamins I can get for the baby.'

When the food arrived, Beth took a large mouthful of garlic bread and addressed the elephant in the room. 'Dee,' she said, still chewing, 'you know that Pete kissed Georgie the other night, right?'

'Beth, leave it,' whispered Georgie, but Beth held up her hand.

'No, girls, we love Georgie and we want an explanation.'

'I think the reason he came here tonight was to see Georgie, not check on Beth,' Sam continued, picking up the baton. 'No offence, Beth.'

'None taken,' said Beth magnanimously. 'Anyway, you're just waltzing in here, Dee, and thinking you can snap your fingers and Pete will come rushing back. You haven't even thought about Georgie.'

Dee gave Georgie a faint smile.

'Fine, let's discuss this like adults. So, Georgie and Pete had a little moment the other night? That's sweet. But the thing is, Pete and I have a connection. We were dating, back in New York. He might be the father of my child.' She rested her hand gently on her midriff. 'There are other fish in the sea, you know, Georgie – including your husband,' she finished with a sting in the tail.

'It really doesn't matter,' whispered Georgie. 'You're right. You were dating Pete long before–'

'Dating? Was it not just a one-night stand?' Kate couldn't resist.

'A one-night stand who probably impregnated me, so let's not minimise what happened,' Dee said, clearly trying to stay calm. 'Why don't you get it? Pete is possibly, no, probably, the father of my child. Why doesn't that count for something?' Her cheeks were flushed now and she looked even more beautiful than usual.

'Dee, you know that I'm not minimising things,' Kate spoke in the calm, authoritative life-coach way that she usually only used with her clients. 'But regardless of who the father of the baby is – and presumably that's something you can only find out with a paternity test – the point is that Pete was calling here tonight to see Georgie, not you.' She finished, taking a sip of her wine.

'Because he obviously didn't know that I was here, Kate,' Dee said. 'You should keep your nose out of my business. Maybe concentrate on your own relationship.'

Kate flinched.

'What's that supposed to mean?'

How dare she, she thought angrily.

'What I mean,' said Dee, 'Is that you've been with the same person since you were nineteen and you still can't commit. You have far bigger problems than me and that's saying something. At least I do something, instead of sitting around wondering if I should. Are you still going to be weighing up the pros and cons in your spreadsheet when you're fifty?'

Low blow. All fell silent. The other girls watched, eyes wide.

Kate rarely lost her temper but when she did, she didn't hold back. Kate gathered herself.

'Actually, your relationship is my business, Deirdre,' she said coldly. 'Because when you're in a bad mood, we all know about it. It affects the group, because you're incapable of dealing with your emotions like a grown-up. And I didn't come on holiday to watch you sink your claws into some guy and give Georgie the side-eye because she had the audacity to flirt with your property.' She took a gulp of her wine, glad that she'd got her feelings off her chest.

Dee gasped and Georgie went paler than before.

'If you want to thrash this out with Pete, do it on your own time,' Kate finished. 'This is our holiday, not the Deirdre Byrne show.'

'Well, would you like me to leave, Kate?' Dee stood up dramatically. Heads turned in the restaurant. She was clearly loving the drama. 'Because I can be on the next flight home.'

'Oh, get off the stage,' Kate said. 'Sit down.'

After a moment, Dee sat down, sulking.

There was a silence. Dee's face was like thunder. Kate wondered if she'd gone too far.

'All I'm saying,' she went on more quietly, 'is that you and Pete will need to have a conversation about the baby and find out if it's actually his or one of the other guys. And if you like Pete, then that's for you two to work out. But you can't just swoop in here and pretend that Georgie didn't like him too.'

'Fine,' said Dee. She turned to Georgie with a tight smile.

'Georgie, I accept that you liked Pete. Before you realised our history. And I know you didn't mean to get involved in all this and I hope you understand how complicated it is.'

'Thanks, Dee,' said Georgie meekly. 'I do understand. There's nothing between me and Pete really, it was just a drunken night, like you said. And I hope it works out for you.'

Kate sighed at the sight of Dee walking all over Georgie as usual. She opened her mouth to say so, but Sam kicked her under the table. Ouch! she thought, glaring at Sam.

'Not now,' Sam mouthed.

The food arrived and for a moment, the row was forgotten: the girls tucked into the juicy pizza with stretchy mozzarella cheese, garlic oil dripping down their chins.

'God, this is amazing,' Kate said, savouring every single bite and sighing with happiness.

'There you go,' said Sam. 'After all this time saying no to pizza, you're finally saying yes.'

Kate smiled. 'If I can say yes to this, what else might I say yes to?'

Sam squeezed her greasy, garlicky hand.

*

When Dee's salad arrived, she picked at it as the others looked on. The atmosphere at the table was chilly once more.

'Why don't we all go into town tomorrow?' said Sam. 'We can have a mosey around the market.' She was eager to change the subject.

'Check out the fake LV bags,' Beth suggested.

Dee shook her head.

'You can always tell the fakes,' she said. 'It's in the lining–'

'Still, be fun to look though, won't it?' said Sam briskly. 'Come on, Dee, don't tell me you're not tempted. Think of the bags, the belts, the bikinis . . . '

'I'm up for it,' said Kate. 'Ariana needs a new wallet. I can say it with Chanel!'

'Me too,' said Georgie. 'Not the bags, but I'd love to wander around and soak up the atmosphere.'

Paying the bill and yawning, they all said, 'Night, love you,' almost in sync, just as they always had from their first night in Irish college. Old habits were hard to break, Sam thought, as they all headed off to their rooms to sleep.

*

Back in her room, Dee sat happily on the bed. Of course, Georgie and Pete had clearly had a moment the other night. But hell, all was fair in love and war, and she'd met Pete way before Georgie had. Besides, whether Georgie liked her husband or not, at least she had one, Dee thought. And Dee needed one. The fact that Pete had come into her life again just when she had discovered she was pregnant was surely fate: Georgie was always banging on about fate. After all, what were the chances of him being in the same area, in the same country, at the same time! It was meant to be. If Pete was the man who had got her pregnant, this could all work out so well. She smiled to herself. She was done with these showbiz types. Done with the glitz and glamour of her life. She needed a solid, salt-of-the-earth type of guy to be the father of her child. And Pete was perfect.

Chapter Fifteen

As soon as the door shut in Beth and Dee's room, Kate followed Sam and Georgie into theirs. They all sat on Sam's bed.

'What the hell is going on, Georgie?' Sam asked.

'What do you mean?' said Georgie, bewildered.

'I mean, letting Dee swoop in and take Pete!' said Kate.

'Oh, for goodness' sake,' said Georgie. 'Take Pete? He's not completely passive, you know. If he liked me, well, he would have said something.' She got up off the bed and went to the bathroom and turned on the tap to wash her face. 'Besides,' she said, her voice muffled, 'he's potentially the father of Dee's baby.'

'So she keeps telling us,' muttered Kate.

'She saw him first,' Georgie replied, coming out of the bathroom in a nightie with her face scrubbed clean. Then she started to laugh. 'Saw him first? I'm as bad as you. For goodness's sake, we're not kids fighting over a toy! Pete can make his own mind up. I don't want some guy who can't stand up for what he wants. If he likes Dee, then he likes Dee. Besides, if he's the one who got her pregnant, I'm backing off. That's like something off *Real Housewives*.'

'Let's just try and get on tomorrow,' Kate said. 'I hate all the drama.'

'You were the one telling Dee off at dinner,' Sam reminded her.

'I know, I know,' said Kate. 'I hate how she always thinks everyone will fall in line. But then, to be fair, they always do. And I guess you're right, Georgie – it might be safest to back off while Dee and Pete sort this out. Okay, night-night,' she said, hugging them, and left.

'I don't know what I was thinking, attempting a holiday romance,' said Georgie miserably when Kate had left. She lay down on the floor and swung her legs up to rest against the wall.

'I should have been taking a good, hard look at my marriage and making a decision about Paddy, not pretending I'm twenty again and trying to snog guys in bars.'

It was typical though, Georgie thought, that the only person that she had found attractive since Paddy had slept with and maybe impregnated her good friend! What were the chances? You had to laugh. But also, she felt sick inside. What she had felt with Pete was surely no normal holiday attraction. It had felt electric. And Dee was tenacious. There was no chance for her and Pete now.

Stop being so pathetic, she told herself. You're just starved for sex and affection, that's what. Pete was the first guy she'd fancied in ages, so she'd clearly built him up into some sort of Disney prince.

'What are you going to do about Paddy?' asked Sam curiously. 'And what are you doing with your legs up the wall?'

'I'm going to end it with Paddy,' Georgie replied, her eyes filling up. 'Do you know what, Sam, I've stuck around and tried but it's my life, too! He has zero respect for me as a person, let alone as his wife. He loves our life, not me.'

Tears ran down into her ears. She drew a shaky breath.

'Oh, and the legs? Lymphatic drainage. It's good for anxiety and sleep.'

'What do you think happened between the two of you?' Sam asked gently.

'Men go off sex, too, apparently,' Georgie replied from her position on the floor.

'But we could work through that. It's more that he's lost interest in me. I don't even think he likes me. I'm not sure he ever did. My yoga teaching, my Insta following – he thinks it's silly. Embarrassing. I think he liked me in my box as a trophy wife and I'm too old for that now.'

She glanced up at Sam.

'It's hurtful, but I can't take it personally. And who knows? Maybe with someone else, he would feel differently. Be a better, kinder husband.'

As she said the words, she knew that it was unlikely, still, maybe she should give him the benefit of the doubt.

'You have to put yourself first, too, Georgie,' Sam said. 'You never do.'

'Right,' Georgie said, forcing a smile. 'I'm learning that. But not when it comes to Pete. Seriously, if he and Dee want to be together, they don't need to worry about me.'

*

Kate could hardly wait to close the door before calling Ariana. She knew it was against the rules, she knew Ariana liked an early night, but she couldn't wait any longer. She had to tell her how she felt.

'I love you,' was her first sentence when Ariana picked up. 'I love you so much.'

'What?' Ariana sounded sleepy. 'Are you drunk?'

'I know I'm not meant to call, I just want you to know that I appreciate you so much.' The words tumbled out. 'There's lots going on over here with the others and it's kind of made me see more clearly. You bring out the best in me and you always have, no matter how hard I tried to push you away. I ate pizza tonight and you know what? I loved every bit of it. I didn't think about my stomach or my thighs, I just loved it. That's because of you, because of how you've made me feel.

We have such a special relationship and there is no one else for me and–'

'Kate,' Ariana interrupted. 'Stop just a sec. I feel the same.'

Phew, Kate thought, relaxing now and sitting on the bed. Her shoulders dropped with relief. She couldn't bear to lose Ariana, and she knew that now.

'I have to go,' she said.

'Are you kidding?' Ariana started to laugh. 'You wake me up, start ranting about pizza and how you love me and now – you have to go?'

'Yeah,' said Kate, smiling. 'We agreed no phones, remember? But I do love you. And I want you to know that I'm making some changes. You'll see. Goodnight.'

She hung up and lay there for a long time, smiling at the ceiling.

After forty-one years, her life was really starting.

*

In Beth and Dee's room, Beth was sitting on the loo and brushing her teeth at the same time. She was used to occupying this position but usually with the bathroom door open, answering questions from her family as people ran around. It was a real testament to her bowels that they were able to get on with their job regardless of the surrounding chaos. Practice makes perfect.

Beth was torn about the events of this evening. On the one hand, she understood why Dee, in the confusing first stage of pregnancy, would want to pin down a relationship with the man who might well be the father of her child. Especially a man with shoulders like that.

On the other hand, why did she have to be such a complete and total bitch about it? No one would judge her if she was just nicer; they were all old friends after all. It was as if Dee was scared to show her vulnerable side. Hiding behind that tough mask, the trappings of fame that none of them actually cared about . . .

'You're going to get piles if you sit on the loo for too long,' Dee said from the other room, breaking into her thoughts.

'Right, yeah,' Beth called back. 'I'm done.' She finished up, washed her face and went back into the bedroom. It was so hot and sticky at night, so she was just wearing a sports bra and shorts. Both had definitely seen better days. She caught Dee, in a silk negligee, giving them a once-over and Beth quickly hopped into bed and pulled the sheet up to her chin. She flicked off the light and closed her eyes. There was a silence.

Then: 'Do you think that I'm a good person, Beth?' Dee said quietly in the dark.

Beth opened her eyes. Of all the questions to answer delicately and to a pregnant woman as well.

'Of course I do, you muppet, we all do,' Beth said firmly. 'We wouldn't be here on holiday with you if we thought you were a bad person.' She thought for a moment.

'No one is a bad person except, you know, the really bad people. We all just have our baggage and sometimes we make bad decisions.'

More silence.

'So, you don't think I'm a bitch?'

'Er.' Beth bit her lip. 'Tricky one, to be very honest, Dee. You are capable of being a bitch, yes. The way you handled this Pete thing wasn't great because you could see that Georgie was hurt and yet you just kept going and wouldn't even acknowledge it. I know you're a strong, powerful woman and sometimes, in this world, that can mean being a bit of a bitch, so I wouldn't change that about you. You could maybe just . . . soften things a bit, you know? Amongst friends?'

She waited a moment. No response, so Beth closed her eyes again. She was just dozing off when Dee spoke again.

'But do you think that I'm a good friend?' Dee asked. 'I would never hurt anyone on purpose Beth, but I did see Pete first, to be fair and what if he is the dad of my child? He could be. There's a one-in-three chance, just like in *Mamma Mia*.'

'*Mamma Mia*?!' Beth laughed heartily, before realising that Dee was serious. 'I mean, that's a story, Dee. But sure, it might be just like that.'

*

Dee stared up at the ceiling in the darkness, trying to remember her night with Pete, six weeks ago in New York. There had been laughing and chatting in a bar . . . and then kissing in a taxi and back to hers . . . and then . . . And then what? The room had been spinning. She had taken a lie-down on the sofa and closed her eyes and . . . She could clearly remember removing her very expensive lingerie, leaving it trailing behind her on her way to the bedroom, so surely . . . ?

She frowned. The next bit was a bit of a blur, but she was sure it had been nice, she could remember the essentials from the night and they were, well, amazing. They'd sat up in bed after, sunlight streaming into her apartment, mugs of coffee in hand, before she'd sent him packing, she remembered. She looked over to the other bed, where Beth was snoring away loudly. Just before she'd nodded off, she'd said, 'If Pete is the father, you need to find that out. But be kind to Georgie, hey? She's having a hard time.'

I'm having a hard time too, Dee thought, feeling a bit sorry for herself. Maybe she did need to be tough in today's world, but where had it got her? She was looking at the end of her reign as queen of daytime news and she was pregnant with a stranger's baby. Could it be, she thought cautiously, that being a complete bitch isn't what is needed right now? Maybe it was time to let her softer side show. If only she could remember what that was . . .

Chapter Sixteen

'Morning, Dee!' Georgie waved from the breakfast table as Dee walked in, looking like she was off to Paris Fashion Week.

'Good morning,' said Dee graciously, walking over to her. 'You look very lovely this morning, Georgie.'

'As do you.' Georgie smiled politely. She looked a bit pale, Dee thought, a bit peaky. As she helped herself to a bowl of plain yoghurt with a sprinkling of seeds in it, Dee felt suddenly guilty. Had she stolen Pete from Georgie? She approached the table cautiously. Georgie was hunched over a green tea, looking a bit lost.

'About last night . . . ' Dee began.

'It's forgotten,' Georgie looked up at her and smiled. 'I mean, who allows a man to come between a long friendship?'

Dee looked at Georgie sceptically, before agreeing. 'You're right. I value our friendship, Georgie. I want you to know that.'

'Oh, I do too,' Georgie said, pushing her food around her plate. 'It's certainly worth more than Pete,' she said quietly.

Dee said nothing, just picked at her food.

The others filtered down slowly. The girls got their food and headed to an outside table to get the morning sunshine. The smell of fresh coffee and pastries filed the air as light music played softly from the pool bar, across the water. The chef was whipping up omelettes and all was good.

Kate took out her notebook. 'I know, I know, you're getting bored with me. But this is a topic I really want to discuss.'

She looked around covertly, like a CIA agent, and lowered her voice. 'Therapy. Who is having it, is it better than any of the therapists I've been to, because I've decided on this holiday that I really want to become a better functioning person for Ariana.'

'Oh, I've been having therapy for years,' said Dee, slicing into her mushroom and Gruyère omelette. 'Everyone in New York does. At one point, I had three different therapists. In Ireland, they're probably a bit behind when it comes to that sort of thing.'

'Three? What do you talk about, Dee? How do you even start or know what to say?' Kate enquired.

'Your commitment issues, of course,' said Dee, waving her hand. 'It's simple. You just talk about anything you want to talk about. It's your money.'

'Give me an example,' said Kate.

'The idea of psychotherapy is that the answer lies within our childhoods, ourselves. So, all of my problems started with my parents, obviously. You all know about my dysfunctional childhood.' Dee shrugged, but her eyes were sad. 'It explains why I have trust issues, connection issues with guys, body issues and quite honestly, it explains why, even though I am very beautiful,' she smirked, 'I don't always see it.'

Dee's parents had been too wrapped up in their own lives to see Dee and had expected her to fend for herself from a young age, to achieve without their support or interest. Maybe it explained why Dee was so ruthless, even with friends. It was like a suit of armour to her.

'Of course,' Dee went on, 'we talked about my relationship with . . . surgical tweakments, too.'

'I can't be doing with that,' Beth said, shuddering. 'Needles in my face, no thank you. I can barely be bothered with eyeliner these days.'

'We can tell,' muttered Dee. 'The thing is, you don't know what it's like being in the public eye. I do and there are times that it's very intrusive. You have complete commenting on your weight, your wrinkles, your body . . . It goes on, guys. Irish charm only gets you so far, you know. My public expect a certain standard of–'

Beth snorted. 'Your elusive public? All right, Angelina Jolie.'

'Do you think that you still have trust issues with men?' Georgie said. 'I find the idea of your past influencing your present really interesting. My parents were lovely, but they valued getting along with other people more than me standing up for myself or fighting for what I want. Maybe that's why I'm such a pushover.'

Dee didn't rise to the bait.

'Definitely,' Dee answered honestly. 'My parents did a bit of a number on me. The men I meet are pretty dire. Either they're terrified of commitment, or they want you to meet their parents right away, settle down and have a ton of babies ASAP.'

She shuddered.

'Gross.'

There was a brief silence where everyone thought about Pete, who was clearly husband material.

Dee cleared her throat and addressed Beth.

'I don't mean that staying at home with the kids isn't a valid choice too,' she said hastily.

'I don't know the exact moment I decided to give up work,' admitted Beth. 'I was lucky I had the choice to quit, I guess. But being a working mum was so hard. Every day, getting a dirty look when I had a doctor's appointment or one of the kids was sick. I felt totally judged. "Oh, Beth's got to go and fetch the kids early again". That kind of thing. Sitting at reception with my coat bundled up under my chair, so I could sprint for the last train to get them from nursery. And you know, if you're a minute late to collect them, you get fined? In the end, I decided it was easier to just stay at home until they don't need me anymore. And believe me, that's work. Anyway, sorry for the kid talk,' she said, 'but it's a lot.'

'It's okay,' said Sam softly. 'Maybe we should have the kid talk. It's clearly important.' She chewed her lip nervously. 'Mind you, all of this isn't selling it to me,' she said. 'Which is lucky, I guess, since nothing is happening.'

'Yeah, sorry. And to you as well, Dee,' said Beth. 'This is probably all a bit tactless. Kids are great,' she added.

But Dee shook her head, taking another sip of coffee.

'It's hard whichever way you look at it,' she said. 'Now Beth, for the love of God, get some fibre in you. You were on the toilet for bloody hours last night.'

'Okay,' Beth laughed, reaching for the fruit salad. 'Let's get stuck in.'

*

The lobby was full of older couples again, mainly English, Beth thought as they waited for their taxi into town for the market. They all seemed to know each other and were laughing and joking. Very good friends, clearly. How sweet it was to come away together every year.

'Where are you lovely young things going? asked Margie. She wagged her finger at Sam. 'You never come to our parties! And you would be such a hit!'

'We're just off to the market now,' Sam said, smiling. 'We want to check out all the fake goodies, like the bags and pashminas. Get some stuff for the hubby.'

'Ah lovely, in that case would you do me a big favour?' asked Margie, seizing Sam's arm.

'Of course,' said Sam, thinking that she couldn't very well refuse such a delicate old lady. Although her grip on Sam's arm was surprisingly strong.

'Would you be able to pick me up some Vaseline? I've run out.' Margie said, smiling sweetly.

'Sure, of course,' said Sam.

'An extra-large tub, if that's okay? added Margie.

'Um, extra-large, okay,' said Sam.

When the taxi arrived, they headed outside into the scorching heat. 'Like who in their right mind would ask a total stranger to get them Vaseline?' Kate muttered. 'Anything else we can get for her? Some sinus meds? A corn plaster?'

'Bit weird, isn't it?' said Sam. 'Maybe we should go along and check out one of the parties they're so desperate for us to come to. Nice glass of sherry and some bridge.'

They climbed into the taxi, Dee and Kate up front and the other three behind, and did up their seatbelts.

'Where can we buy an extra-large tub of Vaseline?' Beth asked the taxi driver.

'She is joking!' Kate said laughing. 'The market, please. And can you drive slowly?' she added, 'I get car sick.'

'Yeah, that would be great actually,' said Sam, whose own stomach was heaving.

'Maybe your car sickness is catching,' she said to Kate, rubbing her queasy stomach. She couldn't understand it: she never so much as suffered from the hiccups and now, she had indigestion all the time. It must be all the food she was eating, she thought. That was all-inclusive for you.

They kept the windows up as much as they could to benefit from the air-conditioning, but Beth liked to hang out of the window like an excitable dog, taking in the Portuguese sights. Waves of hot air trickled in the window. Bliss.

'Do you know what, girls? I feel great today! Up for the craic, know what I mean?'

'Oh, we know,' Sam said dryly. 'Go easy, Beth, won't you?'

'Don't know what you're talking about,' Beth said happily.

'We are here!' Kate said, as they pulled up into a carpark. It was busy, in full market swing, with locals swarming around along with the tourists wearing bumbags and big hats. The market was buzzing with children racing around between the stalls and delicious smells wafting through the air.

They paid the taxi and turned round to face the scorching heat. It was over thirty degrees today. 'God, my thighs are sticking together,' Beth said. 'Not that I'm complaining – it's raining in Ireland. Speaking of which, I must get some more Ventolin inhalers when I'm here,' Beth said. 'Still allergic to everything under the sun. Apparently, they're cheaper than home.'

'I'll go for you,' said Kate. 'I want to find somewhere with decent air-con, and you know how I feel about shopping. I'll catch you guys up.'

'Don't forget Margie's Vaseline,' said Sam as Kate headed off. 'Extra-large. God knows why she needs it so urgently.'

Kate waved in response as the others headed into the market.

*

'How are you feeling, Dee?' Sam asked as they wandered past the stalls. 'Just say if you need to sit down.'

'I'm fine,' said Dee determinedly, 'I'm not going to be one of those pregnant people who make it their whole personality,' she said, picking up the pace and charging towards one of the fake designer bag stalls. It was filled with fake Louis Vuitton, Chanel, YSL . . . no premium brand had been left out.

'Zero interest in haggling,' Dee sternly told the stall holder, who was selling some soft leather bags. 'So, don't even try. I've travelled the world and I'm pretty streetwise, so don't try and pass off a copy as designer . . .'

'There's no haggling,' the stallholder told her wearily. 'Just a set price, on the label.'

'Oh,' Dee said, deflated. 'Well, in that case, can you reach me down that one with the shoulder strap?'

For a woman who didn't believe in haggling, Dee cut a tough bargain, working the stallholder down from €50 for a fake Louis Vuitton purse to €25. The stallholder looked relieved to be getting rid of her as they wandered off. Sam couldn't blame her.

'So, if you're really thinking of going ahead with this pregnancy . . . ' Sam began cautiously as they wandered off to look at the rest of the stalls.

'Which I think I am,' said Dee.

'Right, then what's the plan? Have you got space for a baby? How would it work with your job?'

Sam wasn't sure why she was asking these awkward questions, and she knew she was being a bit of a bitch, but she was sick of Dee and – if she were honest – pretty jealous of her. A baby was supposed to be all that she wanted right now, and it had just landed on Dee's unmaternal lap without her even trying.

Dee shrugged. 'I can get a new apartment if I need to,' she said breezily. 'It's no big deal.'

'And work?' pushed Sam. 'They'll be okay with you taking time off for maternity leave and all that?'

'Why not?' said Dee, holding a shirt up against herself.

'I'm sure Dee will work it all out,' said Beth. 'She's only just found out. She hasn't even seen a doctor yet.'

'Yeah,' said Dee. 'I have plenty of time.'

'Well. You have nine months,' said Sam.

'Thanks Sam,' said Dee through gritted teeth. 'Why are you so interested in my pregnancy?'

Sam shrugged.

'I just want to make sure you're doing this for the right reasons.'

'What would the wrong reasons be?' said Dee, her voice hardening.

'Because a baby is a serious commitment–'

'And you know all about babies, do you?'

There was a chilly silence.

'Ah, Dee,' Beth said. 'That's uncalled for.'

Sam wanted the ground to swallow her whole. It was the truth – she didn't know much about babies, and she was desperate to learn – but that didn't mean she wanted to hear it. And from Dee, of all people. Georgie squeezed her arm in sympathy, her blue eyes soft.

'Yes, well,' Dee said, having the grace to look a bit guilty, 'look, Sam, I know that you're trying . . . '

Then Dee whipped round. Her gaze narrowed as it landed on a small man standing a few feet away, who had his phone out and pointed at her.

'What,' she hissed, 'do you think you're doing?'

*

Kate was heading back to the girls with a bag full of inhalers and an extra-large tub of Vaseline. She stopped at a stall and bought a small leather purse for Ariana for seven euro. It was leather with an embossed floral pattern on it – pretty, delicate and tough – just like her. Stop being so cheesy . . . plus, I could have got that for a fiver, she heard Ariana's voice in her head and smiled. She missed her. She couldn't wait to see her. And oh my goodness, she was going to give her the surprise of a lifetime. A new, improved Kate, ready for commitment, ready to step fully into their lives together–

Kate stopped. She could see the gang over by one of the stalls and . . . what the hell was going on? Oh God, a crowd had gathered around them. There was shouting. Chaos. Gesturing. She hurried over. Honestly, she couldn't leave them alone for a minute. She could hear Beth, trying to calm things down; Sam looked exasperated and Georgie looked stressed. Dee was in

194

full flow, shouting at a small man in a baseball cap, who was holding a phone in his hand.

'Keep nice and calm now, Deirdre, I'm sure there's an innocent explanation for what you saw.'

'What's going on?' asked Kate, looking between Dee and the small man cowering in front of her.

'This man,' Dee was saying, furiously pointing a finger at the bewildered-looking tourist, 'was trying to take my picture!'

Dee's face was red with righteous anger.

'No,' the man said, flapping his hands, 'I wasn't, I–'

'It's an invasion of my privacy,' Dee steamed on. 'I'm trying to enjoy a quiet morning with my friends in this simple local market and yet I am harassed!'

'Why would I want your photo?!' the man cried, scarlet with embarrassment. An equally bewildered-looking woman, who must be his partner, was standing beside him. The crowd was getting bigger.

'To sell to the papers, of course,' said Dee angrily. 'I'm used to it; it comes with the territory – but it's still not on.'

The man laughed incredulously. 'I don't want your photo to sell to the papers,' he said, speaking very slowly and clearly as if he was talking to a child. 'Why would I want your photo?'

Dee frowned. There was an undeniable ring of truth to his protest. 'Because I'm famous,' she said uncertainly.

'I was trying to take a picture of that statue over there.' The man pointed past Dee to a crumbling statue by a fountain. 'You were standing in front of it, with your big hat. I was trying to zoom past you to take a picture. I have no idea who you are. None. Zero.'

There was a pause and then Dee shook her head.

'That's what you would say,' she said. She held out her hand imperiously. 'Give me your phone. I'm deleting whatever creepy photos you took. Come on, hand it over,' she insisted.

'You know who I am now and I'm sure you can see how I feel about my privacy being invaded.'

She put out her hand, at the same time applying more lip gloss with the other. Kate couldn't help but laugh to herself. So much for not wanting to be photographed.

'Absolutely not,' the man said, jamming his phone in his pocket. He turned to walk away, but Dee, rage reignited, leapt like a panther. Before anyone could stop her, she was on his back, trying to grab his phone. A few people started giggling. His partner looked simultaneously horrified and as if she were trying not to laugh.

'What are you doing!' cried the man, trying to prise her off. 'Get off me, you maniac! I'll call the police!'

'Wait. Is that Deirdre Byrne from TV Gold?' someone said. A whisper began to grow in the crowd and Kate saw phones appearing in hands. If no one had been taking Dee's photo before, they would be now, she thought. It was time to take action. Kate pushed through the crowd and hauled Dee off the poor man's back. 'What the hell are you doing, Dee?' she hissed. 'Let's get out of here.'

The man took his partner's hand, and they sprinted down a side street. Kate could see from their backwards glances that they were torn between finding it hysterically funny and calling the police. She hoped it wouldn't be the latter.

'Let's go, Dee,' she said again, more firmly. But as they turned, she could hear the clicking of many camera phones.

'Shit,' Dee said, seeming to come to her senses. 'Let's get out of here – now.' And she, too, started to run. Deirdre never ran.

Kate looked at the others and shrugged. No one was keen to run in this heat, but they did need to keep tabs on Dee. They set off at a brisk walk, sweaty fringes sticking to their foreheads, pursued by a crowd of curious tourists with their phones out.

'Is Dee okay?' panted Georgie to Sam, trying to keep pace with Dee's frantic trot.

'Oh, who cares?' muttered Sam. 'She brought this on herself and now we're the ones being chased.'

Beth put on a sprint and hurried off ahead, darting into a doorway, then sticking her head out to wave. 'Get in here!' she shouted. 'Look! This shop has those fish that eat your feet.' she said.

The others looked at each other and shrugged.

'If it's my only sanctuary,' murmured Dee dramatically, casting a hunted glance down the alley.

'Might as well get a pedicure out of it,' agreed Sam.

*

They sat in a row in the fish salon and dipped their feet into the tanks. The shop owner was delighted with the sudden influx of business and told them all about the benefits: softer, more exfoliated foot skin apparently.

'We're just hiding out from an angry mob,' explained Kate, when he brought them glasses of water.

'From my public,' corrected Dee.

'This is actually quite nice, in a weird way,' Georgie said, as she watched the tiny fish eating the skin on her feet.

'Can you hear anything outside? Do you think they've given up?'

Kate listened. All was quiet. The people outside had clearly lost interest in the bizarre incident, thankfully.

'This is lovely,' Beth said smiling. She closed her eyes.

'Jesus, I'd hate to be famous,' said Sam. 'Like, could you be arsed with all of that shite? People filming you and stuff. Yes, you get great dosh and tables at restaurants but is it really worth it? I don't think so.'

'Yeah,' Beth said, raising her eyes. 'People are like flies on shi–'

'You're not wrong,' Dee admitted. 'I know it's not what most people want to hear, but seriously, it's hard being famous, rich and beautiful.'

'Tell me about it,' Beth said, smiling. Her hair at this point was a big mountain of frizz, the air-conditioning drying the sweat into it.

'But I love my job, delivering news, it's what I do. The rest of this . . . ' Dee smiled bravely. 'Well, it comes with the territory.'

'Sounds tough,' said Sam, mentally rolling her eyes.

'It is. I have no freedom, really. What with TikTok and Instagram, videos get uploaded in seconds–' Dee broke off, frowning.

'Wait.' She took out her phone. 'Oh God. Please tell me they haven't . . . '

She tapped at her phone, then stared at it, her face rigid with shock.

'What is it, Dee?' Beth said.

Silently, Dee held the phone out to them. There she was on TikTok, clinging onto the man's back in the market, arms flailing. You could barely see her face under her massive hat, but the next photo was a different angle and there she was, face red and contorted in rage, gesturing furiously.

Dee scrolled through the results of her Google search:

DEIRDRE BYRNE LOSES IT IN PORTUGUESE MARKET

DEIRDRE BYRNE LIKE YOU'VE NEVER SEEN HER BEFORE

STUNNED TOURISTS HORRIFIED BY DAYTIME DEE'S RANT

Dee whimpered. She handed her phone to Sam.

'The comments,' she whispered. 'What are they saying?'

Sam scanned them and swallowed.

'Um. They're . . . mixed.'

Dee snatched her phone back, peering at the comments through her fingers. She held the phone out to the girls again. 'Here it is,' she said quietly.

The others peered at the comments:

Washed up

Hot mess

Let's not be unkind. Menopause can make women behave strangely . . .

Is she drunk? Or drugs?

Is that a moustache?

Dee touched her upper lip self-consciously.

'Does this look like a 'tache?'

'Of course not,' said Georgie soothingly. 'This photo was taken at a terrible angle and it's all blurry.'

'And what do these weirdos in the comments know?' said Beth stoutly. 'They'll say anything bitchy behind a screen.'

Dee let out a wail.

'I'm going to have to phone my agent right away,' she said, pulling her feet out of the fish tank. 'What time is it in New York?' She stabbed at her phone frantically and then put it to her ear.

'Freddy, it's Dee,' she started. 'I'm on holiday, as you know, and the most terrible thing happened. I was forced to confront a man who was trying to take my photo when – oh. You've seen it. Well then, you'll know that – what? I've gone viral? In a good way or a bad way? Oh, right . . . '

As Dee walked off, with wet feet, still talking, Kate pulled up her socials. 'It's true,' she whispered. 'Dee's everywhere. There are memes.'

'Maybe this will be an opportunity,' said Georgie. 'One door closes, another one opens, that kind of thing.'

'Hmm,' said Sam, peering over Kate's shoulder. 'Washed-up? Jeez, these people are vicious.'

'Ok, well, thanks for letting me know,' said Dee, hanging up and returning, biting her lip. 'My agent's going to do some damage control, and she says that I should lie low while we "see where this goes". And she says I should be patient.' She sighed. 'Patience isn't my strong suit.'

'People are loving the hat,' said Beth, scrolling. 'Someone here says you're iconic.'

'Yes, but everyone else says I have anger issues,' said Dee. 'This could go either way.' She looked down at her feet, which had been thoroughly exfoliated by the fish.

'Can we go back to the hotel now? I think that's enough sightseeing for one day.'

Chapter Seventeen

Back at the Edene, they went straight outside to the pool bar.

'I need a drink after that,' Sam said.

'So do I,' Dee said. 'But it'll just have to be juice, I guess.'

The five of them clambered up onto the bar stools and waited to catch the barman's attention. Nobody said a word, until they spotted someone waving to them from the far end of the bar.

'Hello, girls!' called Margie cheerfully from her perch beside the pool. 'Did you have fun in the market?'

'Yes, thanks,' said Sam. 'Oh, and we got your, um, Vaseline.'

'Excellent! Oh, that will come in handy,' Margie said. She pointed a stern finger. 'Now, you young girls have given us the brush-off too many times. We must insist you come to our little farewell gathering tonight in the boardroom. After all, this is our last night, and we have hardly got to know each other!' She smiled gleefully, the lines around her eyes crinkling.

'Er.' Sam glanced at the others. Dee and the others looked horrified, but Beth was nodding vigorously.

'Of course we'll come,' said Beth. 'I love a party.'

Margie beamed at her.

'Wonderful! The others will be so pleased. I think we're going to have a wonderful, intimate little evening.' She bustled off.

'Ugh, why did you say we'd go?' said Kate, stretching and yawning. 'Now we're going to have to make conversation with Roger about his timeshare and his gout.'

'Don't stereotype the elderly. I thought it would be a nice thing to do,' said Beth. She looked at the others.

'That'll be us one day soon.'

When the barman appeared, Georgie said, 'I'll have a sparkling water, please.'

'White wine for me,' said Beth.

'Just take it easy,' warned Kate. 'I've been reading about it and apparently, it's super common to stop being able to tolerate alcohol in mid-life. And I don't fancy scraping you off the kerb like Georgie had to do the other night.'

'I'm on my holidays, for God's sake, not in school!' Beth forced out a laugh.

'We can't tell you what to do,' said Kate. 'It's for your own head, Beth. But if you're not feeling happy, alcohol is a depressant.'

'I know,' Beth admitted. 'I have been using it too much recently as a way to relax but I know that at my age, with the ol' perimenopause, it's a dodgy combination.' Kate nodded, but then Beth changed tack. 'But I'm on holiday, you know, and I'm not running around after small children.' She raised her glass. 'So let me have some fun, for God's sake.'

Kate sighed. 'Well, you're the adult, Beth,' she said in a 'but-don't-say-I-didn't-warn-you' tone of voice.

Dee's phone beeped and she glanced at it.

'Huh. It's my agent,' she said. 'She's had an offer off the back of that market video.'

'No way, what is it?' asked Sam encouragingly.

'You know the reality one where everyone lives in a house?' said Dee. She frowned. 'Not exactly what I had in mind.'

'Is it good? I don't really watch telly these days,' said Beth apologetically. 'I barely have the time to scroll through my phone and find out what's going on in the world.'

'Doesn't narrow it down much, does it?' said Kate. 'People living in a house? That's half the reality TV there is.'

'Well, this one has a mid-life twist.' Dee consulted the email. 'It's called *Seeing Grey*. You know, instead of "seeing red"? I think they could workshop that a bit more. So, a host of extremely well-known people, like me, are going to live in a house together for thirteen nights and discuss this challenging phase of life.'

Dee sipped her apple juice.

'And we get to know each other and stuff.'

'And you'd be okay with that?' said Georgie, incredulous. 'Sharing your space with randomers?' Dee didn't even like sharing a bathroom.

'Maybe,' said Dee. 'I do like reality TV, you know, just not strangers or shared houses. The rest is fine.'

'What about your actual job?' said Kate, narrowing her eyes.

'Oh.' Dee waved her hand vaguely. 'We go on hiatus, you know? The timings might work out.'

'And are you going to discuss your pregnancy on telly?' Sam asked.

'God, no!' Dee almost choked. 'I'm keeping all of that to myself. Besides, I need to talk to Pete about it. He might not like the idea. He seems like a private sort. Still, I'll bear this TV offer in mind.'

'You're talking like you're in a relationship,' said Kate slowly. 'But you haven't even told him he might be the–'

She looked at Georgie warily. Georgie was flipping a beer mat idly, pretending to look unconcerned.

'Jeez, all in good time,' said Dee sharply. 'Okay, what are we thinking? Are we going to check in on the oldies later?'

'Yes, we should. We can hand-deliver Margie's Vaseline, and they are leaving tomorrow,' Sam said. 'They might be able to give us some older-woman wisdom as well. After all, Margie seems loved up and she's come away with a big gang of friends. I think it would be worth picking up some tips.'

'We'll probably end up chatting about *Coronation Street*,' Kate said. She glanced over at Georgie, who was picking at her drinks napkin now and looking sad. She took out her notebook. 'Okay ladies . . . Agenda time!' She looked at her notebook for a moment, hesitating.

'What is it, Kate?' Beth said. 'Is it about our bunions or warts or something?'

'Well, Kate said. This is a bit tactless . . . ' she said, looking at Georgie. 'I'm sorry, but I wrote the agenda before I left home. The fourth topic is . . . ' She took in a deep breath, 'Sex!'

'Well, obviously I'm not having any,' said Georgie, who was now ripping the napkin into shreds, piling them onto the already shredded beer mat.

Kate looked crestfallen. 'Sorry Georgie,' she said.

'It's okay,' said Georgie, glancing at Dee. She drew a breath. 'I think if this holiday has taught me anything, it's that this marriage isn't good enough, for me, and that's all I'm going to say about it for the moment.'

Kate reached an arm around Georgie and gave her a hug. 'Good for you, love.'

'You can go it alone, Georgie, and be happy again – with someone who appreciates you, rather than the idea of you,' Sam added.

'Thanks,' said Georgie, wiping her eyes on what remained of her napkin.

Sam blew her a kiss.

'Me next!' Beth put up her hand. 'Because I don't have it either. Well, hardly ever anyway. It's not that I don't love Jack, but I'm not in the mood any more. Sometimes, I worry we're just good friends who look after our children together. Which would be fine, only isn't a long-term relationship meant to be about sex, too? Just occasionally we'll organise a dinner out, just the two of us and he'll put on a nice shirt and I'll think how hot he is, and we'll have a shag. But we don't often make the time to do that.'

'Stating the obvious here, but maybe you should,' Sam said. Beth nodded. 'Noted.'

'Fine, moving on. What about you, Sam?' Kate asked.

Sam sighed. She was smiling but looked weary. 'I mean, if you'd asked me a few years ago, I would have said everything was rosy,' she said. 'Both of us have high sex drives and we had the time and money to take romantic breaks, go to expensive restaurants, the lot. But this trying-to-conceive business . . . '

She shook her head.

'You only get a short fertility window and then after that, I'm fretting about whether or not it's worked and . . . well, it's starting to feel a bit regimented. I should have shares in Clear Blue. I wee on a stick to get the smiley face, then two weeks later, I wee on a stick and pray for two red lines and I never see them.' She laughed but the smile didn't quite reach her eyes. 'So, we've stopped. IVF doctor next week. I think it's hanging over us.'

'At least you have each other,' said Georgie. 'You're a team.'

'You're stronger than you know,' Kate told her quietly.

'Right,' Beth said. 'That's enough psychoanalysis for the time being. Let's hit the boardroom for some serious Scrabble!'

'Not for me,' said Kate. 'I'm off to bed. Have fun and don't do anything too wild, I know how these sherry parties can get.'

*

Kate headed out of the room grinning to herself. She didn't have time for parties – she had a proposal to plan. But as Kate lay in bed planning proposals, on the floor below her, Sam, Dee, Georgie, and Beth stood outside the boardroom.

'Wasn't there a special knock? Sam asked. She was holding the XL tub of Vaseline in her hand. 'Oh, feck it,' she said and rapped hard on the door.

A waiter answered, looking a bit flustered.

Beth beamed at him. 'Hi! We're here for the party. I have to give some, um, Vaseline to Margie?' Sam held out the tub as proof. Totally ridiculous, she thought. Who'd need Vaseline for a sherry party?

'Ah, yes,' the waiter said, looking Sam up and down. 'They're in the presidential suite.' He let the girls in and closed the door behind them. 'Er, they let you know what sort of party this is, yeah?' He looked concerned.

'Sherry and games,' said Sam, marching past him.

'Sort of,' the waiter said. 'But did they mention what kind of games?' He was walking beside them a little nervously, a drinks tray in his hand.

'Look, we're only popping in,' said Sam. 'Down here, yeah?' And she marched off, leaving the waiter shrugging.

'Jesus,' Beth said, as they made their way down the corridor. 'The presidential suite. Guys, this is so exciting, I've never seen a presidential suite. Let's go,' she said, actually sprinting along the corridor, so all the others could hear was the sound of her sticky flip-flops and heavy breathing.

'I mean it's the presidential suite at an all-inclusive,' panted Sam, running to catch up with her. 'I wouldn't get too excited, Beth.'

They got to the suite and Sam tapped at the door.

No answer.

A firmer knock at the door and all of a sudden, it swung open and, standing in front of them, was Davey from Essex, wearing a G-string and a tail.

'What the fu–?' Beth started. She peered past him. With the red velvet curtains closed against the sunlight, the room looked quite dark. And what were those noises?

'Good evening,' Dee pushed to the front casually. She did a double take at Davey but kept her cool. 'Deirdre Byrne – TV Gold.'

'Oh, hi. Welcome, welcome to the Games Room,' he said and gave a little bow, letting them in. He gave a little squeak then and melted away into the darkness.

'What sort of games night is this?' whispered Beth.

Just then, Margie walked out, draped in some sort of velvet cloak, an eye mask perched on her forehead.

'Sam,' she said, kissing her cheek. 'You look gorgeous! Glowing! I'm so glad that you and your friends could make it. Welcome to our little games night.'

Numb with shock, Sam silently handed over the tub of Vaseline like it was a party gift.

'Ahh, thank you sweetheart, I'm going to need it tonight . . .' Margie burst out laughing, so Sam did too, a bit nervously.

'Maybe she has chapped lips,' Beth whispered. 'Everyone knows that Vaseline is great for . . .'

'Chafing,' whispered Georgie in reply.

'Come along in, Roger will be delighted to see you,' Margie said. And she flung open the door to the presidential suite. There, right in front of them, was poor little sunburnt Roger, tied up in a crucifix position on the bed, like Jesus himself. At least, they thought it was Roger: he was dressed in black shiny latex, wearing a goat mask. He looked like an extra from *Game of Thrones*.

Georgie squeaked, turned and ran.

Dee screamed. 'What is this? Some sort of torture dungeon? What have you done to Roger?'

Tracey rushed over to her. 'No, don't worry, love,' she said. 'He likes being whipped, don't you, Roger?' Roger gave the thumbs-up and then kind of bleated.

'Tracey, I'm not quite sure what's happening here to be honest?' Sam stuttered. Even Dee, who kept telling them what a world traveller she was, looked shocked. Only Beth was looking around with interest.

'Do you have a bar?' Beth asked casually, as Margie took off her cloak, showing that she was pretty naked underneath, except for nipple tassels.

'Jesus Christ,' Dee said in Sam's ear. 'I've finally figured it out. Took me long enough. These old people are swingers, repeat, swingers, Sam. Let's get out of here, before we end up on the cross like old Roger!'

'Refreshments?' Tracey said, leading Beth to the bathroom, where the tub was filled with ice and alcopops. She offered one to Beth as casually as if she were cabin crew on a long-haul flight.

'This is nice, Tracey,' Beth said cheerfully perching on the side of the bath and cracking open a bottle. 'We had no idea it would be so different. We thought by "games", you meant bridge.'

Tracey laughed. 'That's my fault! I should have been more specific.'

Beth nodded at Roger on the bed in the bedroom. 'So how long has he been there for?'

Dee was heading towards the exit door. 'Come on, girls,' she said briskly. 'Thanks for the invite, Tracey, but we're out of here. Sam, let's go.'

But Sam found that she couldn't move. She felt like everything was blurring in front of her. Was it the heat? The sight of Roger in a goat mask? She felt her ears ringing and then . . . nothing.

*

'Sam? Can you hear me?'

That was Dee's voice. Sam recognised the slightly impatient tone.

'Good, she's okay,' she heard behind her, and she could just see a tassel hanging over her face. So, it hadn't been a dream.

'Are we at a sex party?' Sam whispered.

'Sort of. You're okay, Sam, you've just had a fright, let's get you back to your room,' Dee said.

'Where's Georgie?' Sam murmured, sitting up. An annoyed-looking Dee and a selection of older people in bondage gear surrounded her. 'And Beth?'

'Georgie exited the minute she saw Roger. Beth is inside, giving Roger one. As in, whacking him with a whip. She thinks that it's hilarious. Says this might kickstart her libido or destroy it forever. I gave her three minutes and said then she had to come out.'

As if on cue, Beth walked out, sweating and laughing. 'Guys, this is a bit of craic, isn't it? God, Sam, are you okay?'

'Let's just go,' Sam begged. 'I need to get into my PJs and bed. Thanks for an, er, interesting evening, Margie,' Sam said, remembering her manners as she stood up on wobbly legs.

'Another time perhaps,' Margie said, following them to the door. 'I forget how easily shocked you young people are.'

'Not me!' Beth said cheerfully. 'Thanks for the education, Margie!'

The girls made it back to Sam's room, where Georgie answered the door, pale and in a dressing gown. 'Sorry, guys, that just wasn't for me,' she said. 'From no sex in three years to seeing Roger in a goat mask . . . it was too much.'

Then she caught sight of Sam. 'Sam, are you okay? What happened?'

'Let her just sit down,' Dee said, bustling Sam inside. She settled her on the bed, then went to get a damp flannel.

'It's very weird,' said Sam, letting Dee dab at her forehead. 'I've never fainted before, I'm not sure what's going on.'

'A bug maybe?' said Georgie.

'Yeah, actually, I've felt off for days,' Sam said. 'Totally off my food and wine, which isn't like me.'

'Sam, I think that we should go to the medical clinic or the pharmacy tomorrow and get you checked over, just to be safe,' Dee said.

'Since when did you become so caring?' mumbled Sam. She scooted up the bed and pulled the sheet over herself. 'I don't need a pharmacy, I just need a rest,' she said, closing her eyes before she finished the sentence. In seconds, she was snoring lightly.

The others stared down at her. This was not like Sam.

'She hasn't even done her skincare routine,' whispered Dee loudly. 'She hasn't cleansed.'

Something really must be wrong.

Chapter Eighteen

Beth's shriek from the pool-bar toilets reached them at breakfast.

The others looked at each other.

'I'll go, shall I?' muttered Kate, putting down her coffee. 'Drama and more drama. What's wrong now?'

She found Beth examining herself in the bathroom mirror. Her back was covered in mozzie bites that were red and swollen.

'How the hell did I get so many bites? They love me!'

'Or maybe it was one of the partygoers from last night getting a bit frisky with you Beth?' Kate burst out laughing. 'God, I can't believe they were up to that kind of thing.'

'I didn't participate in that way,' said Beth. 'I'm amazed they can all look each other in the eye in the morning. Bit full-on, eh? I hope I didn't hurt Roger. Although he seemed to like it.'

There had been no sign of the enthusiastic English team this morning but the waiter from the party was walking through reception and turned bright red when he saw the girls, a shade which only deepened when Beth wolf-whistled at him.

Kate and Beth headed back to the others to find Sam gathering her things. 'I'm going for another lie down,' she said weakly. 'I feel rotten.'

'This isn't like you,' said Kate, worried. 'I'm not sure I've ever seen you sick.'

'First time for everything. At least it's the second-last day. I'll be back for lunch,' said Sam, hobbling towards the door. She belched loudly. 'I think.'

*

The girls lay down on their sun beds and tried not to think about it being almost the last day of their break. The few days had just flown by, but then they would, with all of the action.

'Those bloody swingers,' Beth said, scratching one of her bites. 'Maybe one of them gave Sam a cold or something.'

'It can't have been them,' said Kate practically. 'Sam was only there for about five minutes and a cold takes days to incubate. She must have picked something up on the plane.'

'Speaking of which,' Georgie said, 'I saw them all getting on a coach earlier. "Brighton Convention", the sign said. "Brighton Swingers' Convention", more like.'

She laughed.

'Good for them, I suppose. At least they're getting some, which God knows I'm not.'

'What about him,' said Dee, nodding. They all followed her gaze to where the lifeguard was sitting in his chair, surveying the turquoise water.

'The lifeguard?' said Georgie uncertainly.

'Yeah, I saw you eyeing him up earlier this week,' Dee said. 'He's gorgeous. And I'm pretty sure he was checking you out, too, as he should be. You deserve some fun, Georgie.'

Kate narrowed her eyes at Dee. 'Did you organise dinner with Pete yet, Dee?' Kate asked.

'Oh, yes,' said Dee, studying her nails. 'We thought tonight might be good, actually. A quiet, romantic dinner. We'll reignite the spark we felt in New York and then, you know, I'll . . . '

'Tell him he's 66.6 per cent likely to be the father of your baby,' said Beth baldly. 'Simple.'

Kate sighed. 'Look, you deserve some fun, George.' She looked over at the lifeguard. 'Now, he's not exactly my cup of tea, what with me being a middle-aged lesbian, but he's hot. Look at that hair, and that tan! I think you should go and talk to him,' Kate said firmly.

'I don't know, guys,' Georgie answered. 'I should really sort things with Paddy before doing anything extra-curricular.'

'I know, Georgie,' Beth piped up. 'But I doubt Paddy is at home pining for you. If your marriage is really over, then what's the harm? This could be a fun holiday distraction. It's been a while since you were intimate,' she made air quotes with her fingers, 'So why not . . . get back on the horse?'

Beth waggled her eyebrows.

'Let those swingers inspire you to get in touch with your sexuality. Minus the goat mask – for now.'

Georgie hesitated. 'Well, it's been a while, but . . . I'm not sure,' she said. 'Besides, I wouldn't know how to arrange a – a date.'

'You go over there and ask him out,' said Dee, as if it were the most obvious thing in the world.

'Oh, I couldn't,' said Georgie, shaking her head rapidly.

'My confidence isn't all that great. The idea of talking to a man I've never spoken to before – at least without snot running down my face – it's . . . well, no,' she finished lamely.

Shy Georgie back in place.

She did not add that she had managed to speak to Pete without too much difficulty.

Beth stood up.

'Jesus, Georgie, this is giving me flashbacks to our school disco. Do you want me to talk to him for you?'

'Nooooooo! Beth, stop!' Georgie yelped.

Beth gave a devilish smile.

'Better get on with it then,' she said.

'Fine,' said Georgie. 'I'll talk to him. But let me do this my own way.'

'Which is?'

Georgie hesitated.

'Anyone fancy a dip?' she said at last, adjusting her bikini top to accentuate her perfect cleavage.

'You'll all come too, won't you?'

'Not me,' drawled Dee. 'I avoid the midday sun. But I shall be watching with interest.'

'Not me,' said Kate, lifting her head from her thriller. 'But good luck with Mr Hot.'

'I see where you're going with this. Sure thing,' said Beth. 'Watch me do a full *Charlie's Angels*.'

Beth and Georgie got into the pool as Kate and Dee watched, trying not to laugh. The seductive hair-tossing from Beth was something else. 'She's going to take someone's eye out,' murmured Dee.

Two seconds later, though, the hot lifeguard looked over at Georgie and lowered his sunglasses.

'The fly has been trapped, repeat – the fly has been trapped,' Beth call over to the girls – really quite loudly – as she did the breaststroke, badly, past them.

'Beth, stop being so weird,' Kate replied. 'Honestly, have you ever tried being discreet?'

'It's overrated,' Beth said, continuing to swim up and down past the lifeguard.

'Let's just float here,' Georgie suggested.

The girls casually floated past the hot lifeguard, Georgie looking her usual elegant self, as if she didn't even notice the lifeguard above her, checking her out.

'Hey! She didn't want me to say anything, but my friend likes you.' Georgie heard the piercing voice behind her. She craned her neck. Beth was treading water right in front of the hot lifeguard's chair. For God's sake, she thought, mortification washing over her along with the chlorine.

'Sorry, what?' said the lifeguard, leaning forward.

'My friend, the blonde, fit-looking one, likes you. What do you think?!' Beth yelled up to the lifeguard, pointing at Georgie.

'Er,' the lifeguard said, glancing at Georgie and then back to the pool. 'I mean, I'm flattered. Thanks for letting me know. But I'm doing my job now, okay?'

Georgie, too embarrassed to stay floating at this point, swum back over to their area and got out, dripping and cringing. Kate and Dee watched her in silent sympathy. Georgie scurried over to the sun loungers, lay on her towel and closed her eyes.

*

I have never been so embarrassed in my entire life, Georgie thought as the sun began to warm her. What was I thinking, asking the lifeguard out like that? Well, she technically hadn't asked him out – she'd left it to her tactless friend to do the work, not that it mattered. His answer had offered her all the humiliation she needed.

'I'm going to get you a drink,' said Dee, standing. 'This whole thing is too tragic.'

'Are you ok?' Kate said, as Dee stalked off.

'Not really,' said Georgie. 'I've been with one guy since college, and he's lost all interest in me. Then, I fall for a guy on holiday, who it turns out is spoken for by one of my best friends, who just happens to look like Angelina Jolie. And I just tried to throw myself at someone who couldn't be less interested.'

'Georgie, you are the most beautiful person that I know, inside and out,' Kate said, with feeling. 'You're so beautiful that it's almost physically painful to look at you.'

'Calm down,' laughed Georgie. 'What's got into you?'

'I'm grateful to have someone I love and trust at home and I want everyone to feel the same way,' Kate said. 'What I'm saying is, it will all work out for you, I know that. Kindness breeds kindness. You are done with settling and you will meet someone as wonderful as you are.'

'I hope so,' Georgie said. 'I'm not feeling that beautiful at the moment.' She looked down at the old sundress she'd got on holiday in Malta once and had worn on every break since. She felt old and unattractive. Maybe Paddy had a point.

'Well, it's early days yet,' said Dee, returning with a glass of wine and handing it to Georgie. 'You just need to get back on the horse and all that.'

Georgie took a swallow and groaned. 'Feck it,' she said and drained the glass. 'I've been like Sandra Dee, the good girl, my whole bloody life. Maybe I need to go wild for once, just once. Maybe I do need to have sex with a stranger. Get whatever this is out of my system.'

At that moment, Beth came over from the pool, dripping water. She was beaming. 'You're welcome!' she said. 'I think that got the message across. And I was very discreet too, wasn't I?'

They all burst out laughing.

'Beth,' said Kate when she could talk. 'You're about as subtle as a sledgehammer.'

'Seriously, he is primed to ask you out,' said Beth, dropping onto her sun lounger. 'Just you wait and see.'

Dee smiled under her big hat, but said nothing further.

'I'm going to check on Sam,' said Georgie, swinging her legs over the side of her sunbed. 'And then if she's not feeling better, I think we should take her into town and go to a–'

'Olá.'

Georgie turned towards the voice. A deep, attractive, slightly amused and very sexy male voice. It belonged to the lifeguard, Marco.

'Oh, hi,' said Georgie, going pink.

'Olá,' he said again, holding out a hand.

'Georgie,' she reminded him, taking it. His fingers were firm and warm.

'Are you having a nice holiday?' he asked politely.

'Yes, thank you,' said Georgie. 'Very nice. Very relaxing.'

The others watched, eyes darting back and forth as if they were watching a tennis match.

'Your friend,' said Marco, nodding at Beth, 'said you might . . . well, that you might like to go for a drink with me?'

'I don't think that's exactly how she put it, did she?' said Georgie, shooting Beth a dirty look.

He gave a faint smile. 'Well, no, she was quite a lot more direct. But it got the message across, you know? Anyway, would you? Like to go for a drink tonight, I mean?'

Georgie looked up at Marco. Sunlight was surrounding his handsome face like a halo.

Beside her, Beth held her breath. So did Kate and Dee. 'She'd love to,' broke in Beth, unable to bear the tension any longer.

Marco raised an eyebrow. 'Really?'

Feck it, Georgie thought again. Her marriage was effectively over, and Pete and Dee were probably going to be raising a child together. She needed this.

'Okay,' Georgie said. 'I mean, that would be lovely, thank you.'

'Great. We could meet later at the square in the old town,' Marco said. 'Say, eight o'clock? At the henna tattoo stand?'

'I'll be there,' Georgie said, grabbing her pool bag. 'Um, see you then. Bye.'

As Marco walked away, Beth said loudly, 'Told you! In the bag. Now. Have you waxed recently?'

'Oh God, Beth, like he's going to see anything like that!' Georgie snapped.

'Well, I think we should all go into town. I've got my dinner with Pete at eight, remember?' said Dee. 'Drinks, lobby at six?' She dug her phone out of her Gucci beach bag and began to type rapidly. Then she leaned back on her sun lounger with a smile.

Georgie's heart plummeted.

'You couldn't be more obvious, could you?' Kate looked at her sternly.

'What?' Dee said, 'We're just friends. At least, that's what he thinks,' and she gave a little giggle. 'I have other ideas.'

'Oh, Christ,' Beth said, looking at Georgie. 'I'll help you to get ready, shall I?'

'I don't want to look overdone,' Georgie said carefully.

'Don't worry – we don't want to cover up that natural beauty,' Beth said. 'Just give it a little polish,' she said, shooting dagger stares in Dee's direction.

*

Upstairs, the girls spent a good hour getting beautified, shaved, moisturised and prepped for the evening in the old town.

'Are you okay?' Sam shouted from her bed. Georgie had been in the shower for at least twenty minutes.

'All good, thank you,' Georgie yelled back. 'Just having a minor emotional crisis.'

'Do you need me to come in?' called Sam, who was lying horizontal and trying not to be sick.

'No, I'm okay,' Georgie said, and continued her mental back-and-forth. Why shouldn't she go for it with Marco, she thought, scrubbing her legs. Okay, yes, she was technically married, and this was betraying Paddy. But also – she was so tired. Tired of trying to make Paddy fancy her again, tired of talking to couples' counsellors, tired of trying and trying to make it work. Maybe this was her way of holding her hands up and saying, 'enough'. The fact was, she thought miserably, her marriage was over. And this date with Marco only proved that. Paddy might even be looking around, too, for all she knew. She had always blocked out memories of him flirting, or worse, with other women when he was out with the lads, with her there.

'You've been in there for hours!' called Sam. 'Are you sure you're okay?'

Georgie flipped off the shower and grabbed a fluffy towel, wrapping it around herself.

'Okay?' She flung open the door. 'I've never been better. Tonight, I'm going to have sex with someone who isn't my husband.'

'Wow,' said Sam. laughing. She sat up in bed. 'Who are you and what have you done with my friend, Georgie?'

'I'm still Georgie,' Georgie said, tossing her wet hair dramatically. 'But I'm new and improved and I've even shaved my legs.'

'Amazing,' said Sam. 'But for the avoidance of doubt, you know you don't have to have sex, don't you? Beth was just kidding about the waxing.'

Georgie began to towel-dry her hair. 'I mean, I kind of want to, just to remind myself what it's like. Plus, he's gorgeous. But what if I've forgotten what to do?'

'Georgie, you are not twenty-one, you are forty-one. It's like riding a bike – you just need to get back in the saddle.'

'I know,' Georgie said. 'I'm just rusty, that's all. I find it hard to talk to handsome men, let alone do anything else.'

'You seemed to find it easy with Pete,' said Sam tentatively.

'Forget Pete,' said Georgie. She began to dig through her drawer for underwear. 'I just need to remember that I'm still attractive, I'm Georgie, not Paddy's wife, I'm a red-blooded single female who has needs.'

'Amen, sister!' Sam laughed as there was a knock on the door.

When Sam went to open it, Kate was standing there with wet hair and a bottle of pinot in her hand. 'Can I do my makeup in here with you guys? I want to hear all the goss.'

She ran into the bathroom.

'But first, let me wee.'

Sam laughed. No matter how important, mature, professional and wise they were with other people, they will always be the same together. Back to their teenage selves. She loved that they had never changed.

Five minutes and one spilled glass of wine later, they were all crowded around the bedroom mirror. The conversation was in full swing.

'How is your mojo, Kate?' Georgie asked as she shakily applied her liquid liner under Sam's instruction. 'We never got around to you earlier. You and Ariana have been together longer than any of us have been with our partners. Does it get stale?'

'Nope.' Kate stopped blending and looked at the girls. 'I adore her, she is the one for me etcetera. Between us three, do I want to jump her every five minutes? No. We do have busy lives. But do I still fancy the pants off her? Absolutely.'

'Trying for a baby definitely craps all over that,' said Sam dryly. 'We get home knackered. I'm standing there in my bedsocks wanting an early night and Jeff reminds me we need to get on with it because the app is telling us to. All the same, I think he's my soulmate.'

Georgie squeezed her hand. 'I'm so pleased for you,' she said.

'Ariana is my soulmate,' said Kate simply.

'Do you think Paddy ever was your soulmate, George?' asked Sam, frowning.

'I'm not sure now, Sam. I mean, of course I did when I was sixteen but then . . . I don't think I knew what love was really like at that age. I'd never really experienced that instinctive connection . . . '

'The one you felt with Pete?' Sam said softly.

Georgie sighed, her lovely blue eyes filling with tears . . .

'I met this woman on the plane, who was carrying her husband's ashes here to scatter them in the place they'd both loved. I couldn't imagine doing that with Paddy, you know?'

At the mention of Paddy, Kate noticed the mood drop immediately. 'Well, I'm not sure about being your soulmate, but Marco seems like he'll show you a good time at any rate. Let's check what you're wearing and make sure that your knickers match your bra.'

They all laughed.

'You look so gorgeous,' Kate said as Georgie paraded around in her matching bra and undies. 'I'd never have the confidence to do that.'

Georgie did up her robe again.

'Kate' she said, 'I've been saying this to you for the last thirty years and I'll continue until I die. You are beautiful just the way you are.'

'I know, I know.' Kate brushed it off. 'A beautiful soul and all that jazz.'

'Forget the soul business, you're hot,' Sam said sternly. 'And Ariana thinks so, too.'

'I dunno,' said Kate doubtfully.

'I see this all the time in my classes,' Georgie went on. 'Unless you are in your forties, you can't understand the monumental changes that happen at that time. It's almost like you don't recognise yourself anymore, that the body and mind that you've known for forty years, have suddenly been invaded by someone else . . . '

'An anxious, sad someone else,' said Beth.

'Yes, and they're too embarrassed to talk about it.' Georgie sighed. I'm putting a whole chapter in the book about peri- and menopause.'

Just then, Dee appeared in the doorway, looking jaw-dropping in an emerald green halter-neck dress, which, with her over-coiffed hair and long, witchy nails, looked far too much for a casual date. 'Are you guys still talking about menopause?' she said. 'Because I'm calling time on it. Shall we go?'

They wandered down to reception together in awkward silence, aware that Dee and Georgie were going on very different dates.

'What time are you meeting Marco?' Beth asked Georgie.

'Eight o'clock, but I've got the fear. I mean, I don't even know the guy beyond his first name and the fact he looks fantastic in swimming trunks. He could be a serial–'

Sam interrupted. 'I strongly doubt it. But we won't be far away, okay?' She gave Georgie a reassuring squeeze.

'Well, I'll be busy,' purred Dee. 'With Pete, you know.'

Georgie swallowed and looked away.

'Will you tell him about the baby?' Beth asked. 'I was reading about it, and I think you can actually do paternity tests while pregnant. It's non-invasive, they just need–'

'That's interesting,' said Dee, her smile tense. 'Yeah, tonight's the night I break the news. But I told you. I have a feeling it's him.'

'Well, we can hang out first,' said Kate. 'Then you two can go for your dates at eight o'clock and the rest of us can get a kebab.'

Dee visibly shuddered. 'A kebab? God, do you girls have any class at all? Thank goodness I'll be having a nice, civilised dinner with an intelligent and handsome man.'

'Actually, I could murder a kebab,' said Sam, ignoring Dee, snob that she was. 'I'm ravenous. Maybe I'm over whatever bug this is. Shall we call a cab?'

Chapter Nineteen

They found a quiet table in a sweet little bar off the main square, which tonight was filled with English soccer fans, wine was ordered and menus perused. The girls studied the menus in silence for a few minutes, then they all lowered and removed their reading glasses and casually put them into their handbags, no one mentioning them, as if their failing eyesight hadn't happened.

'Shall we just get a few bits? These two are having dinner on their hot dates.' suggested Kate.

'Okay,' Sam replied, 'but I'm having that kebab before I go home. I'm bloody starving.'

They ordered and then Kate began to rifle through her bag, putting sanitary towels, Veet strips and paracetamol on the table, before producing a large notebook.

'Oh, not the agenda,' groaned Dee. 'Can't we ditch it, for once?'

'Tonight, we discuss . . . ?' Kate looked around the table like a game show host. 'Ageing. Do you think we need to get that older-woman haircut? The sensible crop our mums all had?'

'I'm not getting a bob,' Georgie said, and she said bob as if it was rude. 'I'm keeping my hair long until I'm dead.'

'Ariana has a bob,' said Kate.

'Yeah, but a hot Italian bob,' argued Georgie. 'Not a society-has-forced-me-into-this bob.'

'Guys, honestly, we really haven't aged badly at all,' Sam said. 'I mean, yes, Dee, you've had a lot of work done, particularly with those knockers and–'

'Knockers? Please! My breasts. And if you want the full run-down, I've had a semi-lift, baby Botox and fillers. Plus a little polynucleotide. That's nothing in Manhattan.'

Dee sipped her sparkling water.

'I'm just looking after myself.'

'Okay, okay,' Kate put her hands up. 'You look terrific. But what's wrong with ageing exactly? Better than the alternative, isn't it? Each to their own, but I think it's time we got used to seeing real women's faces.'

Georgie touched the skin around her eyes.

'I think I look pretty much the same as I always have, but then I see a photo of myself as I am now and it shocks me. I see the wrinkles, the fine lines around here . . . '

'And that's why you need baby Botox,' Dee said smugly.

Georgie shrugged.

'I'd rather embrace my face,' she said. 'Every wrinkle of it.'

'Easy for you to say when you look like Charlize Theron's prettier sister,' giggled Beth. 'But yeah, I can't be doing with any of it either. Although I might try and get my hair cut more often.'

The small plates arrived, piled high with prawns, squid and octopus.

'Bom proveito, ladies,' their gorgeous waiter said and bowed as he walked away.

'Let's tuck in, it's seven-fifteen already,' said Kate, 'and you two have hot dates! How are we feeling?' she said as she shoved a prawn into her mouth. It was hot but delicious.

'I'm looking forward to it,' said Dee primly.

'God, you give nothing away, Deirdre,' Beth laughed. 'You'd make a great undercover cop.'

'Or maybe a serial killer,' she added, tucking into the squid.

'Gee, thanks,' Dee said, looking dignified.

'What about you, Georgie?' Kate asked. 'You'll have to stay away from the garlic, my friend!'

Georgie laughed.

'Guys, don't be such saddos, it's just a drink. No need to buy your hats yet.'

She sighed. 'But I feel a bit nervous, to be honest. What if we decide that sex is on the agenda for tonight?'

Beth spat out her wine and a bit landed on Dee's shoulder. Thankfully, she didn't appear to notice.

'Well, if you want to, I guess cross that bridge when you come to it,' Kate said reassuringly, 'It's up to both of you.'

They finished their food and looked out over the square, the golden light gilding the stonework. The town looked magical. They ate in silence for a bit, and then Sam glanced at her watch. 'Well, this is it,' she said at last, standing. 'We'll walk you there, check Marco looks nice to you still, and we'll hang around, too. Just call us if you change your mind at any point.' She squeezed Georgie's hand.

They headed to the square, where they could see Marco waiting at a little bar by the fountain, sitting at a table. They stood and watched him from a distance.

'Nice shirt,' Dee said approvingly. 'He's made the effort.'

'I know, I thought it might be the mystique of the pool that made him so hot – but he looks great out and about, doesn't he?' said Beth.

'Yeah,' said Georgie in a small voice. 'Do . . . do I look okay?' She looked down at her simple white shift dress, the opposite of Dee's overdone look.

'You look incredible,' Beth told her. 'He'll be even more smitten than he is already.'

'Well, I think this is it,' said Sam encouragingly. 'Ready, George?'

'Keep us updated,' said Kate.

They hugged Georgie as if she were going backpacking to Australia for a year. Then Georgie squared her shoulders and walked over to Marco.

Marco stood up as she approached. His eyes widened admiringly. 'Olá,' he said.

'Olá,' Georgie replied shyly, trying not to notice the four women peering out at her from one of the trinket shops. They were so obvious.

'I wasn't sure you'd come,' said Marco, smiling. It made his eyes crinkle engagingly.

'Neither was I,' said Georgie honestly, 'It's been a long time since I've had a date.'

Marco held out a hand, 'Still sure you're up for it?'

Georgie hesitated for a second, then took it, 'I'm sure.'

*

Hand in hand, she and Marco walked through the main square, passing families queuing for ice cream and babies screaming in buggies, and up a cobbled street where it became quieter and more romantic. They stopped outside a small winery and Marco said, 'What about a drink here?'

God, the smell of his aftershave is absolutely divine.

'Sure,' she said shyly.

They walked in and were shown to a table up a steep flight of stairs. It overlooked the square, and the room was filled with little tables with burning candles, mandolin music playing in the background. It was simple, beautiful and so romantic. Georgie could feel herself getting into the mood. Here she was with this hunk of man looking admiringly at her, overlooking the old town square of Albufeira. It was a long way from the yoga studio and downward dog.

Or maybe not.

They ordered some lovely Portuguese vinho verde and when it arrived, they clinked their glasses. 'So,' Marco said. 'Why don't you tell me–'

'Oh God.'

Georgie looked around at the familiar voice, and there, standing just inside the door of the restaurant, was Dee – and a shocked-looking Pete.

'Hello, Dee,' Georgie said. 'And Pete.' She nodded awkwardly. 'Um, this is Marco.'

'Hi guys,' Dee trilled.

'Georgie's on a hot date,' Dee added with her fake smile still on her face. 'With the pool guy from our hotel.'

Georgie flinched. There was no mistaking the condescending tone in Dee's voice.

'Lifeguard, actually,' said Marco.

'Same thing, isn't it?' Dee laughed nastily.

Georgie narrowed her eyes.

'Not quite,' Marco said pleasantly. 'We don't really use the word "pool guy". An "attendant" would mostly keep an eye on things, check the pool is clean. A "lifeguard" has a responsibility for the guests' safety and would need to be fully trained in first-aid, CPR and water safety. I'm also training in hotel management in my spare time.'

He smiled at Georgie, his eyes crinkling again in that lush way.

'I'm Pete.' Pete leaned in and extended a hand to Marco, who gave it a firm shake. A little too firm, judging by Pete's grimace. Georgie couldn't believe it – not only was Marco to die for, but he was brainy too.

'Your table is here,' the waiter's voice interrupted them. Dee and Pete turned to see him indicating the table next to Georgie's and Marco's.

Dee frowned at the table.

'Don't you have something more intimate?'

The waiter glanced around at the restaurant, which was completely packed.

'Sorry,' he said, his smile faltering, 'This is the only table we have.'

Dee leaned in to him and whispered loudly, 'I'm Deirdre Byrne? Ring a bell?' She gave her megawatt smile and flicked her hair. Beside her, Pete shuffled awkwardly on his feet.

The waiter looked at her blankly. 'We only have this table,' he repeated, placing down the cutlery and napkins and walking away.

'Fine,' Dee said through gritted teeth.

They all took their seats. Pete ended up sitting across from Georgie, so close their thighs were almost touching. She edged away and forced herself to focus on her date. Her gorgeous, gorgeous date. She could do that, couldn't she?

She looked over at Marco and smiled. 'Cheers,' she said. 'Now, where were we?'

*

At the other table, Dee raised her glass and clinked it against Pete's.

'What are we toasting, babe?' Dee said, smiling seductively and staring right at Pete. 'Our reunion?'

'Sure,' he said, sounding a little distracted. 'It was a surprise to see you here, Dee, after all this time. But we had fun that night in New York, didn't we? Laughed a lot. I really think we could be friends.'

Dee's smile sharpened. There was that word again. Friends. She had to nip this pretence of friendship in the bud – and tell Pete about the baby, sharpish.

*

'How about trying some local food?' said Marco. 'I could choose some things for us.'

'Sounds great,' Georgie said, accepting the large glass of house wine that had been poured for her. She wasn't a drinker, but one or two of these and she'd be fine. She might even be able to tune out the feeling of Pete's leg inches away from hers.

Marco ordered briskly in Portuguese, then turned back to Georgie. 'What is it that you do?' he asked.

'I'm a yoga instructor,' she said. 'I've just bought my own studio. And I've been approached to write a book.'

'Yoga,' he said in a low voice. 'How interesting.'

She flushed as Marco's dark eyes met hers. She could flirt; she told herself. She had it in her, she knew she did.

'It can make you very supple,' she said, lowering her own voice. 'Very . . . flexible.' She had managed to lock out Pete now, as if he wasn't here. He and Dee were making small talk about New York, small talk, which sounded slightly awkward. But still. None of her business.

She noticed Dee get up and make her excuses, tottering over to the toilet in her skyscraper heels. At that moment, a friend of Marco's waved him over.

'Two minutes,' Marco said apologetically. 'I need to sort our shifts for tomorrow.'

'Of course,' Georgie said, smiling up at him, heart sinking. How was it she'd ended up with Pete sitting across from her?

There was a moment's awkward silence across the two tables.

'Look, Georgie,' Pete began. She made the mistake of looking over at him and was struck again by how kind and how handsome, he was. He also looked tense and worried. 'I'm glad that we've finally got the chance to talk. This is pretty awkward, isn't it?'

'Oh, it's not awkward,' said Georgie, trying to sound relaxed.

He frowned. 'It isn't? Only the other night, I thought we really connected.'

'That was just a misunderstanding. I didn't realise you and Dee had history.'

'I didn't realise you were married,' Pete said.

Touché.

'Oh. Yeah, I am,' said Georgie, flushing. 'I mean, probably not for long. I'm here on a date as you can see, so it's not like my marriage is in the best shape in the world.'

'It's not?' Pete leant forward eagerly.

'Well, no,' said Georgie. 'But that's between me and my husband and we should probably sort it out. I'm not even sure why I'm doing this to be honest,' she admitted. She felt like she could tell the truth with Pete. It was as if she had known him for years. He was comfortable in his own skin, had nothing to prove. Unlike Paddy, with his weights and cars and sharp suits.

There was a silence, then Pete said, 'Well, if we're being honest, the truth is that I came to see you the other day in the hotel. So, you can imagine my surprise when Deirdre stepped out of the lift.' He breathed out heavily.

'You came to see me?' said Georgie, her eyes widening. 'Really?'

'Yeah, of course I did.' He stared at her. 'Georgie, tell me if I'm way off base here, but I think there's something between us. Something real, I mean. I know I live in New York, and you live in Ireland, but I can't help wondering if–'

'No,' said Georgie in a strangled voice. 'I'm afraid not.'

Pete might be the father of Dee's baby and so she had to put him out of her mind. For Dee's sake and her own. Pete didn't know that yet, of course, but when he did, he would understand.

'Oh, okay,' said Pete, looking downcast. 'I mean, that's fine, of course. I was just wondering.'

An uncomfortable silence settled over them.

'All okay?' Dee had reappeared and was standing over them, smiling fixedly.

'Fine,' Pete said.

'All good,' said Georgie, smiling up at Dee.

Marco came back too, and brushed his hand across Georgie's back as he sat down.

'Sorry about that,' he said. 'I'm all yours now.'

Georgie smiled and gave him her full attention. She was putting Paddy and Pete out of her mind for now. And Marco turned out to be the perfect distraction. It turned out that they had plenty to say. The conversation flowed nicely, as did the Portuguese wine. He asked her hundreds of questions about her business, listening attentively and seeming genuinely fascinated by the community she was building. He was an interesting guy too, with his travelling all over and his plans to open his own hotel someday.

'I'd love to have a yoga instructor like you for the holiday period,' he said, adding her on his Instagram account. 'This is exactly the sort of demographic I want to appeal to.'

'Middle-aged people?' joked Georgie.

He smiled, gazing into her eyes. 'Beautiful, classy and thoughtful people,' he said. 'Like you.'

Some delicious-looking Portuguese cheese parcels arrived, and Georgie tried one. The filo pastry crumbled in her mouth, the goats' cheese deliciously pungent. She couldn't help laughing at Marco's jokes and his impressions of the tourists. She was dimly aware of the stilted conversation at the next table but, more and more, she found herself able to tune it out. She wondered whether Dee had told Pete about the baby and what he would say – but it was none of her business, she told herself firmly.

At last, the meal drew to a close. Marco was beaming, Georgie was flushed and giggling. Beside them, Pete looked tense and Dee looked pleased with herself.

'The bill please,' Pete asked, looking almost relieved that the meal was over.

The waiter came over quickly with the card machine.

'Me too, please,' Marco said in Portuguese.

Then, in English, he added, 'Perhaps you and I could go on somewhere, Georgie?'

Georgie felt herself flushing deeper. His accent just made her melt. Plus he seemed nice and kind. She was into him. There was no denying it. It was just . . .

He wasn't Pete.

Both couples paid and got up to leave.

The wine hit Georgie as soon as she got up and she stumbled. Marco caught her elbow to steady her, and she laughed nervously.

'I'm not a drinker,' she said. 'I think it's gone to my head.'

Out of the corner of her eye, Pete stood up and his and Georgie's eyes met for one second. It was enough for both of them to pause. They were leaving with other people tonight. Not each other. And that was all there was to it.

'Goodbye, Pete,' Georgie said softly, 'if I don't see you again, have a good flight.'

'You, er, you too,' he mumbled, staring at her as if he wanted to say so much more.

'See you back at the hotel, Georgie,' said Dee, putting an arm through Pete's and dragging him out.

'See you,' said Georgie, looking after them.

That was it, she thought. It would be the last time she ever saw Pete.

'Well, shall we?' Marco said.

'Sure,' Georgie said, taking his arm as they stepped out onto the cobbled street.

'Another drink?' She could feel his hand slide down her back, to rest gently on her bottom. You can do this, Georgie told herself.

'Sure,' she said, stopping on the corner. 'But there's something I'd like to do first.' She tilted her head back and looked up into his eyes, hoping he got the message. He smiled and put his hand up to caress her cheek just firmly enough to make her feel sexy and desired.

She took a deep breath and lifted her face to his.

When his lips met hers, she was drunk enough to imagine that he was Pete, and she reached up and kissed him deeply.

He had one of his big life-saving hands in her hair and the other one on her ass.

YES, she thought. This feels so good – and strange. Marco was the first guy, apart from Paddy, she had kissed in years. But it was definitely good. The question was, did she want it to go further? She tried to blot out all her worries and questions and relax into the kiss–

'Hi guys!'

Georgie pulled away at the sound of the familiar, foghorn, voice, the bubble completely burst and reality kicking in.

'Um, Beth?!'

'Fancy seeing you here!' Beth continued. She was a terrible actor, Georgie thought.

'What are the chances! Now that I am here, though, I may as well check . . . is everything okay? The others are heading back to the hotel, so I thought I'd check in.'

She gave Georgie a look. A look that said, 'Are you sure you want to do this? Because if so, great, and if not, let's go now.' Just like the time Beth had rescued Georgie from the class creep at the school disco, there she was again.

Georgie hesitated, looking back at Marco, who was smiling down at her. She felt torn. On the one hand, here was a handsome, kind, funny man who she could spend the night with if she wanted. The holiday fling she had been hoping for, landed right in her lap.

But it wasn't right. Not because of Paddy, her actual husband, but because of Pete. A guy she had talked to for about ten minutes. It was ridiculous, but she couldn't change how she felt.

'Sorry, Marco,' she said. 'This has been lovely, but I think I'm going to go back with my friend here. Thank you for a great evening and great conversation.'

'Of course,' he said, looking a little disappointed. He squeezed her bum once more in farewell. Maybe it's a Portuguese tradition? Georgie thought.

'See you at the pool tomorrow,' he said. 'I'm serious about a future collab. Of the business sort, of course.'

'Of course. Bye, Marco,' said Georgie.

'Are you sure about this?' Beth hissed as they walked away. 'He's really hot and you probably need a night of good passion, Georgie, it's been a while, eh?'

'I'm sure and thank you,' she whispered to Beth as they walked through the old square. 'I quite fancied the night with him, but it wouldn't have been the right thing to do. I should have closure in my marriage first.'

'So, it wouldn't be anything to do with a certain New York firefighter?' asked Beth sympathetically.

Georgie sighed.

'No comment.'

'Let's get a drink,' says Beth. 'You and me. I'll text the others and say they can head back, and we'll catch them up.' She grabbed her phone, typed the message and then turned to Georgie. 'Right,' she said, her eyes dancing with devilment. 'Tell me everything!'

Five minutes later, they were in a bar with two huge flaming sambucas in their hands, just like when they were in their early twenties. And it turned out the measures in Portugal were much bigger than back home.

'To friendship!' they toasted.

'Can I confide in you, Beth?' Georgie slurred. That shot had gone straight to her head and she didn't even want to think about the damage the toxins were wreaking on her insides, but she didn't care: she was on her holidays. And, as she intended to put in her book, life was all about balance.

Beth nodded.

'Course you can. You can tell me anything,' she said firmly.

Georgie knew that was true and there would be no judgement. That was Beth's greatest, most endearing quality as a friend. She never gave advice unless she was directly asked, and she never judged.

'Beth, the truth is, you're right about Pete. I know how absolutely wild this sounds . . . but I think . . . '

She paused.

'I think I'm in love with him.'

There was a silence. Then Beth said, 'You think you are in love with Dee's Pete. The potential-father-of-her-child Pete. The guy you spent, what, ten minutes with the other night Pete? Pete-Pete, who I really like but don't know if you should, that Pete?'

Georgie nodded.

'Yeah, that Pete, I think I love him,' she said again miserably.

'Oh shit,' was all that Beth said, as the eighties' music blared. This was going to end badly.

Chapter Twenty

In the end, Georgie insisted on leaving after one sambuca because she wanted to do a sunrise meditation on the balcony. She felt a little tipsy and that was quite enough.

'I'll come in with you and Sam, George, if that's okay,' said Beth. 'I don't want to disturb Lady Dee.'

She also had a nagging worry that Dee might have dragged Pete back with her and didn't want to walk in on that. Sam was fast asleep, so Beth slipped into bed beside Georgie, where she dropped off almost immediately, only to wake up a few hours later, heart racing and sheets soaked in sweat.

Oh good, she thought. More of this.

She lay there for a while, terrified to disturb Georgie and Sam, who were sleeping peacefully. At last, she squinted at her watch. 3:53 a.m. She would sneak outside and do one of Georgie's deep-breathing exercises and then, hopefully, go back to sleep. It had worked the other night.

She headed into reception, got herself a glass of water, and then headed out the front where she thought she might get a nicer view of the mountains. She stopped dead. There was a man sitting on the kerb.

'Hi,' said Pete, 'it's me. Again.'

'Why are you here?' Beth said, staring down at Pete. He looks anxious, she thought. 'It's nearly four a.m.! And this isn't your hotel.'

Then the penny dropped. Pete must have just been up in Dee's room and was heading out on the walk of shame. Beth groaned.

She liked Pete, he had a nice way about him, a comfortable ease. But the last thing she wanted was for Georgie to regain consciousness now and find Pete here, in a post-coital haze.

'Look,' she said. 'I totally get that you and Dee have your thing going on. But–'

'Oh.' Pete went pink. 'No. It's not what it looks like. Dee went up to bed hours ago. I've actually been waiting to – well, to see Georgie,' he finished, looking embarrassed. 'And then I gave up and ordered a taxi but it's taking a while.' He patted the kerb. 'Care to join me?'

'All right,' Beth said, feeling very confused. She sat down.

'Well?' she said. 'What's going on?'

'I had an honest chat with Deirdre tonight,' he said gloomily. 'It didn't go very well.'

Beth laughed. That explained why he looked so stressed. 'I can imagine. And my advice to you is to get the next plane out of Portugal. Like, now.'

He blinked at her. 'She's not that scary. Is she?'

Beth shook her head. 'You have no idea. Talk me through what happened.'

'Well. We ended up on a double date with Georgie and that guy Marco. He and Georgie were laughing and talking and getting on so well . . . to be completely honest, Beth, all I wanted to do was swap places with him.' He hesitated. 'Do you mind me telling you all this? I know you are friends with them both.'

'You go ahead,' said Beth, in her best Mammy voice. 'But why don't you pop inside and get us some water first? I'm parched.'

'Good idea,' he said smiling.

He jumped up and headed into reception, returning with a bottle of prosecco in an iced bucket with two flute glasses and a jug of iced water.

'How did you manage to get that?' she said, very impressed. Persuading people to give them booze at all hours – she and Pete definitely had stuff in common!

'I speak Portuguese,' Pete said simply. 'And, well . . . I told the young guy in reception that we had just got engaged.'

'Great,' Beth said, looking down at her sweaty nightie. 'Makes perfect sense.'

Pete popped the cork. 'It was the best idea I could think of at the time. They're delighted for us and wish us all the best for our wedding day etcetera.'

'Well, here's to us officially,' Beth said as he filled her glass to the brim. They could hear the birds singing now. It was definitely late – or, rather, early.

'Ok, go on then. Spill,' she said, sipping the yummy, chilled prosecco.

'Well, we left Georgie and Marco at the restaurant and Dee said I should come back here for a nightcap, and I thought it would be a good chance to straighten everything out. I'd been dropping hints that I wasn't interested romantically, but I didn't want her to get the wrong idea. So, I told her that just to be clear, we were better off as friends. She got . . . annoyed. Said I clearly hadn't understood how much I'd meant to her. Then she told me she was pregnant with my baby.'

'Woah,' said Beth, round-eyed over her drink. 'So, it all came out.'

'Yeah. Only, the thing is, she can't be.'

'What?' said Beth.

'She can't be pregnant with my baby. We'd have to have had sex for that, and we definitely didn't have sex that night in New York. We went back to hers, and, well, she got into bed and so did I . . . ' He had the grace to blush. 'But she fell asleep. We had coffee the next morning and then I left and . . . well, that was that.'

'Woah,' said Beth. 'And you told her this?'

'I did.' He pulled a face. 'And then it came back to her. Which seemed to make her more upset.'

'Yeah,' said Beth sympathetically. Dee had decided that she wanted Pete to be the father and therefore it would be the case. Her fantasy had come crashing down and she couldn't imagine Dee taking it well.

'Anyway, then she absolutely lost it. She was shouting at me that I had led her on and had been staring at Georgie all evening.' He paused. 'That last part might have been true.'

Beth beamed. She felt a mix of things – very excited for Georgie, scared of Dee and nervous for Pete's life. Dee was one of the brightest people that Beth had ever met. She was well-read, well-researched and well able to take on anyone at any time. Very dangerous if you were opposite her in a fight and not on the ball.

'She screamed at me, said I was a loser. Said I was the last person she'd have a baby with.' He shuddered. 'God, it was bad.'

'Here, you should have another drink,' said Beth solicitously pouring him one. 'You sound like you need it.' '

'Thank you,' he said. 'I knew that the minute I met you, that you were a good egg.'

'A drunk one.'

'Well yeah.' He glanced at her curiously. 'You're a good friend; I can tell that. The thing is, at the restaurant I asked Georgie if there could ever be anything between us and she said no. But now I wonder if she said that because Dee had told everyone it was my baby. And if Georgie knew it wasn't . . .'

'She might feel differently?' said Beth.

'Yeah, well, that's what I was waiting around to ask. But now, I'm not sure. Is it too messy? I don't want to hurt Dee. And I mean, Georgie is married. Dee told me that.'

'I'll bet she did,' said Beth. 'But did Dee also tell you that things have run their course there? Georgie is one of the most loyal people you could meet,' Beth went on quickly, in case he was getting the wrong idea, 'but she's been through a lot this last year. Her husband is, not to put too fine a point on it, a complete and total prick.'

Pete looked hopeful.

'Do you really want my advice?' Beth said.

Pete nodded eagerly, fixing her with his brown eyes.

'We have one more day here. It's your last chance to see Georgie. I think she would want you to get in touch.'

'You really think so?' said Pete hopefully. 'What about that Marco guy? She seemed really into him.'

'Georgie's really into you,' said Beth, deciding it was okay to share, in the name of true love. 'She told me so. Ignore Dee. She's used to everyone doing what she wants, but she'll come round.'

If I have to force her into it, she thought to herself.

Headlights swept down the drive. 'My taxi.' said Pete. 'See you soon, Beth.' He smiled. 'I'll call at the hotel for Georgie tomorrow at midday. And Beth? I really appreciate this.'

'Pleasure.' She smiled back.

*

Sam put her hand to her stomach. She was feeling rough again. Her throat was sore from being sick and she felt both restless and exhausted. And she couldn't stop running to the toilet to pee. She tiptoed over to the window to open it. She needed to breathe. As she looked out onto the garden, she could see people stirring below, setting out tables on the patio. She'd go down and have a few hours to herself.

After a thirty-second shower, she threw on a bikini, grabbed two towels and her beach bag with its book, water, Vaseline – a small tub! – paracetamol, an apple and sun lotion and quietly slipped out of the room.

Wow, it was really nice being on her own, she thought as she walked slowly down the tiled staircase. As much as she adored the girls, being away in a group meant that you only had peace on the loo and even that was hard with friends who had no boundaries. Why would they, after all those holidays they'd shared when they were younger, stuffed into a tent at a music festival, Beth's smelly feet in Sam's face, or backpacking through Spain, staying in hostels, fighting over the top bunk? Still, they'd been a lot this holiday. Beth with her insecurities and drinking, Kate at her relationship crossroads, Dee deciding to go full Hollywood diva, Georgie and her marriage breakdown . . .

The smell of sizzling bacon hit Sam's nostrils. Her stomach lurched again. Breathe, she said to herself, channelling Georgie, as she headed through the lobby double doors and onto the pool terrace. It was heavenly here first thing. Just the noise of the waterfall filled the air, otherwise, it was empty, completely empty. Someone was cleaning the pool with a net. Tropical plants were being fed water from sprinklers. Pure relaxation and just what she needed this morning, the last full day of their holidays. She headed over to their sunbeds, relishing the thought of time to herself when she caught sight of a woman in a huge hat and sunglasses. 'Dee!' she said, shocked. 'I don't think I've ever seen you up so early.'

Dee pushed her sunglasses down her nose slightly and looked at her. 'Morning, Sam,' she said tightly.

'Why are you here? At this time, I mean?' Sam said, glancing at her watch as she laid her towel down on the bed beside her. It was only seven o'clock in the morning. 'You're always going on about how much sleep you need.'

'Because I am bloody furious if you must know!' Dee jumped off her bed quicker than a dog hearing the word "walkies".

Sam jumped in fright. Oh God. She should never have asked. She could feel the bile rising again in her throat. Her stomach was rocking. Not here, not now, she thought frantically.

'I haven't slept a wink, Sam.' Dee started pacing around the sunbeds, posing every time. She turned like a model at a fashion event. She was making Sam dizzy, but she tried very hard to focus on her friend. She knew from experience that Dee expected her full attention.

'What about?' Sam asked cautiously. 'I've literally just woken up, so I know nothing, Dee, to be honest.'

'Well, I'll tell you all about it!' said Dee.

'Oh good.' Sam said wearily. She closed her eyes and lay back, trying to keep the nausea at bay.

'So, after we all left each other in the square, I went to meet Pete, the guy that I really like, the guy who could be the father of my foetus!' Dee's voice rose to a shriek on the last bit. 'The guy who–'

'Hang on.' Sam held out a limp hand. 'Dee, let me stop you right there.'

Dee, unused to being interrupted mid-flow, looked at her in shock.

'I am here to listen,' Sam said weakly, 'but NOT to be shouted at, so could you bring this all down a notch, please?'

'Right,' Dee said, winded with surprise. 'Fine, I'll whisper. Now, where was I?'

'Pete, love of your life, father of your foetus,' Sam said. It was only then that Sam noticed that Dee's usually perfect nails had been bitten and gnawed at. Jesus, this must be serious, she thought. Dee's nails were her pride and joy. Even at a young age, Dee had been able to keep her shit together when others would have crumbled. Her technique was simple. She just brushed her hair, reapplied her lippie and kept going. She had an inner steel that was unbreakable. The others all admired it. It was her skill, they thought, her superpower. And now, she seemed to be crumbling. Sam thought back to the unfortunate incident in the town square, where Dee had clambered onto the man's back. Come to think of it, Dee had been losing it for quite some time.

'Continue, Dee,' Sam said gently. 'But quietly.'

'Okay.' Dee sat back down. 'I'm sorry, Sam. First off,' she went on in a whisper, 'Georgie and that random pool bloke from the hotel crashed our date.'

Sam frowned. She had a feeling she knew where this was going now. Dee could not cope if another woman got more male attention than her. She had always considered herself the star, in more ways than one. The only issue was, Georgie was stunning. In spite of her old clothes, bare face and complete disinterest in her appearance she was usually the recipient of admiring glances. This had always killed Dee, but she managed to force the green-eyed monster down most of the time. After all, she had the fabulous celebrity life. She had everything she'd ever wanted. Now, it seemed, the monster was wide awake and ready to roar.

'What does Georgie and her date have to do with your dinner with Pete?' Sam asked.

'Everything, Sam,' Dee said starting to cry, big, dramatic Kim Kardashian tears. She picked up a towel beside her. 'Is this yours?'

'No, it's Georgie's, I . . . ' Sam didn't finish her sentence as Dee blew her snotty nose into the towel with gusto and anger.

Gross, Sam thought.

'What's your problem?' snapped Dee, clearly catching Sam's appalled expression.

Sam counted to ten. She had no experience with children really, but she imagined this was what parents did when theirs were having a tantrum. It worked because her heart rate slowed down and she was able to remain calm.

'Dee, I've already told you. Settle down. I'll listen to you then.'

Dee sat down and hid the snotty towel from sight, looking like a naughty schoolgirl.

'Anyway, we ended up the four of us in the same restaurant. And Georgie definitely likes Pete. I could see it in her eyes. She kept giving him looks. I couldn't believe it. She knew I met him first!'

'Right,' said Sam. 'But that doesn't necessarily mean–'

'She's a shit friend and the reason why Pete doesn't want to keep seeing me, I know it.' Dee put her face in her hands again but this time to scream, not cry.

'Little Miss Innocent,' she snarled. 'She acts like butter wouldn't melt, but she's had her eye on Pete ever since she saw him. And she has a man of her own!'

'Okay, okay,' Sam said raising her hand again. 'Let's not run away with ourselves. You have known Georgie for thirty years, Dee, and you and I both know that she is not like that at all.' She took a sip of her water, trying to steady her stomach. 'Georgie is one of the most loyal people I know, and she backed off from Pete the instant she realised you had history.'

'I'm not so sure that she's the person that you think she is,' said Dee. 'I saw it, Sam! I saw them talking and she was smiling and blushing. She knows what she's doing. I'm not stupid.'

'Good morning,' a voice said, interrupting Dee's tirade. Kate was standing there in a bright orange shift, oblivious to the unfolding drama. She sat on a free bed. 'How come you two are up so early?'

'How come you are?' said Sam. 'You look fabulous, by the way. Orange really suits you.'

Kate began to distribute towels, smiling. 'Thank you! I thought it was a bit much, but now, I like it. I've decided to wear brighter colours.'

'Good for you!' Sam said warmly.

'Anyway, it's a quarter to eight. I always come down to get our beds set up. What about you?'

'I couldn't sleep; I still have a dicky stomach,' Sam replied, letting the sun soak her skin. It was so nice.

'I also couldn't sleep, Kate, because Georgie seduced Pete. My Pete,' snapped Dee, clearly determined to keep the attention fully on her.

'Georgie seduced Pete?' frowned Kate. 'Our Georgie? What are you talking about, Deirdre?'

She used her full name, which they only busted out when things were serious.

'Bloody hell, I haven't even had a coffee yet and you're off on one. Besides, I can't see Georgie seducing anyone.'

'God, here we go again, Georgie the saint, Georgie is so innocent, blah blah blah. Well, I can tell you now that Georgie is not the woman you all think she is. You'll see, if she ever deigns to emerge. Then the truth will be revealed.'

And with this ominous utterance, Dee lay back down and put in her AirPods.

Kate looked at Sam meaningfully. Sam rolled her eyes slightly. Why could they not have one day of peace?

'How about we get some coffees in, Sam?' Kate said.

'Oat latte, low fat, extra hot, heavy on the froth,' said Dee from her bed.

*

'Bagsy not to be the one to ask them for Dee's order,' Kate said, laughing as she and Sam headed into the hotel from the pool. It was quiet today, definitely a lot less lively now that Margie and co. had gone back to Brighton.

As they waited for their order – they compromised on an oat latte, extra foam for Dee – Sam filled Kate in on what she could ascertain from Dee's rant. 'So basically, Dee thinks Georgie made a play for Pete and seduced him just as Dee was about to tell him about the baby. Which I just don't think is Georgie's style,' Sam said. 'She wouldn't go after someone Dee liked. She said as much herself. Not with the baby in the mix.'

'Yeah, it's a load of crap,' said Kate briskly. 'Unless Georgie's had a personality transplant, there's more to this than we realise.'

'Yeah, I hope to God that they'll be down soon so we can move on with the day.' Sam groaned. 'Oof, I feel rubbish Kate, I really do.'

'Oh, Sam. Rotten luck getting sick on holiday.' Kate put her hand on Sam's head to check for a temperature. Her friend felt cool if a bit clammy to the touch. 'I think we should go into town later and get you seen at the pharmacy. You might need some Imodium and stuff.'

They returned with Dee's order; finished their coffee and sunbathed until they heard a slightly croaky, 'Morning guys'. Then they saw Beth and Georgie approaching. Even with wet hair from the shower, Georgie was still beautiful, Sam thought. Georgie waved cheerfully at them. Sam grimaced. Georgie clearly had no idea she'd provoked Dee's wrath.

No sooner had the girls sat on their beds than Dee was up. Hands on her hips, seething. She couldn't wait.

'So, good night was it, Georgie?'

'Um,' said Georgie weakly. 'Yeah. I think so?'

It was like watching a lamb innocently strolling past a starving lion, Sam thought.

'Was it, hmm?! Anything you want to say to me? About Pete?'

'I have no idea what you are even talking about. I left the restaurant with Marco, remember?' Georgie replied, looking puzzled.

'Oh yeah, poor Georgie is so innocent, poor Georgie didn't realise that she was flirting!' Dee spat. 'She betrayed me! Broke my trust! Ruined our–'

'Dee! Stop now or you will say something that you can never take back. You are making a fool of yourself, acting like an angry teenager. You should know better.'

Kate tried to keep her voice calm, but she was furious.

It was check-in time for new guests and curious tourists pulling suitcases passed them as Dee screamed blue murder.

'I am hurt, Kate!' Dee was shouting now. 'I really liked Pete and wasn't expecting my friend to ruin things for me.'

'How did I ruin things?' Georgie asked, bewildered and trying to keep her voice level. 'I said goodbye to Pete in the restaurant.'

'He told me he doesn't like me,' wailed Dee. 'And it's all because of you.'

There was a silence in which Georgie took this in. 'But – but did you tell him about the baby?' she asked softly.

There was another silence. Dee's eyes darted shiftily.

'Er,' she said.

'Go on, Dee,' Beth said firmly. 'Are you going to answer Georgie? What did Pete say about the baby?'

Dee tossed her head. 'It turns out we weren't . . . intimate in New York,' she said. 'But Pete and I had an undeniable connection until she came along and ruined it.'

Enough of this, Sam thought angrily. For God's sake – Dee had fantasised the whole scenario with Pete and now had the gall to blame Georgie because Pete didn't fancy her. 'Dee, I'm going to say this once,' she said, her voice very calm and clear. 'I think you know full well that Georgie is not the sort of person to flirt with a man her friend likes. Now, if Pete isn't interested in you, that's his decision – I know you're used to men falling at your feet, but there's a first time for everything. Why don't you take a good look at yourself for once and stop trying to blame others? It will get you a lot further.'

Dee glared at her.

'Now,' said Sam, 'I'm going to go and do some yoga with Georgie. If you don't mind, George. I think some stretching might do me good.'

'Of course,' said Georgie, scrambling to her feet.

'Oh, I'll come,' said Beth immediately.

'And me,' Kate added. They were all leaving Dee. She stared after them, speechless with rage and hurt.

*

'Nice work, Sam,' said Beth, hurrying after her friends.

'Well, don't tell me she didn't deserve it,' Sam said firmly. 'Pregnancy is no excuse for being a complete and utter tyrant. Are you okay, George?'

'Yeah, I'm fine.' Georgie's face was pale and she looked shaky. 'Come on, we can do some stretching on the grass over there.' Georgie led the group through the searing heat and to a shadowed part of the grass.

'Listen,' said Beth. 'Now that we're over here, I have to talk to you properly, Georgie. About Pete.'

'I don't want to know. Let's forget about it. Sit cross-legged everyone.' White-faced, Georgie crossed her legs and raised her arms up and they followed. 'Now, let's take a deep breath . . . oh, Beth, I can't take it. What did you want to say? We can do yoga while you talk.'

'Thank God,' muttered Kate. 'I'm dying to know.'

'Well. You remember after you went upstairs?'

'Yes. I put my eye mask on and went to sleep. Now, put your legs up, guys, and circle your feet, twirl your ankles left and right and stretch those toes. Now, downward dog girls, and ease yourselves into the plank. So, what happened?'

Beth grunted as she lowered herself into the plank, letting out a small fart. Luckily everyone else was concentrating too hard to notice.

'OK, well I couldn't sleep?' she said, sweat running down her face and into her eyes.

'Right. Now, stretch out your back as you stretch those legs,' Georgie called out in full downward dog, making it look so easy. 'And back into plank.'

Beth wheezed into position.

'This . . . is . . . hard,' she gasped. 'I thought yoga was meant to be relaxing.'

'You're doing great,' said Georgie, effortlessly maintaining the plank, her eyes locked on Beth's, whose face was only inches away.

'Go on. You couldn't sleep and then what?'

Beth's arms were shaking.

'Well,' she started, spitting her hair out of her mouth. 'So, yeah, I was tossing and turning and . . . Georgie, can I take a break? It's hard to talk and plank.'

'Yes,' Georgie said, not moving a muscle. This woman could hold the plank position for hours, it would seem.

Sam and Kate copied Beth and lowered their bodies to the ground with relief.

'So then,' Beth continued, just about able to breathe again, 'I came out here to do some of your deep breathing and then I realised that Pete was here.'

'Pete was here?' whimpered Georgie, her plank wobbling ever so slightly. 'As in, here?'

'Georgie, get yourself together,' said Kate taking over. 'I think we've established that Pete was here! Oh my God. Was he here with Dee? Had they . . . '

'No!' Beth shouted, before lowering her voice.

'That's what I thought at first, but no. He was here for you, Georgie!'

'Me?' Georgie could barely whisper, still managing to hold the plank.

'Yes.' Beth was smiling now because this was the exciting bit. 'He likes you, you dickhead! He was never into Dee. I think she steamrollered him into the dinner last night but it's you he wants to be with. He told her he wasn't interested and also, that there was no physical way he could have knocked her up, which is why she's in such a filthy mood. He waited here till four a.m. to talk to you. I think this could be serious for him, Georgie.'

'Really?'

Sam groaned.

'Obviously he wants to be with you, you are hot and sound and genuine.'

Georgie lowered herself to the ground at last.

'But Dee is so sexy. She's probably a complete animal in the sack . . . Pete likes me? And he's not the father of Dee's baby?' her voice trailed away, before she added, 'Isn't it still a betrayal of Dee?'

'No,' said Kate, Sam and Beth as one.

'Really?'

'Yeah,' said Sam. 'Look, under ordinary circs, I'd say if a mate likes someone, you should steer clear. But Dee wants Pete simply because she can't have him. She is going through it with this pregnancy and is clearly in a bad way. She couldn't even remember Pete's name at the start of the holiday. I can guarantee she'll forget all about him as soon as she's back in New York. If you and he have a real connection – and I think you do – then you should give it a chance and ignore Dee.'

Georgie nodded. 'I really think we do,' she said. 'Have a connection, I mean.'

'Then it's worth standing up to Dee. We just need to manage how pissed off she is,' said Beth. Ugh, I wish I wasn't sharing her room but it's only for one more night.'

'Wait,' said Georgie suddenly. 'I can't even get hold of Pete. What if–'

'Oh no that's fine,' said Beth. 'He's going to call at the hotel later. So, come on. I don't want Dee standing in the path of true love. Who is going to tell her to back off and leave Georgie and Pete alone?'

'I'll do it,' Sam said firmly.

'No. I will,' said Georgie with a new determination. 'You're right. I've done nothing wrong, other than like the guy Dee had her eye on. I can stand up for myself.'

'Are you sure,' Sam said. 'You know what she's like . . . '

Georgie nodded. 'I've done my yoga, so I feel totally empowered.'

'Well let's get on with it,' said Beth nervously. 'We can't hide from her forever.'

Chapter Twenty-one

As they approached the pool area, the music was playing, a low Nikki-Beach beat, and a new group of girls hung out on the opposite side of the pool. They looked the same age as their own group. Behind the pillar, in their area, they could see Dee chatting away on the phone. She ended the call, still smiling, then caught sight of the girls. To Kate's surprise, her smile only widened.

'Dee, I think that its best if we all go for a coffee, maybe to the pool bar?' Sam said calmly. She didn't want this to become a bigger thing than it was. She didn't feel strong enough at the moment to withstand another row.

'Sure, love to.' Dee stood up immediately with an over-bright attitude.

They stripped down to their swimwear and climbed into the pool, swimming over to the café to order coffees.

'So, Dee,' Georgie said, sitting opposite her so she could make eye contact. 'I think we got our wires crossed about last night. You have known me for a long time, and you know that I would never, ever let you down like that. I certainly was not flirting with Pete; in fact, I was enjoying being out with Marco. Yeah, I did like him when we met the other night, but I wrote him off once I realised, he was your Pete from New York.'

'Okay, well that is your side of the story,' Dee started. 'But from where I was sitting last night, you made it pretty clear you liked him.'

'I think he likes me,' said Georgie, lifting her chin. 'And to be honest, I like him back. But I didn't do anything about it over dinner. I only know that because he told Beth the truth after we got back to the hotel. I was asleep at the time. Whether you choose to accept that or not is up to you.' She took a sip of her coffee, her face composed.

'Where does this leave you two then? Kate asked.

Dee shrugged haughtily. 'Well, it all depends, I suppose, whether Georgie here wants to see Pete again. Because I think, as my friend, she owes me some loyalty.'

Beth half-laughed at Dee's pompous tone. Then she coughed.

'Oh, I think I might have wee'd a bit.'

Kate rolled her eyes but giggled. 'Typical.'

Georgie hesitated. 'You know what, Dee?' she said calmly. 'You never gave me a second thought in all this. You knew I liked Pete, and you also knew I'd been having a rotten time lately. It turns out he's definitely NOT the father of this baby. So, frankly, I don't think I owe you anything. If Pete wants to meet again, then I'll see him.' She shrugged. 'This time, I choose me.'

Dee was so shocked, her mouth fell open.

Georgie drained her coffee. 'Now if you don't mind,' she said. 'I'm going to enjoy the rest of my holiday. See you all at the beds.' She set down her cup and got up and swam to the end of the pool.

'See you later Dee,' Beth said and followed Georgie in the pool and Kate followed.

'Well, what a cheek,' Dee huffed.

But Sam wasn't having any of it. 'Georgie has always been a good friend to you – she's just not about to put a guy she likes aside because you've decided your pride is hurt. If you were meant to be with Pete, then you would be.' And Sam swam off too.

Dee stared after her friends for a moment. Then she tossed her head, drained her own coffee and swam to the side of the pool, where she clambered out. She marched up to her room where she began angrily packing. She was done with these bitches. She should have realised they were no longer friends – she'd left them behind a long time ago. They were a tacky bunch, and she had moved on to bigger and better things.

But she would take one, last, parting shot.

Hands shaking, she grabbed her phone and dialled Pete's number. It went to voicemail. Dee took a deep breath.

'Hi Pete, it's Dee,' she said in her most sultry-yet-contrite voice. 'Look, I'm sorry about last night. The whole pregnancy thing, me losing my temper . . . I think I was having a panic, and you were in the line of fire and . . . well, I'm sorry.'

She allowed a note of humour to creep in. 'It's all good, you are off the hook! Go back to New York with a clear conscience. Oh and listen, I spoke to Georgie this morning, too. She wanted me to pass on a message. She really likes you Pete, but she's spoken to her husband today and they're giving things another shot. She was embarrassed to tell you, but I told her not to worry about it and that I know you'll understand. She can be a bit flaky like that. Anyway, see you in NYC some time. Bye-bye.'

That was the way to play it with someone like Pete. Cool and casual. She'd come on a bit strong this week, but she could claw things back, now that she'd scotched things with him and Georgie. As for the girls, she was over them. She'd check flights now. At most, there would be a meal together tonight and then, see you later, girls!

*

Downstairs, Sam had done one lap of the pool and then staggered back to the sunbed looking ghastly. 'I want to die,' she whispered. 'But also, I feel weirdly hungry.'

Beth took one look at her and took charge. 'Right, let's not mess around anymore. Come on, up to reception, we'll go to the pharmacy together now.'

'I'll come with,' said Kate. 'One last potter in town. You too, George.'

'Our friend is sick,' Beth declared when they reached the front of the line at the pharmacy. 'Can you give her something to tide her over, just till we're back home tomorrow?'

The pharmacist, a glamorous woman with her hair in a sleek bun, glanced at Sam. 'What's wrong?' she asked in fluent English, looking bored at the prospect of another tourist tummy bug.

'I feel very nauseous,' Sam said. 'And dizzy. And I keep waking up in the night to pee, but constantly. I thought maybe I'd eaten something dodgy but it's been going on for days. Sometimes I feel okay and I'm starving and then it starts up again.'

'Well, you'll need to see a doctor really,' the pharmacist said, tapping her foot. 'If there is a bug going round, you'll just have to let it run its course – lots of fluids and rest and no heavy foods. You might just have had too good a holiday.' Her tone said that she saw a lot of tourists who also had had "too good a holiday".

'Yeah,' Sam said with a grimace. 'That's what I thought but I haven't touched the booze in days. I travel a lot and I'm normally fine. My husband is always teasing me about my cast-iron stomach.'

'Well, we can recommend some anti-nausea tablets, some travel bands . . . ' The pharmacist frowned and glanced at Sam. Then she lowered her voice. 'Unless . . . there's a chance you could be pregnant?'

Sam gave a short laugh. 'No. I'm not pregnant. I wish.'

'I'm sorry,' said the pharmacist, softening. 'In that case, why don't you . . . '

'Wait.' Sam's mind was racing. She took out her phone and flipped through to the first day of her last period, which she meticulously recorded out of habit. 'Okay, so my last period was June first. That's seven weeks ago. And my periods are like clockwork. I just didn't notice because we'd decided to take a break because of the IVF.'

The girls looked at each other. There was a pause.

'Well,' said the pharmacist diplomatically at last, 'Why not take these anti-nausea pills and buy a pregnancy test? How is it you English say it? "Better to be safe than sorry?"'

Sam didn't correct the woman because she could hear her heart thumping in her ears. She felt dizzy.

'Should I buy a test?' she asked the others. 'I mean, I won't be pregnant, so there's no point. But should I?'

'Yes! Go for it,' Beth almost shouted back.

'Or if you prefer,' the pharmacist said gently, clearly taking pity on Sam, 'you can do a test here. I can ask the doctor from the clinic next door to assist you.'

'Should I?' Sam asked the girls again.

'Why not?' said Kate, trying to sound casual.

'No pressure, though,' she added hastily, looking at Beth and Georgie.

Both women shook their heads. 'Oh no, absolutely no pressure,' Georgie added, unsubtly.

Sam took a deep breath. 'Yeah, ok. I think I've got to know,' she said.

'Sit yourself down then,' said the pharmacist, who had now totally transformed from her earlier reserved self and was now radiating warmth. 'Someone will be with you shortly.'

The girls all sat in a line, expressions tense. Then Georgie let out a small sniff.

'Oh, Georgie, are you crying?' Sam laughed at her friend, whose big eyes were full of tears. 'You know there's such a thing as being too in touch with your feelings? And also, you know I've been trying unsuccessfully to get pregnant for such a long time and the chances of this being anything other than a stomach bug are vanishingly small?'

'Whatever happens, Sam, we're here,' Beth said firmly. She nudged Georgie and nodded at an older lady just leaving the counter. 'George. Isn't that your mate from the plane?'

Georgie looked over. It was indeed Katherine, the lady whom she had sat next to on the flight, the same lady who had come to scatter her husband's ashes. She was holding a wet tissue up to her eye.

'Katherine? It's me, Georgie!' Georgie waved at her.

'Oh, hi!' Katherine said shyly. She came over, still clutching the tissue to her eye.

'Are you okay?' Georgie asked.

'I have a sore eye. Well, this is so ridiculous really, but I'll tell you anyway. So, when I went to scatter my Martin's ashes on the sand dunes, didn't the wind change and now he's in my left eye.'

Kate had to look away not to laugh. But Georgie looked aghast. 'Oh Katherine.' She stood to hug her. 'Sit over here,' she said kindly, and Katherine sat beside Sam.

'The pharmacist gave me some saline to flush him out but with no luck,' sighed Katherine. 'I can tell he's still in there.'

'I suppose in a way,' Beth said carefully, 'Martin will always be with you now, Katherine.'

They couldn't help laughing, including Katherine.

'I hope you girls are all right,' said Katherine. 'No illnesses or anything?'

'Oh.' Georgie glanced at Sam. 'We're just waiting for a . . . '

'A pregnancy test,' said Sam. 'Which will be negative, I know it will. It always is. But all the same, I want to check.'

'Hmm,' said Katherine, eyeing Sam thoughtfully. 'Well, don't be too pessimistic, my dear. You never know.'

'I do know,' said Sam, her voice cracking.

They all fell silent. At last, Sam's name was called and all three women stood up to follow her.

'See you in the airport tomorrow then, Katherine,' Georgie said. It turned out they were on the same flight back as well.

'Good luck, dear,' said Katherine to Sam. 'I'll be thinking of you, whatever happens.'

The girls all followed Sam into the doctor's office, without being asked. The doctor was very handsome with brown eyes, smooth olive skin and white, bright teeth. Plus, he smelt absolutely divine.

'Dishy,' whispered Beth loudly, and Kate nudged her.

'Don't objectify the doctor,' she hissed.

Dr Handsome ran through a few questions with Sam, took her history, her temperature and examined her stomach gently. 'Could just be a bug,' he said. 'But why don't we make sure?' He handed Sam a small cup with a yellow lid. 'Bathroom's just in there,' he said.

Sam stood and so did Beth, Georgie, and Kate.

'If you don't mind,' whispered Sam, 'I'll do this part on my own.'

'Oh, right,' said Beth, sitting down again. 'Sure. Sorry about that.'

Sam took the cup and in silence walked to the toilet door. She came out a few minutes later and handed the cup to the waiting nurse, who removed the lid, dipped in a stick, then set it aside. Then she solemnly handed Sam's test to the doctor.

Why does he have to be so handsome, Sam thought, fighting back giggles, when he's holding my wee!

Morto.

The seconds that passed were agony. Sam closed her eyes and started to pray. She'd never once prayed before but she thought it might bring good luck.

Beth rubbed her shoulder, as if Sam were a champ on a break in the ring.

'I could do some chants to relax you,' Georgie said hopefully.

'Not right now, Georgie,' said Sam. 'Thanks though.'

After about four minutes of silence, the doctor picked up the stick and examined it.

The silence stretched out. Sam licked her lips. She was sweating now and her arm pits felt sticky. She had seen more pregnancy sticks than hot dinners at this stage, but it never got easier.

'Well, Sam,' said the doctor. 'It looks like you're pregnant.'

He held out the stick to show her. Sam burst out crying. Through her tears she could see the two blurry red lines. They were there. They were actually, really there.

'Could be anything from seven to eight weeks' pregnant,' said the doctor. 'When you're home, I suggest making a doctor's appointment and they can try and date you more accurately for a scan.'

Georgie burst out crying now, which started Beth off, and Kate followed. They were hugging Sam fiercely and kissing her head. They were all so shocked and overwhelmed.

'I just love you so much,' Kate wailed wrapping her arms around Sam almost knocking the doctor to the ground.

'This is the nicest news we could have had,' agreed Beth, who was still automatically rubbing Sam's back.

The doctor was also smiling, the handsome devil.

'You take it easy now,' he said. 'The first few weeks can be the worst for some people. Lots of fluids and rest and take care on the flight.' He squeezed Sam's arm. 'Best of luck.'

Beth approached the doctor then. 'Come here' she said to him, folding him into the hug too, resting her boobs on his head.

Chapter Twenty-two

The journey home to the hotel went by in a hazy blur of shock and excitement. Sam could barely remember what the doctor had given her other than the sea-sickness band on her wrist. She was pregnant! PREGNANT! How exciting and terrifying. Her ears were still kind of ringing. It all made sense now though. Her boobs were tender too, more so than usual. The nausea, the dizziness, the hunger! She had never, even in her wildest dreams, considered pregnancy! God, Jeff would be so happy too! Looking out at the bright blue sky she thought that if all went well, she would be a mum in Spring. She could hardly believe it.

'We're home,' Beth said, nudged her. 'Well, home for one more night at least.' What an amazing finish to their trip. Sam was finally pregnant.

The girls got out and headed into reception for a cool drink. Alcoholic and chilled and white for all except Sam. They all clinked glasses.

'To Sam!' they said, and they all laughed, Sam the hardest.

'Will you call Jeff?' asked Georgie.

'D'you know, I think I'll wait,' said Sam. 'I want to surprise him, you know? Tell him to his face. We've had so many disappointments . . . but I know who we should call.' She took out her phone. 'We should all be here for this shouldn't we?'

'Go for it,' said Georgie bravely. 'I'm not scared of her. Much.'

Sam pressed Dee's number. 'Dee, I have some crazy but exciting news,' she said quickly, before Dee could say anything.

'And I want you to put what happened today to one side and just come and listen. We are all down here in reception. Will you join us?'

A few minutes later Dee arrived down downstairs, looking disdainful and elegant in a linen sundress. 'Well?' she said, looking intrigued, in spite of herself. 'Let's hear it.'

'Sooooo, I'm pregnant! I could be eight weeks, Dee. Can you believe it? Pregnancy twinsies!' Sam gushed, still so giddy and on cloud nine.

Dee didn't hesitate; all her rage fell away for the moment, and she flung her arms around Sam. 'Well, that explains why you have been feeling so unwell,' she said. 'Congratulations!'

She sighed.

'What is it?' Kate said sceptically.

'Nothing, nothing.' Dee shook her glossy curls.

As though reading her mind, Sam cleared her throat.

'So, what I would love, if we can, is – could we park all our differences just for our last evening together?' she said. 'Life is too short. Please guys, surely, you're not going to fall out over a guy. You've been friends for so long.'

'I'm very hurt, Sam,' Dee started. Her voice wobbled and the others stared at her in alarm. Emotion was weakness to her.

'Well so am I, Deirdre,' said Georgie firmly. This time she was not backing down, it would seem. 'But I don't think this is the time or place to discuss it. We're here to celebrate Sam's news.'

Dee nodded reluctantly. 'All right then,' she said.

Everyone relaxed a fraction.

'Great. Then where will we go for dinner tonight?' Kate asked. They hadn't had lunch and she was starving. She took some crisps out of her beach bag and, as she ripped open the bag, she smiled, put a handful into her mouth and crunched enthusiastically.

'I'm easy,' Georgie said, smiling at Kate.

'So we've heard,' muttered Dee.

'Deirdre!' Kate snapped. 'We have all made it very clear that we do not want this bullshit to continue today, okay?'

'What about the Portuguese fish restaurant off the square, up the hill? The quieter bit,' Beth suggested hastily. 'One last gambas ao alho and some fresh lemony seabass. Topped off with a bottle of Portuguese pinot maybe and a lemon ice cream . . .'

'Okay, fine,' said Dee planting a fake smile on her face, like the professional presenter that she was.

Just then, Georgie's phone rang, and she glanced at it. Then, expressionless, she muted the call and chucked her phone in her bag.

'You've really made a decision there then?' said Kate. 'I'm assuming it was Paddy.'

'I have,' said Georgie. 'Paddy and I are not a couple anymore, not in the way I want to be. I thought I could cope without sex, without love, without companionship – but I realise now that I can't.'

'Weird how you had this realisation via Pete,' muttered Dee, then caught Kate's eye and shut up.

'So yeah, I'm going to talk to him,' Georgie went on. 'He's always complaining about our cottage, says it's cold, draughty, and expensive – wants to move to one of those swish flats along the river near his friends. He can do that. And I earn plenty now. I don't need him. I think I've been ready for this for a long time.' Georgie drew a deep breath. 'It doesn't scare me anymore. I want to focus on my work and my friends,' she said, squeezing Sam's hand. 'I'm more than some mute little trophy wife.'

'Too right, pal,' smiled Sam. 'Should we go and get ready?' she asked standing up.

'Let's do it,' Beth said draining her glass. This was her favourite part of a holiday. When you had sun-kissed skin and a cold shower.

And it was the last night. Nothing else could go wrong now, could it?

*

Huddled around the mirror applying their makeup, Sam turned to Georgie. 'So, Pete?' she said. 'Has he been in touch like he told Beth he would?'

'Nothing,' sighed Georgie. 'And that's fine. It tells me how he really is. I don't want some flake.' Georgie took a step back and looked at herself in the mirror – not with Paddy's critical eyes, but with her own, loving ones. Blonde hair tumbling about her shoulders, skin glowing with only a dab of coconut oil. She wore an old navy sundress, but it looked effortlessly glam on her. In fact, she looked how she felt – confident, happy, sexy. She still had it, she thought. She was only forty-two and her whole life was ahead of her.

'Well,' Sam said. 'Whether anything happens with Pete or not, you look stunning and worthy of any man. The only problem will be finding one who's worthy of you.'

'Too right. Let's go,' Georgie said, grabbing her battered silver clutch bag. 'I can hear the others. I'm up for a nice, chilled one.'

As they left their room, they could see Beth just ahead, sliding down the hotel banisters, rather than using the lift and Dee tutting behind her.

'Final night!' they heard Beth screech as she disappeared down the banister.

'I hope it is a chilled one,' Sam said uncertainly. 'Because you never know with this lot.'

Chapter Twenty-three

Bags swinging and arms linked, the girls headed to the square towards the hustle and bustle and delicious foodie aromas. When they were all together like this, in spite of their age and their differences, it was hard not to feel a bit giddy. They'd always felt this way, since the day they'd first met. It didn't matter how many rows they had or how much griping they did, their love was older and bigger than that.

'Wait. Should I get my tongue pierced?' Beth asked, as they strolled past a tattoo and piercing parlour.

'Jesus, Beth, what?' said Kate laughing. 'Where did that come from?'

'Or a nipple,' Beth said breezily. 'Not sure Jack will notice and if he does, he might like it.'

'You're not serious,' said Dee dismissively which, of course, was like a red rag to Beth.

'Maybe I am,' she said. 'In fact, yes, I'm going to do it later when I'm more anaesthetised. I've always fancied the idea of having my tongue pierced, so why not now?'

'Beth, I don't mean to judge but are you not a bit old for this?' Sam asked.

'Too old to pierce my tongue? Of course not!' Beth said. 'I can always remove it if I don't like it!'

'The nipple or the tongue?' Kate asked. She may as well go with this as it looked like it was happening.

Georgie shook her head, smiling as the girls bickered. She was trying hard not to think of Pete. Questions whirled around her head. Why had he said all that to Beth if he hadn't meant it? But if he meant it, then why hadn't he got in touch? He knew this was her last night. Maybe he thought it was too much drama and effort for what would only be a holiday fling. Because how could it work anyway, with him in New York and her in Ireland?

The girls walked a little longer and walked past the fish–foot place, remembering the crowd with their iPhones that day in the market when Dee had gone viral.

'Any word on that reality TV house?' asked Sam politely.

'Oh, I haven't checked,' said Dee carelessly.

'You're fibbing,' Sam smiled.

'Yes, I am,' Dee admitted. 'I've checked, and nothing,' she said sadly.

Sam reached out to hug her. 'Don't worry. They'll want you, I know they will.'

'I wish,' Dee said. Now that the holiday was drawing to a close, she could feel the net of responsibility closing in on her. Pregnant. Presumably jobless. How could she tell the girls she was getting sacked while saving face? Her mind cycled frantically through the options.

Then an idea occurred to her. She could tell them she was quitting to pursue something she had always wanted to do. Something classier than reality TV. Something wholesome and fulfilling . . .

'Maybe a fashion company thinks you look so fab in a sarong they want you to model them,' said Sam, trying to butter Dee up a bit.

They stopped outside a steakhouse and decided that the menu had something for everyone. No sooner were they seated, than a waiter arrived over with menus and took their drinks order.

'After we've ordered,' Dee said, perusing the menu, deciding there was no time like the present to announce her image overhaul, 'I have some news for you all.'

'Okay,' said Kate cautiously.

'Five medium steaks please, with side salads and three chips.' Kate ordered, pretending that she couldn't hear Dee fretting about macros and fibre. They could all eat what they bloody well wanted to. The waiter bustled off.

'What's this big announcement then?' asked Kate.

'Soooooo . . . ' Dee toyed coyly with her wine glass. 'I've made a decision.' She flung back her shoulders and announced dramatically, 'I'm coming home.'

There was a silence in which the girls stared at her blankly.

'Coming home?' said Sam at last. 'What – to Ireland?'

'That's right,' said Dee, beaming. 'I've decided that I'm moving home to County Kerry for a few months. I didn't real-ise the toll New York was taking on me. I've had enough of the spotlight. I want to live in nature, right in the middle of the countryside.'

More blank stares. The girls were too shocked to speak. Dee was moving? Back to County Kerry? And the countryside? Deirdre and countryside – those words just didn't go together.

'But – but why? What about New York and your job?' said Kate, the only one who had managed to gather herself enough to speak.

Dee waved her hand. 'I've thought of something far more rewarding than reading other people's news.' She let out a euphoric sigh. 'Home.'

Beth coughed, then said, 'But home isn't County Kerry, Dee. You're from Dublin.'

'Seriously?' said Sam, perplexed. 'Like, what will you do?'

'Well actually, I'm going to film a documentary about our beautiful island of Éire. About the – the beauty of Éire.' Dee's eyes sparkled with excitement as she looked around the girls' faces. For an on-the-spot idea, it was pretty good. In fact, she thought she'd present an amazing doc, even if she said so herself.

Kate spluttered and her wine dribbled right down her chin. 'You?!' She laughed. 'But you think Ireland is a tiny little nowhere place.' She began to dab at her face with her napkin. 'I don't think I've ever even heard you talk about Kerry. Have you even been there?' She laughed out loud, slapping her thigh at the idea.

Dee glared at Kate. 'Real nice, Kate, real supportive.'

'Would you live in Kerry, Dee? I mean, really?' Beth said, straight out. She never remembered even seeing Dee wear a pair of wellies let alone travel outside Dublin. 'You don't really seem to be the country-living type either.'

'Country living is great,' Georgie said, clearly striving to be supportive. 'I love it. But after New York, it might feel a bit . . . quiet to you. Besides,' she said honestly. 'After everything that's gone on this holiday, do you think you'd want to be so close to home?'

Dee scowled. She had a clear vision of herself, cycling along a country lane, wearing an Aran jumper, with fresh bread in her basket, then going home to feed the chickens – and she wasn't about to let the girls ruin it. 'Georgie, I think I know what the countryside is like. I have stayed in many country hotels for shoots. I even own a Barbour.'

'Okay, okay, calm down,' Sam suggested gently. 'We just never realised that you had a dream to . . . eh, live in Kerry.'

'Well, I do. Anyone can write a bloody book, for God's sake so why not make a film about living in Kerry? How hard can it be?' Her eyes darted over to Georgie, who ignored the sly dig. 'And I've always wanted to visit Kerry and, um, cycle around it.'

Kate bit her lip hard so not to laugh. 'Do you know that Kerry is a real place and real people live there? They're not all wearing thick jumpers and milking cows.'

'You once said you'd get a nosebleed if you left the southside of Dublin,' said Beth.

'It will be good for the baby,' Dee said. 'The fresh air. I can be supported by my countryfolk.'

'When is all of this happening?' Kate asked, trying to at least sound like she was taking it seriously.

'In – in six weeks actually,' Dee told her confidently, plucking the time frame from thin air. 'My agent is delighted with the idea.'

Or at least she would be when she told her about it, Dee thought.

'She has publishers biting her hand off for the book.' Again, she was almost certain that would be true at some point soon.

'But what about your actual TV job? What will happen there?' Ever the practical questions from Sam.

'I'll quit,' Dee said breezily. 'My contract is coming up for renewal, so we'd renegotiate now anyway. They'll be devastated, of course – but I need a change and a new challenge, so maybe this is the time. And I want to rediscover Ireland.' She smiled sweetly.

'But you love your job,' said Kate. 'You love having your hair and makeup done and people hanging off your every word. You love commanding the screen. Plus, you're amazing at it.'

'I know I am,' said Dee, her voice cracking slightly. 'But it's time for a change.'

'You'll go from one extreme to another . . .' Sam said, then Georgie nudged her under the table. 'But maybe that's what you need,' she added, having understood the knee nudge. There was no changing Dee's mind, and they had all learnt that over the years. Ultimately, she would do what she wanted anyway. Even if that meant being pregnant in Kerry on her own!

The food arrived which gave them all time to compose themselves. 'Well, good luck with your film about . . . Éire,' Kate said to Dee, unable to make eye contact with anyone in case she would burst out laughing. She kept her head down and looked at her plate instead.

Silence followed.

*

'How do you all feel about going home tomorrow?' Dee asked, for once glad to get the attention off her. She had expected the girls to applaud her returning to her roots and making a film. She had thought they would be impressed and admiring. Their lack of enthusiasm had rattled her. Maybe making a film was hard. Not to mention living in the countryside and the lack of Ubers. But she was doing it, she'd decided. The girls didn't think she could handle not having salad bowls and iced matcha on hand? Well, feck them.

'I haven't told Jeff anything yet about the pregnancy,' Sam said looking around the table. 'It's been killing me, but I want to see his face in real life.' She beamed.

Dee's stomach lurched. Again, she was struck by how different their pregnancy was. She had no one to tell, unless she could track down Mr Exotic Dancer and Mr Boring and she wasn't sure they'd be thrilled if she did.

'I'm going to do another test and put it into a gift bag, as if I've got him a souvenir.' Sam's brown eyes danced. 'Only instead of it being a t-shirt or whatever, it's baby news. He's never seen two lines on a pregnancy test before!'

'Well, I'm excited to go home,' said Kate, slicing into her juicy steak. 'I finally know what I want from life and it's Ariana. I want to commit to a life together, just like she wanted all this time.'

Georgie clapped her hands together. 'I knew something was different about you this holiday. You seem happier, lighter. What changed do you think?'

Kate considered while she chewed. 'I don't know exactly,' she said at last. 'I think it was being here with you guys. We all came here at a bit of a crossroads, didn't we?'

'Me leaving Paddy,' said Georgie.

'Me wondering if there's more to life than kids,' said Beth.

'Me about to become a mum!' Sam squealed.

Dee tossed her head. 'I'd describe my experience as more of an epiphany,' she said grandly. 'But yes, I know what you mean.'

Kate smiled. 'Well, it made me realise I've always had what I wanted, at home. If I was at a crossroads, then I know which direction I need to go in now and it's straight back to Ariana.'

'So, you can start house hunting,' said Sam.

'Screw house hunting,' said Kate, swallowing her wine. 'Ariana needs a bigger gesture after putting up with all my crap. I'm going to propose!'

'Kate!' Beth nearly landed on top of her.

'I'm so happy for you,' she added, as the others stood up to hug her.

'What a wedding that will be!' Sam said, beaming. 'Kate, you will not regret it. You two are soulmates. Go for it! But please phone us as soon as you do.'

'I will,' Kate said smiling. 'And you can all be bridesmaids or maids of honour or whatever people our age call them–'

'Oh my God. Is that who I think it is?' whispered Beth, lunging forward and knocking a glass off the table, which instantly smashed.

They all turned around.

*

'Pete?' Georgie said, peering to look. He was standing with his friends, looking at the restaurant menu, as handsome as ever. Her heart actually skipped a beat. What a shithead though, she suddenly thought. Giving it all to Beth about how much he liked Georgie and then not bothering to contact her. All bloody talk.

Dee was staring fixedly into her makeup compact and had gone rather red.

'You okay there. Dee?' Kate asked suspiciously.

'Fine,' said Dee, trying to sound breezy. Snapping the Victoria Beckam compact closed, she smiled weakly.

'Sorry! Can I get a dustpan and brush!' yelled Beth, seeming to notice the broken glass for the first time. The waitress hurried over with one. 'I'll do it,' said Beth, seizing the handle. 'It's my mess.'

'It's okay, I can–' The waitress hung on. 'If you just let me–'

Georgie tore her gaze away from Pete to see that Beth was now engaged in a tug of war with the waitress. By the time she looked back, Pete was gone.

Shithead, she reminded herself. It was better that she never saw him again.

'Beth, let her do it for God's sake,' Dee hissed. 'Everyone is staring.'

Beth sighed and relinquished the dustpan and brush to the waitress. 'I guess Pete's still here in Portugal then,' she said, sitting back down.

'Guess so,' said Georgie, trying to sound unconcerned.

'Shall we get the bill?' Sam asked as their food was cleared away. 'We could get our final ice cream on the square.'

'And I haven't forgotten my tongue piercing,' said Beth determinedly.

'Oh, I was hoping you had,' said Kate. 'I'm really not sure about this, Beth. It feels like the sort of impulsive mid-life crisis thing you do on holiday and then horribly regret.'

Beth waved her hand. 'It's a piercing, for God's sake. What could go wrong?'

They left the restaurant – Pete and his friends were nowhere to be seen, to Georgie's intense relief. 'I'll come along with you and hold your hand,' she told Beth. 'Do some breathing.'

'Good idea,' said Kate as Beth strode off in the direction of the tattoo parlour.

'Keep an eye on her, will you? I don't want her piercing more than one body part this trip.'

'I'll do my best,' promised Georgie, and ran after Beth.

Chapter Twenty-four

Georgie had to sprint to catch up with Beth, who was marching double time, clearly on a piercing mission. 'Beth, seriously,' Georgie said, trotting alongside. 'A tongue piercing? What about another ear piercing? Those look so cool. Lots of sophisticated women have them all up their ears. All the cool moms. Beyoncé, Cate Blanchett . . . '

'I'm doing the tongue,' said Beth, without breaking stride. 'Seriously, I've thought about this for a long time, and I am ready.'

Georgie didn't have time to point out that 'a long time' time was presumably the last two hours. In Beth's world, that counted as a well-considered decision.

The tattoo parlour looked pretty dodgy to Georgie – ancient price lists, scruffy furniture and one solitary member of staff who looked confused when they marched in.

'There were some really nice-looking places a bit further up,' Georgie whispered. 'Shouldn't we–?'

'I'm doing it,' said Beth. She headed to the counter, where Georgie was sure the guy quickly stubbed out a cigarette. 'One tongue piercing please.'

'Sure.'

The guy jerked his head in the direction of a room behind him and Beth followed him through a cheap plastic curtain. Georgie barely had time to wonder if this was the worst idea Beth had ever had, before Beth emerged, blood trickling from her mouth, the tattooed man behind her.

'Done? Already?' said Georgie. It must have taken all of three minutes.

'I fink sho,' said Beth, drooling blood.

'No talking,' the man said.

Georgie thought that Beth looked like roadkill. Her tongue was hanging out, looking very big and purple. There was a pink stainless steel stud in the middle of it. Beth gave Georgie a thumbs-up and swallowed back blood and spit. She handed over €80 in cash. 'Tank you bery mush,' Beth managed. 'Don' look sho worried, Georgie.'

The girls left the parlour. No mouthwash, no aftercare or advice on what to do next, nothing. Georgie looked back and the shutters were coming down. The guy waved, then slammed the last one down. Beth was clearly the last, if not the only, customer of the day. Georgie had a bad feeling about this.

'Are you okay?' Georgie asked her friend, whose face looked very swollen. 'Will we go back to the meeting spot and see the others?' she said, as she offered her arm so Beth could link her.

'Sure,' drooled Beth.

They walked in silence. Georgie didn't want to ask Beth any questions with her swollen tongue. The others were waiting for them outside a little bar. As they approached, Georgie could see Dee's face contort in disgust. 'Jesus, what's the story?' she asked, straight out.

Georgie looked nervously at Beth. Her face was definitely more swollen now. She also looked a bit green. The kind of green you turn just before you projectile vomit.

'Please tell me that the place was properly sanitised, and the person had accreditations,' said Dee, pressing her fingers to her forehead. 'Honestly, I feel like I'm dealing with children.'

'I feel terrible,' fretted Georgie. 'I didn't check for any of that. It all happened so fast.'

'Beth, what do you want to do?' Kate asked.

'Letsh sit a minute,' slurred Beth, slumping onto a seat. 'Can I shee?'

Dee handed over her compact mirror. 'Jeeeeessshus,' Beth said into it. She tried to open her jaw to see the piercing but couldn't.

*

'I'm sure that this is perfectly fine, normal even.' Kate spoke in her most reassuring voice. 'We should, um, monitor it though. Let's not go back to the hotel just yet. Let's stay here.' Near the hospital. As Kate looked down at Beth, wondering how quickly infection could set in, she felt a sudden, unexpected wave of homesickness. She imagined being back with Ariana, the heating on, a large spaghetti bolognese, bread dripping with garlic butter and a full-bodied bottle of Malbec in front of them. She'd given Ariana a full and complete debrief of this whole trip. And then she imagined going down on one knee, diamond in hand. She imagined the look in Ariana's eyes. She grinned. It was nice having something that good to return to after a holiday. Maybe she hadn't appreciated it enough.

'I'll go get us a drink,' said Sam, eyeing Beth uneasily. 'You guys – watch her like a hawk.'

'Will do,' Kate responded, dreaming of home.

*

Sam headed inside and waited behind a crowd of guys to order their drinks. The smell of Davidoff was quite strong and making her feel a bit queasy. Usually, she loved musky smells.

Then a hand tapped her on the arm and a voice said, 'Hi.'

Sam looked around. It was Pete. Dee's – or Georgie's – Pete. How, she thought, is he always where we are? She hesitated. She didn't want to be rude, but she also didn't want to be too friendly.

This guy had, after all, ghosted poor Georgie after filling Beth's head with shite about his feelings for her.

'I thought that it was you,' he said. 'Are you, um, out with the others?'

'Yes, we are all here,' Sam answered carefully. She wanted to remain polite but not too informative. He didn't deserve it.

'I'll help you bring over the drinks?' he offered.

'Um.' Sam was caught short. She didn't want to say yes – but she did need a hand. Five drinks was hard to carry in one go. Feck it, she thought, they were all adults and Georgie looked hot, so maybe it would be good for Pete to see what he'd thrown away.

'Great, thank you,' she said briskly, handing Pete three glasses of wine. She led the way, slightly regretting her decision as she saw Georgie's beautiful, smiling face fall as she spotted Pete. Dee also looked shocked and then – Sam noticed – uncomfortable.

'Pete!' Dee said standing up. 'What are you doing–'

Before she could finish, Beth stumbled to her feet. 'You, me, outshide,' she said to Pete.

'We are outside,' he said, looking around.

'Hm. Over there then,' she said, pointing across the street.

'Er, okay,' he said, following her.

'Please don't embarrass me, Beth,' Georgie whispered, watching them.

Meanwhile, Dee was biting her lip.

*

When they were out of earshot, Beth started.

'You,' said Beth, pointing a finger at Pete's broad chest, 'you–' Beth had so much to say but her fat tongue was completely getting in the way. Frustrated, she took out her phone and, through slightly bleary eyes, typed a message. She held up the screen for him to see.

'Tongue pierced,' he read slowly. 'Angry. Liar. You told me you liked Georgie, now you've hurt Georgie, not cool.' He looked up at her.

'I wasn't lying! I was telling you the absolute truth! I do like Georgie.'

Beth scowled and typed again.

'Why didn't you text?' Pete read aloud.

'I was going to text! But then Dee left me a voicemail . . .'

Beth held up a hand. Then she typed in block capitals:

WHICH SAID WHAT EXACTLY?

'That Georgie and her husband were giving things a serious shot and that Georgie had asked Dee to tell me to stay away . . .' Pete frowned, as though the truth was dawning on him. 'Er – are you saying that–'

Beth held up a firm hand again and typed:

WAIT HERE

She marched back over the road, grabbed Georgie by the arm, hauled her upright and dragged her back over to Pete.

'What the hell?' Georgie said. 'This isn't actually the school disco, Beth.'

Beth ignored Georgie and positioned her in front of Pete. He opened his mouth to speak, but Beth shook her head vehemently and began typing on her iPhone.

Georgie looked everywhere except for at Pete.

Beth held out her phone:

Tell her EVERYTHING. And sort it out, you two. I'll deal with Dee

Then she walked back to the bar.

*

'Georgie, hi,' Pete started. 'Look, I really don't know what is going on here but maybe I should try and explain my end so that you don't think that I'm a total dickhead? Can we sit for a minute?'

'All right,' said Georgie cautiously.

He pointed to a low wall bordering the square and Georgie followed, her mind in a whirl. Someone was playing the guitar and the square was full of laughter and chatter.

'Dee left me a voicemail yesterday morning,' he said, cutting right to the chase. 'She said she was sorry it hadn't worked out with us but no hard feelings. And then just as an aside, she said that you'd asked her to tell me to back off as you were giving your marriage a serious shot. That you weren't ready.' His eyes searched Georgie's face. 'Was that true or have I been a dickhead twice over?'

Georgie stared at him, at his honest, open face and brown eyes. 'I – I never said any of that,' was all that she could manage. 'I didn't know that Dee was even phoning you. I just thought you'd changed your mind about me.'

'No way.' Pete leaned over, taking her hands. 'I like you so much, Georgie. I meant everything I said. That, as unlikely as it seems, I think there's something here and we should see where it goes. I want to see you again, after this holiday. I want you.'

There was a pause.

'If you'd like that too, I mean,' he said, getting flustered. 'I don't want to freak you out. But I wanted to be really clear this time, in case one of your friends decides to get involved again. Because if you've changed your mind then that's–'

'I would like that too,' Georgie said, putting a hand on his broad chest. 'To see where this goes. And – and I want you too.'

That was all it took for Pete to pull her close. After a few passionate moments, they drew away and laughed. The chemistry was definitely there.

'Pete, Dee wasn't wrong though,' said Georgie breathlessly. 'I am married and while it's over in my mind, I haven't exactly told my husband that yet. It's complicated. And long-distance is hard enough–'

'I don't care,' he said. 'You could have three hundred soon-to-be-ex-husbands, and I'd still fancy you. And I'm done listening to Dee. Can we go on a date? Now?'

Georgie burst out laughing. 'Now? I can't. I have to keep an eye on Beth in case she needs rushing into hospital. Her tongue isn't usually that size.'

'Then tomorrow morning before you go? I'll be outside your hotel at ten a.m?'

'I'd love that.' Georgie beamed. 'Our flight's not till five.'

'Then we'll make every second count,' he said quietly.

They kissed again but then heard someone coughing and they broke their embrace. It was Dee.

A very red-faced, nervous, slightly emotional-looking Dee.

'I – I just wanted to say that I'm sorry,' she said. 'I behaved terribly and I'm ashamed. You don't have to say anything but please know I mean it.' Still stammering, she walked backwards and away from them. Then she turned.

'I love you, Georgie, please forgive me,' she hollered over her shoulder. And with that she ran off towards the taxi rank.

*

As she jogged along, Dee just wanted to go back to the hotel and sleep and pretend none of this had happened. Pretend she hadn't let a guy come between her and one of her best friends. Pretend she hadn't fantasised a whole life with a man she had met just once because she had felt scared and alone. Pretend she hadn't told her friends she was moving back to Ireland to make a film, for feck's sake. Why had she behaved like this? Could she blame pregnancy hormones? Stress around work? Fear about being single mother? Or was she simply a terrible person?

*

Georgie watched Dee go, feeling a deep ache in her chest. They had a thirty-year friendship, and she valued that more than anything. She just wasn't sure that Dee did.

'I hope we can work it out,' she said quietly. She was still wrapped in Pete's arms, still leaning her head against his broad chest. 'I know Dee seems wild, but she's one of my oldest friends. I would never have thought she'd have acted like this.'

'People lose their way sometimes,' Pete said as he inhaled the scent of her hair. 'But old friends usually sort things.' He smiled at her in that way she already adored. 'Shall I get you back to your friends? We can hang out properly in the morning.'

They walked hand in hand across the bustling square, feeling as comfortable with each other as they had the first time they had met. They stopped on the corner and kissed, prolonging the moment for as long as they could. The night felt suddenly full of romance and possibility.

Pete whispered, 'Ten o'clock, outside your hotel, okay?'

'I'll be there.'

In a haze of love-soaked hormones, Georgie watched Pete saunter out of sight, when a voice said, 'Oh, Georgie, thank God you're back. I think we might need to call an ambulance.'

Chapter Twenty-five

'Hurry,' said Sam, bustling Georgie over to where a small crowd had gathered around her table. 'Beth has lost the ability to talk. Something is definitely wrong.'

'Oh, Jesus,' was all that Georgie could manage. As Georgie got closer, she was shocked. Beth's tongue was huge, and she looked wild in the eyes from a mixture of pinot and a piercing.

'Beth, can you hear me?' Kate was shouting in Beth's face. Beth gave the thumbs-up and nodded, but she looked awful.

A waitress was on the phone, Georgie presumed to the emergency services. Thank goodness. 'I blame myself,' wailed Georgie, crouching down in front of Beth. 'I thought that place looked rough, but I still let her go in. I ignored my gut instincts. Beth, are you in pain?'

Beth responded with a thumbs-down. Sam was fanning her with a menu.

'Take her to the corner,' said the waitress, taking charge. 'This crowd isn't helping, and the ambulance will meet you there. She could use some fresh air.'

They girls managed to half-carry, half-walk Beth out into the square. They heard a siren growing louder as the ambulance approached. Thank God, they thought in unison.

'At least we're in it together,' said Kate, squeezing Georgie's hand.

All except Dee, Georgie thought.

When the ambulance arrived, the doors opened and two medics jumped out. These guys were tanned and toned, and wearing uniform, and Georgie felt a moment's sympathy for Dee, who was missing out.

They assessed Beth quickly, attaching a heart-monitor to her finger and taking her temperature. 'Yeah, you need to be in the hospital,' one of them said. 'There's clearly an infection.'

'Yesh, okay,' Beth tried to say. She looked around at her friends with pleading eyes.

'Your friends can follow in a taxi,' one said.

'Thith thould be thexy,' Beth complained, as the buff guys lifted her into the back of the ambulance in a stretcher, muscles bulging. 'But ith not.'

The girls' taxi arrived at the hospital just as Beth was being stretchered inside. In a few minutes, the paramedics were handing her over and she was being examined by a tired-looking doctor. 'Thought you'd fit in last-day piercing, did you?' the doctor said as she took them in – sweaty, red-faced, middle aged, pissed women. 'One final mid-life crisis act before flying home?' She shook her head. 'You'd be amazed how many infected piercings I see in here between May and September. She's lucky she doesn't have sepsis.'

'Sepsis?' Georgie repeated.

God this sounded bad, she thought as Beth handed her over her EHIC card.

'The piercing needs to be removed right away. Under sedation, of course,' the doctor went on. 'Don't worry. We see this a lot, like I say. A lot.' She looked at Beth with a frown. Beth shrugged, looking like a lost child.

Beth was wheeled along behind the doctor, who still seemed spectacularly over this shit, with the girls following. Once they reached a cubicle, Beth was lifted onto the bed, the curtain was pulled and the doctor asked Beth to lie down, and asked her if she was allergic to any medication. 'I'll be right back,' the doctor said.

When she had gone, Beth turned to the girls. 'I'm sho shorry . . . ' She couldn't even continue, but they knew.

'Don't worry about us. Breathe through the pain,' murmured Georgie. 'Align yourself.'

'Beth, you idiot,' said Sam. 'Of all the ridiculous, childish . . . '

'You're going to be okay,' said Kate firmly. 'Just shush, everyone.'

'Why don't you come in with her?' the doctor said when she returned, evidently earmarking Kate as the sensible one. 'You can sign the paperwork in lieu of a family member. In case of emergency.'

Georgie gasped. 'Emergency? Does she mean . . . '

'Let's just get on with it, shall we?' the doctor said wearily. 'We'll take her down to theatre now and she'll be out in about an hour.'

After Kate, Beth and the doctor had left, the girls sat in the waiting room in silence, the tiredness kicking in. The emergency department seemed less busy than expected for a holiday resort. Maybe most tourists were more sensible than Beth.

'Jesus Christ,' Sam said suddenly. 'Is Beth going to die from a bloody tongue piercing?'

'Breathe,' said Georgie reassuringly. 'The last thing you need in early pregnancy is stress. She's going to be fine. Beth is as strong as a horse.'

The wait felt endless, but at last they were allowed round to see Beth, who looked pale and very, very sore. The doctor was reeling off instructions.

'The stud is removed but you have an infection. I will give you IV antibiotics here, then a prescription for tablets. Make sure you take them, okay?'

Beth nodded sadly.

'Right,' said the doctor, glancing at her watch. 'Someone should keep an eye on you tonight.'

'That'll be Dee,' said Kate, trying to keep a straight face.

After another few hours on a drip, Beth was finally good to go. She got up, woozy but able. 'I'm dying to get back to the hotel and just sleep,' she whispered to Georgie. 'Well, maybe after a little nightcap.'

'And lay off the booze, okay?' the doctor said. Clearly, she had good hearing.

*

Kate organised a taxi and the four girls sat in silence, letting the air-conditioning cool them down. What a night they had just had. When they pulled up to the hotel, Beth said, 'DINK?' which made them all laugh uncontrollably. It was the kind of laugh that makes people look insane, but it was all of the tension releasing itself.

'Apple juices all round,' Sam said sternly.

They headed straight for the resident's bar and ordered four large glasses of apple juice. Beth was looking better already and could kind of make sense. 'T'ank you all,' she clinked her glass to theirs. 'You shaved my life. How did it go with Pethe, George?'

'I didn't tell you because of your near-death experience,' Georgie said, 'but I'm going out with Pete tomorrow for a date.' She was blushing furiously, but she looked so happy.

'Yesh!' Beth clapped happily.

Kate beamed at Georgie. 'Glad it worked out for you two. Why did he ghost you in the first place though?'

'Dee,' Georgie said starkly. 'She left him a message telling him I was back with Paddy. Understandably, he backed the hell off.'

'Jeez,' said Sam, shaking her head. 'That's some proper mean-girl shit.'

'She did apologise,' admitted Georgie. 'She seemed properly remorseful, too.'

'Will you accept it?' asked Kate curiously. 'I know how forgiving you are, but has Dee pushed things a bit too far?'

'Of course I'll accept it,' said Georgie, with a wry smile. 'But I'm not going to forget. Something is going on with her and we need to find out what. All this behaviour is very strange. Obsessing over a guy? Moving to the Irish countryside, for goodness' sake? Literally the last thing I would expect from Dee.'

'How long do you think she'll last in the back arse of Kerry?' said Sam. 'I'm not sure she's going to be fighting off the paps in the local pub.'

'Something is wrong,' insisted Georgie.

'Or she's always been a massive bitch, and we've only just noticed,' pointed out Sam.

There was a moment's silence while the others looked at their drinks. Then Sam shook her head. 'No, I think you're right. Something is up.' She laughed suddenly. 'Jesus, I can't believe I thought this holiday would be relaxing. In six days, we've had two pregnancies, a swinger's night, a market run, three big fights and a trip to hospital in an ambulance!'

'Don't forget an imminent proposal, does that count?' said Kate, wriggling on her stool with excitement. 'I can't wait.' They clinked their glasses together. 'Let's go to bed, ladies. I want to make the most of our last day together.'

*

I hope Dee's not awake, Beth thought as she closed their bedroom door. She couldn't talk properly but also; she didn't want to. Dee had been pretty awful on this trip.

Beth didn't have to worry though because as she opened the door, she could hear Dee quietly snoring. Her back was facing the wall so Beth couldn't see Sleeping Beauty's peaceful face, oblivious to all the drama that she had caused the others. Phew, she thought. She got straight into her PJs, tried to kind of brush her teeth, then popped another antibiotic and got into bed, conking out immediately.

Across the room, Dee's eyes were open. She didn't know what to do. She had tried to book a sneaky red-eye flight out in the morning, but they were all taken, so she'd have to face the unpleasant reality of her very best friends despising her in the morning.

She couldn't win. She'd just have to take their shit. She had to admit, she deserved it.

Chapter Twenty-six

It was their last morning together and the girls were gathered for breakfast. The only problem was, none of them knew what to say. There was a lot of awkward scraping of cutlery on plates and sipping of coffee before Georgie took the lead.

'I'm sorry we didn't speak last night, Dee,' Georgie said at last, clearly deciding to be the bigger person here. 'I wanted you to know I accept your apology. It's water under the bridge and all that.'

Dee looked up, very surprised. 'Oh,' she said, picking up the menu so she could hide behind it. 'Thanks for that, Georgie.'

'Are you okay, Dee?' asked Sam, eyeing her closely, thinking that no way was Dee crying behind her menu. She didn't cry. But when she dropped her menu, they all baulked, nearly falling off their chairs. Tears were streaming down her face.

'I'm so sorry, guys,' she started, in between heaving sobs. 'I don't know what is actually wrong with me. I feel so angry and hurt; I feel scared and ashamed. I feel everything. And the last few days, in fact, months, have been really tough for me.'

'The pregnancy must have been a real shock for you,' said Georgie softly. 'It just makes it hard to talk to you when you keep up so many walls, you know?'

Dee looked at Georgie, whose big blue eyes were full of tears. 'I know. And George, I can't believe what I did to you, I'm so sorry, I really am. You of all people. I like Pete but not enough to do what I did. I think that I got competitive because I was scared about being a mum on my own – me, a mum, how crazy is that! – and I don't know . . . ' She trailed off. 'I want you to be happy. He's a nice guy and is perfect for you.'

'As it happens, he asked me out this morning and I'm going to accept,' Georgie said, thinking that honesty was the best policy. 'I'm not asking your permission, Dee, but I would like to know that you're okay with it.'

'Of course,' Dee replied. Then she tossed her head. 'I don't have time for a boyfriend now, anyway. Not if I'm going to be looking after a baby. I'll need to take classes. First Aid, NCT . . . '

'Anger management?' Beth innocently, and they all burst out laughing, even Dee.

'I think so, yeah,' Dee said with a watery chuckle. 'I need to set a good example for the baby.'

'We all care so much for you, Dee, but you never really let us in. You should, we are here for you.' Beth patted Dee's arm.

'Thank you, guys, all of you,' Dee said. 'And I know that you think this whole moving-to-Kerry idea is wild, but maybe it's what I need right now. To realign myself. A fresh start for me and my baby. You know?'

'Er,' said Kate, 'are you sure about that part? I was hoping you'd see sense in the morning. You really do love your job.'

'About that,' said Dee. She took in a deep breath. 'I'm pretty sure I'm going to get sacked when I get back to New York.'

'What?' Sam cried, shocked.

'Why didn't you tell us?' asked Georgie.

Dee continued. 'I was ashamed, to be honest – I know that's ridiculous. We've known each other for such a long time but all the same, I felt embarrassed. I overheard people talking about my future replacements in the toilet, for God's sake. I've never liked my boss, but I didn't ever think that I was so easily replaceable. It's been a hard lesson to learn.'

'Dee, don't get ahead of yourself,' said Sam firmly. 'Wait till you hear it from them. As it is, you can scope out your options ahead of time.' She nudged Kate. 'Care to jump in here, life coach?'

'Absolutely,' said Kate, straightening her back and snapping into professional mode. 'I see this as a new opportunity. When one door closes, another opens. No just stands for New Opportunity.'

'Who said that?' whispered Beth. 'Was it the Dalai Lama?'

'I'm not sure,' said Kate, frowning. 'Oprah, maybe, but the point is, now and again in life, we find ourselves at a cross-roads and we need to choose which way to go. And we've all been at a bit of a crossroads in our lives on this trip. You just need to make a decision.'

Dee swallowed. 'That sounds terrifying, frankly,' she said in a small voice.

'No, this is a good thing,' Kate said firmly. 'You've been stuck in a rut for a long time. A glamorous rut that made you filthy rich, but still. Change can be a good thing. Think of this as a relaunch! Deirdre Byrne two-point-oh.'

'You're going to be a mum, Dee,' said Beth, looking misty-eyed. 'That will change you without you even realising it.'

'Give yourself time, Dee,' urged Kate. 'Change doesn't happen overnight but just keep following the path, it will take you to where you're meant to be.' She pointed at Georgie. 'And while I'm on a life-coach roll, you need to dump Paddy's ass before you ride off into the sunset with Pete.'

'And then burn his ugly shirts,' added Beth wickedly.

'I'll bring the matches,' said Dee.

*

After breakfast, the girls headed to the sun loungers for one last soak in the sun, while Georgie went out to meet Pete. In the dazzle of the bright morning light, she could see her handsome date leaning against the side of a taxi, smiling at her as if she were the most precious and exciting thing in the world.

'Good morning, beautiful,' he said as she approached, leaning in to kiss her.

She kissed him back, excitement racing through her. 'Where are we off to?' she smiled, letting him open the cab door and getting into the seat beside him.

'Have you ever been on a catamaran before?'

She shook her head, her stomach flipping. She was sure of herself on dry land, but on the open sea?

As if reading her mind, Pete said, 'It's okay, I'll be there every step of the way.'

Georgie sighed blissfully, visions of Pete steering the boat while she sat up the front filling her mind. 'Okay then,' she said shyly.

'Great. We're setting sail,' he said. Ten minutes later, they pulled up at the jetty and in front of them was a row of stunning white catamarans, each with a shining navy hull and cream leather interior.

Pete helped Georgie on board. 'So, do you like my boat?' he joked they put on their lifejackets. 'Ok, fine. It's not mine, I just hired it for the hour. And I'm not even going to be sailing it.' He pointed to the crew, who laughed.

'It's perfect,' Georgie said breathlessly, looking around her at the glistening sea.

She heard a pop beside her as Pete handed her a glass of bubbles. They clinked glasses and then he pulled away, looked down at her again as though she were unbearably precious, pushing a strand of hair back from her cheek. Then he bent his head and kissed her.

Georgie swooned. And she'd thought that romance was dead.

The catamaran sliced through the harbour with ease, leaning slightly on the right as the wind filled the sails. Pete slid his arm around Georgie's back, and she relaxed into it. Soon they were out of the bay and surrounded by water, the sun beating down and the waves bouncing. The captain kept them close to the land so that they could see the spectacular cliffs and enjoy the gorgeous scenery. The day was perfect for sightseeing and the water looked so clear: looking down, they could see the white sand underneath.

'I could get used to this.' Georgie smiled out at the sea.

'So could I,' Pete said watching her.

They sailed right up to the cliffs and the captain showed them each of the sea caves, explaining the history. 'They say that people who fall in love here stay in love forever,' the captain told them, smiling.

'Really?' asked Georgie, her eyes huge.

'Well, no,' said the captain apologetically. 'But I have a good feeling about you two. When I see it, I know,' he winked.

Georgie had a feeling that she knew too.

They sailed for another while, enjoying the feeling of the warm sun on their shoulders, finishing the bottle of bubbly and taking photos and selfies, so they wouldn't forget the trip.

'I don't want to go home,' Georgie said to Pete suddenly as the harbour drew near. And she meant it.

'Then don't,' he said, taking her hand. 'I can add a few more days to my holiday. We can go for meals, swim in the sea, really get to know each other.' He kissed her fingers.

She sighed. 'That would be amazing – if I didn't have a husband whom I need to talk to.' She stiffened at the thought. It was horrible, but Kate was right. The sooner that she and Paddy had the talk, the sooner she could begin to live again. She added, without thinking, 'It'll have to be some other time,' and then flushed. Did Pete think she was angling for more dates, straight off the bat?

'Of course. Take your time,' he said seriously. Then he watched her, his eyes dancing, as though he knew exactly what she was thinking. 'Some other time, you say. In which case, we should get a date in the diary. Because I don't want to wait too long.'

Georgie's heart flipped.

When the tour finished, they waved to the crew, walked along the harbour, ate crêpes and kissed some more. At last, Pete glanced reluctantly at his watch. 'I should get you back for that flight,' he said. 'But first,' he said, 'let me finally give you my number.'

*

Georgie arrived back as the girls were packing up their sun-bathing gear, putting their towels away and pushing their sun-beds back. They could see new arrivals pulling their suitcases through the paths around the pool, groups of girls laughing and bickering.

'Is Marco checking them out already?' Beth said.

Dee rolled her eyes. 'If you ask me, this place goes downhill later in the season,' she said. 'I'm sure when we arrived it was a bit less noisy.'

Kate was checking the time and frowning. 'We really need to get ready,' she said. 'I don't want to miss the . . . ' She broke into a smile. 'Ah, feck it. If we miss the flight, we'll survive.'

'Wow, I love this new easy-breezy Kate,' said Sam, grinning.

'Same,' said Kate. 'But, er, let's get a shift on, shall we?'

'Come on,' said Sam, nudging Georgie. 'I want to get this flight over with, too. It'll be my first ever while knowing I'm pregnant and I have a feeling it's not going to be pretty.'

Georgie was watching the new arrivals, smiling. 'That was us when we got here,' she said, her eyes on a gaggle of girls, whooping and laughing, their arms slung around each other. 'I wonder whether they'll have half the week we had.'

Chapter Twenty-seven

'Bloody Brexit,' Dee said, eyeing the queue at passport control in the airport – not that it affected her in any way. 'All it got us is queues.'

'We're over there, Gate A10,' said Georgie pointing at the board. Just then, a text came through. She opened it, read it, and went bright red.

'You look pleased with yourself,' said Sam, and Georgie giggled.

'It's just Pete, saying he's looking forward to hanging out again soon,' she said, giving the PG version of his extremely X-rated text. She glanced at Dee, but Dee was looking deliberately casual. 'We're thinking we'll meet halfway between New York and Ireland. Which, it seems, is . . . Canada.'

'So, when will we all get back together again?' Beth asked. 'Are you still planning your Irish homecoming, Dee?'

'I am,' Dee said firmly. 'I know you all think it's wild, but I need to regroup, think about what I really want and traumatise my parents with the news of a late-in-life grandchild. I'm planning to come home in about six weeks, once I've seen the doctors in New York and sorted things with work. I'll stop in Dublin for a few nights to see Dad and then I'll head to Kerry and stay there then till Christmas. That's three months I mean, how long does it take to make a movie?'

'Er, it can take quite a while, I think,' said Kate, trying to keep a straight face. 'Months? Maybe a year?'

Dee flinched. 'A year?'

'I'm sure you'll manage it more quickly,' Sam said hastily. 'I'll come home for a night out in Dublin to see you. Hopefully, I'll feel less grim by then. Anyway, that's my flight being called.' She kissed the girls and headed over to the boarding area for Heathrow. 'I love you all!' she called, walking away to her line. 'No goodbyes because I'll see you soon!'

Next was Dee. They hugged and kissed her as she walked off to the executive lounge, sunglasses firmly in place. Brave Deirdre Byrne, ready to face up to her uncertain future. Then Beth, Kate and Georgie headed off to the security area. Beth sighed happily. She'd had a great time, but she was dying to see the kids. And Jack, of course.

They removed their belts and shoes as instructed, putting all their valuables into the trays and sliding them along. After a week of glamour, the dingy security area brought reality back to all three of them, who were silent as they shuffled along in the queue.

'You packed the bags yourself, yes?' the security guard asked in a monotone voice, as she looked up at the girls.

'Sure, we did,' said Beth. 'I didn't come on holiday with staff.'

The woman was unsmiling.

'Don't make jokes to the security people,' whispered Kate.

A strict-looking guy in uniform with a large German Shepherd dog was walking over towards them. As the dog approached Beth, it began to strain at its leash. The man pointed to Beth's suitcase on the conveyor belt and the woman whipped it off and brought it to a table.

'Can you open your case, madam?' the security guy said.

'Sure,' Beth said as she pushed her case onto its side and opened it. Within seconds, the dog had jumped up and was sniffing and rummaging with its nose so viciously, that when it popped its head up, Beth's massive grey knickers dangled from its snout.

'Don't worry, they're clean,' said Beth laughing, a little nervously this time. What on earth had the dog found? She'd left the sex toys in the hotel bedroom, a last-minute decision because her suitcase was too full of knock-off designer bags and belts.

The officer removed them from the dog with his gloved hand, like a robot. No emotion. The sniffing and rummaging continued, the dog's tail wagging as he drooled all over Beth's new souvenirs and clothes. All that she could do was watch on in silence. Then the dog started barking, proper, loud security-incident barking. The security guy patted him and pulled him back, before tipping the bag over to empty it onto the table. Among the mess of clothes and knick-knacks, out popped two bright purple balls, each with a little silicone handle attached.

The security guard examined them slowly. 'An ornament?' he asked.

'More of a medical aid. They're for my pelvic floor,' Beth explained. 'Among other things.'

'Let's just pop them in here,' the man said, putting the Kegel balls into a Ziploc bag and handing it to her in front of the crowd who had now gathered to watch.

'Okay, all good,' the officer said, pulling the dog away and walking off.

'Oh great,' Beth sighed loudly with relief. The crowd dispersed, a woman winking at Beth as she piled her clothes back into the suitcase.

'They were for my pelvic floor, girls!' Beth said as she took in their 'judgy faces'.

The other two said nothing, well used to Beth's shenanigans at this stage. 'The flight is boarding,' Georgie said after checking the boarding screen. 'We'll have to run, girls.

'Oh dear God,' Kate said. 'Running for the first time in ten years and in an airport too. I'm far too uptight for this.'

They pounded along to the gate. The area was deserted except for two figures up ahead, who seemed to be arguing and gesturing – a member of the airline crew and a slight, elderly figure. Then the older lady turned.

'Georgie!' It was Katherine.

'I made them hold it for you!' She turned triumphantly to the airport staff. 'I told you my friends were on this flight.' Georgie introduced her and they all hugged.

'Thanks so much!' gasped Kate. 'I hate missing flights.'

'Your eye is clearing up nicely,' said Georgie to Katherine.

'Just a bit of puffiness,' Katherine said cheerfully. 'The eyewash sorted it right out. What about your friend?'

'Pregnant!' cried Beth. 'Isn't it amazing?'

'Wonderful news!' said Katherine, clapping her hands. 'Oh, this calls for a–'

'Could you please,' the airport staff said coldly, 'get on the plane now?'

'Katherine, WAIT!' they heard a voice shouting and all looked around. An elderly gentleman was shuffling along, then joined her and took her hand. 'I just had to use the bathroom,' he said.

Beth nearly fainted. She recognised that man, although the last time she had seen him he had been wearing substantially fewer clothes.

'Oh, this is Davey,' Katherine said casually. 'He was over on a group trip with his friends from Brighton when we met and we, ah, decided to spend the last few days together. Actually, I think he was in your hotel?' she said innocently.

Davey just smiled, a twinkle in his eyes.

I bet you've a lot to be smiling about mate, Beth thought, grinning.

'Oh, lovely. Yes, we met Davey.' Georgie smiled. 'He organised a games night at the Edene, in fact. Very educational.'

Davey gave her the faintest wink.

*

The flight was quick and seamless and before long the captain announced that they were starting their descent.

'Seatbelts, guys.' Beth nudged Georgie who woke immediately and strapped in. She had completely dozed off in the middle of planning her talk with Paddy. She knew what she needed to say though. She had this.

Meanwhile, Beth had been busy on the flight. Midwifery application enquiry filled in and emailed. Beth looked over Kate's shoulder to the window to see the welcoming green land of Ireland. She was excited now to get into her own bed tonight after an evening with her babies – well, children, really! They weren't babies any more, which meant she could start thinking about herself for a change.

At the airport, they all said goodbye and went their separate ways. Lots of hugging and laughing, all complaining about feeling sweaty and manky.

'Till we meet again! This isn't goodbye!' Beth shouted at the top of her voice as she left the building. She could see her husband and kids waiting, clutching a handmade banner. Her throat tightened. 'Love you Mini Breakers!' she called.

Then she turned, ran and jumped into Jack's arms.

*

'KATE!' Ariana shouted over. She was holding a bunch of flowers. So romantic.

Kate's heart flipped; she just adored this woman. She ran over and gave her a huge kiss and hug. It was great to be home.

'I've missed you so much.' Kate gushed. She dropped to one knee in the busy arrivals lounge, for once oblivious to any curious glances. 'Will you marry me, Ariana?'

Ariana stepped back in shock 'What did you just say?' she asked cautiously, searching Kate's eyes in case she was messing.

'I'm buying you a ring tomorrow,' Kate said, lifting up her hand and kissing it. 'Let's make this official. I'm sorry for everything I put you through. I realised what I want and it's you. A life with you.'

Ariana pulled her hand away, her eyes troubled. 'I don't want you to ask me just because I've been nagging,' she said. 'Because I've done some thinking this week too. I don't need to get married; I just need–'

'Stop it,' whispered Kate, looking up at her. 'Just say yes. Please say yes.'

There was a pause.

'Okay,' Ariana said, 'as in, I will.'

And she laughed, her eyes filling up.

'She said yes!'

Kate turned around, shouting to strangers. Cheering and clapping broke out. God, this felt so right.

'What on earth happened to you on that holiday?' said Ariana, bemused.

'I'll tell you all about it,' said Kate, folding her fiancée – fiancée! – into a hug.

'Back at home.'

*

Across the Irish Sea, Jeff was waiting anxiously to see Sam. He had missed her more than usual this time; she had been so low and despondent when she had set off. It wasn't like her, or at least it wasn't like the old Sam. The last few years had really taken it out of them both. As soon as he saw his beautiful wife walking towards him, he fell in love all over again. This holiday has done her good, he thought, waving over to her. She looked relaxed and happy, a little paler than usual, but her gorgeous self.

She started to almost run when she saw him, as she pulled her suitcase behind her and he hurried to meet her.

'Sammy, I've missed you so much,' he said picking her up in a hug and twirling her around. 'You look like this holiday was just what you needed.'

'It was eventful,' she said. 'But fun. Oh and I got you something,' she said, thrusting a paper bag at him. 'A souvenir. And you have to open it now.'

Jeff laughed and stuck his hand into the bag. When he pulled his hand out again, he froze.

'We're having a baby,' she managed to get out as he kissed her though her tears and wet face. 'It's really happening. We're having a baby.'

*

Back in Ireland, no one came to meet Georgie at the airport. She got into a taxi and arrived alone outside her beautiful home, with the wisteria over the door that Paddy always said they should cut down as it might ruin the façade. She stood, looking up at it. She had no choice but to go inside. But then the door opened and she could see Paddy standing there with a scotch in his hand. No kiss, nothing. Sounding bored, he said, 'Oh, you're back. I thought I heard something out here. So how was it?'

He had turned away before she could reply. Georgie swallowed the lump in her throat.

'We need to talk, Paddy,' she said to his back.

*

Dee's flight to New York was prompt and pleasant. She disembarked, got her bag, went through customs and was hailing a cab within thirty minutes.

She checked her flawless makeup in her compact and rehearsed her speech.

She looked out of her cab window at the people hustling on the streets. New York had been fun. Everything she had hoped for as a kid dreaming of stardom. But the network had taken the best years of her life and had given nothing back, bar a bit of fame, priority restaurant booking and free haircare. Did they really value her, as a person? Not a hope.

She had too many eager and desperate people literally waiting for her to resign or die, so that they could take her place in the makeup chair. Well, they could have it. She'd had enough.

She used her pass to get through and went straight to production. 'I want to see Dave,' she told the receptionist, breezing past.

David, the producer (sleazy little shit), looked startled to see her. 'Dee! Did we have a meeting?'

'Nope,' she said, slinging her coat onto the chair. 'I just wanted to have a little chat.'

'Oh, right. Is everything okay? Good holiday?' he asked feebly.

God, she didn't like this little weasel of a man. He gave her the ick, so she took a deep breath and thought of Ireland. 'David, the reason I wanted to see you was to tell you that I'm moving to Ireland to make a film and I'm quitting.' He blinked at her. 'Now, don't pretend you're sorry because I know you were planning to sack me anyway. You can give me eight weeks' salary, and I'll work two weeks of them. Oh, and I want a healthy payout because I'm having a baby and you don't want me to sue you for discrimination, not with your track record with the interns.'

As the door slammed behind her, she smiled to herself. Roll on, Ireland, she thought, I'll be home soon.

Epilogue

One month later

'Twins?! Are you serious?'

Pete swerved the car as Georgie screamed into her phone.

'Isn't it deadly?' said Sam. 'I spent all that time trying for one baby and now look.'

'Oh my God!'

Pete swerved again and nearly crashed into a tree.

'I know, Jeff is beside me and he's in shock!' Sam laughed.

'Sam, I can't believe it! You're going from two to four!' Georgie said, her eyes filling up. 'You guys are going to be wonderful parents.'

'Spread the word for me, will you?' asked Sam. 'Jeff and I need to go home and breathe into a paper bag and consider that loft extension.'

'Ah guys, I'm so happy for you both. Yeah, I'll spread the word. Just take it easy, okay?'

She hung up and turned to Pete, beaming.

'Twins!' she said.

He laughed.

'I gathered. That's great news, isn't it?'

Georgie was already on her phone, pulling up Beth's number. 'Pete, I love you being here and I don't want to miss a second of this time together obviously, but can I just make a few quick calls?'

*

'Georgie! Sure thing I can chat. Let me go up to the attic,' Beth said. 'Back in a sec Jack, you're in charge.' There was the noise of scrambling on the other end of the line and then she said, 'Okay, shoot.'

'Beth! Sam had her scan and she's expecting twins!' Georgie shouted.

'Oh my God!' Beth shouted back. 'What fantastic news!'

'How's all your course stuff going?' Georgie asked.

'My application is done and dusted.' Beth sighed happily. 'And I've nailed it, if I do say so myself. Maybe my brain fog only extends to the home, you know? Although the doctor said we should just keep an eye on my HRT dose.' She lowered her voice huskily. 'How's Pete? Has he started any fires, know what I mean?'

'I've got him for a whole three more days,' said Georgie, giggling. 'And our flights for Canada are booked. My publisher thinks we can do a bit of a speaking tour as well, drive some sales at the same time. Now, would you mind calling Dee for me? Pete and I are nearly at the pub. We're doing all the typical Irish tourist activities.'

Beth hung up the phone and grinned. She was delighted that Georgie's firefighter had visited so promptly and that it all seemed to be dreamy.

Now it was time to check in on their diva.

*

'Good morning, Beth, what's up?' Dee said, sounding out of breath. She was jogging, which would once have been unimaginable. She missed her personal trainer. Exercise was a bit different when you had to drag yourself around the village. Still, she was enjoying herself in Ireland. It wasn't quite what she had expected – a lot busier and a bit less picturesque – but still, she was having a great time reconnecting with her family and friends.

She had left her job with a box of her stuff, symbolising the last ten years of her life. She didn't care. It was all too toxic anyway. She had flown home, taken a lease out on a small apartment and resigned herself to telling her friends and family that Deirdre Byrne, TV personality, was no more.

And then the news had come in.

Her miracle had happened.

'A talk show?' she had whispered down the phone. She was very rarely lost for words but she could barely string a sentence together. 'I'm being offered my own talk show? Here in Ireland?'

'That's right! The network are thinking of calling it *Just Dee*,' her agent had told her. 'Real women, real stories. I didn't want to tell you till the network had sign off. They'll want you to start in just under a year's time, so there won't be much in the way of maternity leave . . . '

'I don't care,' said Dee. 'That's what nannies are for, right?'

Freddy laughed. 'Sounds right. And it's day time, so none of this late night stuff. Apparently, the network wants to see the feisty Dee they clocked in the market in Portugal. Less buttoned-up newsreader, more opinionated, more . . . '

'Unhinged?' Dee said, giggling, recalling that day in the market.

'A bit,' her agent said. 'And the great thing is you wouldn't have been able to do this if the show hadn't let you go. You'd have been sewn up for another five years.'

It had been fate, just like Georgie had said. Georgie, who was the first person Dee had called to tell.

'Go on, Beth, what is it?' said Dee impatiently now, slowing to a walk. Running was harder the more pregnant she was, but she felt surprisingly decent. 'I've got a midwife's appointment in ten.'

'Sam's having twins!' Beth shouted and Dee nearly walked straight into the river.

'Holy shit!' Dee yelled. Bloody hell, that would be hard work, Dee thought, thanking her lucky stars that her own scan had only shown one normal-sized baby. Imagine the stretch-marks . . . Jesus.

Dee had found an Irish, very attractive single OB-GYN who was monitoring her pregnancy. He had dated her at thirteen weeks pregnant. He was great, except that he kept referring her as a 'geriatric mother', which she could quite frankly do without. She had also found a therapist called Valerie, who was older and very firm, and said that Dee could feel all her feelings, she just had to be thoughtful about how she let them out.

'Congratulations, I guess,' she said, turning into her road. 'I'm kidding, that's great news.'

'Sam wants us to spread the word,' said Beth. 'Can you phone Kate? I've still got the rest of this application essay to do.'

'Sure, I'm nearly home now anyway.'

Dee stepped through the front door. Once inside, she kicked off her runners and slid on her new Crocs.

*

'Dee, hi!' said Kate. She was trying to work out if she could sit her very opinionated, golf-playing uncle next to her activist niece at their wedding dinner. Maybe it would be a good thing?

'I'm just trying to sort the seating plan.'

The day after they got home, herself and Ariana went into town and had a romantic morning having coffee and trying on rings. The had both chosen the same. A neat band with three diamonds set into the gold band. Quietly beautiful. It was perfect for them.

'Sam's having twins!' Dee exclaimed.

'What?! I don't believe you!' Kate laughed. 'God, no wonder she felt so sick in Portugal.' She lowered her voice. 'What about you? Has that paternity test come back yet?'

'Not yet,' said Dee. 'But what will be will be, you know? I can build a good life for us here, me and the baby, man or no man.'

'And we'll all help,' Kate said staunchly. 'After the wedding is over and Bridezilla calms down. She's off the vapes too, she finally came clean and told me!'

'I heard that,' Ariana shouted from the kitchen.

Kate laughed. 'Got to go, speak soon, love you.'

She hung up, smiling. Then her phone beeped – as did Dee's in Kerry, Georgie's at the pretty gastropub near Dalkey, Sam's as she and Jeff sat watching a hypnobirthing video in bed.

A new WhatsApp group: 'Mini Breakers'.

GUYS. Anyone fancy Marrakesh in October?

Acknowledgements

To my very best friends Anna, Gemma, Vicks, Joey, Nicola and Nathalie. Totes emosh!

This book is LOOSELY based on our nights out together and the trouble that we get into on our own mini breaks! But we won't name the hotels or restaurants! You can't compete with history and we'll always have that together. Loyalty and friendship are so important to me and that's why you are my very best friends. You are kind, funny, genuine, supportive people and the kind of women that I want on my team forever. Thank you for always being there for me. I love you all.

Joanne Byrne, my good friend and agent that I quite simply couldn't live without! You and I are together for the last nineteen years and you have never, ever let me down. You are one of the kindest people that I have ever met and I always feel strength from being with you and Presence Plus. You and Sinéad have been so good to me and what a brilliant team you have. Thank you for everything.

To Marianne Gunn O'Connor, my literary agent. Thank you for letting me send you ideas and for always being so supportive and patient. I was told that you are the best in the business and you certainly are.

When it comes to Deirdre Nolan aka Dee . . . The second that we met, seven years ago, we clicked and stayed in touch ever since. We started our relationship through *The Friendship Fairies*, as she published my very first children's book. She has always believed in me, so it would seem only fitting that she would also publish my first adult book! We always laugh and I have the utmost respect for her as a person and editor.

Alison Walsh, thank you for your patience and humour. You have taught me how to stretch my imagination and get it down on paper! You have a lovely calm way about you.

Lisa Gilmour, assistant editor, thank you for the astute edit and for being my social media guru and always responding to my eighty-six questions so quickly! I have comfort knowing that you're at the end of a phone line.

At Bonnier Books UK, Sophie Raoufi and Clare Kelly, I promise to behave in public and when representing you!

The team at Gill Hess: Declan Heeney, Simon Hess, Helen McKean – thank you all for everything and for giving me confidence as a first-time adult novelist!

And finally, to all of the people around the hotel pool in Albufeira, July 2024, I was the strange Irish girl that was writing on her sun lounger at 8 am!

Obrigado.

Lucy xxx

About the author

Lucy Kennedy is an Irish television and radio presenter. She first came to public attention co-hosting *The Podge and Rodge Show* on RTÉ 2 and has also presented *The Ex-Files, Livin' with Lucy* and her own chat show *The Lucy Kennedy Show*. Lucy currently co-hosts *Colm and Lucy in the Morning* with Colm Hayes on Ireland's Classic Hits radio show. She is also the bestselling author of *The Friendship Fairies*.